"A story full of brilliantly and cleverly written characters, *The Reluctant Visionary* is a must-read."

– **Readers' Favorite Reviews**

"An intriguing slow burn of a novel, *The Reluctant Visionary* is carefully structured, with well-developed character voices that make it a rewarding read. Recommended."

– **James Artimus Owen**, bestselling author and illustrator of *Here, There Be Dragons*

"*The Reluctant Visionary* is an intriguing novel for driven people who want a gripping read with metaphysical elements. Take a break, dig in, and connect with these challenged and inspiring characters who will touch your heart. "

– **Suzanne Evans**, *New York Times* best-selling author of *The Way You Do Anything Is the Way You Do Everything*

"*The Reluctant Visionary* is the story of two women with gifts that neither they nor the world welcome. This exceptional novel follows the journey of these women finding the support and love they deserve— true empowerment, delivered in a way you can't put down."

– **Dr. Marilyn Walker, PhD**

"The characters, dialogue, and unfolding story of *The Reluctant Visionary* is more than just an entertaining novel of remarkable power. It's a journey that spans the ultimate human potential—from the divine to the evil; and everything in between. Highly recommended."

– **Mark Leslie**, author of *Fear and Longing in Los Angeles* and former President of the Canadian Booksellers Association

"Featuring unexpected heroism, the Reluctant Visionary is a suspenseful novel in which a grandmother and her granddaughter believe they can impact the future."

– **Forward Reviews**

"I love a good story, and Datta Groover is a masterful storyteller. *The Reluctant Visionary* has as many twists and turns as a Texas tornado. Nuggets of homespun wisdom and insight woven throughout enrich the reading experience. Give yourself a gift and get a copy of this book."

– **Dr. Jeffrey Weissmann, M.D.**

"Three women, Anna Mae, Kat, and Jess each confess to being the visionary of her era. They never asked for the ability to glimpse danger ahead, to have the opportunity to save others from a terrifying destiny. These women show how a determination to light a hopeful way forward ignites courage despite threats of desperation and peril."

– **Chanticleer Reviews**

"Datta Groover's writing is powerful, moving, and inspiring. *The Reluctant Visionary* will take you on a wonderful journey through intergenerational trauma, intrigue, and a dash of romance."

– **Karen Collyer**, Author of *Guilt & Surviving Martin Bryant*

"I loved this book! The story and the characters were entrancing; the insights, the responsibilities, the tensions, the sacrifices, and resolutions were woven together expertly; the connections, the humanity, and the care people showed for each other moved me."

– **Dr. Dan Thomsen, PhD**

302
p301 Rifle not pistol

ENTRY LABEL

THIS FORM MUST BE INCLUDED INSIDE THE FRONT COVER OF
EACH BOOK YOU SUBMIT, therefore cut it from here and duplicate
it as often as necessary. Insert the label inside the front cover of
each book submitted (if you enter one book in one category, you
must insert this form into each of the four books sent).

FOR AUDIOBOOKS: please send 3 Audible gift codes to Terry
Nathan at terry@ibpa-online.org. If your book is not available
on Audible, please contact Terry Nathan for additional options.

CATEGORY (NO. AND NAME)

13. Fiction: Mystery & Thriller

TITLE

The Reluctant Visionary

CONTACT PERSON

Datta Groover

PUBLISHING COMPANY

Deep Pacific Press

CONTACT PERSON'S ADDRESS

117 E 37th St. #580

CONTACT PERSON'S CITY, STATE, ZIP

Loveland, CO 80538

CONTACT PERSON'S TELEPHONE

541-301-0537

CONTACT PERSON'S EMAIL

Datta@DeepPacificPress.com

WEBSITE ADDRESS

DeepPacificPress.com

PLEASE INDICATE THE BOOK'S TARGET AUDIENCE:

People who want to read uplifting fiction with

a hint of the supernatural

THE
RELUCTANT
VISIONARY

DATTA GROOVER

Deep
Pacific
Press

LOVELAND, COLORADO   MELBOURNE, AUSTRALIA

ISBN: 978-1-956108-09-5 (Hardcover)
ISBN: 9978-1-956108-08-8 (Paperback)
ISBN: 978-1-956108-09-5 (eBook)
ISBN: 978-1-956108-10-1 (audiobook)

This is a work of fiction. Names, characters, businesses, places, events, locales, and incidents are either the products of the author's imagination or used in a fictitious manner. Any resemblance to actual persons, living or dead, or actual events is purely coincidental.

Front cover images by Shutterstock.
Cover design by Patrick Knowles / PatrickKnowlesDesign.com
Interior formatting by Mark Thomas / Coverness.com

First printing, July 2023

Deep Pacific Press
117 E 37th St. #580
Loveland, CO 80538
DeepPacificPress.com
info@DeepPacificPress.com

DEDICATION

I dedicate *The Reluctant Visionary* to my dear friend and brother, the late Robert O. Groover, III.

Thank you for your friendship, advice, honesty, and love. Thanks for all your great suggestions for *The Reluctant Visionary*, for watching over me through this process, and for your contribution to my world in general.

I will miss you always.
Datta Groover,
March 2023

PROLOGUE

Jessica Atwood groaned and buried her head under the pillow when Kat shouted something from the other end of the farmhouse. She couldn't quite make out her mother's words, but they probably wouldn't have made sense anyway. They never did during her so-called visions. Half a minute of silence passed before Kat yelled again, something about popcorn.

"Dammit!" Jess threw off her covers, climbed out of bed, and pulled on her worn Dallas Cowboys bathrobe. Was living in a normal household too much to ask?

The teasing she endured at Center Point High—especially when one of her mother's visions didn't come to pass—irritated her profoundly. What she hated most was the Little Orphan Annie nickname she hadn't been able to shake since middle school. The rumor floating around school was that she'd been adopted. How else could a person of color have two white parents? Her half-brother Kevin being white as well gave the rumor momentum. Plus, she had the perfect corkscrew curls for the Orphan Annie role—or so the bullies said. There were seventy-three more days until graduation, and she could hardly wait.

Already frustrated by her mother's yelling, Jess swore under her breath when a floorboard creaked as she stepped out of her room. She trudged down

1

the hall, its unfinished knotty pine walls lit by the glow of the armadillo-shaped night-light her stepfather Dave installed after she had a few late-night collisions with door frames.

She arrived at her parents' bedroom just as Kat mumbled something about a family getting out in time. Her mother looked like a wild woman, sitting up in bed with scattered blonde hair covering half her face. Dave had already switched on his Texas flag bedside lamp, and he raised his eyebrows at Jess as she walked in.

"Are we doin' this again?" she asked, feeling a pang of sympathy for him. He tolerated more than anyone could reasonably expect, and as far as stepfathers went, he wasn't half bad.

"Don't reckon we have much choice, though you coulda stayed in bed. Kevin is sleepin' right through this."

"Your son always sleeps through these episodes," Jess said. "I don't know how he does it, but—"

"They're all up there," Kat interrupted, staring at the ceiling.

Jess sighed loudly. "Here we go again."

Kat mumbled something about a store with smoking wires. No point in asking what she meant. The drill was to wait until she was ready. That could mean three minutes—or the better part of an hour.

"Dave, honey, are you awake?" Kat finally asked.

Jess face-palmed herself. Who did her mother think had switched on the light? Gremlins?

Kat told her husband to call Scott Polk, who owned the hardware store downtown. She'd dreamt it was on fire.

Dave yawned. "I'll do it in the mornin'. We all need our sleep. Kale harvest starts Thursday, and we're already behind schedule. Besides, your last three visions didn't even pan out. We might be wakin' him for nothin'."

"Sounds like a plan to me," Jess said, hoping the episode would end before things got too crazy for a change.

"*No!*" Kat shouted, startling them both. "Call him now."

Dave glanced at his bedside clock and shook his head. "It's after midnight.

You know how Polk is."

"Dave Atwood, you call him or I will. You know he sees you as the man of the house. If you think he'd be grumpy with you callin' him this time of night, imagine how he'd be if I called."

He grudgingly picked up his cell phone and searched for Polk's number. "You sure about this?"

Jess dreaded the thought of yet another story about her mother's visions making the rounds. What sane person would wake their neighbor in the middle of the night to tell them about some crazy dream? "Yeah, Mama. If there's a fire, shouldn't we call 911 instead? You could block your number and call anonymously."

"That's not how I envisioned it, and they'd ask if I actually saw the fire, which I didn't. Besides, you can't block your number on a 911 call anyway. They'd still know it was us." Kat nodded at Dave's phone. "It won't work any other way. Please, I'm sure this time."

After a moment's hesitation, he tapped the call button and switched to speaker mode.

A sleepy Scott Polk picked up on the fourth ring. "This better be good."

"Hey, Scott, Dave Atwood from Heart of Texas Farm. Sorry for callin' so late, but—"

"It's not late. It's early. Way too early to be talkin' on the phone, that's for damn sure."

"I know it's not the best time, and I hate to bother you—"

"Then why *are* you botherin' me?"

"Well . . ."

"Well, *what*?" Polk snapped.

Kat took that as her cue. "Tell him his store is on fire."

Polk heard her. "The hell you carryin' on about? Look, I don't know if y'all are drunk or just playin' some cute little prank, but I've got the best remote monitorin' system money can buy, and there's no report of smoke or fire. I'm lookin' at the green 'all clear' symbol right now. Glad y'all think this is funny, but I'm goin' back to sleep. Don't bother me again."

"Mr. Polk," Kat said, "this is no joke. I've seen it."

"What do you mean, you've *seen* it?" He undoubtedly understood exactly what Kat meant. Probably half of Kerr County knew about her visions.

"That family upstairs won't have a chance," Kat said, "unless you call the fire department now."

"You listen here, ma'am. I mean no disrespect, but that is crazy talk. There isn't one livin' bein' upstairs or anywhere else in that buildin' except maybe a few mice. Our system's got smoke detectors, heat detectors, motion detectors, broken water pipe detectors . . . we've got more detectors than you can shake a stick at, all reportin' back to me in real time. If anythin' did happen, it'd wake me right up. So y'all just go back to whatever you were doin' before you rang— or don't—but do not even think about callin' here in the middle of the night again."

Jess heard Polk's wife in the background ask what was happening.

"Nothin', dear, it's just them organic folks sayin' there's a fire at the store when there isn't."

Polk's wife said something else that Jess couldn't quite make out.

"Of course I'm sure," Polk responded. "They're just barkin' up the wrong tree." He came back to the phone with even more edge in his voice. "I've had it with y'all," he said and hung up.

Jess crossed her arms. "That went well."

"Better than you think, sweetie," Kat said. "Go on back to bed. Everythin's gonna be fine."

"Seriously? How is everythin' gonna be fine? Didn't you just tell Mr. Polk his store was on fire? All you did was make him mad. Folks are just gonna think we're plumb crazy."

"You mean they're gonna think *I'm* crazy."

"No, Mama, they already say our whole family's insane. This will just give 'em more ammunition." Earlier that month in biology class, a girl named Rachel had joked that Jess's family probably ate hallucinogenic mushrooms for supper, and a few kids laughed. Jess dumped a jar of wet fruit fly paste into Rachel's lap without missing a beat. It earned Jess a three-day suspension, but hearing that girl scream was worth it.

"Let's call it a night," Dave said. "This drama is officially over."

Jess rolled her eyes. "Is it *really* over? You know it's only a matter of time before she does it again."

"Please don't talk about me like I'm not here," Kat said.

"And what dimension were you visitin' ten minutes ago? 'Cause you surely weren't here."

Dave drew a sharp breath. "Jess! Don't talk to your mama like that."

"It's okay. She's just blowin' off steam," Kat said, giving her daughter a weak smile. "I'm sorry, sweetie. I know how difficult this must be for you."

"Ya think?" Jess glared at her mother and stomped out of the room.

She used the bathroom, hung up her robe, and heard the wail of faraway sirens as she climbed into bed.

* * *

Two days later, the front-page headline of the *Center Point Online Gazette* read: "Family Saved from Hardware Store Blaze." The article described how firefighters arrived at Polk's Hardware moments after a rapidly growing electrical fire had started. They saved a family of undocumented workers living in a second-floor storeroom, hidden there by one of Polk's employees. A shorted-out popcorn maker had been the cause, but the damage was minimal. The *Gazette* quoted Scott Polk saying that a high-tech monitoring system hadn't warned of the problem when it should have. When the *Gazette* reporter asked Polk how he knew about the fire, he simply shrugged and wouldn't say more.

The Atwoods, of course, knew the whole story. Yet Polk still hadn't called to thank them, which Jess thought was weird considering that Kat's vision had saved lives.

"Some folks aren't much good at showin' gratitude, but that doesn't mean they're not grateful," Kat said, putting the plate she'd just dried back in the cupboard.

"Huh." Jess stopped washing and stared at the soapy dishes in front of her. "Does that mean I don't have to thank you for makin' supper?"

"You never have to thank me, honey. You should do it only when you want to practice gratitude and respect." She started on another plate. "The difference 'tween you and Mr. Polk is that he doesn't have his mama there to remind him."

"Lucky me."

Kat slid her arm around Jess's waist and stared out the window a few moments before kissing her daughter's shoulder. "Lucky you."

* * *

Despite the disturbances from Kat's visions and the occasional teasing Jess endured at school, for the next two years, she truly believed she *was* lucky, even when some mean girls started calling her Oreo in her senior year—as if the Little Orphan Annie nickname wasn't bad enough. Her best friend Elena Rodriguez encouraged her to ignore the haters, which helped. People cared about her, and overall, life wasn't so bad.

That was before she wore the wrong shoes and turned her world upside down.

CHAPTER ONE

Center Point, Texas
Present Day

The strange dream about a choking baby had returned and kept Jess awake most of the night. Her greatest fear was not that people would see her as crazy—the way they'd seen her grandmother, Anna Mae, and Kat when they were alive—but that she really *was* crazy. Worst of all, Jess could do nothing to keep these hit-or-miss visions from coming. What was the point of seeing an anonymous baby in distress other than to frustrate her?

In this latest version, the dream included a neighbor's house down the highway, past the fork in the road. She was pretty sure their name was Thornton. They were Yankee transplants from Chicago who owned the Happy Platter Cafe downtown. Jess had never met them in person, but everyone in Center Point knew the café.

She rolled over and eventually fell asleep, but the same dream woke her again around five a.m. She rubbed her eyes with the heels of her hands, thinking about the busy day that awaited her.

They decided as a family to keep the farm instead of selling it when Kat inherited the property from her uncle Rudy, but Jess often wondered if they had made the right choice. Organic production took far more effort than any of them expected. Without Kat and her organizational skills, they struggled to make a profit. They essentially lost Dave at the same time. He was physically

7

present but drunk more often than not. In their first season without Kat, they had hired Jess's old high school friend Elena as their business manager. She was a big help, but she wasn't Kat, and they had been financially strained for the past few years. If they didn't turn things around, they could lose the farm.

More than anything, Jess wanted peace from visions that weren't always accurate—or relevant. Why couldn't she have a vision that would teach her how their farm could make money instead of losing it? If there was a baby choking, wouldn't the parents either deal with it or call 911? Part of her wanted to just leave it alone, but like Dave used to say back when he was sober, there were three kinds of people: those who act, those who react, and those who never act.

The last time she ignored one of her visions and didn't act, a young couple died. Jess's dream about an orange Chevy Camaro with black racing stripes colliding head-on with a trash truck had begun early one May. It returned every two or three weeks, interrupting her sleep and disturbing her days. From the faint light of fireworks exploding overhead, the woman in the car looked like a girl who had been in her high school graduating class. Jess had dismissed it as nothing more than a recurring nightmare. Besides, was she supposed to call every trash company in town and have them warn their drivers to be careful on the Fourth of July based on her dream? They would think she was a prank caller.

In hindsight, if she had warned the sheriff's department in time, it might have made the difference between life and death, but Jess would never know for sure. All she knew was that she didn't act, and her nightmare vision became real. On his way to load up spent fireworks and other trash from the Kerr County public display in Kerrville, the driver had his eyes on the show in the sky and didn't notice when his truck crossed the double yellow line. The couple in the orange Camaro had apparently also been distracted, as there were no skid marks from either vehicle until a few feet before they collided.

She had made no agreement with anyone to report dreams that might or might not come true. However, that did little to lessen her guilt over the couple's death. She never forgot Kat telling her when she was only nine or ten,

"Hope all you want, but the past never changes. Your future, on the other hand, is unwritten until you act." Jess sighed and pulled on her running clothes. Time to act.

Not wanting to wake her brother or stepfather, Jess made her way through the dark and quiet house, wincing every time she stepped on a creaky floorboard. Her great-uncle Rudy had built the place in the sixties, and the Atwoods were often reminded it had been a do-it-yourself job. If she was honest with herself, though, she liked its cozy, rustic feel.

What she didn't like was navigating in the darkness. When Kevin was only eight or nine, he told her she couldn't see well in the dark because her eyes were made of chocolate. Kat told Jess to ignore her annoying little brother.

The eastern horizon had just begun to lighten by the time she got outside, though a scattering of stars still decorated the navy-blue sky, subtly contrasting the moon's pale-yellow crescent. The Kidwells' rooster across the road was already trying to wake the world with its crowing. Wallaby, her Australian shepherd, whined pitifully when she told him to stay and barked angrily when the door closed. Dave and Kevin wouldn't be happy about that, but they would probably be up in the next half hour anyway. She glanced at her watch. At least Kevin would. With Dave, it depended on how hungover he was.

She had thought about asking Kevin to come with her, but he wouldn't have approved. Her younger brother usually splashed cold water on anything to do with her visions, though she felt safer with him around. In her senior year, after a boy in her class started a rumor that he'd had sex with her, Kevin punched him in the nose. It was all anybody talked about for weeks—the gay freshman with a stutter giving a bloody nose to a senior class student twice his size. However, while she liked that he was protective, he was a frequent source of unsolicited advice. The last thing she wanted that morning was to argue with him about warning the Thorntons.

The next-door neighbors' farm took a long time to run past. Crape myrtles, their bright red blossoms gray in the predawn light, lined the road for a thousand feet. Behind them lay three hundred and seventy acres of wheat. Jess could tell from the scent of the gentle summer breeze that it had ripened and was nearly ready to harvest.

She was halfway to the fork in the road when she asked herself why she hadn't taken the pickup truck since the Thorntons lived over a mile away. At least it gave her time to think about what she'd say when they opened the door. "Good mornin', I was wonderin' if your baby might be chokin' . . ." Or better yet, "Hi, I was wonderin' if your baby was chokin', but for some reason you haven't called 911." Or . . . nothing else came to mind.

Kat had earned a reputation as a crazy woman by telling people stories about the future that didn't always come true. Jess had no desire to follow in her mother's footsteps. She slowed to a walk and looked over her shoulder, torn between doing what some dubious vision told her was right and making a fool of herself or going back home and minding her own business. She came to a complete stop. The choking baby dream may have only been a nightmare. *There might be nothing to this.*

Then again, there might be.

She started running again and soon arrived at the Thorntons' property. The sun hadn't fully risen, but there was sufficient light to see the modern three-story brick house—a bit of an anomaly in that part of Texas—set back from the highway, just as it had appeared in her vision. Crookneck squash, zucchini, and Swiss chard grew on either side of the driveway, some of it going to seed. The Thorntons apparently produced just enough so they could advertise locally grown ingredients in their café. Closer to the house, she passed multiple rows of fragrant English lavender, their faint purple hue just beginning to show in the early-morning light.

She knocked on the solid mahogany front door with its fancy decorative trim, first softly, then with increasing intensity. No response. She tried the doorbell and heard a muffled electronic chime deep within the house, but nothing else. She knocked harder and waited.

Still no response. At least she'd tried.

As she turned to go, a faint sound came from inside. Jess pressed her ear against the door and thought she heard a soft noise that could have been almost anything, including the sound of a baby choking.

She tested the door handle, but it was locked. She trotted around the house, feeling a sense of urgency bordering on panic. After knocking on a few windows, she scolded herself for not bringing her cell phone. She pressed her face against the glass side panel of the back door with a "Protected by ADT" sticker and could barely make out what looked like an old-style baby basket in the far corner of the room.

Jess pounded on the locked door with her fist and then checked under the doormat for a key. No luck there, and time was running out for that baby. She picked up a stone large enough to break the glass, and her stomach churned as she thought about her next move. She needed a vision that would show her the right thing to do—but nothing came. It never did when she tried to force it.

She took a deep breath, then hurled the rock at the ADT sticker, scattering bits of glass everywhere. Her hand shook as she reached in, and she swore when her fingers touched a secure deadbolt cylinder. Feeling around the wall to the side, she found a key hanging from a small nail. She used it to unlock the deadbolt, then pushed the door open. Two steps inside the house, she froze at the scent of cinnamon on buttered toast. Maybe they were home and just didn't want to answer the door. She had read about Texas's "Stand Your Ground" law, which gave homeowners the right to shoot an intruder without having to answer too many questions afterward.

"*Hello?*" she called out. With butterflies in her stomach and eyes fixed on the baby basket, she walked across the room in what felt like slow motion. Her heart sank when she found only a white blanket with little blue koala bears on it and a strong odor of talcum. Had she risked so much for nothing? At least the alarm hadn't gone off. Maybe they had forgotten to set it—or perhaps it was the silent kind.

Jess tried the bedrooms down the hall one at a time, her mind desperately urging her to get out of there. The third door she opened was to the master suite. A crib stood on the far side of a canopied four-poster bed. She heard rustling from that direction and crossed the room in a few quick steps. In the crib lay a baby in a charcoal-gray and sky-blue onesie who seemed as surprised to see her as she was to see him. A baby who was definitely not choking.

A silver SUV pulled up out front, and Jess frantically considered her options. If she ran out the back, she would look like a common thief, but trying to explain her misguided vision could be an even bigger mistake. She had to get out of there.

Jess hurried toward the back door and nearly collided with a shocked Lisa Thornton.

"What are you doing in my house? Are you from Child Protective Services? I was only away for a few minutes."

"I was at the door and heard what sounded like a baby chokin." Jess hoped she sounded more confident than she felt.

Lisa pushed past her, ran into the bedroom, and came out holding her baby a few seconds later, her face flushed. "Does he look like he's choking? What are you *really* doing here? How dare you come in here and—" Her eyes widened as she noticed the broken glass, and her voice rose in pitch. "You broke in! What were you thinking? You were planning to kidnap little Jimmy, weren't you?" She shifted the now-whimpering child onto her hip and pulled a cell phone out of the rear pocket of her tight-fitting designer jeans. "I've seen you around town. What's your name?"

"I'm—" Jess began, then bolted out the back door.

Lisa yelled something she couldn't make out, but Jess wasn't about to stick around and find out what. Crossing the neighboring fields, she ran most of the way along the river, as far from the road as possible. She was well into a dense growth of Texas mountain laurel when a sheriff's patrol car raced by with its siren wailing. It had been a mistake to run. Why hadn't she stayed and explained the situation to Lisa Thornton instead of acting like a common criminal? How hard would it be for the authorities to find a woman of color in a virtually all-white town?

The only reason she was in this mess in the first place was because of a stupid dream she'd thought was a vision. She probably would have screamed in frustration if she wasn't so out of breath.

Back home, she waited in anticipation through the morning and into the afternoon, listening for a car in the driveway, which could mean the sheriff arriving to question or arrest her, or maybe one of the Thorntons coming to holler at her. How could she have been so foolish? Who in their right mind would break into their neighbors' house based on a stupid dream?

Elena knocked on her door in the middle of the afternoon. "Ready to go over the accounts?"

"Sure." Jess had forgotten their plan to go over the previous month's profit-and-loss statement. She didn't want to meet but didn't see any way out of it.

"We're not getting the numbers we need," Elena began, "and thanks to you being behind on the accounts, we don't even know how far off those numbers are."

It was difficult to focus, and Jess kept wondering whether she'd be caught for the Thornton break-in. Elena eventually gave up with a dramatic sigh, telling her to reschedule when she was ready to give their meeting her full attention.

By the end of the day, Jess felt relieved that no one had shown up to arrest or yell at her and promised herself she would be more careful in the future. Just the week before, Kevin had said her visions were hopelessly intertwined with her imagination.

Maybe he had a point.

* * *

"Why are you mopin' around?" her brother asked after supper that evening as she watched a video of a national-level paintball competition on her smartphone.

She pulled out one of her earbuds and frowned. "I'm not mopin'."

"Of course not. This is what you look like when you're happy."

"Thanks, I was hopin' someone would come along and say that. Now, if you don't mind, I'm kinda busy," she said, turning her gaze back to the phone. She wasn't about to tell him what had happened at the Thorntons' house that morning, though she'd decided to explain everything to Elena when she saw her next. Their business manager was more understanding and less judgmental. More importantly, she was a friend, while Kevin was . . . an annoying younger brother she happened to be in business with.

"Come out b-back and pop off a few rounds with me while there's still some light left. It'll do you good."

She glared at him. "You should know better than to ask me that."

"Call me a slow learner, b-but I see no reason not to ask you. We walk down to the river, shoot at some cans and targets, and suddenly feel much happier. We could even make it a competition."

"You know I don't touch guns."

"Am I confusin' you with someone else, or aren't you obsessed with a sport that's all about shootin' people?"

"Paintball is nonlethal."

"So is shootin' paper targets and tin cans. B-besides, I don't see any problem with firearms b-bein' lethal, long as you make sure the person on the receivin' end deserves to die."

"Which is probably what the guy who shot my daddy was thinkin'."

"Right. You're mad at whoever killed your daddy and are therefore mad at guns—but only the kind that use gunpowder, not paintball pellets. Maybe it's just an excuse for b-bein' mad at the world."

"I think you missed your callin' as a master psychologist, Kevvy."

"Don't call me that."

"Why not?"

He shook a finger at her. "You know damn well I don't go b-by that anymore."

Jess just shrugged and walked away.

CHAPTER TWO

Wears Valley, Tennessee
May 1964
Twenty-six years before Jess is born

Anna Mae Cole found the sweltering heat and oppressive humidity disorienting. She always felt uneasy when things weren't the way they'd appeared in a vision because it meant something was out of order. The Fraser firs were more fragrant than usual because of the higher-than-normal temperatures, causing them to release extra pitch. The sheen of sweat on her skin made her pale-blue cotton dress cling uncomfortably to her. May wasn't usually so hot.

In her dream-vision, she hadn't seen the rich earthy loam of the woodland floor, soft enough in places for her bare feet to make imprints. The chorus of cicadas around her hadn't been in the vision either. She tried gathering her long blonde hair into a ponytail, but that didn't work because she had nothing with which to tie it back. After struggling to knot it a few times, she gave up when it kept slipping loose.

She came to a campsite and considered the four trails branching out in front of her while attempting to wave away a swarm of gnats, sweat trickling down her back. She'd lost all sense of order, leaving her with a vague feeling of panic. Which way to go? The Great Smoky Mountains National Park had thousands of little paths here and there. Some were made by animals, some by humans—and some by humans no better than animals.

Suddenly, order and direction were back. Anna Mae saw herself following the path off to the left, which would take her along Dakota Ridge and past an old abandoned barn.

Her mother had warned her not to enter the park. The National Park Service displaced the family of her father, Jefferson Cole, from Cades Cove when he was only ten. He said they took homes and livelihoods away from thousands of people so they could create a place for a bunch of fat-assed tourists to gawk at trees.

When her big brother Rudy was in high school, he came home one day arguing that a hundred years before any white people had been evicted from the Smokies, the federal government forced thousands of Cherokees to leave their homes there. They then marched them at gunpoint to reservations in Oklahoma. His father slapped him for saying that.

The senior Cole didn't allow anyone in their family to even mention the park. Anna Mae would be severely punished if he knew she'd been there.

Did she want to make her father angry? Of course not. But neither parent would know since they had gone into Gatlinburg for the day to hear some half-pint teenager named Dolly Parton sing. They didn't ask Anna Mae if she cared to come along, but she had better things to do anyway.

She spotted a patched and tattered army tent when she got to the part of Dakota Ridge that overlooked Redberry Creek. Rudy used to have one just like it. It was down beyond the switchback, so it would take her a while to reach it. She was going to walk right past and not think about her brother too much. Anna Mae missed him but understood why he'd left home. As soon as she was old enough, she'd leave as well. Her father had rarely whipped her when Rudy still lived at home, but now it happened far too often.

She hit a tripwire about a hundred feet from the tent, rattling some empty Campbell soup cans. It had been almost invisible, strung just a few inches above the path.

A short, stocky Negro with a scar on his cheek emerged from the tent, waving a revolver. "Hold up now," he said, "you don't belong here."

Her mind told her to fear, but her heart stayed calm. The man's frown deepened as she came closer. She would pass within a few feet of him, but it'd be all right.

"Where you goin', blondie?"

"Just walkin' by. I ain't here to create no bother."

"Well, that didn't work, now did it? You sho' nuff botherin' me."

She kept her eyes on the path. "I got no bone to pick with you, mister."

"Damn right you don't." He pointed the pistol at her as she came closer. "You stop right there."

She glanced at the gun. Stopping would get her off track and out of order. It wasn't going to happen.

"Hey now," he said, "I ain't done talkin' to you."

"My interest ain't with you today."

"Your interest? You go when I say it's okay for you to go. You're on my land."

"This ain't your land. This is God's land."

He laughed. "Well, you got that right," he said, following her. "But you got no bidness here."

"I *do* have bidness here," she said over her shoulder. "It just ain't with you."

"You see I got a gun. What are you thinkin'?" He paused. "You stop now, chile."

She continued on, increasing the distance between them, sure he wouldn't shoot her.

"You must be crazy," he said. "There ain't nothin' down here for you. You don't even have no shoes on."

She didn't answer. No point in that. At least he'd stopped following her. Did he have anything to do with the girl she saw in her vision? Maybe she was running from him.

But she knew in her heart he wouldn't do anybody harm—gun or no gun. Besides, he hadn't been in her vision, which meant he wasn't the reason she was there. Yet somebody—or something—who *would* do harm was around, and that was why she'd been called to go there. She would be safe if she kept with the order the vision had shown her. Order always kept her safe. She could have just gone to a park ranger or the sheriff, but she got into big trouble the last time she'd done that. Despite her detailed description of where to look, they didn't find a young boy in distress as she'd claimed.

What would she have told them this time? If she shared her dream about a teenage girl running along a ravine, glancing back at something scary, that would go over like a lead balloon, as Rudy used to say. Especially if they had to hike through miles of hot and humid woods to get there.

A thrill surged through her when she reached the barn, its red paint peeling, roof sagging, sections of the siding warped and twisted. She felt validated whenever she experienced something she'd foreseen in a vision. Empty milk bottles, old sardine tins, and other trash littered the area.

She continued along the path for miles, avoiding frequent patches of poison ivy. Even though the trail branched off a few times and became less obvious the farther she went, order stayed with her, and the direction she had to take remained clear. She finally arrived at the ravine with the rock formation high on one side, exactly as it had been in the vision.

She almost tripped over a body covered by branches and bright green leaves, and it took all the self-control she had to not scream. Before her lay the lifeless form of the girl she'd seen in her vision, sprawled catawampus across the path, her blood-stained clothes ripped, eyes opened wide.

The vision's comfort, security, and purpose evaporated as if they had never been. Order—and therefore safety—were also gone. She heard a twig snap and spun around but saw no one. In the space of two heartbeats, she turned and ran back the way she'd come. More than once, she thought she might faint.

Her dress was soaked in sweat by the time she neared the old tent.

"*Hey, mister!*" she called out, struggling to catch her breath. No response. She reached the tripwire and deliberately shook it, rattling the soup cans. The man came out of the tent, his face clouded by anger.

"Why do you think you need to bother me again?"

"You should know the sheriff will be here soon."

"Why? What the hell did you do?"

"I didn't do nothin', but I found a girl's body down near the ravine."

"Don't you be playin' games with me now. That ain't no funny joke."

"I ain't bein' funny, cross my heart. The first house I get to, I'm callin' the sheriff. If he finds you here, it won't be a good thing, especially with that gun of yours."

The man cursed, went back into his tent, and started rustling around.

Anna Mae turned to go, then had another flash of a vision. The man in the tent was part of it, but otherwise, it was vague and dark.

She almost said something but instead hurried back toward safety, civilization, and a phone.

CHAPTER THREE

J ess woke to the lazy rumble of distant thunder, the earthy scent of rain, and the patter of raindrops on the roof. She yawned, pulled aside her curtains, and looked out at the gray morning. This was good. Their crops needed water, and the rain gave her a great excuse to be inside. She felt more secure indoors, though if there were going to be any repercussions from the Thornton break-in, they most likely would have already happened. Besides, it would give her a chance to bring their accounts up to date.

Instead of accounting, however, she spent the first few hours of the day organizing her bedroom. As if it mattered which side of the desk her trash basket with the John Legend sticker was on or whether the pink comforter with little white dots was positioned correctly on her bed. Her brother loved to tease that her room looked like a teenager's, but she didn't really care what he thought. She wasn't going to tell him about the set of Pokémon cards she'd concealed at the bottom of her underwear drawer—or that she occasionally used them as tarot cards. The surprising thing was that they actually worked, though more often than not, she didn't want to know the future if she could avoid it. The problem was that she couldn't stop the visions even if she wanted to. For Jess, they were like unbidden guests who overstayed their welcome.

She had only just booted up her computer when the doorbell rang around ten-thirty, and her heart fell when Kevin yelled her name. Trudging downstairs, she saw Dave hunched over his morning coffee at the kitchen table, red-eyed and unshaven, in his frayed U.S. Navy bathrobe and slippers. His unkempt salt-and-pepper hair used to look good on him, effortless and rakish; now he just looked like a bum. He watched her walk past and grunted a greeting, most likely nursing a hangover. Jess knew that people had to grieve in their own way, but it had been ten years since they lost Kat.

Two somber sheriff's deputies stood on their porch, rain dripping off their ponchos. One of them—a man with hazel eyes—said a woman had broken into a house down the street and asked if that had been her. She could deny it, but then they would probably bring her to the sheriff's office and have Lisa Thornton identify her—and prove her a liar. Few people of color lived in Center Point, so it'd be one of the fastest lineups in history. Kat used to say that while there would be many things in life she wouldn't have control over, she could always choose to act with integrity.

"Ms. Thornton said the woman we're seekin' is around thirty, with your approximate height and weight," the hazel-eyed deputy said. "And color," he added after a pause.

Heart pounding, she raised her chin and looked him in the eye. "Yes, sir, that was me, but I can explain. I thought I heard—"

"Ms. Thornton has lodged a formal complaint." The deputy glanced behind her. "Is your stepdaddy here?"

"He is. *Dave!*" she yelled over her shoulder.

Of course they knew who her stepfather was. They also undoubtedly knew he was a regular patron of Clancy's Cowboy Saloon and had buddies in the sheriff's department. He and the Kerr County Sheriff were both Navy veterans, which was how Dave had connected to the department initially. Before Kat died, he'd perform at their yearly fundraisers without fail, with the whole family there to cheer him on.

After a few seconds, he shuffled up behind Jess.

"I'm sorry, Mr. Atwood," the taller deputy said, "but we're gonna have to arrest your daughter."

"On what charge?"

"Criminal trespass, breakin' and enterin'."

"We hate doin' this," Hazel Eyes said, "but we have to follow through. Mr. Atwood, if you like, you can meet us at the sheriff's office."

Jess noted the conflict on her stepfather's face. At least he felt something. Then the look faded. "No, I'm good. Y'all just do what you gotta do."

With a heaviness in her heart, she watched him pad back toward the kitchen. He used to be so different.

"Do we have to do this?" she asked, turning back to the deputies.

The taller officer pursed his lips. "'Fraid so, miss."

All she had done was to try to save a baby. A baby who didn't need saving, but her intentions had been in the right place.

They handcuffed her and put her in the back of the patrol car. As they drove off, she tried explaining the reason for the break-in to the deputies.

"You know, you're more than welcome to have a lawyer present whenever one of us talks to you," the taller deputy said. "He or she would tell you to hush 'cause we can use what you say against you and enter it as a confession."

"I thought that baby was in trouble."

Hazel Eyes turned in his seat. "You hard of hearin', young lady, or just plain stubborn? For your own good, don't say anythin' more about it. Sometimes we can forget what was said, but that only goes so far. If the judge asks me to tell the truth, I have to tell the truth. You understand me?"

Jess nodded and stayed quiet during what felt like the longest ride of her life.

They fingerprinted her and took mug shots at the sheriff's office, just like they would for a real criminal. She kept thinking about what it would be like to be in jail and have a felony conviction on her record. All because she couldn't leave well enough alone.

After processing, they brought her before a judge who explained that since it was a first-time offense and she was a local business owner, they would release her on her own recognizance. That, at least, was a relief. As tight as their finances were, she didn't know how they would have come up with the bail. The judge set a hearing date for the following Monday.

Jess hated calling Kevin to pick her up, but Elena wasn't available, and Dave might not have been sober. The rhythm of the wipers clearing light rain from the windshield was the only sound in the pickup truck all the way home. As they climbed out, her brother smiled tightly. "Tell me about it whenever you're ready." He raised an eyebrow. "Or not."

* * *

Jess worked on chores around the farm through the overcast and often drizzly weekend. She sprayed a tangy-scented mixture of diluted soap, lemon oil, and cayenne on cauliflower growing in the south field, brought the accounts up to date, and felt mortified over what had happened. All because she'd believed her dreams were real.

She called a lawyer named Victor Carson, whose father had supposedly worked with her great-uncle Rudy back in the sixties. He met her in the sparsely furnished Kerr County courtroom lobby Monday morning. "Well," he began, sitting next to her on the hard wooden bench under a painting of George H. W. Bush. "I have good news and bad news."

"Just give me all of it, please."

"It looks like you drove down here for nothin'."

"Say what?"

Carson smiled. "Which brings me to the good news. Ms. Thornton came in yesterday saying she decided not to press charges after all." He checked his watch. "I would have called, but I only just now found out myself."

"Are you serious?"

"Serious as a heart attack. The sheriff's department can still pursue the matter, but I don't think they will. That's good, 'cause you could've seen up to a year of jail time."

"I don't know what to say."

"You can say you're one lucky woman who can count her blessin's," he said, shaking her hand. "Give me a holler if you hear from the sheriff's office again, but I doubt they'll do anythin'." He winked at her and walked away.

* * *

Jess absently scratched at a spot of dried pasta sauce on the kitchen table while arguing with Kevin over the best way to make their farm profitable and get out of debt. Her brother could be so thick sometimes.

His self-labeled brilliant solution to their financial problems was to grow, process, and package edible mushrooms. He explained how the idea came to him while browsing farming trends on Reddit. As they discussed it, she realized his suggestion might not have been as clueless as she had first thought. But they couldn't just pile on more debt while already overextended. She tried to explain the simple math, but he wasn't getting it.

The doorbell rang, sending chills up her spine. Were the deputies back? "Can you answer that?" she asked her brother.

He gave her a funny look and walked to the door. "*Jess, you need to come here,*" he called out a few seconds later. Maybe she wasn't as lucky as she thought.

She caught her breath at the sight of Lisa Thornton standing on their porch wearing high-heeled snakeskin boots, with her baby in her arms, looking like she'd rather be just about anywhere else.

"Mornin', Ms. Thornton. I'm so sorry about what happened last Friday."

"Don't be. I'm here to thank you. You saved my little Jimmy's life."

The hairs on the back of Jess's neck stood on end. "What do you mean?"

"One reason I got so mad when I found you in my house was because I knew leaving him home was a stupid habit."

Jess slowly let out her breath. "Okay."

"It's just that I don't have anybody to watch him with Rick always off in San Antonio, and it's such an ordeal to get Jimmy to sleep . . . I didn't want to wake him. I'd made a quick dash to the café to get the cinnamon buns rising. All I had to do was take them out of the cooler and set them on the counter. I was only gone from the house five minutes, tops." She examined her bright-red fingernails. "Maybe six at the most. Your visit the other day got me thinking about how wrong that was. The next morning, I put my little boy in the baby basket and carried him into the café. As soon as we got inside the front door, he made a strange sound."

"Oh, my."

Lisa's eyes welled with tears. "He was choking on something. At first, I couldn't tell what it was, but then I pulled out a little metal rattle lodged in his throat." Her voice broke, and she paused. "It looked like a baby toy from the fifties before they figured out babies can choke on small things. It must've been in the vintage basket I bought on eBay, but I never noticed it."

"That was a close call."

"It sure was. I don't know . . . if he'd been home or in the car alone, he might have died, but thanks to your warning, I was much more careful. I probably wouldn't have taken him with me if it hadn't been for you." She pursed her lips. "You saved his life."

"You're the one who chose to bring him along with you."

"Yeah, but from what happened Friday with you in my house . . . well, I think it was a warning from above," she said and kissed her son's cheek. The baby cooed softly, and both women smiled at the sound. "The sheriff made it pretty clear that they could report me to Child Protective Services for leaving Jimmy alone—and I'm so glad they didn't." A tear ran down her cheek. "And he was right. It was . . . I was irresponsible."

Jess opened the door wider. "Won't you come in?"

"No, but thank you. I just wanted you to know." She turned and walked to her silver SUV. After strapping Jimmy in his car seat, she nodded to Jess and climbed in.

Jess watched her drive off, still processing the shock of what had just happened.

Kevin came up behind her. "I caught a few words. I take it that was somethin' good?"

"Oh yeah." She shook her head in disbelief. "Somethin' incredibly good."

CHAPTER FOUR

Wears Valley, Tennessee
May 1964

Out of breath and dripping sweat, Anna Mae frowned at the rundown mobile home as she ran up. The skirting on one end of the dwelling was missing, exposing crumbling, moss-encrusted cinder blocks, and the front porch sagged slightly under her weight.

She knocked on the textured sheet metal covering the door and wondered if they even had a phone. Hearing nothing but a tinny echo, she gave up and was halfway across the crabgrass and chickweed that served as a front lawn when the door opened. A white-haired woman leaned out on a cane and glared at her.

Anna Mae asked if she could use her phone to call the sheriff.

"Don't you have one at your house, honey?"

"Yes, ma'am, but that's a good twenty minutes away, and I need to get the sheriff here soon as possible."

"Why is that?"

"I found somethin' in the woods, and he's gonna want to see it right away."

The older woman looked doubtful. "Jeremiah's at the hardware store. Saturday's his day off, you know. Why don't you come back in half an hour?"

"Please, ma'am, this is an emergency."

"Emergency, huh?" She opened the door wide and led Anna Mae to the kitchen, which had a disagreeable odor of recent pickling.

Trying not to gag on the pungent smell, Anna Mae reached for the phone on the wall, but the older woman grabbed it first. "I'll do it." She eyed Anna Mae as she dialed and waited for the sheriff to answer. "Afternoon, Sheriff Keene. This is Jo Ellen Brower over on Pinecrest. There's a barefoot blonde girl with dark-brown eyes here . . ." She cupped her hand over the mouthpiece. "What's your name, honey?"

"Anna Mae Cole."

"She says her name is Hannah Mae Cole and—"

"That's *Anna* Mae."

Mrs. Brower waved her off. "She's sayin' she found somethin' in the park you need to see but won't tell me what it is."

"Please, ma'am, may I talk to him?"

The older woman ignored her. "Right, I understand. Okay, here she is." She passed her the phone with a hint of a smirk. "He knows who you are."

When Anna Mae told Sheriff Keene she'd found a body, he mentioned the time she'd had them search for a boy who wasn't where she said.

"I saw this girl with my own eyes, Sheriff."

"You sure about that?"

"Yes, sir, one hundred percent." She glanced at Mrs. Brower, who stared at Anna Mae with her mouth open.

"You were sure the last time, weren't you?" the sheriff asked.

"I saw her body less than two hours ago. Cross my heart."

Keene and Deputy Stevens arrived ten minutes later. The paunchy sheriff frowned at her, his cheeks bulging with chewing tobacco. His tall and trim deputy opened the back door of the patrol car for her and nodded politely as he closed it.

Sheriff Keene kept glancing at her in the rearview mirror as she directed them to where she had entered the park. It took them another forty-five minutes to hike to where she'd met the man with the gun. No sign of him—he'd even removed the tripwire—but the sheriff and deputy apparently felt they had to look inside the tent. Anna Mae tried to speed them along, worrying that things were already too far out of order, but Keene just told her to let them do their job. She wanted to say part of their job meant they had to hurry, but she held her tongue. After hiking in for another half hour, they arrived at where she'd seen the body, but found nothing out of the ordinary.

Anna Mae's heart sank. "It was right here."

Keene motioned to where she stood. "You mean right at that spot?"

She glanced around at the thick woods. The background chorus of cicadas seemed louder than before, as if they were mocking her. "Yes, sir, more or less."

Sheriff Keene removed his hat and wiped his brow with a handkerchief. "Honey, more or less don't cut it. You need to tell us exactly where you saw that body."

"I'm tryin'."

"You're *tryin'*?"

"It was right over . . ." Anna Mae felt the pressure of tears. "I swear, it was . . ." She looked up and down the path, trying to remember precisely where the body had been. Order was gone because they had taken too long to get there.

Keene glanced at his watch and scowled. "Ya know, reportin' a crime that didn't happen is a serious thing."

"Of course it is, but that's not what I'm doin'. Her body was right around here."

The sheriff slapped a mosquito on his forearm. "If it was 'right around here,' as you say, I think we'd at least see somethin' suspicious. If not a body, then wouldn't we see some blood? Yet everythin' looks pretty damn normal to me." He squinted at her. "I reckon you've been leadin' us on again."

"I swear I saw her body."

Keene crossed his arms. "Anna Mae, have you ever seen somethin' you thought was real but wasn't?"

"The visions *are* real."

"No doubt they are in your world. But I'm talkin' real in the sense of physical, as in somethin' you can actually touch."

"Well, I . . ."

"Now, listen here, young lady. I've heard stories of you helpin' to locate lost dogs, and there was that tourist lady from Virginia you helped us find last fall. But there was also the time you led us on a useless hunt for a boy who didn't even exist."

"I'm pretty sure her body was right here."

Keene wiped his forehead again. "So now you're pretty sure? Well, I'm pretty sure this is a complete waste of our time. I'm gonna have to tell your pa."

"Oh no, please don't!"

"Look, missy, I don't know where the voices that guide you are comin' from or who or what they are. Maybe they only exist in your head. I ain't the judge of that, but I take responsibility for keepin' Wears Valley safe, and this little boondoggle is interferin' with that."

Deputy Stevens turned toward her. "Body or no body, these woods ain't a proper place for a young lady to be." He paused. "Especially one pretty as you, which makes it much more dangerous for you to be off on your lonesome." He wiped his brow with the back of his hand. "Who knows who's livin' in that hobo camp we passed back there?"

"Well, *I* know who's livin' there. I met him when I was down here earlier."

"You what?"

"A man came out of that tent when I was down here before."

"Now you tell us," Sheriff Keene said. "And he just disappeared too, has he? Here one minute and gone the next, I suppose?"

Stevens frowned. "What'd he look like?"

"He was a short Negro with a scar on his cheek."

The sheriff glanced at Stevens. "A long, fat scar?"

"Yes, sir."

"And you talked to him?"

"I did. He had a tripwire set up that rattled some cans when I went by."

Sheriff Keene spat a wad of tobacco into the bushes. "That sounds like Hobo Bill, but he don't talk to nobody. Do you understand that way out here in the woods, no one would hear you call for help? He might've even had a weapon."

"Oh, he never would've used it on me."

"Used *what* on you?" asked Keene.

"He had a gun, but he's not dangerous."

Stevens cleared his throat. "If someone has a gun, chances are they'll use it if the right opportunity presents itself. You're mighty lucky."

"Indeed you are," the sheriff said. "Colored man livin' in the woods with a gun, and you don't think he's dangerous? I gotta talk to your pa about that, too."

"Please don't. He'll give me the worst whippin' ever."

"Honey, I got no choice. This world can be wicked, and sometimes we find bodies for real. Promise me you won't be goin' alone to out-of-the-way places like this again."

"I was guided to come here. Please don't tell my pa."

"Sorry. Let's go, Stevens. Missy, you follow us."

In her mind's eye, she saw herself looking for the body alone. Her sense of order was back, which meant safety. "I'd like to stay here and look around some more."

The sheriff spat into the bushes again. "Are you pullin' my leg? You just told us there's a colored man with a gun in the area. People with nothin' to lose can be the most dangerous and unstable." His mouth tightened. "Let's say there *is* a body somewhere in these woods. That'd mean a vicious criminal would be around here. Now, ain't that right?"

She nodded.

"Which would mean it ain't safe for you to be here alone."

She stared off into the trees. "When I'm bein' guided and do things in order, I'm always safe."

Sheriff Keene raised an eyebrow. "Honey, I don't care if you want to believe such silliness, but my job is to protect you, bare feet and all. You came with us on official sheriff department business, and it's our duty to get you safely out of here. You understand what I'm sayin'?"

"I do, but if you give me a chance to look around, I—"

"That ain't gonna happen, sweetheart, and I don't have the patience to stand here arguin' about it. We're leavin' now, and you're comin' with us."

CHAPTER FIVE

Center Point, Texas
Present Day

A dream about a meeting at the bank where their refinance application was rudely rejected woke Jess from a deep sleep and disturbed her, as visions usually did. The day got worse soon after breakfast when, sure enough, she received a call from the Central Texas State Bank in Kerrville requesting she be there at noon to discuss their application.

After watering the asparagus, she went inside, picked up her well-worn copy of *The Midnight Library* from the kitchen table, and walked down to the river with Wallaby. With its hazy white clouds and cooler than average temperature, the beautiful September morning made her feel a little bit better. The dusty-sweet scent from the wheat harvest next door reduced her anxiety even further. She'd decided things might not be so bad after all when another vision hit her mid-stride.

Beginning the night before Kat died, more than ten years earlier, visions had only come to Jess in her dreams. In her very first vision, she hadn't recognized the dream about a snake and a funeral for what it was until after the accident, when it was too late to do anything about it.

Her next vision didn't come until a year later—two weeks before her twentieth birthday—then others followed with increasing regularity. Except for the recent one with the Thornton baby, they rarely happened twice in a week and never when she was wide awake.

Until that morning. Her second vision in twenty-four hours came in broad daylight as she walked down the gravel access road that wound through their pecan trees to the river. Not what you might expect on an ordinary day in the life of an organic farmer, but not much that had transpired in Jess's twenty-nine years could be considered ordinary.

The intense vision only lasted a few seconds and showed multiple police cars flashing red-and-blue lights all over their farm. Uniformed cops and agents wearing blue jackets with "FBI" in yellow block letters on their backs ran between strange buildings she'd never seen before. A helicopter buzzed overhead, then the vision was suddenly gone as though it had never been.

It took her a few seconds to realize she'd stopped walking. Trembling slightly, Jess continued on, anger rising within her. So many of these stupid visions had no point. So there would be police all over the property. Who was she supposed to tell about that?

She had experience trying to warn folks that something was going to happen, and they would look at her like she was a nut job. Sometimes she wondered about that herself.

When Kat was alive, she loved telling Jess and Kevin that what they thought of themselves was all that mattered. But Jess noticed times when small-minded gossip bothered even Kat. Folks called her crazy—and worse—behind her back, and somehow those comments always seemed to find their way home to hurt her. The worst rumor was that she'd not only driven her first husband away, but that was proof that interracial marriages can't work. It deeply upset Jess when she heard it, especially since his leaving was probably her own fault.

Her father left their young family when she was only five, about a year before they inherited the farm and moved there with Kat's new boyfriend, Dave. Jess remembered very few things about her father except his last words before leaving. "I'm done with your craziness," he'd said, looking directly at his only daughter before walking out the front door. He didn't say, "y'all's craziness." He said, "your craziness," plain as day.

Her mother said he was only acting out of fear and was talking about Kat's visions. She explained that sometimes grown-ups say mean things to each other, but he'd looked right at Jess when he said it. She couldn't remember what she'd supposedly done, but their father left because of her. At least that's what she used to tell herself, even though he was the one with a few screws loose. That was proven beyond doubt a couple of years later when they discovered he'd been killed in a scuffle at a seedy bar in South Dallas.

The Dallas police said he had overreacted when a trio of bikers called him the N-word, and he said something snarky back. When the bouncer made *him* leave the bar instead of the bikers, it infuriated him, and he kept coming back, yelling obscenities at the large, dangerous-looking men sporting prison tattoos. The bouncer threw him out at least a couple more times until one biker pulled out a 9mm Berretta and shot her father dead. No one was ever charged with the shooting. The police told Kat that everyone there had suddenly developed amnesia about what the shooter looked like.

When she heard that, seven-year-old Jess vowed she would never touch a gun as long as she lived—at least not the kind that fired bullets. Paintball was a whole different story, however, and by her early teens, she'd become addicted to the sport.

She usually loved her walks to the river, past the rows of kale, potatoes, and carrots with their random ladybugs and the rich smell of organic compost. Reading on the dock was one of her favorite things in the world, and it usually calmed her down when she felt upset. But so many things had gone wrong that day. The argument with Kevin ten minutes after she'd gotten out of bed, the call from Central Texas State Bank, and now this new vision that did a fantastic job of shaking her up but gave her nothing to act on left her with an overwhelming feeling of anxiety. The cherry on top that started it all had been the dream about the bank meeting the night before. As Dave liked to say, when it rains, it pours. At least she didn't wake up yelling like Kat used to.

Wallaby came running back, probably to see why she was so slow, and Jess couldn't help smiling. Having him around always lifted her spirits. If it weren't for him, they would be competing with all kinds of critters for their produce. Wallaby loved chasing animals off their property, especially the raccoons that seemed to enjoy taking random bites out of their red bell peppers.

When she reached the dock, she pulled off her cowboy boots with the little blue hearts on each side and her ruffle top socks. She sighed and dangled her feet in the cool, murky water. Thanks to recent rain, the Guadalupe had collected a good bit of runoff, clouding it more than usual.

With the warm Texas sun on her back, she scratched Wallaby behind the ears and opened her book. Dave often warned her about gators, but there was nothing to worry about. Not only did they rarely get so far upriver, but those that did were small and stayed away from humans. The only ones she'd ever seen had been on Instagram.

"Go on now," she said to her dog. "Find someone more fun to be with than me." Wallaby just tilted his head and gave her a puzzled look.

Jess squinted upriver at the sound of distant shouting. A rowboat floated lazily toward her, carrying a couple of teenage boys who laughed, yelled, and splashed water at each other. Shouldn't they be in school? They were probably skipping classes. She felt a flash of anger. When did *she* ever have the opportunity to skip anything?

A few seconds later, the irony hit her. Wasn't she skipping out when she should be preparing for her meeting at the bank? She closed her book, stomped the water off her feet, and pulled on her socks and boots.

Time to face the music.

CHAPTER SIX

Wears Valley, Tennessee
May 1964

Dear Diary,

The past three days have been the worst of my life. I hate it when people think I'm lying. Even worse is when they think I'm crazy. I know what I saw. Thinking about that poor girl has kept me awake for hours these last few nights.

Today, things went from one extreme to the other. I received a wonderful gift at school this morning, but in the afternoon, I got a whipping I didn't deserve for the second time in three days.

This time it was my tone of voice and not showing how happy I was to see my dear pa after him working his fingers to the bone for us all day long. His words, not mine.

If I'm not glad to see someone, how can I pretend that, especially when they're drunk and ugly? He was limping again, so I know his leg was hurting, but still. How we act is up to us. The whipping three days ago was thanks to that fat pig of a sheriff calling Papa after seeing me in the park—even though I was only trying to help him do his job.

I was already sad about turning seventeen tomorrow because no one will notice.

I can't exactly say no one, though. I wouldn't have this diary if

Miss Porter hadn't given it to me after home economics class. She said it was a birthday/graduation/goodbye present, and I love that it's got a lock on it. It's the best gift anyone ever gave me.

Miss Porter might be the only one in the world besides Rudy who doesn't act like something's wrong with me. She also never gave me trouble about graduating early. "Stay in school," my other teachers warned. Even my English teacher, Mr. Harris, thought so. "You have so much to learn," he said with a worried look. I'm glad he cares, but he doesn't understand the order of things. Most folks don't.

Miss Porter thinks doing things in order is something I'll grow out of. "As if," Rudy would say. I miss my brother so much I could almost cry, but the bright side is that in less than a month, he'll be back home. I can't wait.

Maybe Mama or Papa will notice my birthday tomorrow and say something, but I won't be holding my breath. Either way, only a year left until I'm eighteen, then I'm gone from this place.

People say we create our own reality. Some days that makes good enough sense to me, but someone would have to tell me what I did to create this.

Folks think I'm strange just because I know that one thing has to follow another. When baking a cake, you don't put the frosting in the pan and pour the other ingredients on top. No. You preheat the oven, mix the ingredients, pour them into the pan, bake it for the right amount of time, let it cool, and spread the frosting on last. Can you do any of those things out of order? No. When you build a house, you don't add plumbing after the walls are in and painted. Life is like that, too. One thing follows another. Everything has its proper order, and sometimes you just need to follow the divine breadcrumbs to the end of the path.

The other day, those breadcrumbs led me to find the body of that poor girl. I don't know what's worse: that there's a terrible person on the loose or that no one cares.

CHAPTER SEVEN

Jess started the pickup and glanced at her watch. She wouldn't make it by noon. The bank had better be okay with her being late. Part of her didn't know why she was even going through the motions. They needed the refinance to save their farm, but if her vision was accurate, the bank wouldn't let it happen.

As she turned out of their driveway toward town, she saw Travis Kidwell checking his mailbox across the road, just outside the pretentious Kidwell Cattle gates with river-rock columns on either side and a cast-iron lettered arch across the top. How lucky to live directly across the road from the biggest cattle ranch in Kerr County—which represented everything their little organic farm was not. As she drove by, he tipped his hat, very gentlemanly and polite. Without thinking, she gave him the finger. His eyes widened, then he howled with laughter.

Not the reaction she expected, but whatever. Such a player, that one. She watched him shrink to ant-size in her rearview mirror as she floored the old pickup, its modest four-cylinder motor struggling to perform. Travis and his father, Earl, were unfortunate reminders of how successful even obnoxious people can become if they work hard enough.

Parking in front of the bank on Lombard Street, she turned off the engine and stared at the glass doors. The big red "Central Texas State Bank" lettering had faded, and the upper left corner of the "x" in Texas was long gone. Who were these people to call and demand she come in? They weren't planning on discussing the refinance application. It was going to be a turndown, plain and simple.

If she were in a movie, this would be where she'd lose it, maybe by crashing the pickup into the lobby, or better yet, pulling off a holdup, like George Clooney did in *Out of Sight* when *he* went over the edge. She'd also be very polite about it. "Just put the money in the bag, and no one gets hurt. Is this your first holdup? You're doin' fine." Somehow, the idea seemed oddly appealing. Prison had limited appeal, though.

The short bald man who met her inside looked at his watch as she walked up. "You must be Miss Atwood," he said without smiling.

"Last time I checked."

He stared at her for a couple of seconds, his mouth tightening into a thin line. "I'm Fred Wagner, your loan specialist. Follow me, please."

This is off to a splendid start, Jess thought as they walked into his office. *Twelve minutes late, and you'd think I ran over his dog.*

Fred sat behind a desk too big for the room and waved a hand toward a simple beige couch, indicating she should sit. He leaned forward and steepled his fingers. "About your refinance application . . ."

"I know what you're fixin' to say."

"Do you now?" His weak smile was only a mask. The bank had lost money between bad loans and poor management, and his boss blamed him for being too soft. Problems with his marriage stressed him out further. All of this had been in her dream the night before. She had even foreseen his scratched nameplate with "Fred" engraved on it and the faint scent of stale cigar smoke that permeated the room.

Ignoring the little voice in her head telling her to keep quiet, she shifted on the couch. "I know you're under pressure from your manager for approvin' loans that wound up goin' south."

Fred glanced toward his boss's office, then frowned at Jess. "I beg your pardon?"

"And I know you're havin' trouble with your marriage, so I understand if you're—"

"That couldn't be further from the truth," he said, turning slightly pale. "Who told you that?"

"I'm a good guesser."

His frown deepened, and Jess wondered if she hadn't just made things worse. She was usually more careful not to tell people her visions, especially since they weren't always accurate. Still, sometimes the words just spilled out unchecked.

Fred was looking at her, waiting for something.

"Sorry, what was that?" she asked.

He stiffly repeated himself, asking if she understood the inevitable.

Jess nodded passively, and as he droned on, she looked around the room, only half-listening. The file cabinet from Ikea with the black walnut finish, the clock on the wall running two minutes fast, and the papers on Fred's desk with blood-red "DENIED" stamps on them had all been in her dream the night before.

That was something she hated about the visions. They provided plenty of irrelevant details, but nothing that might make a positive difference in her life—or anyone else's most of the time. The Thornton baby had been a significant exception to how things usually turned out, and even that may have been a simple coincidence.

Bald Fred told her that not only had their refinance application been rejected, they had ninety days to get current on their existing equipment loan, including all outstanding late fees. Otherwise, they would have to pay it off in full. Because the Atwoods' property was security against the credit, he warned that the next steps would be foreclosure and the auction block.

When she got home, Kevin asked her how it went. He frowned and shook his head when she told him what had happened. "B-bummer that they're squeezin' us, b-but why would you tell him that? Maybe we would've had half a chance if you hadn't spooked him."

"I got a little upset."

"Why does that not surprise me?"

"He was turnin' us down anyway."

"Which you knew 'cause you saw it in one of your dreams?"

"I knew 'cause our refinance papers all had red stamps saying 'DENIED' on 'em and 'cause the branch manager told him to turn us down."

His eyebrows went up. "Which you got from one of your visions, right?"

She silently counted to ten, determined not to let him under her skin. He wasn't going to win this one.

But Kevin was on a roll. "Some folks already suspect we have an arrangement with the Devil. B-Becky Sue Crowley has been revivin' the rumor that losin' Mom was payment."

"If we had an arrangement like that, wouldn't that mean we'd be rich, powerful, and wildly successful? Or at least one of those? What did we supposedly get out of *that* deal?"

"Your superpower, of course."

"It's not a superpower, and you know it. Everyone has premonitions that people mostly write off as coincidence." She paused. "I just might have a little more of 'em."

"B-bullshit. We b-both know you have a *lot* more of them."

Jess gave him a tight smile and walked out, with Wallaby following close behind. Didn't Gandhi, Confucius, or someone who knew what they were talking about say to choose one's battles wisely?

She hiked down to the river until she got to her favorite place on the dock, wishing she'd brought her novel. Kat had told her that Granny Mae used to love that spot and would also go there to read. Jess's great-uncle Rudy had built it back when he and his wife Molly were peanut farmers there in the sixties.

She plunked a pebble into the water and watched the expanding ripples. Another thing she hated about her visions was that they reminded her of the last day of her mother's life.

Ten years earlier, the warning in Jess's dream had been clear enough, but she missed the hint of an anonymous funeral with a snake crawling through it. It should have made her wary enough to not have been wearing running shoes the following day, working in tall grass where a rattlesnake had been seen a couple of weeks before—especially since Kat was bitten by one when she was only twelve and had a severe allergic reaction. Allergies are often hereditary, so Jess should have been more careful. Her everlasting regret was not heeding the vision's warning because that oversight ultimately cost her mother's life.

Jess had been using a handheld brush cutter out by the equipment garage. She'd had her bright-orange ear protectors on and didn't realize that she'd cornered a rattler, backing into it as she neared the building. When the snake struck her calf, Jess jumped backward and hit her head against the door's metal frame, knocking herself unconscious.

Dave explained later that Kat found her with a swollen leg and a pool of blood around her head. Dave and Kevin weren't around, so Kat rushed Jess to the hospital. On the way, a drunk driver hit them head-on, as Kat had foreseen in her vision many years before. It was why Kat never got behind the wheel of a car—until she needed to save her daughter's life. The daughter who survived the brutal crash without a scratch, unconscious, strapped in her seatbelt. The daughter who slept through the most significant event of her life and didn't wake until the day after when she learned her mother had died saving her.

If Jess had been wearing her knee-high work boots instead of running shoes, the snake wouldn't have gotten its fangs into her, and her mother would still be alive.

* * *

The Atwoods had just sat down to supper when the doorbell rang.

"You should answer that," Kevin said to Jess. "Seems like everyone in Kerr County wants to either thank you or arrest you."

She pushed her chair back from the table and glared at her brother. "You think you're funny, don't you?"

Earl Kidwell stood scowling on the porch.

Jess's first thought was that he'd come to admonish her for flipping off his son that morning. "Mr. Kidwell, what can I do for you?"

"You can keep that dog of yours off our land and away from my cattle."

"Sorry, I didn't realize."

"You didn't realize your dog has no trainin'? Or are you sayin' you didn't realize that he goes anywhere he wants whenever he wants? 'Cause I'd bet my ranch you already knew both of those things."

"I meant I didn't realize he'd been over there."

"He wasn't just over there. He was botherin' my cattle, and I don't cotton to it. Do you think we're raisin' them animals for fun? Unlike some folks, we're runnin' an actual business."

"And we're not?" She crossed her arms. "Just what are you sayin', Mr. Kidwell?"

"I'm sayin' what would you do if your precious dog hurt one of our cattle? Or several of 'em? Bein' untrained and all, maybe he'd run 'em into a fence or somethin'."

"Wallaby would never do that."

"Well, we're not gonna find out 'cause he'll never put his filthy paws on our property again." His frown deepened when she didn't immediately respond. "Is that right?"

"I'll do my best, Mr. Kidwell."

He shook his finger in her face. "Your best better be pretty damn good, 'cause—"

"I'll thank you to not point your finger at me, sir."

"And I'll thank *you* for keeping that goddamn dog on your own property." He shrugged dramatically. "I'd hate to see him get hurt."

"That sounds like a threat."

He narrowed his eyes. "Glad to know those ears are good for more than decoratin' the sides of your head." He turned and strode away.

She clenched her jaw and watched him climb into his shiny red two-ton pickup with its dual rear wheels and a white Kidwell Cattle logo on the door. He drove off without so much as a backward glance.

Back at the supper table, she stared at her plate.

Dave took a long swig of Lone Star beer, his eyes slightly glazed. "Who was that?"

"Earl Kidwell."

"Anythin' we should know about?"

"Just that I have to keep Wallaby off his property come hell or high water."

Dave gave her a crooked smile. "Don't pay him no mind, Jess. He just loves to boss folks around. I swear, that man could strut sittin' down. Probably would be good to make sure Wallaby stays away from there, though," he said, holding up a basket of biscuits. "Eat up, honey, supper's gettin' cold."

She glanced at the biscuits. "If it's okay with y'all, I'll finish up later. I've lost my appetite."

CHAPTER EIGHT

Wears Valley, Tennessee
June 1964

Anna Mae resigned herself to walk the mile and a half to the Greyhound station in the late-morning heat and humidity. Rudy would find a way home without her, but someone should be there to greet him. She'd asked her mother to drive her, but Lucinda Cole said she had to work and couldn't take time off to welcome the son she hadn't seen in more than two years.

Anna Mae knew better than to ask their father.

She arrived, dripping with sweat, and glanced at the station clock high on the wall. Paint peeling off its face, the minute hand slightly bent, it showed 12:17, twenty-one minutes before her brother was due to arrive. She wandered around the musty old building, each minute an eternity in that place smelling of spent cigarettes and despair. What if he didn't arrive? Maybe he'd changed his mind.

The old bus finally pulled in, belching stinky black diesel smoke. Rudy was the third passenger to disembark. Anna Mae ran to her brother and threw her arms around him.

"Whoa there, tiger," he said, "you're gonna knock us both down."

She stepped back, brushing a tear off her cheek. "Well, ain't you a sight for sore eyes?"

"Good to see you too, baby sister."

"Case you haven't noticed, I'm no baby."

"It's all in the eye of the beholder, ain't it?" He smiled and scanned the nearly empty parking lot. "Where are Mama and Papa?"

"They had to work."

"Of course they did," he said after a pause. "You couldn't have borrowed one of their cars?"

"Don't have a license. Our parents forbid it. Though I'm sure if it suited 'em, I'd have one in a heartbeat."

"Reckon you're right." He glanced down at his beat-up suitcase with one leather corner torn half off, his dark green duffel bag, and a third, smaller bag. "There's a lot to carry here."

She lifted the smaller bag. "I can manage this if you can handle those two puppies," she said, nodding at the other items.

He slung the duffel over his shoulder and picked up the suitcase with an exaggerated sigh. "I'd argue with you, but we've no real alternatives. Besides, I know how far that argument would get me."

"At least I'm only half as stubborn as my big brother."

"Sure ya are."

On the long walk home, she asked him about Vietnam.

"There ain't much to tell, really," he finally said.

"You can't be serious."

"Well, the way it turned out, I didn't do any fightin'. The official word was that none of us did, as we were only supposed to be advisors, but that wasn't how it worked out. Sometimes our boys were doin' battle right alongside the South Vietnamese Army. My platoon was assigned to logistics, makin' sure they had food, bullets, and everythin' else they needed to fight the Viet Cong."

"Did you see any dead bodies?"

"Way too many. Why on earth do you ask?"

Anna Mae looked away. "Just curious."

Rudy laughed. "I swear, girl, the things you're curious about."

She didn't respond.

"Anna Mae, what is it?"

"Um . . . I found a body up in the park a few weeks ago."

"No!"

She told him the whole story.

"Anna Mae . . ."

"What?"

"You need to stay away from all that bidness."

"All that bidness? This is some girl's life we're talkin' about. Her family must be worried sick not knowin' what happened to her."

"I appreciate that you care about folks, but part of bein' happy in this world is lettin' go of things beyond our control."

"This ain't about me bein' happy. This is about—"

"You're missin' the point, Anna Mae. Sometimes you just need to leave well enough alone."

"And ignore the visions?"

"Maybe. You get obsessed, thinkin' you have to follow those visions to the letter, and that's not always good for you—or safe."

What could she say to that? She loved her brother dearly, but sometimes he just didn't get it.

"Tell me about Katherine," she finally said.

"What's gotten into you, Anna Mae? First, you talk about dead bodies, and now you're bringin' up . . ."

"The sister we never talk about."

"'Cause it's a painful subject."

"I know it is. But Dr. Ferguson said it'd be good for our family to talk about her. He said it would help my . . . he said it would make me feel better."

"Well, there ain't much to tell. Katherine was our little sister, but she only lived a few days. The doctor said she had a hole in her heart." He glanced at Anna Mae. "You were only five or six, and I was ten. Her death changed everythin'."

"Did it?"

"Oh yeah. Papa's always been mean, but when Katherine died, he got worse. Especially when he's been drinkin'."

"I reckon I might know somethin' about that."

"And Mama, well, she used to be warmer. She'd even hug me when I was little."

"Really?"

Rudy nodded. "And she'd read to me at night. You know, the stuff most mamas do."

"I had no idea, though a couple of months back, she took me aside and warned me that gettin' pregnant would ruin my life forever—as if that'd ever happen. I guess it was just her way of sayin' she cares."

"Maybe, but that carin' don't show much through all the pain she holds inside."

"No kiddin'."

When they arrived at the house, Anna Mae showed him to his old room.

He nodded approvingly, then frowned. "Um, when does Papa get home?"

"Don't you worry. I'm sure he'll be happy to see you."

He gave his sister a thin smile. "Don't bet on it."

CHAPTER NINE

Jess was spritzing young broccoli plants with soap and lemon oil when yet another daytime vision caught her off guard. A teenage girl with white-blonde hair struggled with a man under the hazy yellow glow of a streetlight. After a second or two, another man yelled something and ran up to intervene. With a flourish, the first man pulled a fancy folding knife out of his pocket before the vision quickly faded and was gone.

Stunned, Jess stared at the broccoli, barely able to breathe. She was vaguely aware of Wallaby barking at something in the distance and a car passing on the road. It felt as though she was waking from a nightmare. Her body had flushed with adrenaline, which left her trembling.

She found Kevin in the equipment garage working on their old thirty-horsepower John Deere tractor, parts scattered across the floor. After describing the vision, she asked him what he thought.

"Just leave it alone."

"Don't know if I can do that."

"Now look, we b-both know you've had dreams that never came true."

"This wasn't a dream. I was wide awake."

"Not the point. Sometimes what you envision never happens. True or false?"

"They don't *always* happen, far as I know, but that doesn't mean they *never* happen."

"So, what would b-be the point?" Kevin asked.

"Exactly! What *is* the point of these visions? Other than to drive me insane."

"Wouldn't b-be a long drive, would it?"

"I should've known better than to say anythin' to you."

Kevin held his hands up. "Simmer down, Jess, I'm just pickin'. Okay, let's say you help catch this incredibly b-bad person. Maybe they arrest him, and he goes on trial. Do you think they'd let you come in and testify b-based on what you saw in some vision? There's only one smart thing to do, which is to let it go. B-besides, we've got enough on our hands figurin' out how to make this farm profitable."

She knew that made sense, but sometimes letting go was easier said than done.

For the next few days, whenever she wasn't working, she checked the internet for any news of a stabbing or kidnapping. Nothing unusual came up until day four. In East Dallas, a man had been stabbed to death a few blocks from Fair Park, a place she'd been many times when they'd lived nearby. The article didn't mention a kidnapping but made a vague reference to another crime. Jess wondered if it had something to do with what she'd seen in her vision. But it had happened in East Dallas, far away. It wasn't her table, as the saying went.

Or she could just call in an anonymous tip. They still hadn't caught the perpetrator, according to the article. Maybe something from the vision would give the police a helpful clue.

Her mother had strong opinions about what she'd call making right. "Oh, honey," Kat used to say, "you'll always know what's right. Just decide to do it or not."

* * *

Jess parked the pickup across from the last surviving phone booth in Kerrville, outside the Rite Aid on Goat Creek Road. She could've found a pay phone in Center Point but didn't want to take any chances. Driving to Kerrville gave her extra separation and anonymity. She called directory information for the main number of the Dallas Police headquarters. When she got through, she asked for someone in homicide, and the operator transferred her to a Detective Simmons.

"Are you takin' leads on a case involvin' a stabbin' in East Dallas that was recently in the news?" she asked.

"Why? What do you know about that?"

"I'm not totally sure what I know about it, but—"

Simmons loudly clicked his tongue. "Listen, I'm sure you mean well, but we get all kinds of folks callin' us with helpful suggestions about how to solve crimes. Not that we don't appreciate it, but we need solid facts or clues we can work with. If you heard or saw somethin', tell me."

"I might be able to give you a solid clue."

"I'm listenin'."

She was about to tell him about the girl with the white-blonde hair she'd seen in the vision when another vision began to form in her mind.

"You still there?" the detective impatiently asked after a few seconds.

"A left-handed assailant stabbed the victim," Jess said.

"What makes you think that?"

"It's true, isn't it?"

"Maybe that detail got leaked. How'd you find that out?"

"Well, I kinda see things."

"You kinda *see* things? Are you kiddin' me? Do you have any idea how many psychics have called us with red-hot clues about practically every major crime that's been in the news?" The detective made a popping sound with his mouth. "They find out one little detail and then call us like they heard it directly from the angels. You're not tellin' me anythin' new. Anyway, I need to get back to work. You have a good day, young lady."

"Did anyone else tell you he crawled a few feet away from where he'd been stabbed? Or that he wore a charcoal-gray suit jacket, blue jeans, and cowboy boots? Any of your psychics tell you that? Or that a girl with white-blonde hair was bein' kidnapped when the man got stabbed." She hesitated. "I'm seein' the name Ashley."

"You read about Ashley bein' missin' on the internet, didn't you?"

"Actually, I didn't, and I'm willin' to bet most of what I just said you haven't disclosed to the public."

"That's a good point," he said, his keyboard clicking in the background. "Would you mind comin' in so we can talk about this?"

"I'm not from around there, as you undoubtedly just found out from your trace," she said, glad she'd called from a phone booth away from Center Point.

"Sounds like you've read too many crime novels. I'd still like to hear it from you in person."

"I can see what I could do to get there, though it's not likely since our cash flow isn't great at the moment."

"Do you need help with your travel expenses?"

"It wouldn't hurt."

"You people always need somethin', don't you? We've had so-called psychics give us information that sounded right, but they eventually wanted somethin' in exchange. Once they got paid, most of their so-called insights were useless. Now," he said, his tone hardening, "I've no idea how you got that information, but I'm gonna ask the sheriff there in Kerrville to find out about you and get back to me. Whatever your game is—"

"Detective Simmons, I'm not playin' any kinda game. I called 'cause I thought I could help. Clearly, you're not interested in what I'm offerin'. And you'd better fix your damn tracer, 'cause I'm nowhere near Kerrville," she lied before hanging up.

On her way home, she thought about how she'd tried to do the right thing but simply told that stupid detective what he already knew. It only made him suspicious, which felt like a slap in the face. Kat occasionally had the same problem, though she'd always find a brighter side—even when there wasn't one.

Jess breathed deeply as she drove, which gradually made her feel better. Maybe she could also find a brighter side.

She passed a pair of enormous grain silos at the edge of town, silhouetted by the orange glow of the setting sun. The paint on their enormous red-and-white checkered patterns was peeling, making them look like oversize works of retro art. Even ordinary things could be beautiful if you saw them in the right light.

Jess tried to convince herself that the trip to Kerrville hadn't been a waste of time and energy. She just had to look at it the right way. Elena once told her that sometimes she had to do what she didn't like to find out what she did like.

For sure, she didn't like telling people about her visions or talking to the police.

* * *

Soon after she got home, her cell phone rang with a number she didn't recognize.

"Hello?"

"Is this Jessica Atwood?"

"It is."

"This is Special Agent Ed Mallory of the Texas Rangers."

That caught her by surprise. "Oh?"

"First, let me apologize for the rude treatment you got from Detective Simmons with Dallas PD earlier. I just listened to the recordin'. He said he was havin' a bad day, but his behavior was inexcusable, especially when you did the right thing and came forward to help us with your insights."

"Thanks, I guess. But how did you find me?"

"You called from a public phone on Goat Creek Road in Kerrville. Simmons contacted the sheriff's department there, askin' if anyone in the area had reported havin' visions. Guess what they said?"

"I can't imagine."

"It wasn't exactly high-level detective work. The deputy he spoke to had heard about your family. Your mama was pretty well-known around those parts."

"I'll say."

"I'm callin' to let you know we'd love your help. You gave Simmons accurate information, which is why he rang me."

"I'm sure it was. But listen, Agent . . ."

"Mallory."

"Agent Mallory, I don't want these visions, insights, or whatever the hell they are. They come without me askin' for 'em. I only called 'cause I thought it might do some good."

"Which was a courageous thing to do. We'd love your help in findin' Ashley before it's too late."

She paused. "Thanks, but . . . I don't have anythin' else to tell you."

"Jess, her life may be at stake. You never know what might help."

After a bit of silence, he asked if she was still there.

"I truly don't have anythin' more, though I reckon I could let you know if somethin' else comes up. But next time I get told I'm tryin' to squeeze somethin' out of this, it'll be the last time I talk to anybody about anythin'."

"Of course. The number I'm callin' you from is my personal cell number. Please save it on your phone. You don't have to talk to anyone but me."

She wasn't sure how she felt about that. "Okay."

"If anythin' comes up for you—I don't care how insignificant it may seem—call me day or night. I'll be your liaison."

"You make it sound pretty dramatic."

"Well, it can be. We're doin' important work, and you've just become a significant part of it."

"I'm not sure I *want* to be a significant part of it."

"I understand and promise to make it as easy as possible for you. Ashley needs your help."

"Okay, I'll try." Jess ended the call and wondered what she'd gotten herself into.

CHAPTER TEN

Anna Mae loved that her parents were in a better mood when Rudy was around, which meant less chance of getting hit. Her mother didn't do the hitting, though if she wasn't happy, no one else would remain happy for long.

Lucinda Cole had given up her big dream of becoming a country singer, though she'd made a go of it in Nashville years before. Some so-called promoter approached her after one of her shows and told her she was the next June Carter, from her singing voice and striking blue eyes to how she walked and did her hair. Of course, June Carter had auburn locks, while Lucinda's hair was a natural strawberry blonde. More importantly, June had Johnny Cash, but Lucinda was stuck with Jefferson Cole. Still, the promoter's compliment hit home. Even if he'd only been trying to flatter her, she never forgot his comment and resented that she had to come back to her family. Her singing career had lasted only nine weeks and ended dramatically when her husband drove from Wears Valley to Nashville to bring her home. He was a hard man to say no to.

Jefferson Cole had been a fighter in his early twenties before being drafted into World War II. He claimed to be good in the ring, and Anna Mae had no reason to disbelieve that. His war injury abruptly ended his boxing career, however, handing him one of his life's biggest regrets. With his crew cut, intense close-set dark eyes, and surly demeanor, most people found him intimidating even though he was at least four inches shorter than average. If one believed the rumors, that was how he got good at fighting. When other kids teased him about his height, they'd pay the price. From what Anna Mae heard, no one did that more than once.

Since Rudy got home, the senior Cole hadn't been surly at all and appeared almost happy. He even got his son a job at the Maryville railway yard. At supper one evening, he nodded to Rudy. "How's work goin' in the yard, son?"

"Just fine. Thank you for askin', sir."

The day before, Rudy had told Anna Mae in confidence how much he hated his new job. For $1.25 an hour, he practically broke his back in that filthy rail yard day after day. Their father demanded he hand over half his pay because he was staying there and eating the food. At least he'd give his son a ride to work the mornings he was in town. To get back home, however, Rudy had to ride the bus and walk a mile and a half from the nearest stop so Jefferson Cole could have drinks with the guys from work. He'd made it clear he didn't want his son there for that.

* * *

Lucinda walked into the kitchen one evening just as Anna Mae was pulling a mouthwatering black-eyed pea casserole out of the oven. The thick top layer of cheddar cheese had browned and melted in. It smelled delicious, and Anna Mae considered it close to perfect. She was about to tell her mother that supper would be ready in five minutes when she noticed the frown.

"Everythin' alright, Mama?"

"Everythin's fine, but I don't see why you gotta go cookin' such fancy things all the time."

"But Mama, you told me this is one of your favorites."

Lucinda clucked and turned away. "No need to save any for me. I'm havin' supper with . . . Betsy, from work."

"Yes, ma'am." Anna Mae wasn't about to mention that the friend from work her mother had gone out with the previous week was named Betty. Almost like Betsy, but not quite. More unusual was her mother's makeup and perfume, which she usually didn't put on even when she went out with her husband—

who was currently working as a caboose flagman on a freight run to Santa Fe and wouldn't be back for another day.

Anna Mae felt relieved when her mother finally left the house because it gave her and Rudy time to talk. As they sat down to supper, she told him about the dream she had the night before, when she saw herself getting bit in the calf by a rattlesnake, jumping back, hitting her head against a door frame, and falling unconscious. "And I was a Negro."

He stopped pouring his milk. "You were?"

"Yes."

"Then it couldn't have been you."

"Well," she shivered involuntarily, "it sure felt like me."

"That's weird."

"It is, but that ain't all. I was usin' this crazy machine with a noisy motor on one end and a spinnin' saw blade on the other, cuttin' down bushes like a hot knife through butter. I wore these funny things on my head that looked like big orange earmuffs. That machine was connected to some kind of harness that went over my shoulder, and I held onto its handlebars."

"Handlebars?" he asked, serving himself a generous helping of casserole.

"Yeah, like on a bicycle. The handlebars were attached in the middle, and the saw blade was down near the ground. I tell ya, it was the strangest thing. Never seen anythin' like it, yet it seemed so real. But there I was, runnin' that machine like an expert, right until that snake struck my calf."

Rudy tugged on his earlobe, a sure sign he was upset. "I doubt a machine like that even exists, Anna Mae. Plus, we both know you're not a Negro. You've heard me say this before, but just dreamin' somethin' don't make it true."

"Sometimes it does, Rudy. I could even smell the bushes as they were bein' cut." She stared at the ceiling. "But I don't know what to do about it."

"That's what I'm tryin' to tell you. Maybe you're not supposed to do anythin' with it." He leaned across the table toward her. "You need to let go of obsessin' over every old dream you have."

"This wasn't just any old dream . . . but it wasn't like my other visions, either, where I see the order of things and know what I'm supposed to do."

"So, what was it then?"

She smiled weakly. "Wish I knew."

* * *

Dear Diary,

Maybe it was a mistake telling Rudy about the dream where I got bit by a rattlesnake when I used that strange machine. He's been looking at me funny the past couple of days. With him being one of the few people in the world who believes in me, I should probably be more careful about what I tell him.

Or maybe he's still upset about me graduating early. Far as I'm concerned, I'm happy to be done with high school and have my diploma in hand. Sure, there were some good things, but I swear I've learned more on my own at the Wears Valley Public Library.

In home economics class yesterday, we were putting stuff away and helping Miss Porter clean up. Last day of school and all, so the other girls were chattering about what they were fixing to do over the summer. None of them mind that they're coming back for another year. Me, though, I'm free as a bird.

Miss Porter came over in the middle of all the commotion and told me she was jealous of my hair. She said she always wished she'd had lovely blonde hair like mine. I didn't know what to say to that except, "Thank you, ma'am."

Then she patted me on the head, saying I was pretty and smart and would go far in life. It took all the self-control I had not to ask her to keep her hands off. Mama says I hated anyone touching me ever since I was little unless I was the one reaching out.

At least Miss Porter was saying nice things to me. What people don't say to my face is that if I'm lucky, I'll get a sober husband who makes and keeps enough money to feed his family and doesn't beat me.

Folks ask, "What are you gonna do now? Getting married?

Working somewhere?" I got work to do, but it's not what they're thinking, and marriage is one merry-go-round I'm not getting on for reasons they don't need to know—no point in making folks worry.

Mama worried enough to get me in to see Dr. Ferguson in Maryville a few years back. She did it without Papa knowing, which was a good thing. I didn't like the idea of seeing a shrink, but he was okay.

Mama might be the only married woman in Wears Valley who works full-time at a paying job, and she's quite proud of it. She says she enjoys working as a receptionist for some dentist over in Pigeon Forge, but I don't reckon that's true. What she likes is that she's not fully dependent on a man who'd beat her if he thought for a minute he'd get away with it. Papa doesn't like her working, but he had to promise she could, so she'd come home from Nashville.

"Else," Mama told him, "it ain't gonna happen." Of course, that was right after she lost Katherine, which just about crushed her. I reckon she figured she had nothing to lose after that. She always wanted to be a singer and saw Nashville as her big opportunity. I begged her not to go and was crying and throwing a fit, but it didn't even slow her down. That was twelve or thirteen years ago, but I remember like it was yesterday.

Papa never let it show that losing Katherine mattered much to him, but I'm sure it did. Some folks keep all their pain deep inside and think showing they care is a sign of weakness.

Papa cares about other things, too. He loves his work with the railroad, especially when he does the all-night runs out of Tennessee. He loves to gamble, especially when he's playing poker. He loves chasing women, especially when they're pretty. And he loves to drink, mainly because it helps him forget.

He and Mama both pretend she doesn't know all that. Sometimes telling the truth isn't worth the price you pay.

It's been four years since Dr. Ferguson said I was obsessive and had difficulty telling imagination from reality. He kept talking about my hallucinations, as he called them. I hardly expect him to understand. But he told Mama just to let me be, that there was nothing she could do about how I was. He even winked at me when she wasn't looking.

He also told her I was depressed, which isn't true. I get sad sometimes and might stay that way for a bit, but it doesn't mean I'm depressed. Besides, I'm happy enough most of the time that it all balances out, I reckon.

When Dr. Ferguson asked how things were at home, Mama told him everything was fine. I believe he knew she was lying. I love it when people know the difference, which I told him later in our private session. He said I was insightful for a thirteen-year-old.

Wonder what he'd say now?

Last night, I had a vision of a path I'm supposed to follow, and when I finish my chores, I'm going back to where I found that girl's body last month. I'll be safe, as long as I stay with the order of things.

Chapter Eleven

Center Point, Texas
Present Day

Thoroughly annoyed, Jess closed her eyes and counted to ten. Their meeting had started peacefully enough, but as usual, Kevin complained about how she did the books and managed the budget. Dave was physically present but seemed almost asleep. Elena knew to stay out of their arguments once things got personal, though Jess would've liked her support.

"You've pushed this whole organic thing a little too far," Kevin said.

"Organic thing?" Jess couldn't believe her ears. "This is not a *thing*. We make a small environmental footprint and provide people with healthy food free from pesticides, herbicides, and GMOs. That's why we call this an organic farm, in case you haven't noticed."

"Oh, I've noticed, all right. And have you noticed how many other farms around here have gone organic? Let's see now, there are exactly . . ." Kevin made a show of counting on his fingers. "None."

"Since when do we let other folks tell us what to do?"

"Lettin' them tell us what to do is one thing, but seein' what turns a profit is somethin' else entirely."

"I know," she said sarcastically, "why don't we just partner up with Earl and Travis Kidwell? They make plenty of profit."

"When hell freezes over."

"You haven't gotten over your thing with Travis yet, have you?"

When Kevin was in middle school, he told Travis—who was then a sophomore in high school—that he was gay. Travis later swore he assumed Kevin was telling everyone when he mentioned it to one of his friends, who told all of *his* friends. Soon everyone knew. Kevin was sure Travis did it just to spite him, and held a serious grudge because of it.

"You're the one who hasn't gotten over Travis," Kevin answered.

Jess felt her face flush. "There's nothin' for me to get over."

"Sure there isn't. That's why you're so angry right now."

"I'm not angry."

"Right. And I'm the governor of Texas." He crossed his arms. "You know, Jess, you'd be much easier to be around if you just found yourself a b-boyfriend."

Dave frowned. "That was uncalled for, Kevin."

"That's okay, Dave. He's just lashin' out in his typically immature way." Jess cast an angry glance at her brother. "Like I have time for that kind of nonsense."

"Nonsense? That's the problem right there. Maybe if you spent less time at the arena shootin' guys in the nuts with your paintball gun, you'd have more luck in the romance department. I'm no shrink, b-but looks to me like someone's got man issues."

"You really want to go there, Kevin? Big relationship expert that you are? The only boys you've been goin' out with lately live inside your Xbox."

"Knock it off, you two," said Dave. "We don't have the time or energy for this."

Wallaby whined from his cushion, and Jess turned to him. "You need to go out, boy?"

He rested his chin on his paws, his gaze shifting between Kevin and Jess.

"He can tell when you're uptight," Kevin said.

"Hush up. I reckon that brings us to the business at hand."

"It doesn't b-bring us anywhere."

Ignoring her brother, she picked up the financial report in front of her. "We lost money again last month."

"How much?" Dave asked.

"We wound up in the red by nearly two hundred dollars."

"So? We can't expect a clean profit every month, can we?" Kevin asked.

"We sure can't, but September was a great month for weather, bein' cooler and wetter than normal, and we had a bigger than usual harvest in October. We should have been well into the black, yet we're typically in the red," she glanced at her report, "an average of a hundred and seventeen dollars a month. If we weren't doing so well at the farmers' market, we'd be out of business in three or four months."

Elena shook her head. "We need to find a solution before we lose everything."

Kevin tapped the table. "I still say we need to grow mushrooms. It'd be a great year-round crop."

"I don't think so," said Jess. "I googled it, and thirty percent of folks don't even *like* mushrooms. Hate to break it to you, dear brother, but successful farmers don't just grow what they like. They grow what will make them money if they want a business that turns a profit."

"You mean the opposite of what we're doin', right? 'Cause accordin' to what you just said, we're not reapin' any profits at all. Somethin' has to change."

"You might just get the change you want," she said, "cause yesterday some guy from the bank called sayin' we've got sixty days to catch up on our equipment loan before they start the foreclosure proceedin's."

"How can they do that without giving us a fair warning?" Elena asked.

"That's why they wanted to see me back in September. They said it was to discuss our refinance application, but I reckon the main purpose was to put us on notice. They hinted they might call the note on our loan 'cause of too many late payments—as I told y'all then." Jess paused. "But there may be a way out. The bank guy said someone was interested in buyin' part of our farm."

"Seriously?" Elena asked. "How would the bank know someone was interested?"

Kevin's eyes narrowed. "I'd b-bet you my Xbox somebody at that b-bank is sellin' information about vulnerable properties."

"That may be, but we should consider it."

"No way," Kevin said.

Jess glanced at Wallaby, who was whining again. "That's what I said at first. But he suggested we seriously consider it unless we want to face foreclosure."

"What part of the farm are they interested in?" Elena asked.

"That would ultimately be up to us, but they mentioned the two acres by the river."

"Our two most b-beautiful acres," Kevin said, "and the b-best trees we have on the entire property. That's a b-brilliant plan, Jess. Don't know why I didn't think of that." He snapped his fingers. "Oh, that's right, maybe 'cause that's our source of irrigation water."

"We'd keep water rights, with an easement for pipes and pumps, like the Kidwells already have on our property. Sure, they may be our prettiest two acres, but we hardly use 'em. Harvestin' and maintainin' those pecans isn't worth the labor involved for the small quantity of nuts those trees produce, as we've learned the hard way. And sellin' that land would be smart. There's already the access road that could be their driveway. The bank guy said it was a solid cash offer and would be a workable plan."

"That plan sucks," Kevin said.

"I'm open to hearin' somethin' better," Jess replied.

"How much are we talkin' about?" asked Dave.

"He didn't know for sure, but he thought the buyers could go as high as $125,000."

Elena looked surprised. "Are you sure? There's decent land all over the county for $20,000 an acre—or less." She thought about it for a moment. "With our Guadalupe frontage, it might be three or even four times that, but it still doesn't add up, especially with the real estate market being slow as it is. I've heard that people just aren't buying right now."

Jess shrugged. "I repeated it back to him, and he said he couldn't guarantee that amount, but that's what he thought they'd be willin' to pay. He said they have the cash on hand."

Elena leaned forward. "That's a lot of cash. But that part of our land is probably only worth . . . I don't know, maybe seventy to eighty thousand tops.

And that's a stretch."

"Which is why I'm seein' this as a real possibility. Even if we put it on the market this week, it could be a year or more before it sells, way too late to get us out of our current financial crisis. Besides, it'd never sell for the price they're offerin' us right now."

"You know what they say when somethin' sounds too good to be true," Kevin said.

"You're just bein' pessimistic."

"No, I'm bein' realistic. Just 'cause there are sharks circlin' doesn't mean you jump out of the b-boat and into their mouths."

"But what if that boat is sinkin'?"

"Kevin has a point about this sounding too good to be true," Elena said.

"That's why we do everythin' through lawyers," Jess insisted. "We make sure it's one hundred percent secure."

"You know," Dave said, "you may be on to somethin'. This could be the perfect opportunity for us."

She gave her stepfather a grateful glance before continuing. "I'd love to keep the entire property, but we have to be practical. Otherwise, the bank will just take it all and walk us out."

Kevin abruptly stood. "They wouldn't do that."

"Oh, yes, they would. If we're not caught up within thirty days, more penalties kick in, and a month later, they'd start foreclosure proceedin's."

Kevin paced the room like a caged tiger. "All we have to do is make our damn mortgage payments."

"And pay down the equipment loan. That is assumin' the bank would let us keep makin' payments." She tapped her pen on the table. "Which we're already strugglin' to do 'cause we also have to pay for biofuel, equipment upkeep, and dozens of other things."

"What if we pay off the loan and use the rest of the money from sellin' the two acres for Kevin's mushroom operation?" Dave asked.

"Well," Jess said after a surprised pause, "that would use up a huge part of whatever buffer the sale would create. Before long, we'd be right back where we started."

"Except that we'd have another stable source of income," Kevin said.

"A source that would take a long time to see a positive return," Jess replied, "if ever."

"Of course. Nothin' is ever gonna b-be okay with you if it's my idea."

"It has nothin' to do with it bein' your idea."

"Like hell. You just like b-bein' in control."

Jess smiled grimly. "I'm open to any solid ideas you may have, dear brother. When you find a solution that might actually work, please let me know, 'cause I'm dyin' to hear it."

They needed something, but it certainly wasn't mushrooms.

CHAPTER TWELVE

Wears Valley, Tennessee
July 1964

Even though they had earned her a whipping the last time, Anna Mae trusted her visions and knew she should follow them without judgment. It was hotter in the park than when she had been there two months earlier, but the familiar scent of goldenrod felt like an old friend and had been part of the vision, which comforted her. She passed the army tent again, but it had long since collapsed, and the Negro with the scar on his face had moved on. Good for him.

She'd thought about asking Rudy if he wanted to come along, but he had to work, and he only would've told her not to go. He didn't understand that everything would be fine if she stayed within the order of things.

The vision from the day before didn't tell her why she had to be there, but that didn't matter. Visions never showed her the why, only what she had to do. They frequently didn't show her all the details, either. This particular vision didn't show her she'd have company, but there stood Deputy Stevens, sweat dripping off his chin.

His eyes momentarily widened at the sight of her, and he almost smiled. It didn't require second sight to see that he liked her, and Anna Mae wondered why she hadn't noticed it before.

"Anna Mae Cole, what in the Sam Hill are you doin' back here?"

She paused. "I, uh . . ."

"Please don't tell me you were guided to come here."

She gave him a tight smile and remained silent.

He raised an eyebrow and pointed at her feet. "No shoes again?"

"I feel more connected when I'm barefoot."

Stevens looked at her skeptically and shook his head. "Believe what you want, but listen to me, child. You can't be here alone."

She raised her chin. "I ain't no child. I'm eighteen in less than a year, which practically makes me an adult."

"That's a long way off, and besides, bein' eighteen don't make you an adult."

"By law, it does," she said, noticing for the first time that his eyes were even darker than hers. With him, though, they made more sense because of his black hair.

"Well, the law ain't always right, and besides, it's not safe for you to be here. Didn't Sheriff Keene tell you not to go to dangerous places like this alone?"

The rumor around school had been that Stevens was engaged to Peggy June Morris, who had a reputation as a floozy. She also wasn't a pleasant person, which Anna Mae had experienced firsthand back when she was a sophomore, and Peggy June was a senior. Deputy Stevens deserved someone who didn't sleep around. Someone who'd be nice to him. Someone who'd take care of him in sickness and in health. Someone who'd—

"Anna Mae, are you listenin' to me?"

"Yes, sir." She pursed her lips, trying to recall the last thing he'd said. "The sheriff may have mentioned somethin' about that," she finally answered.

"You know damn well he did."

Sweat rolled down her back, but it didn't matter because everything was in order. "I felt called to come here today."

Stevens shook his head in disgust. "I can't tell you what to believe, Anna Mae, but you could get yourself hurt or even killed thinkin' like that."

"'Cause this place is more dangerous than you thought?"

"Well . . ."

"Did somethin' else happen?"

He hesitated. "Back in May, around the time you led us down here, a girl went missin' from Gatlinburg. For whatever reason, the family didn't report it 'til a couple of days ago. They're a troubled bunch. Lots of issues goin' on, if you know what I mean."

"Reckon I might."

"They assumed she'd run away and would return when she wasn't mad at them. But that never happened. Sarah Jacobs. That name ring a bell?"

Anna Mae shook her head. "Not that I recall."

"Well, I'm here lookin' for clues, and you're in the midst of a possible crime scene, which means you could hinder the investigation."

"I could help you search for those clues."

"Who do you think you are, Nancy Drew? In real life, things aren't always capped by happy endin's the way they are in books."

"Maybe not, but I notice you're lookin' in the area I saw that body."

He rubbed his chin. "Fair enough, but you could help us best if you were safely out of here," he said with a twisted smile. "And by lettin' us know if you have any more insights."

"So now you believe me?"

"Let's just say a good investigator leaves no stone unturned. But this is sensitive law enforcement work, and you shouldn't be here."

"'Cause you care about my safety."

"Of course I care. It's my job."

"Well," she said, "I'm here now, and to keep me safe, you'd have to walk me all the way back. Or you could let me help."

"There's not much you could do."

"I might surprise you." Anna Mae wasn't sure, but he seemed to redden slightly.

"I'm about done here anyway."

She just nodded and smiled.

He said little on the hike back except to scold her, but she didn't mind. People had different ways of showing they cared. She felt safe and protected around him. When they got to his patrol car, he opened the passenger door and gave her a slight smile. A faint scent of cedar greeted her when she climbed in.

"Why does your car smell so good?" she asked as he put his key in the ignition.

He laughed. "Cedar shavin's in a nylon stockin' under my seat. It's a great trick, but don't you dare tell Sheriff Keene."

"I won't. Cross my heart."

They were about half a mile from Anna Mae's house when they passed a tall man with dark hair covering his ears and a red tattoo on his right forearm. He smirked at them as they drove past.

"That's a wicked man," she said without thinking.

Stevens watched him in the rearview mirror as the distance between them increased. "Why do you say that?"

"Just a sense I got."

"Just a sense, huh?"

"Well, isn't he?"

Stevens chewed his lower lip. "I think so. But you didn't hear that from me."

"I didn't have to. Some things you just know."

He nodded. "Yep, some things you just do."

"But what's with that haircut?"

"It's the latest fad. Folks call 'em Beatle haircuts, after some newfangled English band. Tell you the truth, their music ain't bad, but those mop-top hairdos are ridiculous." He glanced over at her. "Wonder if you could do me a favor?"

"Anythin' you want, Deputy Stevens."

"You see him anywhere, find a phone and call me immediately. His name is Phil Daley, son of Congressman Sam Daley."

"You're kiddin' me."

"Wish I was. That privileged little snot gets away with far more than he should. All he has to do is make one quick call to his daddy, and the breeze suddenly blows his way. I'm kinda keepin' an eye on him."

"As well you should." She turned to stare at him. He glanced at her, but instead of looking away like she'd done when other boys cast their eyes on her, she just smiled, which seemed to make him nervous.

When he dropped her off at home, he leaned over and rolled down the passenger window. *"Anna Mae!"*

When she turned, he shook his finger at her. "Now, don't you forget what I said."

She smiled and took a few steps back toward the patrol car. "Yes, sir." This time, his blush was unmistakable. She came closer. "Thanks for not tellin' my pa about this."

"Who says I'm not gonna tell him?"

She smiled again, turned without a word, and walked to the front door. He didn't drive away until she was inside, making her even happier. She put her apron on and thought about what she'd make for supper, humming to herself. When she glanced at the kitchen clock, however, her heart sank. It was nearly half past five, meaning her parents could be home any minute. In a panic, she rushed to prepare things, heating leftovers from the day before, hoping no one would notice.

* * *

No one else arrived home until almost six. By then, she'd effectively disguised the leftovers and put together a proper meal. Rudy was the first one in, and he helped her set the table. She loved that he didn't ask why she was late and considered herself lucky things had worked out the way they did.

They had nearly finished supper when her father set his fork down and took a swig of beer. "I don't know about y'all, but I'm ready for some of that sweet potato pie."

Anna Mae froze, unable to breathe. How could she have forgotten? "I'm sorry, sir, but I didn't make any," she finally said with a trembling voice.

He tilted his head toward her. "You didn't *what*?"

"I'm terribly sorry, sir, but I—"

"Did I not say when Rudy came home we're gonna have sweet potato pie for Friday night supper?"

"You did, Papa, but I forgot."

"You hear that, Lucinda?" he asked his wife as he spooned gravy onto what remained of his mashed potatoes. "She forgot." He turned back to Anna Mae. "You mean you forgot what my favorite food is, you forgot Rudy was comin' home, or you forgot I asked you for exactly what I wanted?"

"I don't know, Papa."

"You don't know, huh?"

"No, sir." She focused on her plate but could see him turning red from the corner of her eye.

"*Of all the damn fool things to forget!*" he yelled, slapping the table.

"Don't holler at her, Papa," Rudy said.

He squinted at his son. "You stay out of this, boy!"

"I ain't no boy."

Their father jumped to his feet, his chair falling back and clattering against the floor. "You ain't, huh?" He walked around the table toward Rudy, who also stood.

Lucinda watched passively, chewing slowly, her face expressionless. Anna Mae widened her eyes at her, hoping she'd say something, but Lucinda simply shook her head slightly. Anna Mae turned to watch her father and brother face off.

Rudy squared his shoulders. "She just forgot, Papa. It's not that big a deal."

The senior Cole put his face inches away from Rudy's, his crew cut even with his son's nose. "Not that big a deal? You callin' me a liar?"

Rudy stepped back. "No, sir, I was just sayin' that—"

"You better learn to keep your mouth shut when it ain't none of your bidness."

Anna Mae noticed her brother's chest heaving. While it might look like he was backing down, she knew Rudy was close to lashing out physically. That wouldn't end well.

"It's okay, Rudy," she said.

"*Hush up, you little bitch!*" her father yelled, pointing a quivering finger at her. "You're the one who started this."

"I was just tryin' to—"

"You hard of hearin', girl?" He took a step toward her.

"No, sir." She turned back and stared at her plate. "I'm sorry, Papa." She waited for a slap or a punch to the back of the head.

"Y'all get out of my sight," he said. "I don't wanna see either of you the rest of the day."

Rudy and Anna Mae stared at him with their mouths open.

Their father narrowed his eyes. "Did y'all not hear me?" he asked, his voice rising again. "You got ten seconds to get out of here if you know what's good for ya."

They were out the door in eight.

CHAPTER THIRTEEN

Center Point, Texas
Present Day

"Jessica Atwood?"

"That's me." A sense of unease settled over her as she puzzled at the two men on her porch, one of whom looked Latino and wore a cowboy hat and boots. The other was tall, wiry, and had cold eyes. He sported a Philadelphia Phillies baseball cap and Nike running shoes. His demeanor reminded Jess of a coiled snake, ready to strike.

"How may I help you?" she asked.

A sudden bark behind her made her jump, and she just barely grabbed Wallaby's collar as he tried to lunge past, causing both men to flinch.

"Whoa there, boy." She frowned at the snarling animal trying to break free from her grasp. "I'm sorry. He's normally not like this. Wallaby, hush."

The dog calmed slightly but continued to growl, the hair on his back standing up.

"Can y'all give me a sec? I need to get him situated." She put him in the laundry room, where he barked wildly from behind the closed door. "Sorry about that," she apologized again when she returned.

The man with the cowboy hat held his hands up in mock surrender and smiled. "No problem. Your dog is just doing his job. I am Santiago Ramos from Central Texas State Bank." He extended his hand. "We spoke on the phone."

Jess nodded and shook his hand, noticing that when they touched, he looked away. Was that a sign of insecurity—or insincerity? "I remember."

The wiry man with the Phillies hat also extended his hand. "Johnny Jenkins, at your service." The hairs on the back of her neck tingled, and she had to force herself to reach out and take his hand.

"Jess Atwood, pleased to meet you," she managed, though truthfully, she was anything but pleased. Who did these people think they were, showing up on her doorstep without warning?

Santiago cleared his throat. "I know this is inconvenient, but I thought it would be great for you to meet Johnny in person, so you know he's sincere."

Johnny nodded and smiled. "I just love your property, ma'am."

"He means, of course, the two acres by the river," added Santiago. "The part you said you'd be willing to sell."

"I said we'd consider it."

"Of course you did." Santiago made a placating gesture. "That's what I meant to say. And I thought it would be more friendly for us to come by instead of just sending you an email or talking again on the phone."

Jess wondered what was coming next.

"Remember when I told you our buyer," Santiago gestured toward Johnny, "may be willing to pay as much as $125,000?"

"I do." She crossed her arms. "Are you here to negotiate a lower price?" It looked as though Kevin was right about the deal sounding too good to be true.

"Oh, no. Johnny and his brother Carl are serious about this transaction."

"We can go as high as $165,000," Johnny said.

Jess's jaw dropped. That was a crazy amount of money for such a small piece of land. She tried to remember every bit of negotiating advice she'd ever heard. "I'll take it to my partners and see what they say. If everyone agrees, how soon do you think this would happen?"

"That's the best part," said Santiago. "If we agree soon, we could close as early as next week." His smile widened. "And everything would go smoothly." He winked at Jess, apparently indicating they'd avoid the additional penalties the bank had threatened earlier.

"Are you serious?" she asked, failing to contain her growing enthusiasm.

"Totally serious. That's why we wanted to come by, so we can get things moving in a way that works for everyone."

Jess frowned, thinking about the kickback Santiago would undoubtedly receive from the buyers. "If we agree, we'll need an easement for the ten feet of river frontage our irrigation pipe feeds from and for the electric lines and the pumps themselves. The Kidwells across the road already have a similar easement through the property, which has to continue."

Johnny raised both hands, palms toward her. "That's all good with us. As long as we have our privacy, we're okay."

Santiago agreed. "They will be fine. Johnny's uncle in Houston is setting them up with a landscaping business."

Jess's bullshit detector went off immediately. Were these men lying to her? She nodded mechanically despite herself. Liars or not, they were making a proposal she'd never see anywhere else. "Okay, write up a formal offer, and we'll take a look."

"We'll bring that to you by tomorrow at noon," said Santiago. "If everything seems good to you, we can close a week from Friday. How does that sound?"

It sounded fantastic, but they were a little too friendly and eager. "Like I said, I have to ask my partners."

Santiago gave her a smug smile. "Your partners, of course."

Once they'd left, she let Wallaby out of the laundry room. He immediately ran to the front door, barking frantically. Jess stood at the window and watched them drive away. Part of her felt elated by their good fortune, while another part wondered if Wallaby knew something she didn't.

CHAPTER FOURTEEN

Wears Valley, Tennessee
July 1964

Rudy admonished his sister once they got outside. "You shouldn't have said anythin', Anna Mae. You know how Papa gets."

"I had to. He was fixin' to hit you."

He tugged on his earlobe. "I could've managed that. You just about got hit yourself."

"But I didn't, did I?"

They walked down the road, letting the oncoming twilight soothe their emotions, eventually passing the high school, its "Home of the Mighty Wears Valley Wolverines" sign still visible in the deepening dusk. Rudy nodded toward the building. "So, what's with you and school?"

"Oh, school and I are just fine. I got straight A's in all my classes and on my finals."

Rudy stopped and stared at his sister.

"What?" she finally asked.

He shook his head and resumed walking. "You know exactly what. Your grades have always been good. I'm talkin' about you graduatin' early."

"It wasn't early, not really. I was finished with my education."

"That's the thing about education, Anna Mae. The day you stop learnin' is the day you stop growin'."

"That so? Maybe I'm gettin' you mixed up with someone else, but aren't you the one who ran off and joined the Army soon as you graduated high school? I don't see you goin' to Harvard."

"Tell you what. If I'd known I'd be comin' back to Wears Valley and livin' with Mama and Papa, makin' $1.25 an hour at that stinkin' rail yard, I guarantee you I would've found a way to go to college—which is what you should do."

"You name me one woman in town who's been to college and has done somethin' with it."

"I know of at least four or five women from around here who went to college."

"But not one of 'em is doin' anythin' with their diplomas. They may have college educations, but all that gave 'em was the opportunity to meet a man they could cook for, clean up after, and take care of for the rest of their lives. Maybe pop out a few babies while they're at it. Do you think Marty Stevens is usin' her fancy diploma? All she's got to show for that is a runaway boyfriend and a little toddler with no daddy. Lucky for her, she's got a brother who cares. Who knows where she'd be if Deputy Stevens hadn't taken her in? That life ain't for me. Besides . . ."

"Besides what? Don't you start again with that nonsense about dyin' young. You're gonna live a long, happy life with a good husband and lots of beautiful and obedient kids."

"Ain't gonna happen."

"Hush." He stopped and gently turned her shoulders to face him. "Tell me this ain't about another one of your visions."

"It's one I've had several times."

"Anna Mae . . ."

"I'm gonna die on your doorstep."

"I seem to remember you had another vision a few years back that said you were gonna die in childbirth. Ain't that right?"

"Yeah, but I don't always get what the visions mean."

"Of course you don't. But if two different visions contradict each other, they can't both be true, can they?"

She twisted her mouth. "Maybe not," she said after a few seconds.

"Seriously now, Anna Mae, I know you see things in your dreams and such, but that don't mean for sure they're gonna come true."

"Yeah, but they most always do."

"Most always don't mean always. You need to get this obsession about death out of that fool head of yours. None of us know when we're gonna die, includin' you. Isn't doin' what we can with what we have and not worryin' about the millions of things that might go wrong the best way to live life?"

She paused. "I suppose."

"And about that body you think you saw in the woods—"

"I most certainly saw it."

"But no one else did." He put a gentle hand on her shoulder. "All I'm sayin', Anna Mae, is that if we think about somethin' too much, we can start imaginin'—"

"I wasn't imaginin' anythin'." She twisted away from him and started walking. "I saw that girl's body, plain as day."

"Now, don't get all riled up. Maybe you did see a body, but we both know you think about death a lot. And once you get somethin' in your head, you sure have a hard time lettin' it go."

They continued in silence for a few minutes.

"I'll let you in on a little secret," he said, "but you gotta promise me you won't tell no one."

"Cross my heart."

"Remember how I was goin' cross-country with that Greyhound travel pass back when I had to get outta here to save my own life?"

"Of course I do."

"Well, by the time we got halfway through Texas, I was itchin' to get off that big noisy bus. Around noon one day, we came to the outskirts of a little town called Kerrville. Ever hear of it?"

"Don't reckon I have."

"Neither had I, but I was just starin' out the window at the farms and ranches goin' past when these two massive silos caught my attention. They were the

83

biggest I'd ever seen, and each had a huge red-and-white checkered pattern. Tellin' you this now, it seems a little strange, but I told myself those silos had purpose. That got me thinkin' about *my* purpose. Not ten minutes later, we made a lunch stop downtown. When I stepped off the bus, the first thing I saw was an Army recruiter's station. You could say I took that as a sign from above. Once the driver got my suitcase from the luggage bay, I walked straight across the street into that office."

"You're kiddin' me."

He smiled ruefully. "More than anythin', I reckon I was just lookin' for an excuse to get off that damn bus. Far as the Army was concerned, I was only gonna ask some questions, then take time to think about it. But when I walked into that recruiter's office in Kerrville, I came face to face with the most beautiful woman I'd ever seen, workin' there as a secretary. I couldn't take my eyes off her, but she didn't pay me no mind. Or so I thought. I can't say what came over me, but as that sergeant kept talkin', I wasn't gonna say no when she was in the room. Once I'd signed on the dotted line, that beautiful secretary handed me my enlistment papers, looked me straight in the eye, and smiled, sayin' 'Congratulations, Mr. Cole, and welcome to the United States Army.'" He chuckled. "I know that may not sound like much, and I even told myself later I'd imagined the whole thing. After all, why would a woman that gorgeous be interested in the likes of me?"

Anna Mae clicked her tongue. "Maybe 'cause you're a handsome man with a heart the size of Tennessee."

"Spoken like my adorin' little sister. Anyway, I got the surprise of my life the next day as I was lookin' over my paperwork. On the second page of the instructions, handwritten at the top in the most beautiful cursive you've ever seen, was the name Molly, along with her phone number."

"How is it you never told me any of this?"

"I'm tellin' you now, ain't I?"

"After you've been home almost a week." She stopped in her tracks. "And this happened more'n two years ago, right?"

"Nearly two and a half. But some things have got to be told in the right way at the right time. We met for coffee a couple of times and took some walks around town before I reported to basic trainin' at Fort Bennin' in Georgia. I only saw Molly three or four times before I left, but I tell you what, Anna Mae . . ."

"What?"

"You ever fall in love?"

"Do you not remember what the boys at Wears Valley High are like?"

"Just 'cause they're beneath your standard doesn't mean you couldn't have fallen in love with one or two of 'em."

"Hilarious, Rudy, but the answer is no."

"Fallin' in love is like nothin' else in the world. Every time I got one of Molly's letters in Nam, I fell more deeply." He stopped walking and turned to face her. "I wanted to make it home alive so I could see her beautiful face again. That kept me goin' through some of my toughest days."

"That's sweet, but does this mean you're plannin' to support a family on $1.25 an hour? Is that what I'm hearin'? Are you bringin' Miss Kerrville here to have her move in with Mama, Papa, and me?"

"Not on your life. I haven't told you the best part. Her daddy is regional manager for the Central Texas State Bank. When they get their new Center Point branch opened, he said he'd get me set up with a good-payin' job. Plus, there's this thing called the G.I. Bill where they give loans to veterans at low interest rates."

"Why would you need a loan if you're gonna have a good-payin' job?"

"Well, Molly's always wanted to start a farm."

She laughed. "A farm? You know I adore you, Rudy, but you couldn't even grow zucchini in our backyard. By the time you worked your magic on 'em, they weren't fit for anythin' but pig food, though I can't imagine what the pigs would say if they had a choice in the matter."

"You are so funny it's killin' me. It's true my zucchini failed 'cause I didn't know what I was doin'. But like I keep tryin' to get into that hard head of yours, education is everythin'. Under the G.I. Bill, I can get schoolin' on how to be successful at farmin'. Molly's daddy says peanut farmers do the best around there."

"You seriously thinkin' about growin' goobers?"

"Why not? It's the perfect environment for 'em. Plus, land out there is cheap, and we're gonna build ourselves a beautiful home with room for plenty of kids."

Anna Mae stopped again. "Rudolf Augustus Cole, I swear you could knock me over with a feather right now. Sounds like you got the rest of your life planned out." What she didn't say was that in her mind's eye, she saw Molly crying in her bedroom after being told by her doctor she'd never be able to have children.

"I've only got part of my life planned, Anna Mae. The rest I don't know about, not yet. What I know for sure is that as soon as I get enough money set aside, I'm outta here."

She forced a smile. "And what am I supposed to do when you leave?"

"You're gonna do what you always do. Land on your feet like a cat." He nodded to her. "The sooner you get away from Mama and Papa, the better. But don't even think about it 'til you turn eighteen."

For the next few minutes, the only sounds around them were the leaves on the trees rustling in the breeze, the calls of birds out for the evening, and the sound of their footsteps on the still-warm pavement.

"Ooh, smell that honeysuckle," she said, before noticing her brother's frown. "Is there somethin' else you're hankerin' to tell me, Rudy?"

He looked at her for a long moment. "Well, one time after we'd set up base south of Da Nang, we started gettin' hit by mortar fire. It was supposedly a safe area. Sanitized, as they say. But somewhere around two o'clock in the mornin', the Viet Cong caught us completely by surprise. Everythin' was blowin' up all around us, and I swear I thought that was it for me. I promised myself that if I lived through it, I'd be sure to tell you how much I love you."

"I already know that, Rudy."

"Well, it's still important for me to say it. It seems like all I've been doin' since Da Nang is thinkin' about love. Nothin' like almost dyin' to make you consider what's worth livin' for."

"I'm sure."

"And I've got a new aim in life."

"What's that, pray tell?"

"What I want to be . . ." A dog barked at them from a nearby porch. "What I want to be is unconditional. I reckon everyone needs love as much as they need oxygen. You, me, even that dog over yonder. We all need it. But mostly, we only give love if we think we're gonna receive it." He glanced at her. "I'll always be there for you, Anna Mae. Lovin' you is easy. With most folks, it's much harder. For example, lovin' someone like—"

"Our parents?"

"I was gonna say that Oswald bastard who shot President Kennedy, but yeah, also people like our parents. I aim to give and receive love unconditionally. I want to judge less and forgive more."

"You sound like Pastor Blaine."

"Anythin' wrong with that?"

"No, not at all. Um . . ."

"Yeah?"

"Are you sayin' you'd forgive someone like Oswald?"

He thought about that for a bit. "Yeah, I reckon I would. But then I'd shoot him like Jack Ruby did." He shrugged. "After all, justice has to be served."

* * *

That night, once the house had gone quiet, Anna Mae took her diary out of its hiding place and sat on the edge of her bed for a long time, thinking about what to write.

> *Dear Diary,*
>
> *I know Rudy wants nothing but the best for me. He's trying to help with good advice, which is lovely. But he still doesn't understand that I'll be okay if I stay within order. I don't always know what the visions mean, but I know they're here to guide me, and that can't be a bad thing.*
>
> *When my visions first began, they scared people, especially my parents. I learned that telling folks about things before they happened would get me in trouble. That's why when Mama asked*

me a couple of weeks later if I'd had more visions, I lied and said I hadn't.

Most people lie, far as I can tell. Papa likes to say he killed a lot of Nazis in the Second World War. That's not true, but it's something he tells people, especially when he's had a few beers. That lie is only there to say he's not really a bad person. Papa's scars don't lie, though. Both the ones that show and the ones that don't. He came home from that war with shrapnel in his right leg and lots of shame because he didn't get to finish what he calls the good fight. Mama says the pain in his leg is what makes him so mean. I reckon his meanness might also have something to do with the shame he packs around.

My flashlight is almost out of batteries, but here I am, writing like there's no tomorrow. "Time is life's currency," Rudy says, "so spend it wisely." Most people don't know how much of that currency they got left, yet they go about their lives like they got all the time in the world.

But here's something you can set your watch by: I ain't like most people.

CHAPTER FIFTEEN

Kerrville, Texas
Present Day

"This is a no-brainer," Johnny said as he paced the cramped living room with its peeling wallpaper and a pervasive odor of onions. His brother wasn't getting it.

Carl looked up from his Sudoku. "That's not a no-brainer. That's a lack-of-brainer. You offered those organic hillbillies $165,000 for two lousy acres! Now we look desperate. I should've gone with you."

"We talked about that. No one should see you, ever."

"But you obviously need me with you so you don't make crazy fucking offers when there's no need."

"Listen, bro, this is the property we loved, remember? It's perfect in every way. Far from the road, river frontage, big trees, and best of all, privacy."

"At what cost? We're talking double its worth, at least. We told that Santiago clown to offer them 125 grand, which was already way too much." Carl raised his hands in exasperation. "Why the hell would you make it so much more?"

"Because the black chick was about to say no."

"Are you sure? We've talked about you being impulsive and how that gets you in trouble."

"Sometimes you just have to act in the moment."

"Which saves the time and trouble of thinking things through." Carl sighed.

"There are other properties available for far less money."

"What does it matter if they're not what we want?" Johnny gestured around him. "Look at this lousy rental. There are places like this for sale, sure. But how safe do you think they are? At least three neighbors can see the house and barn. Even though we're on a few acres, it's not nearly private enough. Do you like this room that's hardly bigger than a kitchen and stinks like some old lady cooked onions here every day for the last hundred years? And yet, if we got something out in the middle of nowhere, it would look even more suspicious. The property in Center Point won't call attention to us, and it's private enough that people can't see what we do. It even has a dock. We can come and go by car or boat and set it up exactly the way we want. It's a perfect balance."

"We don't have a boat."

"We can get one. That's why I'm the visionary here. Try to see the positive for a change."

"But we're talking way too much money. Plus, we've got a run coming up in three days."

"Which is perfect. We make the run; we get back; we buy the property. We'll be more flush with cash then anyway. You think we'd do better down by the border?"

Carl looked uncertain. "I don't know, maybe."

"Yo, have I taught you nothing? That's the first place they look. Immigration, DEA, Homeland Security—they're all looking for hard-working people like us they can bust. But none of them are looking up here." He shrugged. "At least not as much. You remember our argument about the Sprinter van?"

"Of course."

"If you had your way, you would've gotten the Dodge, which might break down somewhere when we don't want it to. I looked it up on the internet, remember? The Mercedes Sprinters rarely break down. That investment already paid for itself many times over."

"The property we're talking about isn't a van. It's three or four times the price," Carl said with less conviction.

"Which is not much difference in the grand scheme of things. We pulled in almost a half-million dollars last year, and we'll do more this year. Would you take a chance on a property where there's more possibility of getting caught? Or would you rather go back to driving an Uber in Philly?"

"Hell no!"

"Exactly. This will be a big investment, but it's safer and more private, so we'll be less stressed and happier." Johnny walked over and put his arm around his brother's shoulders. "Life is good, Carl. We make excellent dough and don't have to work for the cartel."

"What are you talking about? Of course we work for them."

Johnny shook his head. "No. We only transact business with them, nothing more. Just because you have your precious MacBook Pro doesn't mean you work for Apple Computer. We're businessmen, first and foremost. We have to look at what works in the long run, which means not going to prison and retiring rich."

"What about the organic farmers?"

"Fuck them!" He sat on the couch and stretched back. "They're just small-timers who don't know shit about business. Santiago says they pay late almost every other month, which is why they have to sell those two acres to us. When the time is right, we'll make them an offer they can't refuse for the entire property." He smiled. "Meanwhile, we'll have our own driveway and can come and go as we please. What we do is none of their business, and we'll make that clear from the beginning. There'll be no problem with them."

"You sure about that?"

"Of course I'm sure. They'll pay no attention to us. We're gonna be good as gold."

Carl sucked in a breath and sat next to him. "I hope you're right."

"I'm always right, bro." Johnny chuckled and mussed his brother's hair. "Sometimes, you sound like an old lady. Everything will be fine, and no one's gonna get in our way."

CHAPTER SIXTEEN

Wears Valley, Tennessee
July 1964

Phil Daley checked himself in the pickup truck's mirror. The barber had done his work well, and he looked better than ever. That wasn't the problem. With his embroidered shirt and Beatle haircut, anyone would think he was a goddamn rock-and-roll star. Elvis himself would be jealous if he saw him.

He'd driven around Pigeon Forge for a couple of hours without success and was annoyed. The right location mattered, and there weren't many choices nearby. He told himself he would give it all up after the Jacobs girl, but he'd been compelled to start a new hunt after losing Bella. After a whole week of searching, he'd had no success. Not that having his way with some empty-headed girl would ever be a suitable replacement for such a loyal, trustworthy dog, but he needed the means to ease his grief.

He'd even gone to the fireworks event in Maryville on the Fourth of July, hoping to get lucky, but left alone and disappointed. His daddy had delivered a heartwarming patriotic speech he hoped to cash in on, but none of the girls he talked to afterward believed his father was the congressman—even though that was the honest-to-God truth.

The problem was that Maryville and Sevierville were too big, while places like Pittman Center and Wears Valley were too small. In the bigger cities, people were overly careful, especially young girls. In the smaller towns, it was too easy to attract attention. Pigeon Forge should have been perfect, but he was apparently the only one willing to brave the oppressively hot, muggy August day. He drove down Wears Valley Road for another ten minutes without seeing a single living creature other than two chipmunks and a lethargic squirrel. He'd try Gatlinburg tomorrow. Time to call it quits.

He was almost to Wears Valley, ready to turn back, when he glimpsed a young girl up a side street, walking away from him. He slammed on his brakes and turned, slowly driving up behind the young wavy-haired brunette wearing a white sleeveless top tucked into a tight-fitting green plaid skirt that showed off a gorgeous rear and barely covered her knees. From behind, she reminded him of Judy Garland, his childhood crush. He slowed next to her and rolled down the passenger-side window. She was even more beautiful than he'd expected. "Excuse me, miss?"

The girl walked on in silence, eyes to the front.

"Oh, miss?"

Still no response, though she walked a little faster.

Heart racing, Daley tried what had never failed him in the past. "Sorry, but I'm completely lost."

She stopped and looked at him, her eyes widening slightly. No doubt she found his haircut intriguing. Everyone did. Still, she said nothing.

Daley assessed her, carefully keeping his eyes fixed on hers. Glancing at the bra strap edging out onto her bare shoulder would spook her faster than anything—as he'd learned from previous experience. She had an innocent, feminine demeanor and was developing into a luscious young woman. She was a ripe peach, ready for picking.

"I'm late for band practice," he said, "but I can't seem to find Black Crow Drive. Would you kindly point me in the right direction?"

The girl glanced at the guitar case in the back of his pickup. "Is that in Pigeon Forge or Wears Valley?"

"I don't rightly know, but I assume Wears Valley." He gave her a puzzled look. "They said it was off Wears Valley Road."

"That still means it could be anywhere 'tween here and Pigeon Forge. But I never heard of a Black Crow Drive." She started walking. "Sorry I can't help you, mister."

He rolled his truck forward, keeping pace with her. "They said somethin' about it bein' off a Hatcher Mountain Road."

She stopped again. "Then you're close. Just head toward Pigeon Forge on Wears Valley Road, and you'll see Hatcher Mountain on the left."

"Thank you kindly, miss." He intentionally pointed in the wrong direction. "So, I just go that way, and I'll find it?"

The girl shook her head. "No, the other way, toward Pigeon Forge."

Daley rolled his eyes and tried to appear disgusted with himself. "I feel so stupid. I'm just terrible with directions. The fellers in the band always make fun of me, and now I'm late. We're playin' the Grand Ole Opry tomorrow and are supposed to go over our songs this afternoon." He had to keep her talking.

She took another glance at the guitar case and frowned. "You're a long way from Nashville."

He sighed heavily. "Don't I know it. We were tight with time as it was, and now I've ruined everythin'."

"Well . . . good luck."

"I don't suppose you could show me where Hatcher Mountain Road is? Once I get that far, I'm sure I can find Black Crow on my own."

"Just go back out to Wears Valley Road and take a right. Hatcher Mountain is less than a half-mile down on the left-hand side. You can't miss it," she said and resumed walking.

He rolled forward, again matching her pace. He couldn't let her get away, not after coming this close. "Thanks, but I get lost so easily. If you could just show me where that is, I'll bring you right back here, I promise."

"I'm sorry, but I have to get home."

"Please?"

Her response was to walk faster.

He kept pace with her for a few seconds before squealing his tires in a quick U-turn and driving back the way he'd come, watching her shrink in his rearview mirror. He slapped the steering wheel. "Fuckin' little bitch."

* * *

Deputy Stevens took a call from a distraught man who lived a mile northeast of Wears Valley. He said his daughter had come home in tears after a long-haired man in a beat-up white pickup had tried to get her to show him where Hatcher Mountain Road was, even though she'd already explained it to him, plain as day.

"Did he have a red tattoo on his forearm?" Stevens asked.

After the man said he didn't know, Stevens thanked him and hung up.

"That was Duke Jones from over on Antioch Street sayin' a man with one of them Beatle haircuts pretended to ask directions but was tryin' to pick up his daughter," he told the sheriff.

Keene frowned. "Beatle haircuts. What'll they think of next?" He stuffed a fat pinch of chewing tobacco into his mouth. "Those beatniks are ruinin' music. Saw 'em on Ed Sullivan a few months back. They were screamin' and carryin' on, shakin' their heads like they'd gone mad, but can't sing to save their own lives. Bunch of animals, you ask me."

"Speakin' of animals, we need to do somethin' about Daley."

"You don't know that was him."

Stevens frowned. "Why wouldn't it be?"

"'Cause you're obsessed with that man and think he's everywhere."

"I just talked to the daddy of an upset girl who—"

"I heard. I also heard you ask about the red tattoo. What've I told you about lettin' folks volunteer information 'stead of spoon-feedin' it to 'em?"

"I wasn't spoon-feedin' him."

"I reckon that's exactly what you were doin', Deputy."

"Who else would it be with a haircut like that?"

"Honestly, it coulda been anybody. Maybe a tourist tryin' to get some local action."

"He told Duke's daughter he played in a band that was gonna perform at the Grand Ole Opry tomorrow. Bet you that dog won't hunt."

Keene closed his eyes and rubbed his forehead. "Don't get carried away with this. All we know is that some feller asked a young, impressionable girl for directions. She got hysterical, and her daddy called us." He furrowed his brow. "Ain't it about time you let this thing with Daley go?"

"Just tryin' to do my job, Sheriff."

"Sure you are, but sometimes we gotta make sure we keep our personal stuff separate. I know Daley made you look bad, but—"

"That ain't it. Besides, it was his daddy's influence that turned the trial south and got him off the hook."

Keene spat a stream of tobacco into the trashcan next to his desk. "Well, don't forget what I told you about leadin' folks to remember things that may not have happened."

"No, sir, I'll not forget that."

CHAPTER SEVENTEEN

Center Point, Texas
Present Day

Jess sighed. "We're runnin' out of time, Kevin. Santiago called from the bank again, sayin' the buyers are losin' interest. If we don't act quickly, we'll miss a once-in-a-lifetime opportunity. He said they're away for a few days and will want a definitive answer when they return."

"This farm—and I mean the entire farm—b-belongs in our family. That was Great-Uncle Rudy's vision."

Wallaby watched them cautiously from the safety of his cushion on the other side of the room.

Jess closed her eyes and rubbed her cheek. "Either we let some of it go, or they'll take it all from us. This isn't a thing that might happen. This *will* happen unless we do somethin' to stop it."

A flicker of doubt crossed his face. "We'll get lawyers on it. Didn't you say you liked Victor Carson?"

"I said he was good, and that his father had worked with Great-Uncle Rudy. But that's neither here nor there. The bank is operatin' within the law, and there's nothin' we can do to stop 'em." She closed her eyes for a moment. "You can think about it, but that guy from Philly could change his mind any day. If that happens, there's no way we'd find another buyer in time before the bank forecloses on us. Is that what you want?"

"Of course not. B-but do you hear what I'm sayin'? This is our land, our property . . ." He made a broad sweeping gesture. "Our legacy."

Jess chewed her lower lip. "What if we use part of the money from the land sale for your mushrooms like Dave suggested?"

"They aren't *my* mushrooms. They're for all of us," he said, then cocked his head to one side as what she'd just offered sunk in. "I thought you were dead set against that idea."

"This is me compromisin'. I want you to be on board with sellin' those two acres. I think the best thing would be to have the extra money as a buffer, but . . ." Jess looked at him thoughtfully. "You're right. We should agree on these things. Who knows, it might even eventually make us money."

"Ya think? It'll be a freakin' cash cow."

"We'll see about that." She looked at her brother for a few seconds. "You good to move forward with the sale, then?"

He paused, then nodded. "I am."

* * *

The closing took place on an unseasonably warm late-November day, with temperatures up into the low eighties. Things started off well enough—apart from the air conditioning in the escrow office being cranked down to arctic temperatures.

They all sat at a long, laminated table that smelled strongly of lemon furniture wax.

Jess nodded to Johnny. "Where's your brother?"

He squinted at her. "He doesn't have to be here. Do you have a problem with that?"

Jess forced herself to smile. "No, I just thought it'd be nice for us all to meet since we're gonna be neighbors."

Johnny's eyes narrowed further. "Just because we live nearby doesn't mean we have to be neighbors."

"Mister Rogers wouldn't b-be happy to hear that," Kevin said.

Their buyer glared at him. "I'm not here to make anyone happy."

"Sorry," Kevin said, "that was a joke. Mister Rogers was a children's TV host—"

"You may think you're doing us such a big favor, but we have chosen this investment and are saving your pathetic farm, which isn't pulling enough profit to survive."

Jess shifted uncomfortably in her chair. "What do you suppose you know about that, Johnny? I mean, if we have any issues with finances—"

"That's Mr. Jenkins to you, and doing business doesn't mean we have to chat."

Jess glanced at Dave, whose mouth hung open. She imagined their deal going right out the window, their farm along with it. If they weren't so desperate for the money, she would have walked out herself.

The escrow agent cleared her throat and nodded to Johnny. "I've marked all the places for your signature with these yellow tabs." She gave him a halfhearted smile. "There are quite a lot of them, I'm afraid." She reached over and patted the thick bundle of documents in front of him. "You can start signin' those any time."

He scowled and picked up his pen.

She turned to the Atwoods. "Who's signin' for you?"

"I am," Jess said, hating that her voice squeaked. Part of her didn't want to sign at all. She felt nauseous, and it took all the willpower she had to stay in her seat.

Trying to appear cheerful, the agent motioned to the sellers' packet of papers and smiled. "Then you can begin signin' as well."

They finished nearly forty-five minutes later. The escrow agent handed Jess a certified check for $148,732, the total amount for the two acres minus closing costs and taxes. The agent gave the deed to Johnny, who stuffed it into a manila folder and walked out without thanking anyone or saying goodbye.

"I'm sorry," said the agent. "It's usually easier than this."

"I should hope so," Dave said.

* * *

Back home, Jess felt good about the sale on one level, but something felt off.

"Seller's remorse," Dave told her.

"Is that even a thing? I've heard of buyer's remorse . . ."

"Oh yeah. People have it all the time, especially when they sell somethin' they love." He closed his eyes for a moment. "A few years before I met Kat, I found myself strapped for cash and sold my 1960 Gibson Hummin'bird for fifteen hundred dollars. It was exactly like the one Jimmy Page played for 'Ramble On.'"

"Ramble On?"

He gave her an incredulous look. "Only one of the most underrated songs in rock 'n roll history. That was an okay price back in '93, but now it'd be worth more'n three times that." He sadly shook his head, "I never felt good about losin' the best guitar I ever laid my hands on."

"Is that supposed to make me feel better?"

He shrugged. "Just tryin' to help."

* * *

Jess saw Kevin walking purposefully from the barn to the house that evening. She nodded and forced a smile. "We got your mushroom money."

"Whatever." He didn't look at her or break stride.

Supper was quiet that night, and Jess mulled over the closing. Her anxiety would have been far less if Johnny had been the least bit civil.

Kat used to remind her to take whatever cards life had dealt her and play them the best she could rather than wishing she had other cards. While Jess hadn't asked for the Johnny card, at least the Save the Farm card was included in what life had given her.

Considering the circumstances, that seemed to make it a winning hand.

Chapter Eighteen

Wears Valley, Tennessee
September 1964

After breakfast one Saturday morning, Anna Mae curled up on her bed to read *To Kill a Mockingbird*. She'd checked it out of the library the day before, based on the enthusiastic recommendation of the librarian. That night, planning to get through a chapter or two, she read more than half the book and only stopped because her flashlight ran out of batteries. She finished another two chapters that morning and was imagining that Boo Radley probably looked something like Deputy Stevens when a knock on the door made her jump.

"Who is it?" she asked, stuffing the book under her bed as quickly as possible. Her parents usually didn't bother her when the bedroom door was closed. It was her little sanctuary, except when her father was upset about something, which meant there would be no refuge anywhere.

The door opened, and Rudy stuck his head in. "Hey, what're you up to?"

"Readin' *To Kill a Mockin'bird,* which has made me think about things," she said, motioning him in. "It's good you stopped by, 'cause there's somethin' I want to ask you."

He closed the door behind him and sat on the bed. "I'm all ears."

She took a deep breath. "How old were you before Papa stopped hittin' you?"

"How old was I when I left here?"

"Eighteen, less than two weeks after you graduated high school. You know that."

"Of course I know that." He gave her a wry smile. "But that's your answer. What about you?"

She avoided his gaze. "Well," she said after a while, "how old was I the week before you got here?"

His face darkened. "I was afraid of that, especially seein' the way he reacted when you forgot his sweet potato pie."

"I know."

"That is *so* not right. I assumed Papa stopped hittin' you a long time ago." He paced the small room. "Want to know somethin' I decided?" he finally asked.

"What's that?"

"No one's ever gonna use me as their punchin' bag again." He paused. "I ain't gonna tell you what to do, but feel free to make the same decision. It's your choice, but I can tell you one thing . . ." He gazed out the window.

"What?"

"I've seen girls who got hit by their pa or grew up in the house of an alcoholic or womanizer." He smiled grimly. "And you've been blessed with all three in Papa."

"I'm well aware of that."

"I know. I'm just sayin' that some girls unconsciously seek out a husband like their pa and wind up gettin' abused in similar ways." He looked at her sadly. "It doesn't always happen, but I've seen the pattern more than once or twice and wouldn't want that to be you."

"Do you think I'm crazy? Like I'd go out and find someone who'd treat me that way?"

"Of course you wouldn't. I don't reckon anyone would on purpose. Imagine a handsome young man comin' up to a girl's house for a first date with a bouquet of beautiful flowers, ready to take her out. She answers the door, surprised and happy to get the flowers, seein' that her date has dressed himself nicely and even trimmed his fingernails. He smiles and hands her the bouquet, sayin', 'Hey there, I'm ready to go out on a date with you and hopefully have sex, which might be okay now, but later on, when I'm chasin' other women, becomin' an alcoholic, and beatin' you whenever I feel like it, it's all gonna be quite different.'" Rudy shook his head. "It'd never happen that way. He most likely wouldn't know what his future will look like."

He tapped his temple. "It all happens up here. We seek out a partner who's gonna be like our opposite-sex parent. That's what they call a psychological mechanism."

"You mean to tell me this wonderful woman you found, this Molly, that she's like Mama?"

"In most ways, no. She's warm, affectionate, and lets people around her know what she's feelin'." He chuckled. "Maybe sometimes a bit more than I'd like."

"So, she's the opposite?"

"Not that either. But Molly's hard-workin' and dedicated like Mama."

"I'd never marry a man like Papa."

"That's the point I'm makin', Anna Mae. You may not—"

"It'll never happen. Cross my heart."

CHAPTER NINETEEN

Center Point, Texas
Present Day

After an hour of tossing and turning, Jess decided that she'd made too much out of what had happened at the closing. Johnny was probably nervous about spending so much money and possibly having second thoughts. Rather than react to his hostility, she could choose to take the high road. With that in mind, she finally fell asleep.

The next morning, she taped a welcome note with her phone number to their new neighbors' gate.

The note remained on the gate all week, undisturbed and unread, until a midnight-blue Chevy pickup truck with extra chrome drove up their new neighbors' driveway one morning. Jess thought about walking down to talk to them in person but decided to wait for their call.

As she worked through her day, she obsessively checked her cell phone to ensure the ringer was on.

In the middle of the afternoon, a contractor in a dirty red van pulled into Johnny's driveway to work on the gate. From what Jess could see, he was putting an automatic opener on it, with a keypad and a solar panel for power.

Another three days passed with no contact from their new neighbors until they drove in again one afternoon and parked down by what used to be her dock. This time, Jess chose to take the initiative and properly greet them.

Leaving Wallaby in the house, she walked around the gate they used to keep wide open but was now firmly closed. Someone had pounded T-posts into the ground on either side, but they hadn't installed the fencing itself.

She walked over to the truck, barely able to see the outlines of two figures through the heavily tinted glass. She waited for the driver to roll down his window, but nothing happened.

Did they not see her? She finally tapped on the glass. A few seconds later, she'd almost given up when the driver's window slid down a few inches. "The hell do you want?" Johnny asked.

"Nothin'. I just—"

"You came down here to bother us for nothing?"

"I'm just tryin' to be a good neighbor."

"Good neighbors don't come onto other people's property without permission."

"I thought it would—"

The window slid back up, abruptly ending the conversation. Jess pictured herself hurling a rock right through that fancy tinted glass. Instead, she turned and walked away, determined to not let Johnny get the best of her.

Back home, she slammed the door behind her as Kevin walked out of the kitchen. "Hey Jess, do you—" He studied her as she headed up the stairs. "You okay?"

"Just fine, thanks," she said through clenched teeth.

Over the next two weeks, they saw nothing of the new neighbors, which Jess considered a blessing. That changed quickly when a bulldozer, a backhoe, and a massive excavator showed up late one afternoon, carried in on flatbed trailers.

"What are they doin' b-back there, b-buildin' an office park?" Kevin asked Jess at breakfast the following day.

"I have no idea."

The deep rumble of large diesel engines and annoying brattle of revving chainsaws had shattered the usual quiet of their morning at six o'clock sharp. From the second floor, Jess watched as the tops of their beautiful pecan trees shook, then fell, leaving only a thick double tree line separating the two properties, with a mere scattering of other trees here and there.

By mid-afternoon, the chainsaws finally stopped. At least eighty percent of those beautiful trees were gone forever.

* * *

Later that evening, the doorbell rang just as the Atwoods started watching a recorded episode of *Yellowstone* in the family room. Dave waved his bottle of Lone Star in the general direction of the front door. "You want to get that, Jess?"

"Not really. It's probably just one of the neighbors complainin' about all the noise today, thinkin' it was us. Kevin should talk to 'em, 'cause he's more diplomatic than me."

"You got a point there," her brother said, standing up. He nodded toward the television. "B-but do me a favor and pause that 'til I get back."

A few minutes later, Jess went to check on Kevin and found him in the middle of a heated conversation with Earl Kidwell on the front porch.

"The point is, Mr. Kidwell," he said, "they came to us with a great offer, and we took it. We didn't know you wanted that land 'cause you never told us you were interested."

"Are you pullin' my leg? Our family has had an easement across that land for the last fifty-some-odd years. In what world would you think we'd not be interested?"

"Like he said," Jess interjected, "we didn't know you wanted it, and the buyers put a substantial offer on the table. If you wanted it so bad, how come you never made us an offer yourself?"

Earl exhaled sharply. "'Cause we didn't know it was gonna be for sale," he said, emphasizing each word slowly and loudly. "Which is what I've been tryin' to tell your g-gay brother, but he's just not g-gettin' it."

Jess stepped out onto the porch. "That's ugly, Earl Kidwell. I knew you were rude, but I had no idea you'd—"

"Forget it, Jess. He's just b-bein' petty," said Kevin.

"I don't care what he's bein'." She turned her attention back to Earl. "I ever hear you talkin' about my brother like that again . . ."

"Then what? Just so you know, I'm scared to death of some skinny-armed black girl half my size."

Jess's hand involuntarily curled into a fist. "You seem pretty sure of yourself, Mr. Kidwell."

"Oh, my, what you gonna do? Hit me?"

She sucked in her breath. "I'm gonna tell you to get off our property."

He smirked at her for a few seconds, then turned and walked back to his fancy red pickup truck.

Kevin and Jess watched him drive away.

"Motherfucker," she said under her breath.

CHAPTER TWENTY

Wears Valley, Tennessee
September 1964

Anna Mae sat on the edge of her bed, listening to the unanswered call of a whippoorwill searching for her mate somewhere off in the distance.

Maybe Rudy was right, and she wouldn't die young and single. Perhaps she could even find happiness in a relationship. If her recent dreams were any indication, that was indeed possible. She picked up her pen and began to write.

Dear Diary,

I've been thinking a lot about love lately. It might have something to do with a vision I had last week about me and this boy Andy who used to tease me at school. I even woke up touching myself. Mama warned me to never do that, but I don't see why because it felt great. In the vision, I saw Andy making love to me in my bedroom, which was terrific.

Rudy says I'm overly obsessed with my visions. I know he only wants what's best for me, but he doesn't understand that knowing something is going to happen doesn't mean I'm obsessed.

The part of the vision where Andy and I lie together after making love, happy as pigs in mud, was nothing short of beautiful.

Speaking of pigs, Andy works at the Piggly Wiggly. He's said

"Hey" to me a few times and always makes me laugh. A few days after I had the vision with him, Mama and I were shopping there. As she paid the checkout girl, Andy set the groceries in our buggy and casually asked me out to the football game against Pigeon Forge next week.

"Maybe," I told him. "I have to ask my pa."

Right there in the store, he raised both hands and spun around like he was celebrating something important. I couldn't help giggling. If Mama noticed, she didn't let on.

When we got home, I asked Papa, sure he was going to say no, or maybe even get riled up. He told me I could go provided I was home by ten. I could hardly believe it. What are the odds of him saying yes to anything that might make me happy? If that's not a sign, I don't know what is. I never thought this could happen, but look at me now, world. I'M GOING ON A DATE to my first football game ever!

* * *

Anna Mae felt a growing sense of happiness in the days leading up to the game. She was a little disappointed that Rudy didn't share her excitement, but that was just him playing his protective big brother role.

When the day finally arrived, her mother refused her any makeup—Anna Mae was not allowed to have any of her own—and gave her yet another lecture on the dangers of teen pregnancy. Anna Mae managed to sit through it without rolling her eyes once. Afterward, she changed into her favorite calf-length indigo dress. She tied a light-blue ribbon in her blonde hair, which she had put up in just the right way.

Andy arrived in his Ford Fairlane half an hour before game time. Anna Mae was surprised that her father was civil to him and even shook his hand. She'd been half-expecting him to call the whole thing off at the last minute, yet here he was, greeting Andy as though he were an old friend.

Everything was in order, just the way it should be. When Andy finally looked at her, though, he frowned.

Anna Mae had a sinking feeling in her stomach and looked down at her dress. "What?" she asked.

He gazed at her for another few moments. "I just can't get over how fine you look when you're all gussied up," he said.

Relief flooded through her until she noticed the scowl on her father's face.

"Papa says you need to have me back home by ten o'clock," she said, trying to change the subject as quickly as possible.

"Yes, sir," he said, looking her father in the eye. "I promise to have your daughter back by that time, Mr. Cole."

When they got to his car, she noticed her father watching them from the window, still scowling. Andy opened the door for her, and the scent of stale potato chips, motor oil, and spent cigarettes wafted out. She was tempted to say something but didn't want to ruin the evening by complaining.

They arrived fifteen minutes before the game started and found seats halfway up the bleachers. The excitement in the air made it feel more like a party than the dry sporting event she'd imagined. Twenty Wears Valley High marching band musicians were on the field, roughly half of them playing in tune. Anna Mae watched the cheerleaders in their red-and-white knee-length skirts, doing their high kicks while going through their routines. Then she noticed how carefully Andy watched them.

"Make sure you don't drool on your shirt," she said.

"You are funny as all get-out." He gestured at the cheerleaders. "Why do you think they're out there? So people will look at 'em. Which is exactly what I'm doin."

Shrugging it off, Anna Mae scanned the people around them and was surprised to see Deputy Stevens sitting with his arm around Peggy June Morris, a few rows up and on the other side of the center aisle. She had never seen them together—or him out of uniform.

Anna Mae spun her attention back to the field when she realized she'd been staring. Stevens probably hadn't seen her. But what did it matter, anyway? He'd already asked Peggy June to marry him.

She turned, as unobtrusively as possible, to take another peek. They were laughing about something, having a good time.

Anna Mae respected Stevens, but she'd had an unpleasant experience with Peggy June a couple of years before at the library. Most of the seats had been taken, and Anna Mae left her spiral notebook in one of the few remaining chairs when she'd gone to find another book. When she returned, Peggy June was sitting in her seat and had put Anna Mae's notebook on the table.

"Excuse me, but that's my chair," Anna Mae said as politely as possible.

"Bless your little heart," said Peggy June. "I didn't notice that it had your name on it."

"I believe you know what I meant."

"And I believe you're pesterin' me. Should I ask the librarian what to do about someone who won't quit talkin' to me even when I've asked her to stop?"

But that had been two years past, and Peggy June might be nicer now. Of course, if the rumors were true, the problem was that she'd been too nice—to too many boys.

Once the game started, Anna Mae would sneak an occasional glance at Stevens and his fiancée. Around the fourth or fifth time she looked, however, she saw Peggy June glaring at her, so she snapped her attention back to the playing field.

"The hell you keep lookin' at?" asked Andy. "You're missin' half the game."

"I'm just worried about that deputy back there," she lied.

"You're worried about *him*?" He gave Stevens an appraising look. "Trust me, he ain't nothin' to worry about." He turned back to Anna Mae. "He caught a bunch of us drinkin' in the park last summer and let us go with a warnin'. Sheriff Keene would've taken us to our parents or maybe even locked us up for a couple of hours to teach us a lesson. Besides, you and me ain't doin' nothin' wrong." He winked. "At least not yet."

Anna Mae turned away so he wouldn't see her roll her eyes. "What do you think of that girl he's with?"

"You mean Peggy June?" He squinted at Stevens and his date. "I swear, she is one hot number. What I wouldn't give—" he said before catching himself. "I mean, what some people wouldn't give to be in his shoes."

"No doubt." There went Andy's chance for a second date, vision or no vision.

Wild cheering erupted from the visiting team's bleachers. "Damn," he said, "that's the third touchdown Pigeon Forge has scored tonight." He waved his hands in exasperation. "And it ain't even halftime."

"Why don't you fetch us a couple of cokes to ease the pain?"

He stood and bowed. "Your wish is my command, your royal highness." He took a few steps before turning back around. "What kinda coke do you want?"

"Dr Pepper would suit me just fine, thank you."

Ten minutes later, Anna Mae wondered what had happened to her date and went looking. She found him near the snack bar, without drinks, talking to a long-legged cheerleader wearing artfully applied makeup.

"Did you lose your way, Andy?" Anna Mae asked.

"I was just fixin' to get our drinks, waitin' for the line to die down first."

Anna Mae nodded toward the snack bar. "Well, it looks like your timin' is perfect 'cause there ain't nobody in front of you now."

She gave the cheerleader a wry smile and turned back toward the bleachers, almost bumping into Phil Daley, his arm around a pretty raven-haired girl who couldn't have been more than sixteen.

"Whoa there, little lady," Daley said. "Where's the fire?"

"Sorry," she said and hurried back to the bleachers. Deputy Stevens had to know. As she climbed the stairs and approached him, Peggy June gave her a dirty look, which Anna Mae did her best to ignore.

"Deputy Stevens . . ." she began, then wondered if she should say anything in front of his date. She cautiously glanced at Peggy June, who narrowed her eyes.

Stevens smiled, oblivious to his fiancée's upset. "Why, Anna Mae, what a pleasant surprise seein' you here." He didn't seem to hear Peggy June's sharp intake of breath but frowned when he noticed the look of concern on Anna Mae's face. "What is it?"

"I just saw that Daley guy with the funny haircut."

He immediately stood. "Where?"

"Over near the snack bar with a black-haired girl."

Stevens told Peggy June he'd be right back and went down the bleacher steps two at a time without waiting for a reply.

"Thanks a lot," Peggy June hissed.

Anna Mae couldn't tell if she was directing that at her or Deputy Stevens. She smiled weakly and walked away, passing the row where she'd been sitting with Andy just as he returned with the drinks. He held them up, looking at her with a puzzled expression as she continued purposefully down the steps.

"I'll be right back," she called out without slowing down.

"Where're you off to?"

She waved in his general direction and kept going. When she got to the snack bar, she saw Stevens looking around, but no sign of Phil Daley or the girl. The deputy raised an eyebrow at her, but she just shook her head and returned to her seat.

"Did somethin' interestin' happen while I was away on my coke mission?" Andy asked when she returned.

"As a matter of fact—"

Cheering from the other side of the field interrupted her.

"Damn," Andy said, "another interception. They are simply killin' us." He stood and cupped his hands to his mouth. *"Come on, Wolverines, get the lead out, will ya?"*

When Stevens started back up the steps, he glanced at Anna Mae and shrugged. Daley must have gotten away. There was probably not much Stevens could have done anyway, even if the raven-haired girl was under eighteen. There weren't any laws she knew of preventing an adult from putting an arm around a teenager.

At least she'd tried. Hopefully, Daley had been spooked and left empty-handed.

CHAPTER TWENTY-ONE

Center Point, Texas
Present Day

"What do you think about our rude neighbors?" Kevin asked Jess as they finished breakfast.

"You know damn well how I feel about the Kidwells."

He shook his head. "I'm talkin' about our *other* rude neighbors."

"You mean Johnny and his brother?"

"Duh. Our friendly landscapers who drive a shiny new pickup that never has any landscapin' tools in it or a smudge of dirt on it—ever. In the three months they've b-been b-back there, I've never once seen it pull a trailer like every other landscapin' rig in the State of Texas." He leaned across the table toward her. "And how about them drivin' in and out at all hours of the night, sometimes with their lights off? B-bet you they're manufacturin' drugs. Probably meth. They got some strange-lookin' b-buildin's b-back there."

"All you need is a single-wide trailer to make meth. Like in *Breakin' Bad*, remember? They cooked meth in an RV."

"Then you tell me what they're up to. I'd b-bet you my Xbox it has nothin' to do with landscapin." He shrugged. "B-besides, we've never even seen the b-brother. I'm b-beginnin' to wonder if he even exists."

"I've wondered the same thing."

* * *

Bald Fred from the bank stopped by one afternoon, telling them late payments would no longer be tolerated. The new mushroom facility would take another couple of weeks to be up and running and at least an additional month before they'd even know if it would turn a profit. It was way over budget, and Jess wished everyone had listened to her and paid down the loan. But the visit from Fred didn't quite add up. They had only been late with one payment out of the previous four.

When the shiny black-and-chrome Ford pickup with the KC Ranch logo on the side pulled into their driveway an hour later, it all made more sense, especially when Travis Kidwell got out and came to the door.

Despite her misgivings, she invited him in.

"I just want you to know—"

"It's nice to see you too, Mr. Kidwell." She closed the door behind him and glared. "How on earth have you been?"

"Well, Earl wanted me to come over here first and—"

"First? Do you mean to tell me we have more visitors on the way? How delightful. I should set out some snacks."

"Now Jess, Earl sent me over here to . . ."

"To what, pray tell?"

"He's gonna ask you to sell your farm to us."

"There isn't a snowball's chance in hell of that happenin'."

"That's what I told him, but once my old man gets an idea in his head, he holds onto it like a dog with a bone."

"Then why don't you just leave before he gets here?"

"I'm on your side with this, Jess."

"Are you now? Didn't you come over here as your old man's messenger boy?"

"He wanted me to . . . soften you up first."

"Soften me up? Like that'd work."

"Exactly what I tried to tell him. Sometimes havin' history with someone makes it harder to—"

"We have no history."

"We obviously do, Jess, or you wouldn't be so riled up right now."

"I'm riled up 'cause you're standin' in my house, schemin' to take our property away."

"If you'll just listen up for one split second, I'm not—"

The doorbell startled them both. Jess opened the door to find Earl Kidwell on the porch. No surprise there.

Earl touched his hat. "Afternoon, Miss Atwood. Mind if I come in?"

"Actually, Travis here was just leavin', and I've got a lot of work to do. Maybe some other time."

"I'd be much obliged if you could spare five minutes for a neighbor."

Jess stared at him a few seconds, then opened the door wide. "Fine, five minutes," she said, leading them into the living room, already doubting her decision to let them in.

"Saw that y'all had someone over today," Earl said, settling back on the living room couch.

"And I'm sure you had nothin' to do with the bank payin' us a visit, did you?"

"Hey now, I don't mean to go stirrin' things up, but—"

"Happy to hear that. Y'all just have a great day, now."

Travis moved toward the door, but Earl didn't budge.

"Mr. Kidwell, if you don't mind, I have work to do."

He stood and turned as if to leave. "Did you know I helped build this house?"

"I wasn't aware," she said with genuine surprise.

"I used to come over here and help your great-uncle Rudy back when I was in middle school."

"That's nice, but—"

"When y'all are ready to sell your property, I guarantee I'll give you the best price possible."

"Ready to sell our property? The hell are you sayin'?"

"You know very well what I'm sayin', honey. I'm just offerin' you a way out."

"We're not lookin' for a way out. This is our home and our farm, and we're stayin' right here." She narrowed her eyes at Travis, who waited by the door.

Earl gave her a smug look. "That's not what we've been hearin'. People are talkin' about how y'all aren't makin' payments on time."

"What business is it of theirs?"

"This was all Kidwell land before my pa sold it to Rudy Cole," Earl continued, ignoring her question, "who turned it into a damn peanut farm. Excellent pastureland, too. Biggest mistake of my daddy's life." He wagged a finger at her. "You need to know that you might be up for a zonin' review 'cause of transferrin' commercial agriculture property and all that." He nodded sideways toward the back of the property. "And," he said, raising an eyebrow, "you might not pass that review. You're obviously sellin' to people doin' commercial development, which makes you a commercial developer if you look at it in the right light."

"You wouldn't dare."

"Wouldn't I? All I'm sayin' is, you'll save yourself a lot of trouble by sellin' to us. Remember, I'll offer you a fair price."

"That is so unbelievably kind of you."

"It is, 'cause I can squeeze you hard as I want. The zonin' review would just be a start." He tipped his hat and gave her a rattlesnake smile. "Nice talkin' business with you today, honey. Let's go, Travis."

She stood in the doorway watching the Kidwells walk back to their pickup trucks. Travis glanced back toward her, looking uncertain and . . . apologetic? She glared at them as Earl gave her a confident little wave before climbing in and driving off. *He* was the biggest mistake his daddy ever made. No wonder his wife left him.

Jess only wished he wasn't right about their lack of choices.

CHAPTER TWENTY-TWO

Anna Mae thought about Andy as she dusted the living room. He hadn't called since their date five days earlier. Rudy told her that's how boys are sometimes, and she should take it as a blessing to find out he's not interested early on rather than down the road after they'd been married four years and had a couple of kids. It didn't feel like much of a blessing, but she'd decided at the football game that she wasn't going out with him again, so what did it matter if he called or not?

She heard a car pull up and watched from the window as her mother climbed out wearing a deep frown. Her unhappiness was never a good sign. If her mother wasn't happy, her father would soon be unhappy—which always meant trouble. He'd been in an especially foul mood after he and Rudy traded angry words a few days before. Rudy had mentioned the upcoming anniversary of President Kennedy's assassination, and their father said he deserved it.

Rudy got terribly angry, and Anna Mae feared they'd come to blows. Once Jefferson Cole had a certain look in his eye, someone was probably going to get hit. Rudy knew that too, but he stood his ground. The senior Cole wanted everyone to know he was in charge, and neither he nor his son were the type to back down. Lucinda had stepped in and got them both to simmer down.

Although no one got hit, Anna Mae couldn't help but wonder if it was only a matter of time.

Her mother was almost to the house. Anna Mae ran into her room and closed the door. Sometimes staying out of sight was the best strategy. Seconds later, the front door slammed.

"Anna Mae Cole!" her mother yelled.

So much for staying out of sight. She hesitantly came out of her room. "Yes, ma'am?"

Lucinda glared at her daughter. "Guess who called me at work today?"

"I don't know, Mama."

"Lulu Morris, that's who. Can you imagine why she rang?"

Anna Mae wondered why Peggy June's mother would have called. "I don't know, Mama."

Lucinda shook a finger in her daughter's face. "Don't you even think about lyin' to me, girl. You know *exactly* what I'm talkin' about. Looks like you were a busy little beaver at the football game you went to with that good-for-nothin' boy."

"I didn't do anythin' wrong, Mama. I was just watchin' the game with Andy, and—"

"And you were hittin' on Paul Stevens, right in front of his fiancée, with all the grace of a New York City hooker. I can't even imagine why Lulu would've called me. Wait, I know, maybe 'cause she's concerned about you tryin' to upset her daughter's engagement."

"I wasn't tryin' to do that, cross my heart. I saw a man Deputy Stevens told me to watch out for, so I—"

"She told me about that, too. Said you sent him off on a wild goose chase searchin' for someone who wasn't even there. Do you have any idea how that makes me look?"

"That man was there, Mama. I saw him with my own eyes."

Lucinda put her hands on her hips. "Yet no one else did, not even the deputy. How peculiar is that? And you followed him off on that little goose chase of yours once you got him away from Peggy June."

"I swear, Mama, it wasn't like that."

"You swear a lot, girl. I don't even know what's the truth from you anymore, or if you even know the difference. Maybe you believe you saw a girl's body in those woods last May, and maybe you think you saw a man Deputy Stevens supposedly told you to look out for." She shook her head. "Dr. Ferguson called them persistent hallucinations. We've told you time and again to keep 'em to yourself. Unless you're just lyin' to us. Maybe you were up to some hanky-panky with that deputy under the bleachers. Either way, you got some serious correctin' to do. If you think for one red-hot second I'm gonna let you embarrass me like this, you got another thing comin', girl."

Anna Mae opened her mouth to speak, but Lucinda angrily clapped her hands. "Not another word out of you. Wait in your room until your pa comes home."

"Please, Mama, don't tell him. You know what he'll do."

She nodded slowly. "I do indeed. Now you get in your room and close that door. Another word out of your mouth, and I might just give you a whippin' myself."

* * *

Rudy was the next one home, and Anna Mae could hear the muffled sound of his conversation with their mother. Sooner than she'd hoped, another car pulled up, followed shortly by the front door opening. Cold fear growing inside her, she listened carefully for signs that her father was drunk. That always made it so much worse, but she didn't notice it this time. She couldn't hear his words, but he sounded almost happy—at first.

"*Anna Mae!*" he bellowed less than a minute later. "*Get out here now.*"

She opened her door to see him glaring at her from less than ten feet away, her mother standing behind him with arms crossed.

"What's this I hear about you interferin' with Peggy June's engagement?"

"I wasn't, sir. I—"

"You callin' your mama a liar?"

"No, sir, it's just the way things were told to her that—"

"So you weren't givin' the evil eye to the deputy's wife-to-be at the football game? Maybe you didn't even look at her, did you?"

"No, sir. I mean, maybe I looked at her, but—"

"Maybe you did, huh? And did you send that sheriff's deputy off lookin' for somebody who wasn't even there?"

"Papa, I saw him and—"

"Looks to me like everybody's lyin'." He rubbed his jaw and nodded at his daughter. "Except you, of course." He pulled out his belt in one smooth motion.

"Please, Papa. I didn't do anythin' wrong."

"You didn't, huh? Let's say you believe all that horseshit and truly think you saw that man. Didn't we tell you not to discuss your imaginations with anyone?"

"You did, Papa, but it wasn't my imagination."

"Right." He pointed to the floor in front of him. "Get over here now."

She took a halting step toward him, then another. "Papa . . ."

"You know how to count to twenty, Anna Mae?"

"Please, Papa . . ."

He aimed a quivering finger at the dining room table. "Bend over."

Her eyes flicked toward the door. If she bolted, she might make it.

"Don't even think about it. You know we'd catch you sooner or later."

Anna Mae hesitantly walked toward him just as Rudy came out of his room. "What's goin' on?"

The senior Cole squinted at him. "Nothin' that concerns you. Just get on back in your room."

"Please, Papa, tell me. I'm part of this family, too."

"Anna Mae's been tellin' lies again. I don't know whether they're hallucinations or she's just makin' up stories. Either way, she needs to stop, and I aim to help motivate her." He nodded back toward Rudy's room. "Now leave us be."

"I can see why you're angry, Papa, but what if she's tellin' the truth?"

Cole scowled at his son. "Even if she believes her little story, she needs to learn to stop upsettin' folks."

Rudy stepped closer. "I know sometimes folks get upset, but—"

"You need to step back, boy. You're right in the way. If you want to stay and watch, that's fine. But you gotta move. Now."

Rudy squared his shoulders. "There shouldn't be anythin' to watch, Papa. She told me what happened at the game, and I believe her."

"I don't give a good goddamn what you believe. Now get out of the way."

Rudy moved directly between them. "Don't hit her, Papa. That just ain't right."

His father nodded and began putting his belt back on. In the blink of an eye, he whipped it around and caught Rudy in the side of the head with the buckle, creating a deep gash and knocking him to one knee.

Anna Mae pressed her hand to her mouth, careful not to cry out. Their father was like a raging bull when he got like that, and one thing she'd learned from years of experience was that he could always get worse.

Jefferson Cole stood over his son. "I warned you, boy," he said. "Don't be messin' with what's none of your bidness. Now get on outta here."

Rudy touched his head, then stared at the blood on his fingers. He began to rise, then pivoted into an uppercut that connected with his father's midsection. It knocked the wind out of the older man, who gasped and stumbled back.

"*Rudy*," Lucinda cried, "what have you done?"

He looked uncertainly from one parent to the other. "I was only defendin' myself," he nodded toward Anna Mae, "and my sister."

Lucinda rushed to help her husband, who was bent over, hands on his knees, trying to catch his breath. When she touched him, he slapped her hand away and stumbled out of the room.

She glared at her son. "You think that was such a smart thing?" she asked, ignoring the trickle of blood from his wound.

"I can't say if it was a smart thing, but it was the right thing. There's no way I can stand by and—*holy shit!*"

His father had come back into the room with a 12-gauge pump shotgun. His face red, he looked menacingly at his son, who held up both hands in surrender.

"Please don't shoot."

Cole's response was to pump the shotgun and point it at Rudy's heart. "Sucker punchin' me in my own home. Never would've expected that of you, boy."

Rudy inched away from Anna Mae, his hands still raised. "I'm sorry, Papa, I—"

"When I say get, you better believe you're gonna get. Last chance. Now get."

"Yes, sir," he said, starting toward his room.

"*You stop right there.* You're goin' out the front door, boy."

Rudy froze. "I just need to get my things."

"Your darlin' sister is gonna put your stuff out on the porch in the next two minutes."

"I'm goin'," he said as he went out, closing the door behind him.

Cole lowered his gun. "What're you waitin' for?" he snarled at Anna Mae.

Heart pounding, she ran to Rudy's room and stuffed everything that would fit into his dark green duffel bag with "Cole, Rudy A" stenciled on it in three-inch white letters. She tossed the rest of his things into his beat-up suitcase with the torn leather corner. The duffel was too heavy for her to lift, so she dragged it across the floor and set it on the front porch, avoiding Rudy's eyes. When she brought his suitcase and the smaller bag, she whispered, "I'm sorry."

"Ain't nothin' for you to be sorry about." He took her gently by the shoulders. "Anna Mae, come with me. You know he's never gonna stop."

"Probably not, but you yourself said I should stay at least another six months 'til I turn eighteen."

"I did say that, but what happens if he goes too far? What happens if he hurts you more seriously?"

"And what would happen if I went with you, and he called the sheriff sayin' you kidnapped a minor?"

He thrust his hands into his pockets. "I'd take that risk for you, Anna Mae."

"I'm sure you would, but *I* won't take the risk. No way you're goin' to prison on account of me." She placed a hand on his arm. "I've survived seventeen and a half years with him. I can manage another six months."

"Well then, it kills me to say this, but you should probably get back inside. Anythin' you face now won't be as bad as it'd be if you kept him waitin." He hefted the duffel bag onto his shoulder and picked up his other two items. "You better believe I'll be seein' you later, sis. My door'll always be open to you."

"You don't even have a door."

"Not yet, but I will." He winked at her, which made him wince.

"Rudy, you're still bleedin."

"I'll be fine. It's already slowin' down."

She watched her brother walk across the front lawn and hoped he wasn't walking out of her life.

CHAPTER TWENTY-THREE

Center Point, Texas
Present Day

Jess was on her way back from the feed store with a roll of fencing in the back of her truck when she saw Johnny's dark-blue pickup turn into his driveway. Something white flew out of the cab as the truck pulled up to the keypad. A few seconds later, the pickup continued through the automatic gate.

Her curiosity piqued, she also turned into Johnny's driveway and drove up to where he'd stopped. On the Atwoods' land beside the driveway lay a large, half-empty soda cup.

Jess hopped out, picked up the cup, and looked toward Johnny's house. She knew better than to go on their property again. And yet . . .

She walked around the gate through the still-unfinished fencing, soda cup in hand.

Johnny answered his door on the fifth knock, and his eyes widened at the sight of Jess. "You again. Maybe I didn't tell you clearly enough to not come on our property." One corner of his mouth turned up slightly. "Or maybe you're too stupid to understand."

Jess tried to hand him the cup. "I think you lost somethin', neighbor."

He glanced at it disdainfully. "That's not mine, *neighbor*," he sneered, then stepped out and pulled the door closed behind him. "I'll tell you what *is* mine, though," he said with spittle on his lips, his face inches away from hers, "and that is the property you're trespassing on."

She took a step backward. "It's not trespassin' if you don't have a sign up or I don't climb over a fence."

"You think you're pretty fucking clever, don't you? Next time I see you on my property, I'm calling the sheriff." His eyes narrowed. "Unless I feel I'm in immediate danger and need to take action myself. We'll see how much your black life matters then."

"You're threatenin' me."

"Maybe you're not as stupid as I thought." As she opened her mouth to respond, he held up a finger. "Wait here. There's something we need to finish our conversation." He went back into the house, slamming the door behind him.

Jess ran back to her truck, afraid he was going for a gun. As she backed out of Johnny's driveway, she wondered if she'd just made a difficult situation worse.

* * *

Jess watched through the living room window the following week as a small white pickup with "South Central River Authority" on its door pulled into their driveway. Everyone in Kerr County knew a visit from the SCRA was not usually a good thing.

A short, middle-aged man with a prominent potbelly squeezed out of the pickup, pulled on a black ten-gallon hat, and sauntered toward the front door, clipboard in hand.

"Where's Elena?" Jess asked Kevin.

"Out b-back b-by the pumpkin squash."

"Can you get her, please? She's dealt with these damn fools before."

Kevin ran from the room, and Jess opened the door a half-second after the doorbell rang, surprising the river authority man.

"Oh," he said, "is the man of the house home?"

"I'm one of the property owners here, so you can either talk to me or wait a minute for our business manager," she said, nodding toward the back door. "She's dealt with you people before."

His eyes narrowed. "Us people? You mean us white people?"

"That's not what I meant at all. It's just that she's talked with folks from your agency before and—"

"What's going on?" Elena asked, coming up behind Jess.

Their visitor gave her a scornful look. "Now, who's this?"

"Elena is our business manager and the one who deals with anythin' that has to do with our water rights."

Dave and Kevin walked up next. "What's all this about?" Dave asked.

"Well, well," the SCRA man said, "looks like the gang's all here, though I reckon y'all might not wanna hear what I have to say."

"Isn't that a surprise," Jess said.

The man frowned at her. "It's been reported that you're runnin' a three-inch irrigation feed down to the river."

"That's right," Elena said. "Rudy Cole, the former property owner, put that in over forty years ago. But there's nothing wrong with that."

The SCRA man shook his head. "Well, that's where y'all might be wrong." He cleared his throat and read from his clipboard: "Per Texas Revised Statute TRS 412.23, irrigation plans approved for less than five hundred acre-feet per year shall use no greater than two-and-a-half-inch pipe or tubing for any parcel of land greater than 100 acres and less than 200 acres."

Elena held her hand out. "Our allotment is grandfathered in. May I see that, please?"

The river authority man held the clipboard against his chest. "I'm just tellin' you what's there in the statutes. You can look it up whenever you like."

Elena shook her head. "First off, we've only got ninety-two arable acres, so that wouldn't even apply."

The man scribbled something down. "Really? Says right here you got one hundred sixty-three arable."

"A hundred and sixty-three is how much we used to farm before we scaled back," Dave said. "Some of the crops we tried weren't worth the time and effort."

"Yet accordin' to this, y'all are still gettin' a water allotment for one hundred sixty-three acres."

"Hold up a cotton-pickin' minute," Jess said. "The hell are you gettin' at?"

"What I'm gettin' at is that y'all are usin' more water than you're supposed to, robbin' other farmers around here of what they need for their crops and animals. I'm just glad we caught you at it."

Dave frowned. "There was nothin' to catch. We haven't done anythin' wrong, mister . . ."

"Conklin. Jeremy Conklin." He scratched the back of his neck. "You know, the prisons are full of people loudly declarin' their innocence."

"Which doesn't necessarily prove their guilt," Jess said. "Some people who say they're innocent *are* truly innocent."

Conklin considered that for a moment, then shrugged. "Well, I'm here to enforce the rules, and I'm tellin' y'all like it is. I've got a cease-and-desist here." He pulled a paper out from his clipboard. "Now, who wants to take this?"

Elena reached out. "Let's have it." She scanned the document with the three Atwoods crowded around, reading over her shoulder.

"I know there's a lot of fine print, but let me simplify," Conklin said. "Basically, y'all need to stop pullin' from the river 'til we can do a proper water use audit."

"You can't be serious," Jess said. "We've got a major cauliflower harvest comin' up in three weeks. If you knew anythin' about farmin', you'd know the last weeks before harvest are crucial."

"Which is why it's always a good idea to follow the rules."

Jess rubbed her forehead. "This isn't about rules, though, is it? This is about the Kidwells puttin' a squeeze on us, usin' you and your department as their tools."

He stared at her, his face expressionless. "Y'all need to understand this cease-and-desist is in effect from this moment onward. We'll get back to you about the water audit."

"Give my best to Mr. Kidwell," Jess said.

"I'm sure Earl would be thrilled to hear that." He touched the brim of his hat and turned away.

"Oh, so you *are* familiar with Earl Kidwell."

"Honey, just about everyone in Kerr County is familiar with Earl Kidwell," Conklin said over his shoulder.

"Yeah, but you seem to be intimately familiar."

Conklin opened the door to his pickup and nodded toward Jess. "Good luck with that one," he said to Dave.

CHAPTER TWENTY-FOUR

Wears Valley, Tennessee
October 1964

Anna Mae opened her eyes to a dark and still room. Something had awakened her from a dream in which Deputy Stevens protected her from a raging monster. She'd thrown off the covers in her sleep, and her night slip did little to keep her warm against the late October chill. She shivered and pulled her blanket up to her chin.

A pebble hit her window. She got up and looked through glass decorated by tendrils of frost, saw no one at first, then made out the silhouette of a man less than ten feet away.

She stepped back, stifling a surprised yelp. When he came close to the window, she recognized Andy by the dim glow of her night light.

"What are you doin' here?" she whispered, not immediately realizing he couldn't hear her through the window. He motioned for her to slide it up. Flustered, it took her a few tries to get it unlatched and open.

"Just came by to wish you a happy Halloween, my dear," he slurred, his breath a cloud of mist.

"You're drunk," she whispered. "And keep your voice down. Trust me when I say you do not want to wake my mama up."

"Oh, I trust you. When I called you after the game, she told me if I ever rang again, your pa would be more than happy to beat me senseless. Think she meant it, too."

"You called here?"

"Several times. The first time, you were out. The second time, she said you were busy. The third time, she gave me the bidness."

"I had no idea. I just thought . . ."

"You thought I forgot about you." He shook his head, barely perceptible in the dim light. "You done stole my heart, Anna Mae. Ain't no forgettin' that."

"I don't quite know what to say."

"Well, you could start with 'It's so good to see you, Andy. Why don't we go cruisin' in your car?'"

"Of course it's nice to see you, but it might not be such a good idea to go drivin' around in your condition."

He waved off the implication. "I just had a beer so I could get up the nerve to invite you out, seein' how it's Halloween and all. I even saved you a couple of cold ones."

"Papa would kill me if he knew I snuck out." Besides, she'd told herself she wasn't going out with this joker again.

"His car ain't here."

"He's workin', but Mama's here, and you'd best believe she'd tell him." She didn't really want to go with Andy, though if she did, it would be in order with her vision.

"All the reason to be quiet as a church mouse when you climb out of this here window." He extended his hand. "Come on now, time to live a little."

She hesitated, torn between what a vision had shown her and common sense. Maybe she'd just gotten the wrong idea about Andy. He *had* tried to call her.

"Give me a minute to put some proper clothes on."

"What you have on now is simply fine."

She couldn't help smiling. "You just hush up and wait while I change." She closed the curtain, threw a dress over her head, and pulled a sweater on. When she reached out to Andy, he pulled to help her through, but her body resisted as though it had a will of its own. "You sure this is a good idea?" she asked.

"Are you kiddin' me? This is a great idea."

After another moment's hesitation, she climbed through the window with his help, and he released her hand when her feet touched the ground.

"Let's get on out of here," he said, sliding the window back down.

She stood frozen for a second, expecting more. Maybe a kiss on the cheek or at least a hug. That's just how boys are, she rationalized on the way to his car, frosty grass crunching slightly under her feet. They get caught up in an adventure and forget everything else. No need to get her feathers ruffled.

He held the door for her like last time, but when she climbed in, his car not only reeked of stale potato chips, motor oil, and old cigarettes; now it also stank of beer and something she couldn't quite put her finger on—the combined scent much worse than the night of the football game. She'd already pulled on the door handle to get out when Andy handed her a can of Budweiser.

She looked at it doubtfully. "I don't know if I'm really—"

"Beer's included in the grand tour package." He waved his arm in her direction. "And give that door a good slam, will ya? You can't chicken out on me after I went through all the trouble to come get ya."

"How impressive that you drove all the way across town," she said sarcastically, rolling her window down to let in some fresh air. "What'd it take to get here, seven minutes?"

"Nine, but who's countin'?" He nodded at her beer and put the car in drive. "Go on, now. We're partyin' tonight."

She hesitated. "Okay then, where's the church key?"

He pulled away from the curb. "You don't need no church key, Anna Mae. These cans have them new flip-top openers."

"Papa says those things will take your finger off. He uses his church key to open everythin'."

"Yeah, sometimes old folks don't like 'em, but they're much easier to use." Taking his eyes off the road, he nodded at her beer again. "Just pull that little tab up and make sure you don't cut your finger on the edge of the hole. You'll be fine."

When she pulled the tab up, it opened the can with a pop, a half-second before foam spewed out and into her lap. "*Dammit!*" She glared at Andy, who was laughing heartily. "You think this is funny? If my mama smells beer on me, I'm gonna be in enough trouble to last into the next decade."

"Just hide your dress in the bushes before you go in and wash it out tomorrow when she's at work. Problem solved. I'll even stay there to make sure you get in all right."

"You'd love gettin' a peek at me without my dress, wouldn't you?"

"Oh yeah," he said with a wink.

Hoping her blush didn't show in the dark, she took her first-ever gulp of beer. "This tastes funny."

"It's supposed to taste funny, silly. It's beer."

"If it's supposed to taste like this, why do people like it so much?"

"Two reasons." He burped loudly. "One, the more you drink, the better it tastes. And two, it makes you feel great."

"I guess I'll take your word for it."

"You don't have to. It might take a while to acquire the taste, but by the time you're on your second or third can, you'll know just how good you feel."

She took a sip. "I'm not feelin' any better yet."

Andy laughed again. "You've hardly started. It takes a lot more than that."

She took another sip. "So, where're we goin'?"

"I know this amazin' spot up on Foothills Parkway where you can see clear to Maryville and beyond."

Three and a half beers later, watching the sparkling lights in the distance from the front seat of the Ford, Anna Mae began to understand what Andy meant about feeling better. At first, she thought she might be lightheaded because of the kissing but realized it had to be the alcohol. No way Andy's sloppy kisses would make her head swim. She almost didn't notice when he began running his hand up the inside of her thigh.

"What are you doin'?" she slurred, thinking about her vision with him and whether it would come true after all.

"I figured this was our next big step."

She pulled his hand out from under her dress. "I think makin' out has been a pretty big step."

He stroked her hair. "Of course. I just get so overwhelmed with you bein' a celebrity and all."

"Celebrity? What're you goin' on about?"

"You know, you bein' the object of Roy Orbison's affection."

"Huh?"

Andy began singing, loudly and off-key, about a pretty woman walking down the street who looks so sweet.

"I think that's 'kind I'd like to meet,'" she interrupted.

"That was my special interpretation." He leaned in and gave her a long kiss. "'Cause you *do* look so sweet," he continued once he came up for air.

Excitement, fear, and doubt rushed through Anna Mae all at once. She'd written Andy off for good only a few days before, but he *had* tried to call her, and of course, she'd had the vision of making love to him, which had to account for something. Yet the commonsense part of her wanted him to take her home immediately. "Andy . . ." she began.

"Oh, Anna Mae," he said, placing his hand on her knee and leaning in for another kiss.

She removed his hand and pulled away from the kiss, puzzled by the fear she felt. There was nothing to be afraid of. This had been in her vision. Or at least something close. Yet she felt unsure.

"I've got an idea," she said. "Why don't you come by the house tomorrow when Mama is at work? I could make lunch for you." That would make her feel less rushed.

"Can't happen. I've got a double shift at the Piggly Wiggly." He gently took her by the chin and turned her face toward his. "Anna Mae, I've fallen for you hook, line, and sinker." He put his hand on her knee again. "And there's no time like the present."

She put her hand on his to push it away, then hesitated. He leaned in for another kiss. She let the kiss land, took her hand off his, and let him work his way up. It was in keeping with what she'd foreseen, and she only had to surrender to it. She gasped when his hand reached all the way up between her legs, wishing she'd taken the time to pull on some underwear, but the thought didn't last. Her vision would come true that night, and there would be no stopping it.

"Would you like to get in the back?" she asked.

"No," he said with a gleam in his eye. "I want to stay up front with you."

"You're a funny boy."

"Don't I know it," he said, opening his door. He jogged around to her side of the car and held out his hand. "May I have this dance, m'lady?"

Determined to stay within the order of her vision, she took his hand, letting him guide her first out of the car and then into the back seat, not understanding why she was shaking. *It must be the beer,* she thought, and closed her eyes as he climbed in next to her.

CHAPTER TWENTY-FIVE

Center Point, Texas
Present Day

"What if we only watered late at night?" Jess asked as she walked into the kitchen, where Dave, Elena, and Kevin were discussing the irrigation problem.

"That would earn us some serious fines if we got caught," Elena said. "I don't think that potbellied pig from SCRA would hesitate to come down on us as hard as he could."

"Not only that," added Kevin, "b-but it would give them the right to rip our pipes out. Replacin' them would be an expense we definitely can't afford."

"I understand," Jess said, "but it could be a couple of weeks before we get that cease-and-desist lifted, which would be more than enough time to give us a total crop failure." She folded her arms. "There's not much chance they'd catch us. We'd start after midnight and finish at least two hours before sunrise, so everythin' won't be lookin' all shiny and wet when the sun comes up. Let's vote on it and see what we want to do."

"There's four of us," Dave said. "What if we have a tie?"

"We'll cross that bridge when we come to it," she said, raising her hand. "Those in favor?"

They all stared at her for a few moments, then Dave slowly raised his hand. "It's risky, but it may be our best shot."

"Risky isn't the word for it," said Kevin. "Stupid is more like it. If we get caught doin' that, it'd destroy us."

"With our finances the way they are, if we lose that crop of cauliflower, I guarantee that would destroy us," Jess said. "How stupid would we be to let *that* happen?"

"I'm fairly confident we can get this overturned with the help of a lawyer I know of in San Antonio," Elena said. "From what I've heard, she's not cheap, but is excellent at this kind of thing. I've already called her office and am waiting to hear back. We're not watering in secret. There's too little to gain and far too much to lose. A crop failure would surely hurt us, but getting caught violating SCRA's order would kill our business—and declare to the world that we're cheaters."

"We can't let the Kidwells win this one," Jess said.

"It's not about winning. We're not doing it unless you want to find yourself another business manager."

* * *

Jess's vision that night wouldn't let her go back to sleep. After hours of trying to push it out of her mind, she finally called Agent Mallory just after two in the morning, reminding herself that he had asked her to call him anytime, day or night.

"Mallory," a sleepy voice answered.

"I'm sorry to call you so late. I mean, early."

"It's okay, Jess," he said with a yawn. "What've you got?"

She hesitated. "Well, now it seems ridiculous."

"Don't worry about it. This is the work I do, remember? I'll bet you a hundred dollars you have somethin' important to share with me."

"Well . . ."

"You have my undivided attention, young lady."

"Okay. First off, this vision was different from any of the others."

"How so?"

"It was through the eyes of a perpetrator."

"Interestin'."

"I know. And I saw that perpetrator gun someone down in cold blood. But it was so dim, I could hardly see the room they were in. That's why I may not be tellin' you anythin' useful. I might've woken you for nothin'."

"Nah, you're doin' the right thing." He yawned again. "You okay if I record this?"

"Sure, if you need to."

"Yeah, I'll want to listen to it when I'm bright-eyed and bushy-tailed, with at least two cups of coffee in me."

She described how the victim came toward the gunman with raised hands, got shot in the chest, then stumbled backward as the vision faded.

"That's significant. What'd the victim look like?"

"He had sideburns, a handlebar mustache, and a blue-and-white bandana around his neck, outlaw style."

"Outlaw style?"

"You know, like a Wild West outlaw would wear before pullin' it up over his face."

"I see. Anythin' else?"

"That's all I saw."

"What kinda gun was it?"

"Pretty sure it was a revolver."

"That's useful. You did the right thing, Jess. If anythin' else comes up—and I mean the smallest little thing—give me a ring, will you?"

"Okay." She ended the call and stared at the dark ceiling, her mind too agitated to sleep. Doing the right thing was overrated.

* * *

The following Friday, Kevin left for the farmers' market in Kerrville around six a.m. so he'd have plenty of time to be ready for the seven o'clock opening. He'd loaded the pickup truck the night before with carrots, beets, spinach, squash, and strawberries—all packed with great care so nothing would get damaged in transit.

Jess loved it when he went to the market because it gave her extra time alone. Unlike Kevin, Dave rarely bothered her. Elena also gave her space, and sometimes they would hang out when things were slow.

She heard a vehicle pull into the driveway just after she finished breakfast, around half past seven. She walked to the window and saw her brother parking next to their storage shed.

Curious, she went out to see him. "Back so soon, Kevin?"

"I'll need some help to unload," he said tersely, swinging a case of produce down from the truck.

"Why?" she asked. "What happened to the farmers' market?"

"What happened is that those damn fools runnin' the market denied us access."

"What? How can they do that?" she asked, lifting down a case of beets.

"'Cause of some supposed new rule that you need to have a special license—which everyone else seemed to already know about."

"Are you serious?"

He paused to give her an exasperated look. "No, I just came b-back here and thought I'd unload all this produce just for fun." He lifted a case of butternut squash down.

"That's crazy! Did they say for how long?"

"You are full of insightful questions today, aren't you?" He turned back to his work. "They said until we get that license."

"Then why don't we just get a license? Without that income from the market, we're done. Especially with our mushroom sales off to such a slow start."

He swung a case of cauliflower out of the truck, slamming it to the ground. "I applied before I left, b-but they said the process would take at least a month. I'm sure no one else had to wait that long, if at all."

"That is so damn unfair."

"Ya think? I'd bet you a hundred dollars Earl Kidwell is b-behind this."

"I sure as hell am not takin' that bet."

Chapter Twenty-Six

Wears Valley, Tennessee
November 1964

The thing Anna Mae liked best about Saturday mornings was reading time alone in her room. Of course, she could do that any day of the week when her parents were at work, but mostly she had to clean the house or get things ready for the next meal. With her plan to graduate early, she hadn't calculated that with more time at home, her mother would give her extra work to do. Suddenly, the house had to be far cleaner than it had ever been, with things more organized and in their respective places. Meals had to be more complex, which meant extra preparation. During the week, there was always the threat of what would happen if her parents came home and things weren't perfect, but they mostly left her alone on the weekend.

She hadn't heard from Andy since Halloween, almost two weeks before. The thought of it made her sick with regret. Rudy had repeatedly warned her how boys would take what they wanted and move on. Andy had indeed gotten what he wanted, but the way it happened wasn't even close to what her misguided vision had shown. He probably hadn't even tried to call her after the football game. Everything with him had just been one big lie, including the vision that betrayed and misled her in the first place.

"Anna Mae Cole!"

Her father's angry tone made her jump. She opened the door, fearing the worst. "Yes, sir?"

He glared at her, open beer in hand, and Anna Mae's heart sank. He was in a foul mood and drinking before noon—the worst possible combination.

"Get your ass out here. We're goin' to the store to pick up some plaster. It seems like your mama can't be bothered to help," he said, scowling at the closed master bedroom door, "even if it's to fix up her own damn house."

"Of course, Papa," she said, relieved that his anger wasn't focused on her for a change.

Tires squealing as they pulled away, he tossed his beer can out the window not twenty feet from their house, but Anna Mae knew better than to say anything.

After a tense and wordless drive to the Wears Valley general store, they parked near the main entrance.

"Go find us a buggy and meet me by the plaster," he barked as they got out of the car.

"Where's that, Papa?"

"Why're you askin' stupid questions, girl? You think I buy plaster here every day?"

"Sorry, sir. I'll find that out and meet you there right away."

"You'd better."

She hurried toward the entrance of the store, her father limping along behind. It was one of his painful leg days.

She opened the door into a crowd of Saturday shoppers and the faint smell of mothballs. Looking up and down the rows of supplies, she didn't see a single shopping cart. A hand truck would probably work, but she didn't see one of those, either.

The only staff person in sight was a harried-looking woman checking out a long line of customers waiting to pay for their goods. Anna Mae walked up to the counter and tried to get her attention until the woman finally gave her a severe look. "You're gonna have to wait in line like everyone else, honey."

Anna Mae walked to the back of the line and imagined her father standing next to the bags of plaster, getting angrier by the moment. Rudy once said that when their father got that way, he was like a forgotten pot on a hot stove, ready to boil over any second. She sidled back up to the counter. "Excuse me, ma'am?"

No response.

"Ma'am?"

"Did I not tell you to get in line like everyone else?" The clerk waved her hand toward the waiting customers. "What makes you more special than these folks?" A few of them nodded in agreement. "Sorry about that," the clerk said to the man directly in front of her. "Some pretty girls think they have all the right."

Anna Mae knew she was going to make someone mad. It would either be her father or this fool clerk. Not a hard decision. She slapped the counter, startling the clerk and everyone in line. "*Please* tell me where your hand truck is. My pa needs plaster, and he can't wait." There was a time to be nice and a time to put one's foot down.

The clerk pointed toward a set of stairs on the far side of the store. "Why didn't you say so? It's in the cubby under the stairwell."

"Thank you, ma'am." Anna Mae nodded and hurried off. She opened the door to the cubby, pulled out the hand truck, and wheeled it back toward where the plaster should be in the back of the store. As she came around the end of an aisle, however, she nearly ran into Phil Daley and a tall teenage girl with freckles and long brown hair.

Daley made a show of grabbing the freckled girl as though he was saving her from the path of a runaway train. "Whoa there," he said. "You might hurt somebody if you're not more careful."

Anna Mae held her tongue and pushed the hand truck around them.

Daley was incredulous. "And that's it? No 'excuse me' or 'sorry,' or even a 'pardon me, I didn't see you there?'" He turned to the girl he was with. "See, Amy, that's what I was tellin' you before. Some people don't understand the meanin' of respect."

Anna Mae stopped. "Like you know somethin' about respect, Mr. Daley?"

That caught him off guard for a moment, then a smile of recognition crossed his face. "I know you. You're one of Deputy Stevens' girlfriends."

"I most certainly am not," she said, hoping she sounded more indignant than she felt.

"Really? Is that why you're red as a tomato right now? Yeah, I've seen you ridin' around with our pure-as-the-driven-snow deputy. And weren't you with him at the football game against Pigeon Forge a while back? You nearly ran into me then, too."

"I was not with him."

"Yeah, Stevens might've been there with another girl, but you couldn't take your eyes off him."

"Wrong again," she said, wondering how he knew that. She turned her attention to the girl. "I don't know what this man's been tellin' you, honey, but I promise it's a lie. He's dangerous. Trust me on that."

"Hey now," Daley protested, "you'd better watch what you're sayin' there, missy."

She ignored him and kept talking to the girl, who looked concerned. "The best thing you can do is to get yourself as far away—"

"Listen here, you little bitch," he snarled, "do you think you can get away with—"

Anna Mae yelped in surprise when her father came out of nowhere, grabbed Daley by the throat, and shoved him violently against a shelf, knocking a few rat traps and a can of DDT to the floor. The freckled girl gasped, and Anna Mae's eyes widened. Though Daley was a full head taller, her father was stockier, and the other man seemed truly frightened. Cole put his reddened face inches away from Daley's. "Was I hearin' things, or did you just call my daughter a bitch?"

"No. I mean, I did, but—"

Cole tightened his grip. "How about I mop up the floor with you?"

Daley squirmed in his grasp. "She insulted my friend, sayin' all kinds of nasty things to her."

Cole's eyes narrowed. "That true, Anna Mae?"

She shook her head, too shocked to speak.

Cole turned his attention back to Daley. "You say one word other than 'I'm sorry, ma'am' to my daughter, and I swear I will crack your head open in front of all these people."

The store manager ran up. "Can I help you folks with anythin'?" he asked nervously. Cole glanced at him without releasing his grip on Daley's throat. "No thanks. One of us was just gettin' ready to say somethin' important."

Daley's eyes bulged as Cole tightened his grip even more. "I'm sorry," he choked out.

But Cole didn't let go. "I didn't quite catch that last part," he said through clenched teeth. "Who were you talkin' to?"

Phil Daley looked around wildly and drew a breath with great effort. "I'm very sorry, ma'am," he squeaked, looking directly at Anna Mae.

Cole released Daley, who fell to his knees, clutching his throat and gasping for breath.

Jefferson Cole turned to his daughter and motioned to the hand truck. "You good steerin' that thing?"

She nodded wordlessly.

"Alright then, let's get that plaster," he said.

One thing Anna Mae knew about her father was how fast he could change gears. Still, it never ceased to amaze her. As they walked off, she glanced over her shoulder at the manager hurrying to place items back on the shelves and Daley arguing with the freckled girl.

"Down this way," her father motioned to an aisle just ahead, "then we can get the hell out of here."

As they turned the corner, Anna Mae glanced back again and saw the girl walking determinedly away from Daley.

"You comin' or what?" Jefferson Cole asked sharply.

"Sorry, sir." She hurried to catch up, profoundly surprised at how good she felt.

CHAPTER TWENTY-SEVEN

Center Point, Texas
Present Day

Jess shook her head in frustration. Kevin hadn't bought enough charcoal for the dehydrator again, which meant another unnecessary trip to Polk's Hardware. He should be the one to go but was working on the tractor again. She looked forward to the day they could afford decent farm machinery that wouldn't break down all the time.

She slammed the door of the pickup, popped in her Alicia Keys CD, and cranked up the volume. "Girl on Fire" had been one of her favorite songs back in the day and always made her feel better.

On the way to town, a white Mercedes Sprinter van approaching from the opposite direction sped past her. It was driven by a man with a handlebar mustache and sideburns, wearing a blue-and-white bandana around his neck, outlaw style. It had to be the shooting victim from her vision.

She watched the van shrink in her rearview mirror and considered her options. The safest choice was to mind her own business, but as she'd learned the hard way, there could be serious consequences for not doing the right thing. No one else was going to die because of her.

She braked and made a quick U-turn but lost sight of the van in the trees surrounding Logan's Bend. It could take her five minutes or more to catch up. She watched her speedometer creep up past eighty-five, then ninety, but had to slow down for the curve. She'd make it up on the stretch that passed their property and went on for another half-mile before the next bend.

When she reached the straightaway, however, she saw nothing. No cars, vans, or any other vehicles on the road. The driver might have floored it and made it around the next curve, though that made little sense. Maybe he'd pulled into the Kidwells' place.

As she turned into the Kidwells' property, she tried to convince herself she was doing the right thing. The smartest move would be to just turn around and forget it, yet she had the vision for a reason, and a man's life was at stake—if what she'd foreseen was accurate. Driving around to the side of the house away from the road, she didn't see the white van, but there were several garages it could have pulled into. She sat in the truck, staring at the Kidwells' front door. There was nothing about being there she should feel emotional about. Travis Kidwell was nothing but a player, and he'd done her a huge favor by ending their doomed relationship before it even really started all those years ago.

She walked up to the door and knocked. After a half-minute with no response, Jess finally turned away.

She was getting back in the pickup when the front door opened, and Travis walked out onto the porch, looking sleepy and annoyed. "*What do you want?*" he called out, walking toward her.

"Well, this may sound stupid . . ."

"Why do I find that so hard to believe?"

"You know what, never mind." She slammed her door and started the engine.

He tapped a knuckle on her window and waited for her to lower it.

"Hey," he said, "you just came onto our property and woke me from a nice nap when I was dreamin' of beautiful women." He grinned. "Now that I think about it, one of them kinda looked like you."

She almost smiled despite herself. "Spare me."

"The other one looked like Taylor Swift."

"Yeah, well, sorry to spoil your little fantasy."

"So am I. But I know you came over for a noble reason."

"It's nothin', I just—"

"Felt like knockin' on my door to see if I was takin' a nap." He grinned again. "I get it."

"I was followin' a white van and thought it might have pulled in here."

He made a wide, sweeping gesture. "And do you see this alleged white van?"

"No, but I thought it might have gone into one of your garages."

"Nope, no white vans today. You're out of luck." He frowned. "Why are you chasin' vans, anyway?"

"If I told you, it'd sound weird."

"Try me."

"Well, when I passed this van, I recognized the driver from a vision I had a few months ago."

"Yeah? Let me guess, he then gets abducted and probed by aliens. Am I gettin' warm?"

"I'm gettin' out of here," she said, putting the pickup in drive. "Should've known better than to ask for help from some two-bit player."

"Vision or not, this is Texas. You'd better be careful who you go chasin' around."

"*Thanks, I'll keep that in mind,*" she yelled out her window as she pulled away. Travis Kidwell was a jerk, just like his old man. Earl was probably the one who'd messed with their water rights, but Travis always seemed to go along with whatever his daddy did.

When she reached the highway, she looked to her right, the way the van had gone, before taking a left and heading back toward town. So strange. Why had he driven so fast after the curve?

She parked across from the red brick storefront of Polk's Hardware and thought about what it would take to not let Travis upset her. Somehow or other, she needed to get him out of her system. She waited for a couple of cars to pass before she crossed the street and was thinking about the white van as she walked into the smell of hot buttered popcorn that permeated Polk's store. An idea suddenly hit her. What if the Mercedes Sprinter had turned into Johnny's? Of course. Why hadn't she thought of that before?

When she returned home with the charcoal, she drove up to Johnny's gate. A new sign warned "No Trespassing," and barbed-wire fencing now stretched along the property line. She decided to not climb the gate and risk another confrontation. She looked through the trees but saw no van.

She thought about calling Mallory, but what would she tell him? That she passed a white van that might have been driven by a shooting victim from her vision? Some things weren't worth the trouble, vision or no vision. Maybe the van had gone onto the Kidwells' property after all, and Travis was lying to her—besides being rude. It wouldn't surprise her in the least. The more she thought about Earl and Travis Kidwell, the madder she got.

* * *

The following week, Jess and Kevin sat in the living room one evening discussing their developing mushroom operation—which was finally making a profit—when Earl Kidwell's bright red pickup truck raced up their driveway and came to a dramatic stop, spraying gravel.

They both walked to the window for a better look just as Earl slammed his door and marched purposefully toward the front porch.

"Looks like somebody's upset," Jess said. "You want to handle this one?"

"Hell no." Kevin frowned and tilted his head slightly to the side. "I don't suppose this has anythin' to do with your trip down to the river the other day?"

"I'm sure I have no idea what you're talkin' about," she said sweetly as she opened the door and found herself eye to eye with a red-faced Earl Kidwell.

"Why, Mr. Kidwell, what a pleasant surprise. If I'd known you were comin' over, I'd have baked some cookies."

"You must think you're funny as all get-out, but I ain't gonna tolerate you fiddlin' with our livelihood."

"Whatever do you mean?"

"You know exactly what I mean. Y'all been messin' with our irrigation pipes."

"I beg your pardon?"

"The inlet of our irrigation pipe mysteriously wound up above the waterline," he said, narrowing his eyes. "I wonder how that could have happened."

"Well, I certainly am sorry about that, but I'm sure no one here messed with it," she lied.

"Right," he said. "It probably just jumped out of the river by itself."

"Maybe a log bumped it."

"Sure it did. Yet *your* inlet is still well below the waterline. Ain't that just the funniest dang thing?"

"Now, Mr. Kidwell, I can assure you—"

"I can assure *you*, Miss Atwood, that there ain't no way in hell you're gettin' away with this. It could have been a disaster for us if I hadn't noticed the hay in our southwest field turnin' brown. If the pump hadn't shut itself down when it went dry, that alone would've cost us a fortune. Plus, that line supplies water tanks for 150 head of cattle. Some of them could've died."

She hadn't thought about that. "I'm sorry that happened, but we had—"

"This flagrantly violates our easement agreement."

"Like I said—"

"Next time this happens, I'm takin' y'all to court."

"Don't you think that's a bit extreme?"

"No, and that's not all. First thing tomorrow, I'm puttin' in a formal complaint to the South Central River Authority. We have a right to our fair share of the Guadalupe, and y'all have no business interferin' with that."

"I love hearin' you talk about fairness, Mr. Kidwell. It almost gives me goose bumps."

"Well now, ain't you precious?" He turned to go. "Don't you forget what I said," he barked over his shoulder.

"He's madder than a wet hen," Jess said with a giggle after she closed the door.

Kevin raised an eyebrow. "I can't imagine why."

She smiled and shrugged.

"Come on now, Jess, do you reckon that was the b-best thing to do?"

"What? You think it would've been better just to pretend we weren't home?"

"Don't b-bother playin' games with me. You know what I'm talkin' about.

You shouldn't have messed with their intake."

"Why not? Didn't he mess with ours?"

"Of course, b-but he did it legally, and Elena had it overturned the next day. What you did was illegal and would've caused us a lot of embarrassment if you got caught."

"But I didn't get caught, did I? Honestly, Kevin, you can't just lie down and take it when people attack. If you don't stand up to 'em, they're gonna keep doin' whatever they're doin' to you."

"Yeah? What do you think Elena would say to that?" He paused. "Or Dave?"

"I guess it would depend on whether he was sober."

"Not the point, is it? B-besides, he's doin' b-better since he started goin' to AA. I think you know that Dave or Elena would've stopped you if you'd told them about your little plan."

"Maybe, but the look on Earl's face made it all worth it."

"Did it really? Elena is gonna be furious that you escalated things with the Kidwells."

Jess shrugged. "She loves me. She'll let it go."

Kevin shook his head. "Don't b-be too sure."

CHAPTER TWENTY-EIGHT

Wears Valley, Tennessee
December 1964

Sevier County had received a light dusting of snow the night before. Although there had been no white Christmas, December was about to end in splendid beauty.

Mary Beth Perkins had to get herself out of the house. Earlier that month, a Negro named Dr. Martin Luther King had received the Nobel Peace Prize. Mary Beth's father, a Gatlinburg city councilman, had spoken of nothing else for weeks, and she was sick of hearing about it.

"They're just trying to appease them colored folk," she heard him say at least a dozen times. They were still on Christmas break from school, which she usually loved, but his racist rants drove her crazy. His comments that morning were the last straw. "President Johnson's the one who deserved that prize," he'd said. "He's the man restorin' order in Vietnam. Leadership is what we need to reward, not troublemakin'. This King feller ain't doin' nothin' more than raisin' a ruckus in the monkey house."

Rather than argue with her father—which was always a losing battle—Mary Beth just walked out.

A beat-up white Ford pickup slowed next to her, but she knew to keep moving and ignore it. Gatlinburg had more than its fair share of weirdos. Earlier that week, a bunch of boys in a light-green station wagon had yelled crude things at her as they sped past. This character had one of those strange mop-top hairdos covering his forehead and ears. He was either very cool or very weird.

The truck matched her walking speed, and out of the corner of her eye, she saw the driver lean across the seat and roll down the passenger window.

"*Are you Mary Beth Perkins?*" he called out, his pickup staying even with her.

"Who wants to know?" She turned to face him, keeping a wary distance. How on earth did he know who she was?

"Name's Phil Daley," he said, bringing the truck to a stop, "son of Congressman Sam Daley. I live in the blue house on Coombs Road, on the west side of Cove Mountain. Sarah Jacobs told me you live around here, and she needs your help."

"You talked to Sarah?"

"That's what I'm tryin' to tell you." He cut his engine. "She ran off with a boy named Mickey Ray Price from Pigeon Forge last spring, and they've been livin' in an old barn on my property. It just ain't workin' out the way she thought it would. The whole thing is my fault since he's the drummer in our band and was stayin' with me when he met Sarah."

Mary Beth stepped closer to the truck. "She never told me about seein' any drummer and hasn't so much as called me for months."

"There ain't no telephone nearby, and Mickey Ray hardly lets her out of his sight. Anyway, she needs your help to gather her things and get out of there but is afraid of what he might do. Got a helluva temper, that boy. Seen it myself more'n once durin' band practice."

"So why don't you help her?"

"I tried tellin' Mickey Ray to get lost, but he wouldn't pay me no mind. I told Sarah this mornin' I'd protect her while she gets her things, but she said she needs you for emotional support. Says you're her best friend in the whole wide world."

"I am, but . . ." There was something strange about this man. "I reckon it'd be better just to tell the sheriff."

He raised both hands in exasperation. "Exactly what I told Sarah. Just go to the cops. I even offered to get 'em for her. We can always find another drummer. But she said she was already in trouble, and her parents would kill her if they found out she ran off with a boy. All she wants is to quietly go back home. Plus, she doesn't want to see Mickey Ray put in jail. She just needs to end it and said you'd understand."

Mary Beth considered that. "Reckon I might."

"I tried to get her to help me find you, but she wanted to wait there." He raised his hands in surrender. "Well, I did my part. I found you and delivered her request." He shrugged dramatically and started the engine. "Who knows, she'll probably be in school once Christmas break's over, and you can see her then."

Putting the pickup into gear, he nodded to her. "You take care now," he said, slowly pulling away.

"Wait!" She ran up to the passenger window. "Promise you'll take me right to her?"

He leaned over, pushed the door open, then reverently touched the USMC medallion hanging from his rearview mirror. "You have my word as a master sergeant in the United States Marine Corps."

She hesitated a few seconds before getting in and pulling the door closed. "My cousin Lou is a Marine." She smoothed her skirt and patted the dashboard. "Let's go get Sarah."

* * *

A week into the new year, the doorbell rang at around three in the afternoon. It surprised Anna Mae to find Pastor Blaine on their porch, his faded green 1956 Studebaker station wagon parked out front.

"Afternoon, Miss Cole."

For a few moments, she was too stunned to speak. Had somebody died? "Pastor Blaine, I didn't know . . . won't you come in?"

"Love to, but I don't have the time. I've got somethin' here from your brother."

"You do?"

With a grin, he glanced around before pulling a white envelope out of his back pocket and handing it to her.

She stared at the return address from Center Point, Texas. "Oh," she said, her heart racing at the thought of hearing from Rudy.

Pastor Blaine cleared his throat. "I have to get goin', but he sent this to me inside another letter and asked if I'd deliver it to you personally. When your parents weren't home, of course," he said with a wink as he turned to go.

January 1, 1965

Dear Anna Mae,

I doubt you got my last two letters, judging by your lack of response. They probably wound up in the fireplace. Today is New Year's Day and an excellent time for new beginnings. So, here goes.

When I punched Papa, I didn't practice the unconditional love I said I wanted in my life. If I hadn't done that, I'd still be there with you, listening to your crazy ideas. Molly says it's great to know where you want to go, but you have to be patient with yourself until you get there.

Sometimes, things that seem like they're going to be lousy catch us by surprise and turn out for the best. Soon after I arrived in Texas, I started working for Molly's daddy at his bank's new branch in Center Point. I don't love it, but it's making us four times the money I got at that hellish rail yard in Maryville. With Molly's income from the recruiting office and a generous gift from her parents, we made a down payment on our own farm twelve days ago. We moved into a run-down mobile home on the property a few days before Christmas, and we've already started building a proper house.

Center Point is north of San Antonio, west of Austin, and pretty much in the middle of nowhere, which suits me just fine. It's not far from Kerrville, so we can easily visit Molly's family.

I'm still thinking peanuts are the best way to go, and everyone says they'll give us the fastest turnaround, cash-wise. Folks around these parts have warned me that farming is more work than I think it will be. What do you say, Anna Mae? Am I the type to dodge hard work?

Getting started is the toughest part. There was nothing but cattle here before. The mobile home that came with the land only has a kitchen, a bedroom, and a bathroom not much larger than a broom closet. The roof leaks like a sieve when it rains, but it's something to live in while we build our home. It's already got a well, septic, and electric service we can use for the new house.

The land's beautiful, and part of it goes right along the Guadalupe River, which will give us what we need for irrigation since goobers need lots of water.

We bought it off a rancher who lives right across the highway, a fellow named Kyle Kidwell, middle name Kaleb, making his initials KKK. I swear I ain't making that up. He's been nice enough to us, but I can't help but wonder what his parents had in mind with those initials.

He's got a mouthy kid named Earl, maybe 11 or 12 years old, who used to come over on his little Honda 50 motorbike, telling us how we should build the house and pointing out all the things we're doing wrong. I gave him some work with the construction, but that only made him bossier. We call him Little Earl, which he hates. He wears cowboy boots, a big belt buckle, and a ten-gallon hat that looks huge on him.

One evening, we were sitting on the front porch when he rode his little motorbike over. As he came up the drive with a purposeful look on his face, that enormous hat blew right off his head. We coulda died laughing. He turned around, went back to pick up his hat, and headed straight home without so much as a glance at us. We haven't seen him since. I swear his ego's twice the size he is.

Don't forget that I love you unconditionally.

Rudy
P.S. Soon as we get the house finished, you'll be welcome anytime.

CHAPTER TWENTY-NINE

Center Point, Texas
Present Day

On her way home from a long run, Jess saw a patrol car pull into their driveway. When she arrived at the house, the hazel-eyed sheriff's deputy on the porch asked if she was Jessica Atwood.

"You know I am. You once gave me a ride in the back of your patrol car."

Without meeting her gaze, he nodded and handed her an official-looking envelope with a Kerr County seal. "You've been served. Sorry." He turned and walked back to his car.

She opened the envelope and saw it was another cease-and-desist notice, this time from Kerr County. Elena had gotten the last one from the river authority overturned quickly enough, but this looked more ominous. It said things in legal language about violating their water quota, land use parameters, and details from transferring the two acres that were not right. The complaint also said that they'd sold the property knowing it would be used for commercial and/or industrial development, nearly word for word what that prick Earl Kidwell had said.

Less than an hour later, she sat in Victor Carson's law office. He told her she had to get a variance.

"How long will that take?"

"Well, a variance of this type must be approved by the town council, which means a public vote. Long story short, it could take a couple of months."

"Seriously? You mean we're supposed to stop runnin' our business for two entire months?"

"Theoretically, yes." Carson steepled his hands. "But this isn't the first time this has happened to anyone, and the law has a safety valve. You can request a stay on the cease-and-desist once you've applied for the variance hearing from the town council. You're looking at a day or two to get that request filed, and then I ask for the stay, which is an automatic process. You can keep farming and using water from the river until the public vote on the variance. Does that make sense?"

"Kind of. How does it work?"

"The town council holds an open meetin', and one of the agenda topics would be your request. If the majority of those in attendance approve, the stay becomes permanent—which means you could go back to business as usual."

"What if the majority doesn't approve?"

"That would be unfortunate 'cause the stay would then be nullified, and the cease-and-desist would remain active until everythin' got resolved, which could take several months."

"Meanin' we couldn't work our farm."

"That is correct."

"And it'd ruin our business."

"If that happened, then yes, it might."

"Jumpin' through all those hoops sounds near impossible."

Carson shook his head. "It's far from impossible, but y'all gotta make sure you take the right steps. Request that variance hearing at the courthouse today. Soon as the confirmation comes through, I'll prepare a brief asking the judge to stay the cease-and-desist until the hearing so you can go right back to work. As I said, it's an automatic process. Won't happen before Monday at the earliest, though. It looks like you have a nice extended weekend coming up." He smiled. "You can probably use a few days off."

Jess was too upset to return the smile.

* * *

The following day, the doorbell rang three times before Jess could answer it. "*I'm comin*," she called out. "Just hold your horses."

She opened the door to find Earl Kidwell glaring at her. "Oh, Mr. Kidwell, how good to see you. Have you come over to gloat about the new cease-and-desist?"

"I'm here about that damn dog of yours."

"*Wallaby!*" Jess yelled over her shoulder. "You come here right now and talk to Mr. Kidwell." When he didn't appear, she gave Earl a tight-lipped smile. "I'm sorry, Mr. Kidwell, but he's not home. May I take a message?"

"Well now, ain't you precious?"

"I must be, or you wouldn't keep tellin' me that."

He glared at her for a few long moments. "Your dog has been over botherin' my cattle again," he said, "and I'm here to tell you I'm not about to stand for it. He even chased Bucky the other day."

"Bucky?"

"Our rooster. No doubt your dog would love to have one of our chickens for breakfast."

It was time to play nice, be a good neighbor, and apologize. Maybe she'd try that on the next go-round. "Are we supposed to stand for you gettin' the County on us?"

"Honey, y'all gotta play by the same rules as everyone else."

"We play by the rules."

"Sure you do. At this moment, I don't give a damn. What I do give a damn about is your dog comin' over and tryin' to herd my cattle. Didn't you tell me last time you were gonna try your best to keep him off our land?"

"I honestly thought he'd stopped going over there."

"Sure you did. If this is tryin' your best, I'd hate to see your worst. If I see that dog on our property again, the very least I'm doin' is callin' animal control." His mouth tightened. "We shot two coyotes last week. Sure would hate to mistake your dog for one of them mangy bastards."

"Does that make you feel big, Mr. Kidwell, threatenin' a helpless dog?"

"Helpless? It seems your damn fool dog can do no wrong, and apparently neither can you."

"That's not it at all. We just—"

"You just keep that animal off our property." He turned away. "You've been warned."

CHAPTER THIRTY

Wears Valley, Tennessee
February 1965

The afternoon unfolded like most others at the Wears Valley sheriff's office until the phone rang around two-thirty. Keene picked it up, then rapped his knuckles on the desk, a signal demanding absolute quiet.

Stevens stopped typing and watched his boss frown and shake his head, calling the party on the other end of the line "sir." Only a couple of people received that acknowledgment from him. One was Keene's father, a retired Memphis Police captain, but the more likely party was Sevier County Commissioner Harold Baker. As one of seven elected sheriffs in the county, Keene represented the area between Gatlinburg, Wears Valley, and Pigeon Forge. However, as an outsider from Memphis, he'd gotten the job only because of an endorsement from Baker, who would occasionally call the sheriff telling him to do one thing or another. The unspoken agreement was that as long as he did whatever the commissioner wanted, he could count on being reelected.

The conversation seemed typically one-sided, with Keene getting interrupted practically every time he opened his mouth. Stevens wondered what he was getting called out for. The last time Baker had called was with a warning that the sheriff needed to find himself a wife, saying it would sit better with the voters. After the call, Keene mentioned to Stevens that the commissioner should mind his own damn business. Deputy Stevens considered suggesting

167

to the sheriff he say that to the commissioner but wisely kept it to himself. This call was obviously not a friendly chat, either, but Baker was not the friendly type. Not even close.

When the sheriff hung up, he closed his eyes and rubbed his forehead.

"What's up, boss?" Stevens asked.

"Baker's puttin' his nose into our business, demandin' clues about those two missin' girls. The girl who disappeared from Gatlinburg in December is the daughter of a city councilman named Kenneth Perkins. Ever heard of him?"

"Don't reckon I have."

"He's a loudmouthed, obnoxious bigot, but his sixteen-year-old daughter Mary Beth is an excellent student with lots of friends, leader of her Girl Scout troop, and by most accounts was happy at home." He rubbed his forehead. "All makin' the possibility that she's a runaway not that likely. We know Sarah Jacobs was unhappy and would've had a motive to leave home. The Tennessee Bureau of Investigation reckons there might be foul play with Mary Beth— and possibly with the other girl." Keene shook his head. "Can't say I disagree with them. I just wish they'd given us this information sooner. You never know what's gonna help solve a case, right?"

Stevens frowned. "Right."

"The Perkins girl was friends with Sarah when she disappeared back in May, so there's a slight chance she ran away to join her. Anyway, Councilman Perkins is rattlin' any cage he can, including the commissioner's."

"You already know what I think, boss."

"I do. Believe me, if we had one shred of evidence against Daley, we'd bring him right in."

"We both know we have more than just a shred."

"But not enough to convict the bastard. The last thing we want is a repeat of that fiasco from two years ago. And there's more. Remember that colored feller with the scar the Cole girl said she talked to up in the park?"

"Of course I do. Had to have been Hobo Bill."

"I'm sure it was. Anyway, the commissioner read our incident report and said we should've arrested him on the spot since the alleged perpetrator was seen with a gun in the body's vicinity. If that was Hobo Bill, he's a convicted violent felon who's done hard time for assault with a deadly weapon."

"But we didn't see him, a body, or a gun. What the hell were we supposed to do?"

"Don't know." Keene scratched his head. "Anyway, now he expects us to arrest him."

"Did he really say that?"

"Yep. I tried to talk Baker out of it, but he said we need to revoke Hobo Bill's civil rights. Might've been half-kiddin', I don't know. If not, he said he's got some boys who'll take care of things for us."

"*Damn!*" Stevens slapped his desk. "Those people need to stay out of our bidness."

"I agree, but that there's part of the problem. The KKK thinks it's *their* bidness."

Stevens waved his hand dismissively. "The Klan's been throwin' their weight around here for nearly a hundred years. I say it's too easy for them to get what they want."

"Maybe so, but it's the reality we have to deal with."

"What's also a reality is that Hobo Bill has been around since I was a kid. Everyone knows he's harmless."

"Is that somethin' you'd bet your life on? You know he wounded a white man back in fifty-six."

"From what I heard, he was bein' attacked and properly defended himself, though if he hadn't been arrested the same day, he probably would've been lynched by the Klan. He got five years at Brushy Mountain only 'cause he's a Negro. Didn't he fight in the Korean War? The man served his country and received a Purple Heart. I heard he got his scar from bein' grazed by a bullet. Folks say he came back shell-shocked, which is why he stays away from everybody."

Keene frowned. "You think I'm not aware of all that? But what about that gun? Maybe it gave him a sense of power."

"Come on now, Sheriff. We both know he wouldn't hurt anyone unless he was provoked. Anna Mae said she walked right past him, and he didn't do nothin'. If he was some dangerous character who preyed on innocent young girls, well, they hardly get more innocent and beautiful than her."

"Deputy Stevens, I do believe you're sweet on that girl."

"Am not. I'm just sayin' she was the perfect bait to test Hobo Bill."

Keene smiled. "Oh, she's bait, all right. You'd just better watch yourself."

"There ain't nothin' to watch. I'm already engaged, and besides, I got no interest in some underaged, jail-bait girl."

"Sure you don't." The sheriff stood and put on his hat. "Ridiculous as it seems, we'd better get Hobo Bill his own private room where he's safe from them that wear the white robes." He rested his hand on the doorknob. "You comin', or what?"

Stevens pushed back his chair. "Do we even know where we're goin'?"

"I got me a pretty good idea."

* * *

They found Hobo Bill in the third place they looked, up in the park outside Elkmont. At first, he assumed they were arresting him for vagrancy.

"I ain't botherin' no one," he protested.

"That's not why we're here," explained Sheriff Keene. "Hands behind your back."

Stevens saw fear in the man's eyes. "Just stay put, Bill. Runnin' would only make it worse. You know we'd just find you again."

He frowned at the deputy but allowed himself to be cuffed.

"Where's your gun?" asked Keene.

"Don't have one."

"That's not what we heard."

Hobo Bill just shook his head.

Nothing more was spoken until they'd returned to the sheriff's office and locked him in the holding cell.

"We'd better keep a close eye on things," Keene said. "You good to sleep here on the cot tonight in case of any unexpected visitors?" he asked his deputy. "We'll take him to county lockup in Sevierville tomorrow."

"You sure about this, boss?"

Keene nodded but didn't make eye contact with Stevens. "Yep, I'm sure."

* * *

February 27, 1965

Dear Rudy,

I got your letter, full of love and caring, over a month ago. I've been trying to think of something nice to write you about, but I just come up dry. You've told me you love that I'm honest and don't hide what I'm feeling, so here goes.

Things with this boy named Andy ended in the worst possible way, with him being disrespectful and bragging to all his buddies. One of them even called the other day asking me out, even though we've never met. Andy must have told him I was easy, which makes me want to cry. Dr. Ferguson would say I'm depressed, but it's more than that. Order is gone, and I can't find it to save my life.

It's not like I didn't hear what you said about how girls can be attracted to boys who are like their daddies. I just thought that didn't apply to me. Now I wish I'd listened. You were also right about me reading too much into my visions. If I hadn't taken what I thought was a vision as gospel truth, I never would've gone out with Andy on Halloween night, and I wouldn't be feeling so awful about myself right now.

Mama and Papa are getting along worse than ever. It seems like they have hot words between them almost every day. You know Papa isn't about to stand up to Mama, so he takes it out on me. Sometimes I get smacked without even a pretend reason.

The worst news is that a few days ago, the sheriff arrested an innocent Negro named Hobo Bill, on some terrible charges. It's all my fault. I only found out because somebody at work told Mama, and she mentioned it at supper.

I've been calling the sheriff's office, saying they should let him go, but all I'm doing is getting on their nerves.

Sorry to be such a whiner. I don't want to get on your nerves, either. I'm having the worst old time, and you're the only person who understands me.

Love you so much,

Anna Mae

CHAPTER THIRTY-ONE

Center Point, Texas
Present Day

One thing Jess loved about Saturday mornings was that the Kerr County paintball diehards gathered at Blitz Paintball Arena in Kerrville for an advanced-level shootout and the occasional tournament. Keith Rose, the owner of Blitz, had asked her to come in an hour early every week to train whoever wanted to improve their competitive game and was willing to pay the fifteen-dollar fee. Her little class was becoming increasingly popular, especially since she won every paintball competition at Blitz. It earned her a lot of attention and a few envious remarks. During the contest that morning, she'd rated first on the Blitz leaderboard by eliminating seven opponents for every time she'd been taken out—her best kill ratio ever.

Before they started, an obnoxious guy with a huge black beard had been making snide comments about her not belonging in a man's game. Once the tournament was underway, she hit him three times before he signaled surrender. With her first hit, he pretended she'd missed and that the fluorescent pink paint splat she gave him was old. She removed all doubt when she double-tapped him with two follow-ups. The third shot hit him directly in the crotch, and after spending a minute curled up on the ground, he limped off the course, having received exactly what he deserved. She felt elated until she returned home that afternoon to find a dark Chevy

Suburban with heavily tinted windows in the driveway.

Inside the house, a tall, ruggedly handsome black man with an athletic build and clean-shaven head sat in the recliner, talking to Dave. He stood when Jess walked in, his eyes sharp with an intensity she found intriguing—and a bit scary.

"Jess, this is Special Agent Mallory of the Texas Rangers," Dave said.

Mallory chuckled at her surprised look. "You thought I was a white guy, didn't you?"

Jess shook her head and blushed, hoping it didn't show.

"Lots of folks make that mistake," he said. "Not that long ago, there was no such thing as a black Texas Ranger. In fact, there was a time when simply not being white was a reason to fear the Rangers." He winked at her. "Speaking of fearful, I never would've guessed you were a paintball champion."

It took her a moment to recover and smile. "I'm not a champion, I just . . . I didn't know you were comin' by," she said, changing the subject.

"I thought it'd be good for us to meet in person since you have so much to offer."

"I don't know about that."

He sat back down, waving off her comment. "Sure you do. The trail has gone cold on the stabbin' you told us about. However, interest in the case is high 'cause a seventeen-year-old girl named Ashley from that neighborhood went missin' around the same time. You knew her name and that she has white-blonde hair."

She sat on the couch across from him. "Okay."

"That information wasn't public when you called Detective Simmons. The big question on all our minds is why a woman way out here in Kerr County would envision somethin' that happened in Dallas."

She shifted uncomfortably. "I wish I knew."

"Me too." He paused. "Are your visions usually connected to you in some way?"

"Mostly. But with some visions, I never found out whether they came true or not."

"But of the ones you *know* came true," he persisted, "has there always been some kind of connection to you, however slight?"

She considered the visions she'd had over the years. "From what I remember, yes."

"Interestin'." He tapped his pen on the clipboard before scribbling something down. "We can't save the man who got stabbed, but we'd love to find the girl who got kidnapped and catch the bastards behind it. I'd like to think you can help."

"I'd like to think that, too."

He frowned. "About your arrest for breakin' and enterin' . . ."

She swallowed hard. "They dismissed those charges."

"Yes, they did. Can you tell me why?"

"I don't know, I just—"

"Huh," Kevin said from behind her. She hadn't heard him come in. "Just tell him everythin', Jess."

"There's nothin' more to say, really."

Mallory smiled. "'Cause people think you're crazy when you tell them about events that haven't yet happened?"

"Sometimes."

"I've heard some of the things folks used to say about your mama. From what I understand, she was truly somethin'."

"She certainly was," Dave said.

Mallory scanned his notes. "People say she kept Polk's Hardware from burnin' down more than a decade ago. Accordin' to the report, she knew there was gonna be a fire when even a sophisticated alarm system didn't detect anythin'." He glanced at Jess. "And then there's the story of the missin' Davidson boy. She provided the clue that enabled Search and Rescue to find him back in '02, probably savin' his life. That was a pretty big deal." He looked up from his notes. "But sometimes she missed the mark."

"*No!*" Jess's intensity startled everyone in the room. "Sometimes people didn't believe her, or she didn't see enough for them to figure out what was goin' on. But that wasn't her fault. She'd just get a picture or a scene in her mind and would pass that information on as best she could. She never missed any stupid mark."

"I get it. Sorry." He smiled. "Can you tell me more about what brought you to the Thorntons' home that day?"

She nodded at his clipboard. "Didn't you already find that out from the sheriff?"

"Of course. I just want to hear it in your own words."

She told him about her vision with the Thornton baby, the break-in, and the apology from Lisa Thornton.

Mallory tapped his pen on the clipboard. "When the deputies asked why you broke in . . ." He glanced at his notes.

"I told them exactly what happened."

"You said it was to save a baby's life."

"Precisely. I was only tryin' to help."

"Of course you were," Mallory said. "I'm just lookin' for a greater understandin' of what you do and how you do it."

"It's not really anythin' I do. More like somethin' that just happens. You already know my mama had this so-called gift of prophecy . . . as did my grandma."

"From what I heard, your grandma Anna Mae once lived here in this house."

"That's true. Some folks claimed Granny Mae was a witch, while others say she was an angel. Same things they said about our mama. There was even a nasty rumor goin' around that Granny Mae killed someone, which Mama said isn't true. But the stories made their rounds." She paused. "And they still keep poppin' up every once in a while."

"That must be hard."

She shrugged. "Sometimes. I would have loved to have known Granny Mae, but she passed away long before I was born. My mama and grandma both did good things with their gifts, so it doesn't bother me when people talk . . . at least not that much. Sometimes their visions made a difference, like with the fire at Polk's store. That saved the lives of an entire family," she said, staring at the ceiling. "I had a dream about a chokin' baby. I acted on it, and it worked out for the best, though it could have been a coincidence for all I know. My visions don't always make sense. They might only be clues, which sometimes go right over my head."

Mallory stroked his chin. "You never know what little detail might matter, which is why I wanted to talk to you in person. Anythin' else about that stabbin' and kidnappin' you've remembered since we first talked?"

"What I told you and that rude detective was all I saw. The older the vision, the less I remember, except when there's somethin' I still need to act on. If that's the case, I remember it in full detail."

"So there's nothin' else you can tell me about that case?"

"Well, that right there is the problem."

"What do you mean?"

"When I feel pressured to come up with somethin', the visions don't cooperate."

He nodded slowly, not taking his eyes off her. "I don't want to pressure you, but this is a bigger case than we realized initially, and there's a good chance it connects to other unsolved kidnappin's." He stood and handed her his card. "If anythin' else comes to you, please call me. Promise me you'll do that?"

"Okay," she said, following him to the door.

"It was good to meet you in person, Jess." He smiled warmly. "Don't forget to call me whenever somethin' comes up, even if it's one or two in the mornin'."

Jess watched him walk to his Suburban. He gave her a quick smile before climbing in and driving off.

Wallaby chased Mallory's SUV to the end of the driveway, barking furiously and making Jess laugh out loud.

CHAPTER THIRTY-TWO

Wears Valley, Tennessee
March 1965

Anna Mae tensed when she heard the front door slam and waited for her father to yell her name. Instead, she listened to the muffled exchange of her parents' voices, followed by the black-and-white RCA television coming to life in the family room. Except for weekly football games in the fall and Bonanza on Sunday nights, the TV was always off.

She poked her head out after a few minutes and heard an announcer's voice saying something about the domino effect and preserving democracy. She walked down the hall to the family room and saw her parents riveted to the TV, watching soldiers stream out of landing crafts onto a tropical beach.

"What's goin' on?" she asked.

"Hush," her father said, staring at the TV.

The week before, the *Maryville Gazette* had carried pictures of American planes dropping vast loads of bombs on North Vietnam.

"President Johnson announced today that the United States of America has opted for a quick and decisive end to the conflict in Vietnam," the announcer excitedly said. "The president has sent in two full battalions of Marines: 3,500 troops in all. In a statement from the Oval Office this afternoon, the president said, 'We're not fooling around here. We've sent in the Marines to stop Communist interference in the sovereign and independent country of

South Vietnam. Last week, with Operation Rolling Thunder, our bombers flew unopposed into the very heart of North Vietnam, where we effectively crippled the enemy's will and ability to continue this conflict. This will be over soon, with our boys home by Christmas.'"

"I'm glad Rudy isn't there anymore," Anna Mae blurted out.

Her father turned slowly toward her, like a snake preparing to strike. "What kind of chickenshit talk is that?"

Trying to hide her fear, she nodded toward the television. "I just meant that it seems to have gotten so dangerous over there. I'd be worried sick."

He scowled at her. "Is that a reason not to fight the good fight? What would've happened if we'd worried about standin' up to Hitler? You think we should've just sucked our thumbs and let them Nazis take over the world?"

"No, sir."

"Damn right."

She waited for him to turn red or hit her, but he just turned back to the television and shook his head.

"Sometimes you just gotta stand up to what ain't right," he said. "And Rudy, well, I think he would've been proud to fight the good fight had this happened when he was still there."

Anna Mae sighed quietly and slipped out of the room.

* * *

A couple of weeks after they'd arrested Hobo Bill, Sheriff Keene glanced at Stevens when the phone rang for the sixth time. "I swear to God, this better not be that Cole girl again." On the second ring, he raised his eyebrows and rested his hand on the phone. "I'll bet you my car keys if I answer this time 'stead of you, there won't be nobody on the line." He picked it up. "Keene here."

Nothing but silence on the other end. The sheriff exhaled loudly after a few seconds. "Now, you listen to me, Anna Mae Cole. We've asked you many times to stop callin' here. It ain't doin' you or anyone else any good." After another few seconds of silence, the line clicked off.

Keene hung up and shook his head in disgust. "Told you so."

"Glad I didn't take that bet, boss."

"I'm sure you are. The deputy on duty at county lockup in Sevierville called me and said she came in to see Hobo Bill last week. Don't know what the hell good she thought that would do." He chewed his lower lip for a moment. "That's it. I'm done." He picked up the phone and dialed.

* * *

His footsteps heavy, Jefferson Cole marched into the house, slamming the door behind him. *"Anna Mae! Get out here right this second!"*

Full of dread, she stepped out of her room and walked toward him. If his tone of voice hadn't revealed his intentions, the belt in his hand was a dead giveaway.

"Please, Papa, I didn't do anythin'."

"That so? Then why'd the sheriff call the rail yard today and have my supervisor hunt me down?"

"Papa, I—"

"Did I ask you to speak?" he said with barely contained fury, waving his finger inches from her face, the unmistakable odor of bourbon on his breath. "You called the sheriff's office time and again askin' them to let go some low-down colored hobo who kidnaps and kills young girls. That sound like anythin' wrong to you, Miss Anna Mae Cole?"

"No, 'cause he's an innocent man."

"Ain't no coloreds that are innocent. That's why God made 'em black."

"You can't—" Anna Mae stopped herself two words too late.

"I can't *what*?" he demanded, his eyes narrowing.

"I just meant, aren't we all created equal?"

"Is that what the Good Book says?"

She gulped. "I think so."

"You think so, huh? It don't say nothin' of the kind. It says to let the wicked atone for their sins. Does that sound to you like we're all equal?"

"Um . . ."

He cupped his hand to his ear. "What's that? I can't hear you."

"I guess not, sir."

"Elbows on the table."

"Papa . . ."

"You hard of hearin'? Do it *now*."

She leaned on the table. "Please, Papa, this hurts my elbows."

"Well, don't you worry. You'll forget about that real soon."

"Papa, please d—" The first slap of the belt surprised her so much that she yelped, tears welling in her eyes.

"*Count!*"

"One."

He hit her again. "*Louder!*"

"Two." Her thin cotton underwear already offered very little protection, but when her father lifted the back of her dress, the slaps from the belt became almost unbearable.

By the time they got to ten, she could barely speak. While the physical pain was intense, it wasn't as great as the anger and humiliation she felt. However, her anger toward her father wasn't half what she felt toward her mother, who sat silently in the next room.

CHAPTER THIRTY-THREE

Center Point, Texas
Present Day

Jess almost didn't take the call when she saw who it was. She was working on the accounts and didn't want the distraction. By the fourth ring, however, she gave in. "Jess Atwood."

"Hey Jess, Ed Mallory here." He paused. "Just wonderin' if you have any more input on the East Dallas case we talked about."

"I need to be the one to call you, remember?"

"Of course I remember, but my superiors are squeezin' me. Time could be runnin' out for this girl."

Ironically, she'd planned to call Mallory later that day once she had things clear in her mind. The vision from the night before wasn't like others she'd experienced. The details were fuzzy and came from images that didn't make much sense when put together. The whole episode only lasted a couple of seconds.

"I may have somethin' for you but need time to think about it," she said.

"I understand. But remember, a young woman's life is at stake here."

"I know. I just need to find equilibrium with this."

"Equilibrium is an excellent target to shoot for, Jess, but sometimes the world is too chaotic to allow for that, and it might be an unreasonable goal much of the time." He paused. "You know, my great-great-granddaddy Abraham was an emancipated slave."

"For real?"

"Yep, and like many other folks after the Civil War, he was lookin' for equilibrium. At one time, he stuck up for some black sharecroppers who'd been cheated out of their homesteads. Folks in El Paso didn't like that one bit. People repeatedly threatened him, and more than once, his children were frightened by men yellin' at 'em in public. Eventually, a rumor started that he fought on the side of the Union Army—even though that never happened. One Sunday, when he was in church with his wife and three kids, the shack they called home was burned to the ground."

"Unbelievable."

"Certainly is. At least they didn't torch it with everyone inside. Abraham moved with his wife and kids to Dallas, where his brother took 'em in. That's where our family's been ever since."

"That's an amazin' story. I'm afraid I don't know much of our family history from either side. Granny Mae died when my mama was just a baby, leavin' no sign of who the daddy was. Accordin' to her, if my daddy knew who either of his parents was he never said anythin' about 'em. That's three grandparents out of four I know nothin' about. You could say there's a lot of mystery in our family."

"Sounds like it. I reckon I'm lucky in that sense. I learned that our unofficial family motto for generations was 'Leave well enough alone.'. My mama used to say that doing the right thing was not always easy but was always best. My daddy told me the story of Great-great-granddaddy Abraham when I was ten. That was when I decided I'd become a lawman and do the right thing for people. My parents tried to talk me out of it, sayin' it was too dangerous, but . . . here I am." He chuckled. "I got off on a bit of a tangent. Sorry."

"Don't be. That's all fascinatin'."

"Anyway, equilibrium will eventually come, but it might not be accordin' to the timeline you expect."

"You shoulda been an inspirational speaker, Agent Mallory."

"Believe it or not, I have spoken in public occasionally." He cleared his throat. "Anyhow, I'd love to hear about your vision, jumbled or not."

She took a deep breath. "Last night, I dreamt I saw a boy bein' taken out of a car trunk."

"Hmm. Any specific details? The color of the car would help."

"That's why I hadn't called you yet. There were only a few quick flashes of different images that came and went. Another was of a Gila monster hissing at something. I wanted to get it all sorted out in my head, so it made sense before I talked to you."

"You never know what might make sense in the long run. A Gila monster could indicate Arizona, New Mexico, or Mexico itself."

"Another of the images was of a room thick with plants."

"Strange."

"I know. That's why I wanted to think about this before I told you."

"I understand. What else?"

"Well, the boy wore a yellow shirt with white stripes."

"Huh. Any clues as to where this happened . . . or where it *will* happen?"

"Sorry, that was all that came to me."

"Don't worry about it. I'll put this in the NCIC database, and if there's a match for yellow shirt and boy, it'll spit out anythin' that fits."

* * *

A week later, Jess stared at Agent Mallory's caller ID on her phone. She answered on the third ring. "Agent Mallory—"

"I know, Jess, I wanted to wait for you to call me, but I had to let you know about an Amber Alert that went out today. Remember the boy you told me about with the yellow shirt?"

Like it was yesterday. "Of course."

"A boy wearin' a yellow shirt went missin' early this mornin' outside Santa Fe."

"Did his shirt have white stripes?"

"The report didn't mention it, but he still might be the same boy you saw in your vision last week."

"Maybe. That is—" She stopped midsentence as an image formed in her mind's eye. In her vision she saw a blue school bus with a white top parked down a long sandy road, next to a dried-up pond surrounded by cacti, with a mountain in the background.

"Jess, are you still there?"

She told him about the new vision.

"That's useful, thanks. I'll pass it along to the New Mexico authorities."

"Sounds good." She felt better than she had in a while—until she remembered how fast things could go south.

CHAPTER THIRTY-FOUR

Wears Valley, Tennessee
March 1965

Deputy Stevens hung up the phone and listened to the tat-tat-tat of Keene's typewriter.

"What?" the sheriff finally demanded, without looking up from his report. "You know I hate it when you sit there stewin'. Don't tell me it was that Cole girl again."

"That was Jo Ellen Brower."

"I swear, that busybody complains more than the next two dozen people combined. You ask me, I'd say her cornbread ain't quite done in the middle." He shook his head. "What'd she want this time?"

"Said she saw a tall man with a mop-top hairdo walkin' past her place with a young girl."

The sheriff stopped typing and frowned. "So?"

"You know Phil Daley has a haircut like that."

Keene resumed typing. "You need to let that go, Stevens. We got our kidnapper."

"You mean we got Hobo Bill. We both know he had nothin' to do with any of that."

"We know nothin' of the kind. Besides, accordin' to Commissioner Baker, the Klan thinks he's guilty, so the safest place for him now is right where he is.

We haven't had a lynchin' in this town in over a decade, and we're not about to have one now if I have anythin' to say about it." He frowned at Stevens. "You need to drop this thing with Daley. It's been well over a year since the trial."

"You know he was guilty, Sheriff."

"I don't know that, not for sure. The jury didn't seem to think so."

"Only 'cause of that damn fool judge pushin' things his way. I'd bet you anything he got a call from Daley's old man before the trial."

The sheriff squinted at his report. "How do you spell accomplices? One 'c' or two?"

"Three. First two, then one."

"Smartass."

"You asked, boss." Stevens stood. "I'm gonna go check this out."

"You're wastin' your time."

The deputy removed his hat from the back of the door. "We'll see about that."

* * *

Stevens was almost to the junction of Pinecrest and State Route 17 yet saw no sign of Daley or anyone who looked like him. He was about to head back when he came around a curve and saw a tall, long-haired man carrying a guitar case walking beside a teenage girl, almost to a path leading into the deep woods of the Great Smoky Mountains National Park.

Switching on his roof beacon, he floored his patrol car up to where they were and climbed out, sliding his billy club into his utility belt.

The girl looked fifteen or sixteen and seemed frightened by Stevens' presence.

"What do you think you're doin', Daley?"

"We're just out for a stroll on a beautiful spring day." He glanced at the girl next to him. "Ain't we, Kimmie?"

She gave him an uncertain nod.

Daley smiled, displaying straight white teeth. "Not that it's any of your concern, Deputy."

"It certainly *is* my concern." Stevens pointed at the guitar case. "What's in there?"

"A guitar, of course. Like that ain't the most obvious thing in the world." Daley winked at Kim, who nodded and managed a weak smile.

Stevens gave her a stern look. "Have you been drinkin', young lady?"

Kim swallowed and looked at Daley.

"I asked you a question, girl," Stevens persisted.

"Look, Deputy, ain't no point in gettin' all bowed up," Daley cut in. "We both know I've done nothin' wrong, and all you're gonna do is embarrass yourself again. Anythin' you do, you know I'm just gonna walk," he said with a smirk.

"You're not gonna walk this time."

"You were sure about that last time, weren't ya? I'm surprised that you still have a badge after that mess."

"Here in Wears Valley, we don't take kindly to kidnappin' girls." He narrowed his eyes. "Not to mention the other terrible things you do."

"What in heaven's name are you carryin' on about? I ain't kidnapped nobody. Kimmie agreed to take a little hike with me. Fact is, I'm writin' her a song."

"That so?"

"Phil is a famous songwriter," Kim said enthusiastically. "He's written two songs for the Beach Boys and one for the Rollin' Stones." She looked at Daley admiringly. "He's even workin' on somethin' for the Beatles right now."

Daley smirked at Stevens. "See? You're gettin' all riled up over nothin'." He turned to Kim. "You weren't supposed to tell nobody about that Beatles song, though," he admonished, waving a finger at her. "That was our little secret, remember? They need to see what I come up with before they make their final decision."

"Sorry."

Stevens gave her a stern look. "Kim, this man's been lyin' to you. I guarantee he couldn't write a song or play guitar to save his life."

"Oh no," she said enthusiastically. "With respect, sir, he's terrific. He was playin' guitar in Little Bear Park when I came by, warmin' up for band practice tonight." Her eyes widened. "He's gonna let me come and listen, long as I don't ask anyone for autographs."

Stevens rolled his eyes. "Young lady, there ain't no band."

"This is what I was tellin' you about these small-town sheriffs and their deputies," Daley said to Kim. "They'll do anythin' to keep folks from havin' a good time." He turned back to Stevens. "We were havin' a great time 'til you showed up and put some clouds in front of our sunshine. Ain't that right, Kimmie?"

She nodded nervously, keeping her eyes on Stevens.

"You're not gettin' away with this, Daley, not on my watch."

"Ain't nothin' to get away with, Mr. Deputy Sheriff."

Stevens silently seethed, his fingers caressing the grip on his billy club. "Kim here can't be more'n sixteen." He glanced at her. "That right, honey?"

She nodded again.

"Plus, she's obviously had somethin' to drink, which means you're contributin' to the delinquency of a minor."

"I thought she was actin' a little funny. She must've had a beer or two with some of her friends earlier." He winked at Kim again. "He's got nothin' on us."

Stevens fumed, hating that Daley was right. He walked over, opened the back door of his patrol car, and motioned for Kim to get in. "Let's go, honey. I'm takin' you home."

He glared at Daley, who just smirked. The man obviously saw himself as invincible.

CHAPTER THIRTY-FIVE

Center Point, Texas
Present Day

"What's this great new business idea?" Carl asked, unwrapping his hamburger. He wondered what Johnny had up his sleeve this time.

His brother looked around to make sure no one was listening. "I got a call from Jorge this morning."

Carl took a big messy bite out of the burger. "Yeah?"

"He's been on the phone with some guys in New Mexico who were going to make a delivery, but they apparently chickened out."

"What does that have to do with us?"

Johnny shook his head. "If you knew how fucking gross you look talking with your mouth full, you'd never do it again."

His brother never missed a chance to put him down. "Then why did we meet in this joint for lunch?"

"Never mind." He leaned back in his chair and looked away. "Jorge wants us to meet them before our next run. They give us the goods, and off we go with an extra package."

Carl shook his head. That would never work. "New Mexico is too far out of our way."

"Of course, but it gets better. They deliver to us." He pointed a french fry at Carl. "That's why this is so perfect."

"How old is the girl?"

"Well, that's the other thing."

Carl rolled his eyes. "*What's* the other thing?"

Johnny glanced around before answering. "It's a boy."

Carl set his hamburger down and shook his head vigorously. This had to be some kind of sick joke. "No way."

"Hey, now don't get salty on me. He'd be easier to manage."

Carl was still for a few moments, stunned by the suggestion and all it implied. What kind of twisted person would want to keep a young boy for a pet? "How old?"

"I dunno, maybe seven or eight. This is a—"

"Forget it."

Johnny scowled at his brother. "Why forget it? This is a golden opportunity. We just turn him over, and they pay us ten grand for the delivery."

Carl closed his eyes and shook his head again. This was way over the line. "That's just too young. We have standards, you know."

Johnny pushed his french fries to one side. "Listen," he hissed, leaning in, "this is opportunity knocking. Do you want to talk about standards? Some of our girls have been as young as fourteen. What difference does it make if this boy is a few years younger?"

"Not just a few years, more like six or seven. That's too young," he repeated with less conviction.

"Dude, it's all relative." Johnny snapped his fingers for emphasis. "It's the same operation."

"But it's not. A young boy is not the same as a teenage girl."

"No?" Johnny stuffed a french fry in his mouth. "Remember when we started with that one girl? She was what, eighteen?"

"Seventeen."

"Same difference. She was a fucking prostitute no one cared about. Remember?"

Carl picked up his hamburger again and nodded glumly before taking another bite. "Of course I remember."

"We had all kinds of arguments about that piece-of-trash girl, and you said we couldn't do it. But now you're fine with it."

"Who says I'm fine with it?"

"Thirteen girls we've delivered so far. I would call that being pretty fine with it."

Carl stared at the table, not sure of how to respond.

Johnny leaned back in. "If we hadn't picked her up, bro, she'd be dead by now, either from an overdose or her pimp. All our girls are more or less the same, from bad homes or living on the street like dogs."

There he goes again, Carl thought, *exaggerating to prove his point.* "Not all of them."

Johnny waved off the comment as though it were an annoying fly. "Almost all of them. But that's not the point. They get better treatment from us than they've had their entire lives."

When Johnny got like this, he never relented or backed down. He always wanted the first word, the last word, and all the words in between. Some battles weren't worth fighting. "Well . . ."

"You'll get used to this, Carl, I promise. It's easier and safer than taking him off the street, which is the riskiest part."

"What about the guys in New Mexico? Maybe they're FBI or Interpol."

"Jorge said they've done business with them before, and they're fully vetted. It's totally safe."

"So you say."

They stopped talking and watched a teenage girl in a crisp uniform smile and set a large milkshake in front of a morbidly obese man at the next table.

"How do they get their money?" Carl asked once she had walked out of earshot.

"It was prepaid. Jorge said they already have the money in hand and just need the delivery."

Carl shook a finger at him. "No, I mean the guys from New Mexico. How do *they* get paid?"

"That's the other thing."

"Of course there has to be another thing."

"No big deal. We just pay them directly, and the cartel pays us back."

"Are you serious? They want us to go out of pocket on this? How much?"

"Another ten grand."

"Are you trying to tell me someone will pay $20,000 for one boy, sight unseen? We rarely get that much for one girl at auction, and that's only if she's pretty."

"I'm telling you the $20,000 has already been paid for the boy, and you can bet it's more than that, so the cartel gets their profit. Besides, I'm sure they sent photos, so it wasn't really sight unseen." Johnny grinned. "Everybody wins."

"I don't like it. What if the cartel changes us up?"

"It won't happen. They like doing business with us because we bring them easy money. We're good at what we do and always deliver the goods." He reached over and squeezed his brother's arm. "Listen, bro, this is easier, safer, and more profitable. We can't lose."

* * *

Dave stood by the front door. "Jess, honey, you comin'?"

It was the night of the public vote on their variance request. With Earl Kidwell stacking the deck by actively campaigning against them, she saw little chance of it passing. Only one vote per household was allowed, so what was the point of her being there? She'd rather have time to be alone and unwind.

"Don't reckon so," she said. "I plan to make do with a quiet evenin' by myself."

"Come on, Jess," pleaded Kevin. "The more people we have there, the b-better. You could help us get some positive energy goin'."

"I got nothin' positive to add right now. Besides, the idea of being the only person of color in a room full of hostile white folks isn't exactly my idea of a fun evenin'."

Dave opened the door and nodded to her. "They may not be as hostile as you think, but suit yourself and wish us luck. Hopefully, we'll see you in a few hours with some good news."

She stood at the window and watched them pull out of the driveway. Someone once told her that, contrary to common belief, optimists are not the happiest people because they get disappointed more often.

Jess opened the floor hatch in the hall and descended the stairs to the cellar. She clicked on the light and breathed in the earthy scent. Brushing cobwebs out of the way, she ducked the low ceiling beams and walked across the hard-packed dirt floor to the wine rack. Kat once said that her uncle Rudy and his wife Molly had taken shelter there with Granny Mae back in the sixties when a tornado threatened to demolish their house.

Kat had also been there in Granny Mae's womb the day before she made her dramatic entrance into the world. Jess glanced around the cellar—potatoes stacked in a bin on one side, some long-forgotten tools piled in the corner—and shivered. That must've been scary, especially in such a tight space with no windows. What if the house had collapsed on them?

She picked up a bottle of organic Pinot Noir and headed back up, closing the hatch behind her.

She poured herself a full glass, which she usually wouldn't do when Dave was around, though she hadn't seen him drunk in months. His AA meetings seemed to be paying off.

The buzz she got from the first glass made her feel better, so she had another. She was working on her fourth when a loud knock made her jump, spilling wine on her Paintball Rocks T-shirt. She got a bigger surprise when she opened the door.

"Travis Kidwell, of all people. What in tarnation are you doin' here?" she asked, trying to stand as straight as possible.

He gave her a funny look. "Seems like someone's been gettin' loaded."

"In case you didn't notice, this is my house. If I want to have a coupla glasses of wine, I have the right."

"Of course you do. I just came by to let you know you won the vote on the variance."

"What?"

"Y'all got the variance! Dave and Kevin are beside themselves."

"I bet they are. But wasn't your old man there?"

"He was, but I reckon people are sick and tired of him throwin' his weight around. He bitched and moaned, but people didn't listen. Some folks spoke on your family's behalf, and your mama's name came up several times. Seems like she did more than her share of good for people."

"And pissed off a few others while she was at it."

"No doubt." He smiled. "Anyway, I just wanted to let you know. Your guys were still shakin' hands and gettin' congratulated when I left."

"So, why are you happy? Doesn't it undermine your plans for takin' our property?"

"Earl and I don't see eye to eye on many things." He rubbed the back of his neck. "You and your farm are one of our big disagreements, as I've told you before."

"I'd like to believe you, but—hold on, that means they'll be home soon."

"Yep." He glanced at his watch. "The meetin' finished about fifteen minutes ago."

"I thought the vote wasn't happenin' until eight?"

"That was the original plan, but Polk from the hardware store pushed it up with the help of Rick Thornton, the lawyer whose wife runs the Happy Platter. They made it the first item of business and used Robert's Rules of Order to speed things along. So, congratulations." He touched his hat and turned to go.

"Wait a minute; you can't leave me here like this." The last thing she wanted was for her brother and stepfather to see her in that state.

"Hate to contradict you, honey, but I certainly can."

She walked past him onto the porch, closing the door behind her. "Get me out of here. You can bring me back after I, um . . ."

"Sober up?"

"Somethin' like that."

"Drivin' a drunk woman around is not my idea of a fun evenin'."

Ignoring him, she walked to his pickup truck and climbed into the passenger side. "They could be here any second. Get in and drive, cowboy."

"You know, cowboys are good with ropes," he said, walking toward the truck. "We could make this interestin."

"In your dreams, buddy. Get me out of here, now."

"As you wish," he said, hopping into the driver's seat.

Chapter Thirty-Six

Pastor Blaine had dropped off another letter from Rudy earlier that morning, but Anna Mae decided she wouldn't open it until she stopped for lunch. Dr. Ferguson had called that delaying gratification, and it would be good for her to learn to choose the best time for something instead of always acting spontaneously. At noon, she unplugged the vacuum, made herself a grilled cheese sandwich, and opened the letter.

April 17, 1965

Dear Anna Mae,

There were days in Nam when I didn't know if I'd live to see another sunrise. I saw people die in front of my eyes and have heard grown men crying for their mamas at night.

One thing that kept me going was something Pastor Blaine once told me. "This too shall pass," he said. "Good or bad, things will come, and they will go."

And so they have. No matter how dark the day may seem, there'll be another that's brighter. And vice versa.

Before my unit got close to the fighting over there, I was out with some of my buddies drinking beer in Saigon, having a good old time, thinking, "This too shall pass." And sure enough, it did. The chaos and misery started not more than a couple of weeks after that. For us, that is. It had started long before with the locals.

These tough times you're going through will be gone one day as if they never were.

That Andy character doesn't have the good sense God gave a turkey. I'd be happy to teach him a lesson if I were there. The good news is that not every boy is so thoughtless and irresponsible.

Don't take those visions too seriously, Anna Mae. Like you yourself once said, they can't all be true. Sometimes there's order in this world, and other times there's nothing but chaos. Dreams don't always make sense, and you can get into trouble trying to squeeze order out of them.

Put this Greyhound bus coupon in a safe place. When the timing is right, get yourself a ticket, hop on one of those buses, and come join us. We'll be pretty cozy until the house is finished, but there'll always be room for you.

Sending you oceans of love,

Rudy

P.S. From what I've heard about Hobo Bill, I agree that he's harmless. But let the sheriff figure that out on his own. He's a bit of a grump, and the last thing you want is him calling Papa to complain.

* * *

Anna Mae woke gasping for breath, her heart pounding, awakened by the same dream she'd had four times in the past five months. Once again, she'd been falling, the ground rushing up at her, and had a sense that her life would soon end. It had been way too real.

The vision with Andy had also seemed real. Making love, getting pregnant, feeling the glow of a new soul inside her, and the happiness of him lying next to her. But sex with him on Halloween night had been nothing like she'd foreseen.

In her vision, it had been gentle and loving, remarkable in many ways. Not cramped and painful in the dirty back seat of his Ford Fairlane, with empty beer cans and other trash scattered on the floor. Immediately afterward, he just got in the front and drove away before she'd even pulled herself together. She wasn't held and loved the way her vision had shown, and he dropped her off at home without so much as a goodbye. "This is your stop," was all he'd said.

The vision of the fall conflicted with two other visions she'd had: one of her dying while giving birth and another of her dying in front of Rudy's house. Her brother was right. They couldn't all be correct, and when considered together, they made no sense.

And why all the morbid visions anyway? Anna Mae shook her head. She'd lied to Dr. Ferguson years ago when she said she wasn't sad often. How much happier would she be if she never had any visions? Thanks to her, they sometimes messed up other folks' lives as well.

Earlier that day, she'd stopped by the sheriff's office, imploring them to let Hobo Bill go, even though bugging the sheriff had gotten her a terrible whipping last time. But his being arrested was all her fault since she didn't have to tell them about his gun or that he'd been living in the tent.

Sheriff Keene seemed to think her coming in was a joke.

Deputy Stevens was more sympathetic but told her there was nothing they could do.

"Nothin' you can do? You can let that poor man go."

The sheriff clicked his tongue. "Not until we've committed to the due process of law, young lady." He'd waved his hand at her dismissively. "You run along home now. This here is grownups' work."

"Grownups' work, are you kiddin' me? If it was truly grownups' work, then I think you'd be actually *followin'* due process 'stead of just givin' it lip service. Isn't he entitled to a hearin' at least?"

"You think you know more about the law than us? We *are* the law, and don't you forget it. That boy's hearin' is long over. He's just awaitin' trial now."

Anna Mae could barely contain herself. "And he's been waitin' for what? Nine, ten weeks?"

Stevens cleared his throat. "These things take time to set up, especially when—"

"Especially when no one who has the power to do anythin' gives a good goddamn if he's denied his civil rights."

Keene stood. "Hey, now, watch your language. And what do you think you know about civil rights?"

"Apparently more than you," she said and walked out, slamming the door behind her.

Back home that evening, she waited for the call from the sheriff that would guarantee her another whipping. She regretted having lost her temper, but the phone never rang.

Sitting on the edge of her bed, she thought about Dakota Ridge. Years before her visions began, a man who'd lost his brother in the Korean War had jumped from there after drinking all night. "Probably died instantly when he hit the rocks," someone said. Pastor Blaine asked them to pray for his soul that Sunday, and she did so with all her heart.

The rocks must have rushed up at him. The way they would if she fell. Or jumped.

Anna Mae closed her eyes. As Rudy said, this too shall pass. If he could survive Vietnam, she could survive this. Maybe it was time to use the bus coupon.

She lay down and closed her eyes, but tears came instead of sleep.

CHAPTER THIRTY-SEVEN

Center Point, Texas
Present Day

Travis drove up the road toward Logan's Bend, where another set of headlights came around the curve. As they got closer, Jess realized it was Dave's pickup.

"Shit, it's them." She giggled and ducked down.

"You know they can't see you in the dark."

"Jus' makin' sure." She slowly poked her head up, looked back, and saw them turn into their driveway. "Told you we had to get outta there."

He chuckled. "That you did."

"Where are we goin' anyway?"

"Thought you knew. You're the one who had to get out of there with your pants on fire."

"They most certainly were not on fire. It's just that—wait a minute, did you say they approved the variance?"

"So that's why folks call you Speedy, 'cause it only takes fifteen minutes for information to sink in."

She punched him in the shoulder.

"*Ow.* Careful, I'm drivin'." He rubbed his arm with his free hand. "It's not technically approved yet, but they voted down the opposition to the variance, which is the next best thing. It just needs to get rubber-stamped through zonin'."

"You know a lot about those things for a cowboy."

Travis didn't answer for a while. "You know, I'm honored to fulfill your cowboy fantasies," he finally said, "but it doesn't accurately describe who I am. I know about this stuff 'cause I've done a lot of property deals with Earl, that guy nobody likes."

"That's right; we don't. And for good reason." A minute passed before Jess spoke again. "I want to ask you a question."

"Bring it."

"Why're you such a player?"

"That's easy. I'm not."

"I beg to differ with you, Mr. Travis Kidwell. You have quite the reputation around town."

"Havin' a reputation doesn't make somethin' true."

"Sometimes it does. How many ladies have you dated in the past year?"

"I date someone until I see it's not gonna work, then I end it."

"In other words, until it's not gonna work for you."

"If a relationship isn't gonna work out for either partner, that means it isn't gonna work out, period."

"Is that why you dumped me?"

"Those were different circumstances."

"Which I really don't need to know."

"I figured since I was turnin' eighteen, and you were only—"

"I *said* I don't need to know." She turned to look out the window so he couldn't read her expression. "You call that a reason?"

"Like I was tryin' to explain—"

"Sorry," she interrupted. "I should have asked you somethin' safer, like why do you do such crazy things?"

"Crazy things?"

"You know, like racin' your Camaro up and down the highway as if you were late for an appointment with the Devil himself."

"It's a '68 Pontiac GTO. Different animal, and a true classic."

"So?"

"Are you pullin' my leg?" He smacked the steering wheel. "Of course you wouldn't know the meanin' of speed with that pint-sized pickup you drive."

"It's reliable and does the job."

"Only if your job is pickin' up groceries at the supermarket. It's an old folks' truck. You obviously don't know what I'm talkin' about. It's like tryin' to explain to a virgin what sex is like."

Jess felt her cheeks get warm. "Leave it to you to come up with that analogy."

"Just trying to explain things in the clearest possible way. I'm tellin' you, though, acceleration and speed are almost as good as sex."

"I guess that depends what kinda sex you've been havin'."

"Ha!" He braked suddenly and made a U-turn.

"What are you doin'?"

"You'll see," Travis said.

Neither of them spoke until they turned into the Kidwells' driveway.

"You givin' me a grand tour of the family homestead?" she asked.

"Better than that."

They passed the house and pulled up near one of the garages. He pushed the button on a garage door opener clipped to his visor. They both got out and stood in front of his truck, watching the door roll up to reveal a gorgeous emerald-green car with tiny sparkles in the finish and two white racing stripes down the middle that Jess had only previously seen from a distance.

Travis jumped in and started the engine, which roared in response. He backed the car out, then leaned over and rolled down the passenger window. "Get in. What're you waitin' for?"

She opened the door and climbed in. "This is nice," she said, glancing around.

He explained that he'd completely redone the interior. "Some of it's original, and some was refabricated," he explained.

"You certainly did a beautiful job."

"Thanks. Now close the door, and I'll show you what this baby can do."

"Fine. I'll let you know if I'm impressed or not."

He laughed and revved the engine. To Jess, it sounded like a purring tiger that suddenly roared. "There'll be a survey after the demonstration," he said.

She rolled her eyes but felt pleasantly surprised by his happiness. He put the car in gear and had started across the parking area when Earl drove up, exited his truck, and stood in the glare of Travis's headlights for a few moments before walking up to the car.

"Hey, Dad."

"What in tarnation do you think you're doin'?"

"Just goin' for a drive."

The older man leaned down to get a look at Jess. When he realized who it was, he jumped as though a snake had bitten him. "*You!*" He stepped back and glared at his son. "Is this why you didn't stand behind me on the vote? 'Cause you're chasin' *pussy*?" He shook his head. "Especially this colored hippie from across the road." He leaned in to take a closer look.

"You have the wrong idea, Mr. Kidwell," she slurred.

"And how precious, she's drunk. Good work, boy, but wrong material."

"I don't think you mean that," she said.

The older man laughed meanly. "Bless your little heart. Yeah, I know my boy."

"You don't know shit, Dad," Travis said.

"What'd you say to me?"

"You heard me."

His father grabbed the handle and yanked his door open, but Travis stepped on the gas and let out the clutch, throwing gravel and leaving the senior Kidwell yelling and cussing at them.

As they drove down the driveway, Jess looked back. "He's pretty mad."

"Yep, that's how he beats his chest. At least he's not as bad as he used to be." He glanced over at her. "Sorry about his 'colored hippie' comment."

"I try not to let that kind of thing bother me."

"Which doesn't make it right."

"No, it doesn't. But my mama used to remind me that my skin color has nothing to do with the color of my soul."

"Your mama was a wise woman." He gave her a wry smile and gunned the engine, which made a deep-throated growl. "How's that sound?"

She closed her eyes. "Pretty nice. Sexy even."

"You got that right." He pulled out onto the road and stopped, facing Logan's Bend. "Watch this!"

He revved the motor again and popped the clutch. The car squealed its tires and took off like a rocket. The acceleration pushed Jess into the back of her seat, and she whooped with glee as the speedometer climbed to ninety, then a hundred.

"Don't you think you'd better slow down?" she asked.

"Oh, I will. If we took Logan's Bend this fast, we'd wind up wrapped around a tree."

"You know that curve is named after a guy who died there, right?"

He grinned. "Don't worry, Granny, I'll get you home safe."

"I'm not your granny, and—hey, you really need to slow down." She sucked in her breath. "Seriously, Travis, we're goin' way too fast."

"Relax, I got this." He downshifted to third, taking the curve in the high seventies, way faster than she'd ever experienced it. When they were almost to the next straightaway, Travis mashed the gas pedal to the floor, and the engine responded instantaneously. As the road straightened out, he smoothly shifted back into fourth.

She had to admit he knew how to handle the car, which was unquestionably sexy. No doubt he took all his dates out in it, which probably worked out well for him.

"Your turn," he said.

Jess frowned. "My turn for what?"

"Well, it's either your turn to ask another one of your silly questions or your turn to drive."

"Seriously? There's no way I'm drivin' in my condition."

"I know. That part was a joke."

"Forgive me for not laughin'."

"Oh yeah, that's right. Sorry."

"Don't be. This has nothin' to do with my mama dyin' at the hands of a drunk driver. Anyone with a lick of sense knows *it's stupid and crazy* to drive when they've been drinkin.'"

"Okay, got it, no need to yell."

"I'm not yellin.'"

"Maybe not this second, but you were. Anyway, it's no big deal."

"No big deal? Do you have anythin' resemblin' a brain in your head? What kind of idiot would let someone drive their precious car while drunk?"

"Like I said, that was a joke. Don't be so dramatic. Besides, you don't look all that drunk. I reckon you might be pretendin' more than anythin,' maybe hopin' I'd try to get into your pants."

"Are you kiddin' me?" She snapped her fingers. "Such arrogance. Like father, like son. Take me home, *now!*"

"Right away, Princess."

When they arrived, Jess hopped out of the car, held the door open, and leaned in. "Thanks for the ride, Two-bit," she said, slamming it before he could reply.

CHAPTER THIRTY-EIGHT

Wears Valley, Tennessee
September 1965

That fall, Jefferson Cole left on a three-day freight run to the West Coast one dreary, overcast afternoon. It was always safer when he wasn't home, but Lucinda's small talk could drive Anna Mae up the wall. Her vision of falling had returned at least once or twice a month all summer long. It put her on edge, and she wondered if she was being guided to end it all.

During supper, she listened to her mother rattle on about nothing in particular for at least ten minutes before she finally interrupted. "Mama, why do people kill themselves?"

Lucinda frowned. "Pass me the cornbread, please."

"Yes, ma'am." Anna Mae complied and waited.

"They ain't nothin' more than cowards who don't have the guts to face reality," her mother said after a long silence. "They just want to escape and don't give a damn about who they leave behind."

"Do you know anyone who did that?"

She gave her daughter a withering look. "Heavens to Betsy, Anna Mae, this is not an appropriate supper table conversation. You just mind your manners."

"Yes, ma'am."

The rest of the meal was uncomfortably quiet.

Anna Mae had a hard time sleeping that night. The falling dream had returned for the second time that week and the seventh time in six months. She lay awake staring at the ceiling, thinking about suicide.

She'd caused Hobo Bill to be arrested and spend more than seven months in jail—so far. They might keep him there for another seven months or more for all she knew. Back in March, when she'd taken the bus into Sevierville and visited him at the Sevier County lockup, the jailer had said it was for his own good.

"How in the world could keepin' a man in jail be for his own good?" she'd asked.

"Let's just say he's safer inside than out," he answered.

Rusted metal showing through peeling paint, the pungent smell of old sweat in the stale air, and the unmistakable feeling of intense suffering when she visited the jail were bad enough. She'd hoped Hobo Bill would be happy to see her, but that wasn't the case. When she told him he'd be getting out soon, it only made him angry, and he called the jailer to take him back to his cell. She'd lied, trying to make him feel better, but he saw through it, which only made things worse. Since then, he'd spent another six months behind bars.

Her visions sometimes made things worse, often contradicting each other, making order difficult—if not impossible—to find. They frequently caused her nothing but pain, like with Andy the previous fall. She'd been so sure but turned out to be so wrong. It seemed her greatest skill was making herself— and others—miserable.

Dakota Ridge wasn't far. She'd hike out there that afternoon and end her misery. It would take courage, but enough was enough, as Rudy would say. She hadn't answered his last letter and couldn't even respond with the slightest bit of love. He'd surely miss her, but at least he had Molly and all they shared between them. She thought about using the bus coupon he'd mailed her to go stay with them. But why burden her brother and his wife with her sadness?

She considered leaving a note for her parents, then thought better of it. Let them think it was an accident. They'd shake their heads and wring their hands at her funeral. At least her mother would, mainly because of how it would look to lose her only remaining daughter.

After her parents went to work, Anna Mae did her usual chores around the house, leaving everything clean and tidy. At three-thirty in the afternoon, she left for Dakota Ridge, the screen door slamming behind her. The sense of order started clear as day the minute she left the house. Strangely enough, it showed her path cutting through town rather than going the shorter way along Wears Valley Road. So be it. She followed and soon saw the path leading her into the sheriff's office.

But why on earth?

She walked in and found Deputy Stevens alone at his desk.

"Hello there, Anna Mae. Come to help with my paperwork?" He stood and gave her a warm smile. "Or are you here to nag me about Hobo Bill?" His smile faded when he noticed the look on her face. "Hey, sorry, I'm just pickin'. I know gettin' him free means a lot to you." He motioned to a well-worn chair. "Please have a seat. I'd offer you coffee, but we're fresh out." He glanced around theatrically, then lowered his voice as though someone might be listening. "Let you in on a little secret if you promise not to tell the boss."

Anna Mae sat and smiled, but just barely. "Cross my heart."

He opened his desk drawer and pulled out a couple of tea bags. "Peggy June got me hooked on green tea last summer. It's why folks in Japan live so much longer than we do." He winked at her. "I still have coffee when the sheriff's around, though."

Anna Mae's eyes widened as he pulled a strange-looking device out of the coat closet.

"What's that?"

"It's an electric teakettle from Sears and Roebuck." He held it under the tap in the back of the office. "Peggy June ordered it from their catalog as a Christmas present for me last year." He set it on the counter and plugged it in.

"That was right nice of her," Anna Mae said.

"Indeed, it was." He looked at her with a raised eyebrow. "Tell me what brings you in today, Miss Cole." He set out two mugs and dropped a tea bag in each.

"Oh . . ." She felt the pressure of tears and shook her head. "I just happened to be passin' through . . . and thought I'd stop in."

"Well, I'm glad you did," he said carefully, settling back in his chair. The only sound for a while was the noise of the teakettle heating up. Stevens cleared his throat. "I don't mean to pry, but . . . how's everythin' at home?"

Anna Mae tried to speak, but words wouldn't come. Tears rolled down her cheeks, and she covered her face with her hands.

"Here you go." He handed her a Kleenex, then poured hot water over the tea bag in one of the mugs and passed it to her. "This'll make you feel better."

She sniffed and took it, wiping her eyes with the tissue in her free hand.

"You be careful now. That's pipin' hot," Stevens cautioned as he poured from the kettle into his own mug. "I'd let it sit a couple of minutes before sippin' it." He waited patiently for her to say something. "I'm happy to hear anythin' you want to share, Anna Mae."

Another minute passed in silence.

"You know," Stevens said, "sometimes we find ourselves around people we don't like. That's part of life." He gestured at Keene's desk. "The sheriff and I get along like a cat and a dog sometimes, but he does his job well, for the most part. Maybe he'd be happier if he found himself a wife, but that's none of my bidness. He's part of the work I'm meant to do here in Wears Valley, at least for the time bein'."

"That's fine and dandy, Deputy Stevens, but you can quit anytime you wish. That's not an option for me, is it?"

"You know, we always have choices open to us. If we find ourselves in an unpleasant situation, we can do somethin' to make that situation better, or we can leave." He smiled and sipped his tea. "At least most of the time. The main thing is that we get to make new choices based on what we've learned through experience."

"You sound like Rudy."

"Your brother's as good as he is wise. Like his kid sister."

"You know Rudy?"

"Well enough. This ain't a big town we live in, you know. I was a senior when he was startin' out at Wears Valley High. We weren't close or anythin', but

I broke up a fight he was gettin' into once."

"You wouldn't be talkin' about the time those three boys bullied him on the playground, would you?"

"There might've been three of them."

"I was only nine or ten, but I remember him comin' home, feelin' happy that this older boy had saved him." She shook her head and managed a faint smile. "I didn't know that was you."

"I'm sure he would've done the same for me were the circumstances reversed."

"I'd bet on that. Rudy is also . . . a good man."

"I'll take that as a compliment."

"You should. 'Cause if there's one thing I've learned, it's that not every . . ." Tears welled in her eyes again.

"Boy trouble, huh?"

She nodded, and the tears rolled down her face. "I just feel so . . . stupid."

"I know exactly what that feels like. But you know, one thing you got to understand is that we've all done things that were . . ."

"Damn foolish."

Stevens grinned. "Lookin' for a nicer way to say it, but yeah." He leaned forward. "You need to be cautious around boys of any age who might be driven crazy by their hormones. The most important thing is to learn the difference 'tween those who put your interests first and those who don't. The more beautiful you are, the more careful you gotta be." He raised his mug. "You need to be very careful, honey."

She blushed and realized she'd stayed too long. It was time to move on, keep things in order, and complete what she'd planned. "There might not be any of those boys out there. At least not for me."

Stevens chuckled. "Oh, they're out there. They're just harder to find."

She stood. "Well . . . thank you, Deputy Stevens."

"Sure. Stop by any old time." He also stood. "Look, let me give you a ride home."

"Oh, thank you kindly, but that won't be necessary." It would be out of order and out of line with her big plans.

He glanced at his watch. "If I remember correctly, your pa will be home in the next half-hour or so. I doubt you'd be back in time to make supper."

"He's on an out-of-towner and won't be back before tomorrow. It's alright. Truly it is."

"I'm sure it is, Miss Anna Mae. But I'm guessin' he ain't gonna be too happy if your mama tells him you were out and about 'stead of gettin' supper ready."

"I'd rather walk. Thank you all the same."

"I'd love it if you'd let me be of service," Stevens persisted. After a long pause, he gently took her elbow. "C'mon, sweetie, let's get you home."

CHAPTER THIRTY-NINE

J ess walked in the front door and found Dave and Kevin in the living room, laughing over a joke between them. As Travis thundered away, Kevin walked to the window and let out a low whistle. "Wow, look at that goat."

"It's a GTO," she corrected, relieved that Travis went back up the road instead of turning into his driveway.

"I know what it is. Goat is the nickname. Kidwell has one like that he tools around in." He frowned. "Who was that anyway?"

"Oh," she shrugged, "just a friend."

"Is it my imagination, or are you a b-bit tipsy?" Kevin took a step back and frowned. "You're drunk! What the hell is goin' on?"

"Nothin's goin' on. And I'm not drunk. I just had a few glasses of wine by myself."

"B-by yourself, huh? Then who was that in the GTO?"

"Kevin, go easy. She doesn't have to say," Dave admonished.

Jess avoided her brother's stare. "I think I'm gonna have an early night, y'all."

Kevin's face hardened. "Tell me that wasn't Travis Kidwell!"

"Well, if you really must know . . ."

"*Jess!* Those people are our enemies."

"Kevin, don't yell at your sister."

"Why not, Dad? Don't you see how stupid she's b-bein'?" He looked at his half sister with disgust. "That would explain the wine." He paused. "Did you sleep with him?"

"No! Not that it's any of your business who I sleep with."

"It is *totally* my b-business."

"You are completely misunderstandin' this, Kevin. There is nothin' goin' on 'tween Travis and me." She paused. "Plus, I think you might underestimate him."

"He did vote to remove the objection to the variance," Dave said. "And you know Earl will go ballistic on him. Besides, it was Travis who—"

"Forget it." Kevin stormed out of the room. "*I don't need this,*" he yelled from the hallway.

* * *

The call from Mallory came on a Saturday afternoon. He told Jess that the New Mexico State Police found the boy with the yellow shirt, white stripes and all, shaken up but unharmed. She'd answered the phone on the way home from paintball, where she'd once again annihilated her opponents. She knew she'd be happy hearing good news about the boy but was genuinely surprised by the joy she felt.

The conversation came through her phone's speaker, but she pulled to the side of the road anyway. As Mallory spoke, happy tears rolled down her cheeks.

He explained how a helicopter pilot had seen the bus while searching areas Gila monsters were known to exist. Unfortunately, the trooper on the ground who reached it first had entered without a warrant or consent, jeopardizing the case. The attorneys for the defense were already trying to get the whole thing thrown out. At least the boy was safe.

"Want to hear somethin' funny?" Mallory asked. "They said the bus was like a jungle inside. Those kidnappers loved plants, which was in line with your vision."

As Mallory continued, Jess felt herself drifting away. Another vision was coming, and she was glad she'd pulled over.

She interrupted him midsentence as he said something about lawyers who'd do anything for money.

"Tell them to check the car up on blocks. Under the rear seat."

"What car are you talkin' about?"

"That's for you to figure out." The image was already fading from her mind. "I see pink and white."

"Meanin' what?"

"The color of the paint maybe?"

"That color combo isn't likely, but we'll put a watch out. If we find this car, what would we be lookin' for?"

"I don't rightly know, but check under the back seat when you find it."

* * *

Later that week, he called again, excited and almost giddy, saying there had been an old red-and-white Plymouth Valiant up on cinder blocks behind the house of the mother-in-law of one of the perpetrators—and the red had faded in the bright New Mexico sun to a pinkish hue.

They'd been granted a search warrant based on a tip from an anonymous but credible informant.

"That was you, of course," Mallory said.

Under the back seat, they'd found a padlocked steel box welded to the floor containing incriminating information on the yellow-shirted boy and two other unsolved abductions. They had exchanged those kids for six-figure ransoms, alive but not well. One hadn't been fed for days.

That had been the kidnappers' M.O. They would reveal the child's location two days after receiving the ransom, so if the parents didn't want their kid to starve, they had to hurry.

The discovery would enable more search warrants and hopefully give the police enough evidence to get multiple convictions. They were already playing the bad guys against each other, telling one that the other had ratted him out.

"Their public defender advised them to cooperate and go for reduced sentences," Mallory said. "One kidnapper already revealed they were meetin' up with someone in San Antonio and had planned to turn the boy over to them. He claimed he didn't know any details, but we found the number of a pay phone in Kerrville on his cell, which brings us back to the question of why this was in your vision."

"I wish I knew."

"With all the crimes committed around the entire country, what are the chances that this one would have a major connection right up the road from you? It could be a random coincidence, but I'm thinkin' it's more than that. We'd love to find the people they planned to meet in San Antonio."

"Of course."

"So, how does it feel to be a hero, Jess?"

"Oh, I'm definitely not that."

"I beg to disagree with you, Ms. Atwood. This victory was only possible 'cause you told us what to look for. We both know you didn't have to come forward."

"I was just tryin' to do the right thing." At that moment, though, she felt a greater sense of fulfillment than she had in years. Maybe in her entire life. And yet . . . "Agent Mallory?"

"Yeah?"

"I appreciate you givin' me this wonderful news, but I don't know how much longer I can do this."

"Sorry, you lost me there. I thought you loved helpin' people."

"Of course I do, but I get anxious when I feel the pressure to perform on cue."

"I understand. Just let it happen whenever you're ready. Meanwhile, think about the future happiness you've given this boy and his family that they never would've experienced if you hadn't helped us."

She was silent for a few moments before taking a deep breath. "Thanks. I reckon I needed to hear that."

* * *

Johnny slammed the front door behind him and slapped his phone on the kitchen table. He opened the cupboard above the stove, pulled out a bottle of

Jose Cuervo, and poured himself a double shot.

"So, what happened?" asked Carl with a frown, wondering what was up with his brother this time.

Johnny downed the tequila in silence and sat at their kitchen table, head in his hands. "That's the problem. Nothing fucking happened."

"What do you mean, nothing happened?"

"What do you *think* it means?" he snarled. "I went to the phone booth in Kerrville and waited half an hour, but those idiots from New Mexico never called. I texted Jorge, asking what was up, and he didn't respond. The motherfucker is ghosting me."

"Maybe he was busy."

"*Maybe he was busy?* How stupid are you? He always gets right back to us. We've got five girls ready to go, which took us two months of hard work and tons of risk. With the boy, we would've had a full load. *Fuck!*" He threw his glass against the wall, smashing it into a hundred pieces.

"*Yo!* Relax, Johnny. There's no—"

Johnny's phone chimed with an incoming text from Jorge. He stood and read it aloud. "*Hey, old friend. Looking forward to seeing you, but things are hectic right now. How are the wife and kids?*"

"*Damn it!*" he yelled, pounding his fist on the refrigerator. "He wants us to wait. 'Wife and kids' means it's a sensitive situation, and 'old friend' means there's extra danger in it for us."

"How long are we supposed to wait?"

Johnny started texting furiously. "That's what I'm asking him now."

He set his phone on the table. They stared at it in tense silence for a few minutes before it chimed with another incoming text:

"*Unfortunately, Peter and Simon are sick, and it looks like it might be serious. Maybe we should hold off on our party plans? It seems like we all have so much to do. This winter will be better for us, and not so busy. We look forward to seeing you then. Please stay in touch.*"

Johnny rubbed his forehead. "This is fucking insane!"

Carl pointed at the phone. "Who are Peter and Simon?"

"*Seriously?* Did you forget everything we went over about these codes? That means the idiots who were bringing us the boy. They're in some kind of trouble, probably arrested. The rest is obvious."

"Does Jorge think we're running a hotel here?" Carl asked. "Are we supposed to take care of five girls for another three or four months?" He paced the floor. "You told me we'd only be holding them a week or two, and it's already been seven. Plus, if those morons who let themselves get caught start talking—"

"They'd have nothing to say. The only potential link they have to us is through the pay phone at the Rite Aid in Kerrville, and we're not going anywhere near there again."

"I thought you said this was going to be easy and safe? Maybe we should start thinking about ditching. We could drive the girls far away and let them go."

"No fucking way." Johnny glared at him. "By saying 'we look forward to seeing you then,' Jorge is demanding we follow through."

"But . . . what kind of shape will the girls be in months from now?"

"We have to tell them something they'll believe. Something that will motivate them to take care of themselves. Maybe say we're waiting for their families to raise the ransom money."

"They won't believe it would take so long."

Johnny shook his head. "Maybe not, but unless you have something better, it's what we do. We don't have much choice in the matter unless you think disobeying the cartel could possibly have a favorable outcome. Those guys don't fuck around."

Carl nervously fiddled with his mustache. "We better treat the girls like princesses."

"Definitely. And we need more privacy. Just yesterday, the black bitch left a note on the gate complaining that we drive too fast on *our* driveway. She said she's worried we'll hit her dog. Can you believe it?" He shook his head in disgust. "It's time we help those organic hippies decide to leave," he said, stroking his chin. "Something needs to change, and I have an idea."

CHAPTER FORTY

On the drive to her house, Stevens asked Anna Mae if she'd like to listen to some music.

The question startled her out of her thoughts. "Okay."

He turned on the radio and tried a few stations until he heard a song he liked.

Anna Mae couldn't believe her ears. "What's this?"

"Are you tellin' me you don't know the Beatles?"

"Of course I do," she said, staring at the radio. "I just don't know the song."

He chuckled. "That's 'I Want to Hold Your Hand,' as you might have eventually guessed from the lyrics."

"It's amazin'. No wonder this is Rudy's favorite band."

"He's got good taste," Stevens said and began slapping the side of the steering wheel along with the music.

Anna Mae hovered her fingers over the knob. "Mind if I turn it up?"

"Please do." He sang along, and Anna Mae stared at him open-mouthed.

He glanced over at her and stopped. "What?"

"Please don't quit. I was just admirin' your singin'."

He focused on the road. "You know, people have compared me to Tony Bennett."

"Really?"

"No, not really." He made a funny face and turned down the volume as a commercial began. "I sing about as well as a bullfrog in matin' season."

"I'm sure any bullfrog who sang with half as much confidence as you would have any girl frogs in the area all over him."

He laughed. "Well then, if I were a bullfrog, I'd be set for life, wouldn't I?"

"You would be. And honestly, I love your singin' . . . and your confidence." She blushed as the words left her mouth and was thankful his eyes were on the road.

She felt better, more than anything because he cared. That much was clear. She looked straight ahead, discreetly glancing sideways at him every once in a while. Peggy June was a lucky woman.

"Stuck On You" by Elvis Presley started playing.

"I've heard this one before," she said. "It's one of Mama's favorites."

Stevens turned the volume back up and sang along. Anna Mae couldn't help giggling.

"Are you laughin' at my singin'?" he asked.

"I just love that you feel free enough to sing in front of me."

He pulled up in front of her house and clicked off the radio. "My car, my rules."

"Whatever you say, Mr. Deputy Sheriff."

He winked at her. "That's exactly what I say."

Her mother's car still wasn't home, and if she hurried, she might even have supper ready in time.

"Thank you so much for the ride," she said, but she was really thanking him for caring.

He gave her a mock salute, told her it was his pleasure, and to have a great evening. When she opened the front door, she glanced back and saw him waiting for her to go inside, just like last time. She waved, closed the door, and listened to him pull away.

Halfway to the kitchen, she realized how much he looked like Andy. What if it had been Deputy Stevens in the vision making love to her?

Anna Mae switched on the kitchen light and told herself she was being silly. Sometimes she just let her imagination carry her away. Even though she was already behind schedule to have supper ready, she went to her room and got her diary out of its hiding place. She stared at it a few moments, then wrote in big, bold letters down the front:

This
Too
Shall
Pass

That was a good thing to remember.

* * *

A few days later, Sheriff Keene left before noon. There was too much paperwork in the office for the sheriff's liking, and his deputy would have to do it all if he wasn't there.

Stevens glanced at his watch and sighed. Five-and-a-half more hours before he could call it a day. He was typing out a shoplifting report about an incident at the Rexall drugstore when Anna Mae walked in with a picnic basket.

He stared at the basket, then at her. "What can I do for you today, Miss Cole?"

"Oh, nothin'. I just wanted to see if you'd like to join me for lunch. I was thinkin' we could go over to Little Bear Park, where the grass is nice and soft."

He tried not to smile. "There are two reasons that can't happen."

"And what would those be, Deputy Stevens?"

"One, I've got a ton of work to do, and two . . ."

She gestured at the papers on his desk. "I'd be happy to help you with that work."

"This is official sheriff business," he nodded at his paperwork, "and that is highly sensitive material."

"That's okay. I'm great at keepin' secrets."

"And two . . ."

"You're engaged."

"Exactly."

Anna Mae held up the basket. "It's just a thank-you for protectin' the citizens of Wears Valley. Besides, I've got a jar of sweet tea in here. I reckon you can't say no to that."

He felt the pull. "I appreciate you comin' down here and makin' such a kind offer, but . . ."

"It's just lunch, Deputy Stevens. I'm willin' to bet you were gonna eat somethin' anyway."

"Of course, but as a sheriff's deputy on active duty, my behavior needs to be exemplary. Folks would talk."

"That didn't stop you with Jennifer Brownstone."

He caught his breath. "What do you know about that?"

"It doesn't matter. I ain't tellin' nobody."

"That was a complicated situation."

"I'm sure it was."

"And she wasn't a minor like you, making it a nonnegotiable issue."

"I turned eighteen last month," she said coyly, "so I'm no longer a minor. But I understand."

"I hope you do, Miss Anna Mae."

"Guess I'll be off, then." She opened the door and paused. "You know where to find me if you change your mind."

He nodded and stared at the door long after it had closed.

* * *

Anna Mae loved the soft green grass of Little Bear Park, the soothing gurgle of Redberry Creek in the background, and the spectacular view of Cove Mountain.

The day was unusually cool for June, and a gentle breeze blew through the trees. The gardenias the Sevier County Lions Club had planted around the park were in full bloom, their intoxicating scent mixing with the gentle fragrance from the surrounding Fraser firs. She chose a spot that was fairly private and not easily seen from the road, though if someone were looking, they'd be able to find her without too much trouble.

She spread the red-and-white picnic blanket on the grass and started laying out sandwiches and other food from the basket.

A memory surfaced of her being in the same park as a young girl. Her mother was also there—and happy—though she kept telling Rudy to stop being such a clown. He wouldn't stop running around in tight circles, making little Anna Mae laugh.

Closing her eyes, she tried to remember other times she had seen her mother happy, but nothing came to mind. After all, the memory in the park was from before Baby Katherine had come and gone, when dark clouds appeared across Lucinda Cole's sky—and stayed there.

Anna Mae glanced at the road. Deputy Stevens should have been there by now. Unless he wasn't coming, meaning a vision was wrong once again. After another ten minutes, she bit her lower lip and started putting things back in the basket. She'd done everything in order, but it didn't work out the way she'd foreseen.

"You givin' up on me that easy?"

Startled, Anna Mae turned to see Stevens behind her, hands on his hips and a smile on his face. She hadn't heard him walk up. That was smart because parking his patrol car nearby would make people wonder. She smiled nervously. "I declare, Deputy Stevens, I was beginnin' to think you weren't gonna show up."

"My friends call me Paul," he said as he pulled off his shoes, "and I always show up when somethin' is worth showin' up for."

CHAPTER FORTY-ONE

Center Point, Texas
Present Day

Wallaby's wild barking jolted Jess out of a deep sleep. She sat up in bed, disoriented by the red and blue lights strobing through the window. Grabbing her bathrobe, she pulled it on and rushed into the hallway, calling for Kevin. He hollered something from downstairs she couldn't make out. She arrived at the stairs to see Dave hurtling down them three at a time and followed behind. "*What happened?*" she yelled.

"*Fire,*" he called back over his shoulder. "*Must be one of the outbuildings.*"

Jess pulled on her boots and ran out the back door after him. She saw an orange glow on the equipment garage and frowned in confusion. It wasn't until she came around the corner of the house that she saw their new mushroom facility on fire, colorful flames licking out from the roof vents. Kevin watched helplessly, hands at his sides.

"*Hurry,*" she called out, running past him. "Don't just stand there."

He jogged to keep up with her. "Jess, there's nothin' we can do. The firefighters are—"

"There's always somethin' we can do, even if it makes the tiniest difference."

But when they got closer, a firefighter waved them away.

"We want to help," insisted Jess.

"Then stay out of our way," he said roughly, pointing at the burning building. "Any fuel stored in there?"

"No," Kevin said, "b-but there's a feed from our propane tank to the ceilin' heaters."

The firefighter spoke into his shoulder mic, "All fireground units, we've got a propane feed into the buildin'. Keep your distance 'til we get that shut down." He turned back to Jess. "Where's the tank located?"

"On the other side of the house," she said.

The firefighter jogged off in that direction. "*I assume you don't keep it locked?*"

"*No,*" yelled Kevin, "*it should b-be pretty straightforward.*" He turned to his sister. "Why don't you go with him?"

Jess felt numb as she ran after the firefighter. The facility they had invested nearly $25,000 in, which had enabled them to hit number four on Whole Foods Market's fast fulfillment list only three weeks earlier, was on fire. Their profit on the mushrooms from that month alone would have been more than a thousand dollars. Kevin had been over the moon. "Told ya so," he'd said to Jess after their first successful harvest. "Maybe I'm capable of a good idea every once in a while."

She rolled her eyes but had to admit it had been a brilliant idea. An idea that was literally going up in smoke.

The firefighter said something she didn't hear as he closed the propane tank shutoff valve.

"Sorry, what was that?" she asked.

"I need your full attention, please. Any other fuel feeds to that buildin'?"

"No, this is it."

He started back toward the fire and motioned Jess to follow. "Are you absolutely sure? What about storage? Any portable propane tanks, gas cans, or anythin' of that sort in there?"

"Nothin' but mushrooms, chicken manure, and hydroponic irrigation equipment."

"Then what's makin' it burn so hot?" he wondered aloud as he jogged off to join the rest of his crew.

Kevin stood at a safe distance. "I'll b-be damned," he said as Jess walked up.

"What good are these stupid visions if I can't foresee somethin' like this?" she asked. "Mama saw a fire in Polk's store all those years ago before it'd even started. A fire that had nothin' to do with us."

"But her vision saved that family."

Jess watched as the gradually diminishing flames turned the firefighters' water into billowing steam. "Yeah, but this sucks," she said, hot tears streaming down her cheeks.

"You got that right."

* * *

On the scene that morning, the Kerr County fire chief said it looked like arson. He'd told them the fire marshal would be out to investigate in a few days, but the fire would never have gotten so hot and spread so quickly without an accelerant. They would test the ashes and hard surfaces to make sure, but it was most likely gasoline. He asked the Atwoods who would have had something to gain by destroying their facility.

"The Kidwells across the road have had their eye on our property for a long time," Jess blurted out.

"Hey now," Dave said. "You need to think before you speak."

"I've thought about this for the past three hours. The chief here asked who might have somethin' to gain, and I answered him." She gestured angrily toward the steaming debris that used to be their mushroom facility. "Who else would've had a motive to do this?"

Once the firefighters left, the three Atwoods went back to bed after four a.m. With her mind racing, there was no way Jess would get any more sleep that night.

* * *

Kevin passed Jess his iPad during breakfast a few hours later.

"What?" she asked, with puffy eyes and a tired brain.

He nodded at the black screen with a play button in the middle. She tapped

229

it, and a video of a burning building that looked way too familiar began playing on Kevin's Instagram feed. "Are you kiddin' me?"

"Courtesy of Mr. Travis Kidwell." He nodded at it again. "Did you see the title?"

"Where is—" she abruptly stood. "*Smokin' mushrooms!*" she exclaimed, waving the iPad wildly. "I can't believe he'd stoop so low."

"Whoa there," Kevin said as he took the tablet out of her hand. "Careful with the equipment."

"He's makin' fun of us. I swear, I could kill him."

"Last time I checked, they had laws against killin' people."

"That only matters if they catch you."

She was still angry about the video as they sifted through the rubble after a subdued breakfast. Elena had been kind enough to come in on a Sunday. They all looked through the remains of the mushroom facility together. There wasn't much more than wet ashes, some melted metal, a few sections of pipe, and the concrete pad—the only thing that looked reusable. A pungent odor of burnt toast in the air deepened the despair she felt.

Jess announced she was going to have a chat with their beloved neighbors and marched off toward the Kidwells' property.

"*Hey,*" Elena yelled, "*you need to cool off before going over there!*" Jess's only response was to raise a hand high above her head.

She walked up the long driveway and pounded on the Kidwells' door. Earl and Travis answered it together.

"Hope you enjoyed our little bonfire last night," she said, focusing on Travis. "Glad we could provide some entertainin' content for your social media."

Earl grunted. "You're welcome."

"For what?"

"For callin' the fire department."

"Of course, since it did so much good. If you hadn't, we might've had a total loss. No, wait, we *did* have a total fuckin' loss. At least we wound up on your son's Instagram feed, so maybe the loss wasn't a hundred percent," she said, glaring at Travis.

Earl frowned. "I'll be damned if that ain't a funny way of sayin' thanks." He turned to his son. "You see how it is with transplanted city folk? They don't know the meanin' of good manners."

"I've been livin' here twenty-five years. That doesn't exactly make me city folk, now does it?"

"It kinda does. It's more how you think than where you live."

"Funny you should mention where I live, 'cause I told the fire chief this mornin' you want us to fail so you can get our property."

Earl's eyes narrowed. "Like that's some big secret? I told you directly we want your property. No mystery there." He held her glare. "But I don't like what you're implyin'."

"What if I implied that you're interferin' with our irrigation rights?"

Earl crossed his arms. "As someone who draws water from the same river as you, I have every right to report any infraction of water use to the river authority. That is completely ethical, unlike pullin' someone's intake out of the river and endangerin' the lives of their cattle."

"Ethical, my ass! Just 'cause you might be doin' what some damn fool lawyer says is legal doesn't make it ethical. You said you'd squeeze us, and here you are doin' exactly that."

"Squeezin' you a bit is one thing," Earl said, "but accusin' your neighbor of somethin' as low-down as arson is altogether different. I should ask you if that buildin' was insured. Maybe you were takin' a loss on your little mushroom business and wanted to collect a nice fat insurance claim on it."

"That's ridiculous. We were makin' a decent profit with that operation."

"Right. Make sure your statement of accounts and insurance policy are ready when the fire marshal stops by, 'cause he's gonna ask you some pretty tough questions. Now, if you'll excuse us, we'll be gettin' back to our Sunday mornin'."

"Mr. Kidwell, I don't think you—"

He slammed the door before she could finish.

She walked back across the road, trying to convince herself she'd done the right thing. She kicked off her shoes covered with mud and ash and marched into the kitchen, where Dave, Kevin, and Elena were deep in conversation. They all stopped talking and stared at her.

"How did our favorite neighborhood diplomat do with the Kidwells?" Kevin asked. "Did they confess? Did they b-break down in tears and say they were sorry?"

Jess silently poured herself a glass of orange juice. She didn't have to respond to his sarcasm.

Dave crossed his arms. "Seriously, Jess, tell us what happened."

"They didn't take it so well."

"They didn't take *what* so well?"

"Me talkin' about the fire."

Her stepfather shook his head. "Talkin' about it or accusin' 'em of startin' it?"

She sipped her orange juice and looked at him over the top of her glass. "They got overly defensive."

"That's so weird," Kevin said. "I can't imagine someone b-becomin' defensive just 'cause you accuse 'em of second-degree arson on their neighbor's property."

Elena watched silently, arms folded, her face grim.

"I didn't exactly accuse them," Jess said. "Besides, someone had to do somethin'."

"Actually, Jess," Dave said, "no one had to do anythin'." She opened her mouth to speak, but he held up his hand. "What you do affects us all, and unless there's been a change we don't know about, we have a partnership here, and Elena is our business manager. Somethin' like what you just did should never happen without agreement from all of us."

"It felt like the right thing to do."

Elena stared out the window and shook her head. "Honestly, I don't give a damn what it felt like. You can't just jump to conclusions like that about people." She turned to face Jess. "And if you make that jump, you definitely can't go making wild accusations. You don't know the Kidwells started the fire."

"Who else—"

"We. Don't. Know," Elena said, emphasizing each word with a rap of her knuckles on the tabletop. All three Atwoods looked at her with surprise. They rarely saw Elena angry.

Jess felt flustered. "I was just—"

"You just made a bad situation worse. As Dave said, we all need to agree on these things." Elena nodded toward the river. "For all we know, it could have been those people out back. Whatever they're doing, it's not landscaping. Yet I didn't see you going over and yelling at *them* this morning." She raised her eyebrows. "Maybe 'cause they're scarier than the Kidwells?"

"I wasn't exactly yellin' at 'em."

"Sure you weren't." Elena stood and glared at her. "If anybody needs anything, you know how to reach me," she said, walking out the door.

Jess stared after her, open-mouthed.

"What I want you to ask yourself," Dave said, "is whether goin' over to the Kidwells was the right thing to do or just an angry thing to do."

"I thought that—"

"Give it a rest, Jess, and think about what I just asked." He paused. "While you're at it, consider whether you want to continue our partnership, 'cause I'm not willin' to go on like this."

CHAPTER FORTY-TWO

Wears Valley, Tennessee
September 1965

The night after her picnic with Deputy Stevens, Anna Mae dreamt of a baby girl floating in the air. The baby laughed and said, "I see like you," which made no sense since babies neither talk nor float in the air. Anna Mae felt frustrated after the same dream woke her three nights in a row. If it was a vision, there should have been a clear sense of order so she'd know what to do. But as Rudy had told her repeatedly, sometimes dreams were just dreams. So why did that one keep coming back?

Over the next couple of weeks, she visited the sheriff's office more often. When Keene's patrol car was there, she'd go right on past. She walked there one day after preparing a picnic lunch with spicy black bean pate, lettuce, and tomato sandwiches. The sheriff's car was out front, so she kept going to the pay phone in front of the Rexall drugstore, grateful that she'd thought to bring a dime for such a contingency. Luckily, Deputy Stevens answered the phone. Anna Mae reported an out-of-control picnic in Little Bear Park that urgently required his attention.

"Okay, ma'am," Stevens said, apparently trying to sound bored. "I'll check that out right away."

Ten minutes later, he met her in the park, where Anna Mae already had the picnic blanket laid out for them. She thought her sandwiches were some of the best she'd ever made, but the company of Deputy Stevens and the way things had warmed up between them was what she most enjoyed. Stevens was kind to her in ways she'd never experienced. It had something to do with his tone of voice and glances that said more than words. When they finished eating, he winked and told her he had to get back before Sheriff Keene became suspicious. He shook her hand as he said it, but it wasn't really a handshake. It was more of a hand *holding*—gentle, caring, and affectionate. It thrilled Anna Mae to her core, giving her hope that his engagement to Peggy June would soon be ancient history.

* * *

That night, the dream with the floating baby girl was back, and like before, she laughed and said, "I see like you." The difference this time was how much the baby looked like Deputy Stevens. That was understandable, considering their connection at the picnic that afternoon. The best thing about the dream was how much peace and comfort it gave her.

As she did her chores the next day, she tried to figure out what the dream meant. She had just finished wiping down the kitchen counter when she had a flash of insight: What if she was supposed to have a baby with Deputy Stevens? Every time that thought popped up, she felt warm and happy. Perhaps the dream was more than just a dream.

The following morning, however, she scolded herself for her immature fantasies and for letting herself think the dream could have been a vision. She was falling for Stevens and allowing her imagination to carry her away—which was stupid because he was engaged to Peggy June. Just because they'd had a few lunches together didn't mean they'd have a baby and a life together.

The fifth time the dream woke her was in the early-morning hours the next day, and she knew without a doubt what it meant. The only question was whether she dared to go through with what it was guiding her to do.

* * *

Anna Mae sat beside the kitchen phone, thinking about order. Her father was out of town on a freight run to Colorado Springs. Earlier that afternoon, her mother had called to say she was going to see *The Sound of Music* with her friend Betty from work and have supper with her afterward. She'd probably forgotten that she'd said she was going to see that movie two weeks before or that her friend from work had changed names again. It was a bit after four in the afternoon, and Anna Mae was confident she'd have the house to herself until early morning.

For the third time in forty-five minutes, she got up, walked to the kitchen, and looked at the clock. Almost four-thirty. That cranky old sheriff probably would have gone home already, leaving Deputy Stevens on his own. She went back to the bathroom mirror and checked her makeup. It wasn't bad for the first time, considering she'd figured it out herself.

She stood next to the kitchen phone and fiddled with the belt on her mother's pink and white silk kimono. She needed to act while everything was still in order.

With a shaking hand, she dialed the number.

"Wears Valley Sheriff's Department, Stevens here."

"Deputy Stevens, I . . ." She willed the words to come, but they wouldn't cooperate.

"Anna Mae, is everythin' all right?"

It would be easy to make an excuse for why she called. Or she could stick with the plan. "I'm scared," she finally said. That much was true.

"Why, what's the matter?"

She hesitated. "I'd just gotten out of the shower and was gettin' dressed when I heard a noise outside the window. When I went over to look, I saw a man runnin' into the woods. I think he might have seen me naked."

"Can you describe him for me?"

"I only caught a glimpse of him, but he wore a white T-shirt and blue jeans."

"How tall?"

Anna Mae's heart pounded. She'd just crossed a serious line. "Hard to tell. I think he was around your height or taller."

"Hair color?"

"Black, I think. Or maybe dark brown."

"Anythin' else you can tell me?"

"I didn't get a very good look at him." She had a sudden inspiration. "I think it might have been that Daley fellow with the mop-top haircut."

Stevens rang the doorbell less than five minutes later. Her heart still beating hard, she opened the door and noted his surprise at the kimono.

His eyes flicked downward for a moment before returning to her face. "Wait here while I check around back."

Anna Mae ran to her window and watched him from there. When she saw him coming around toward the front, she met him again at the door.

With his eyes fixed on hers—no downward glance this time—he spoke slowly and deliberately. "I didn't see signs of anyone out there, Miss Cole. I reckon you're probably safe, but call again if you see or hear anythin'." He pursed his lips. "When do your parents get home?"

"Miss Cole? That sounds so formal. It's Anna Mae to you, Mr. Deputy Sheriff, who goes by Paul when he's not on duty. Papa's on an out-of-towner, and Mama's out for the evenin' with . . . one of her lady friends."

He looked like a deer in the headlights, then quickly composed himself. "If you like, you can come down and wait with me at the station 'til your mama gets home. But you'd better get properly dressed first."

"Oh, this," she gestured down at the kimono. "I didn't want to finish dressin' with that Peepin' Tom around." She stepped back and opened the door wider. "If you'll come inside, I'll show you the window he was lookin' in."

Stevens glanced behind her. "I'm not sure that would be necessary, Miss Anna Mae."

Was it her imagination, or did he want her? "Oh, please," she said, hand to her heart, "I'd feel *so* much safer if you would."

He paused. "Okay, let's have a look."

She showed him the window in her bedroom with a view of the backyard. He spent a minute looking through it, and when he turned around, Anna Mae had her kimono unbelted and open. This time, Stevens' eyes did more than just a quick downward glance. He raised both hands, palms facing her. "Now, Anna Mae, this is not—"

"You know I've been sweet on you for the longest time, Deputy Stevens."

"I appreciate that, but I'm on duty and . . ."

"You're engaged, I know. But sometimes, when you want somethin' so bad, you just gotta have it." She slipped the kimono off her shoulders and let it fall to the floor, watching him take in her full nakedness, his breathing deeper and faster. What surprised her was that for her first time being fully naked in front of a man, she felt a warmth over her entire body instead of the shame she'd expected.

"Anna Mae . . . there wasn't any Peepin' Tom, was there?"

She shook her head. "But this is a no-strings-attached offer, Deputy Stevens. I promise to never bother you again or tell a soul about this. Cross my heart."

"But why?" he asked. "A young woman as beautiful as you could have your pick of anyone you want."

"Thank you." She drew a breath, deep and slow. "Well, you are my pick." There was no need to tell him it was in keeping with the order of things she'd seen in her vision.

"Um, I don't have a condom."

She reached under her pillow and pulled out a small foil packet, feeling his eyes on her the whole time. She held it up and smiled. "Good thing Papa keeps a supply of these around."

He stared at it. "Anna Mae . . ."

Placing the condom on her nightstand, she sat on the edge of the bed, hoping he wouldn't notice the pinholes in the foil, and smiled at him. "Time to do your civic duty, Mr. Deputy Sheriff."

* * *

Lying with Paul Stevens after making love was just as it had been in the vision she'd mistakenly thought was about Andy. Everything she'd wanted. Everything Andy was not.

She turned toward him and placed her hand on his bicep. "Thanks for this."

"You're thankin' *me*?"

"Of course. What kind of girl would I be if I didn't show a little gratitude?"

He gently brushed the hair out of her eyes. "You're special, Anna Mae."

Suddenly flooded by emotion, she turned away, unsure of what would come next. What was the correct order of things? What about his engagement? "Thanks," was all she could manage.

"Did I . . ."

Anna Mae swung her feet off the bed and stretched, hoping it would hide her nervousness. "That was wonderful," she said as she pulled the kimono back on. "Was it good for you?"

"Of course."

Yet she heard the concern in his voice. The pinholes in the condom must have done their trick and caused it to break. He was probably too embarrassed to mention it, or maybe he was already regretting their tryst. "Don't worry, I'm fine," she said with more conviction than she felt.

"I wasn't worried," he said, but she knew it was a lie.

* * *

Dear Diary,

Months ago, Rudy asked if I knew what it meant to be in love. I didn't then, but I do now. You hear how incredible love is, with people talking and singing about it all the time, but it's something words can't describe. I imagine it's what heaven feels like.

I'm hopeful about Deputy Stevens and our future. Just thinking about him, I couldn't sleep last night. I pretended he was in bed with me. I even took off my night slip, stuffed it under my pillow, and lay naked under my covers for the longest time. I touched myself after a while, then fell right to sleep. Part of me feels a bit naughty but in a good way.

I know I should be careful. I thought things were right with Andy when they weren't. But Deputy Stevens wants what's good for me, and I never had that feeling with Andy.

Will he break off the engagement to Peggy June? How could he not if he feels the way I do?

Is all this in order? I don't know, but it feels way too good to be anything but right.

I may have finally figured out where my dreams about falling were coming from. A few days ago, I went to the library and felt inspired to read a book called Bartlett's Familiar Quotations. On the first page I opened to, I learned that Confucius said, "The greatest glory in living lies not in never falling but in rising every time we fall." What are the chances that I would open the book directly to that? Those dreams of me falling were probably telling me that sometimes in life, you fall, but you just have to get up again, dust yourself off, and keep going. Maybe Rudy is right, and I read too much into what I think are visions.

Or maybe I'm just losing my mind, and the visions are only hallucinations like Dr. Ferguson said.

Chapter Forty-Three

Center Point, Texas
Present Day

Carl sat at the kitchen table with his arms crossed and glared at his brother when he walked in.

"What?" Johnny asked.

Carl thrust a wrinkled piece of yellow paper at him. "The fire marshal left a note on the gate. He wants to talk to us again."

"So?"

"So this guy is on our case. Setting that fire was a bad fucking idea."

Johnny shrugged. "Seemed like a good idea at the time."

"Anything can seem like a good idea if you don't think it through." Carl gestured at the note. "What are we supposed to do now?"

"Just ignore him." Johnny crumpled the paper and tossed it in the trash.

"That's stupid. If we ignore him, he'll be even more suspicious."

"We talked to him once, and there was no problem. He doesn't suspect us."

Carl rubbed his temples. "But he *does*, or he wouldn't have left the note. Besides, your plan didn't work. The organic farmers are still there."

"Give 'em time." Johnny smiled. "And maybe another nudge in the right place."

"No way. Have you not heard a word I said? We have to keep a low profile, especially now." He narrowed his eyes. "Or did you forget who we have in the holding rooms?"

"Of course not. But those are soundproof, remember? Besides, they'd need a search warrant to come on our property, which they can't get without a good reason."

"What if they do that? Or what if they invent a reason? Maybe we should seriously think about ditching."

"Quit being such an old woman, will you?"

"Quit being such an asshole," Carl snarled as he left the room.

* * *

Jess had a few errands to run in town one afternoon the following week. She dropped her tailgate and whistled for Wallaby. When he didn't turn up, she wondered if he was over terrorizing the Kidwells' cattle again. She hated the idea of tying him up or installing one of those invisible dog fences. As obnoxious as Earl Kidwell was, though, she had to give the Devil his due and keep her dog away from his cattle and chickens.

Jess checked her watch. She was supposed to already be at the bank to discuss their credit options. Wallaby would eventually return, and if Earl Kidwell complained again, she'd sincerely apologize.

Once at the bank, it didn't take her long to find out their credit was further extended than Central Texas State Bank wanted it to be. They even made some threats about demanding additional payment. It was the same tired story she'd heard several times before.

On the way home, Jess wondered if the day could be any worse. Then she arrived and saw Earl Kidwell's big red Dodge pickup in the driveway. Her thoughts immediately went to Wallaby. She'd have to keep him on their property no matter what.

Both Kidwells were talking with Dave at their kitchen table, though Travis looked like he didn't want to be there.

"We're here to make you a serious offer," Earl said to Jess. "We'll give you $150,000 cash for your land and another hundred and fifty grand for your house, outbuildin's, and equipment."

"You call that a serious offer? How *dare* you! As I've told you before, our farm is not for sale, though it'd be at least three times that if it was." She glared at them and noted that Travis looked away. At least his daddy had the guts to look her in the eye.

Earl clicked his tongue. "It may not be for sale today, but it will be soon." He stood, and Travis followed suit. "You get to decide whether you sell it for a reasonable price, or your bank will auction it off on the courthouse steps. Either way, I'll be the one to buy it. Frankly, buyin' it at the courthouse would get me a much better deal. I just thought I'd be fair."

"Like that's fair? Your little offer isn't even close to market value."

"Honey, market value is what people are willin' to pay. I don't see folks linin' up to buy your property."

"'Cause it's not for sale—and never will be."

"Oh, I beg to differ with you on that. Y'all bought yourselves some breathin' room sellin' that piece by the river, but your time's about to run out. It's too bad about your fire, but you need to face reality, sweetheart."

"I'm not your sweetheart. *You* need to face reality and get your fat white chauvinistic ass out of our house." Travis still wasn't meeting her gaze. "*Both* of you!"

Earl Kidwell sneered and shook his finger at her. "Such language! Y'all think about our offer, but you'd better decide before it's too late. The clock is tickin'." He tipped his hat and went out the front door, his son following behind.

* * *

Jess yawned and rubbed her forehead as she reviewed their accounts the following day. Wallaby still hadn't returned, and she didn't sleep well without him in her room. He brought her a certain comfort that was hard to put into words. Even though he didn't wander often, she was always worried about his safety. Earl Kidwell might have made good on his threat to call animal control, though when she'd dialed the pound at around three in the afternoon, she only got a recorded message telling her to call back during business hours. What the hell kind of hours did they keep, anyway?

Jess also worried about the accounts. As much as she wanted Earl to be wrong, the numbers agreed with him. If something didn't change, they might lose the farm. Their mushroom operation had burned to the ground five weeks earlier. While the insurance company had implied they were planning to cover the loss, they still hadn't done so, citing the ongoing arson investigation. It was frustrating because they desperately needed that payout to rebuild the mushroom facility and collect the profits that would come from it. They even consulted with Victor Carson, who told them that in Texas, insurance companies had the right to withhold a claim if there was an ongoing investigation and "sufficient" evidence of foul play.

But Earl's so-called fair price? Three hundred thousand dollars was way too low. The county tax assessors had valued their property at $517,400, which didn't even consider the value of the business. Until their mushroom operation burned to the ground, they'd had a productive and profitable farm. Once the insurance company paid up, they'd rebuild, and the mushrooms would make them money again. The challenge was for them to get to that point without collapsing financially.

Earl Kidwell and his talk about fairness galled her to no end, especially coming from a man who caused them as much trouble as he could. She felt bad about the fat white chauvinistic ass comment, though. That was a bit over the top.

"I'm busy," Jess called out in response to an urgent knock.

Kevin opened the door anyway.

Jess groaned and turned toward him. "Did you not—what's wrong?"

He shook his head, tears running down his face.

"Kevin, you're scarin' me."

His chin quivered. "It's Wallaby."

Jess was on her feet in half a second, heart in her throat. "What's wrong with him?"

"Well . . ."

"Come on, buddy, out with it."

"I'm so sorry."

"You're sorry about *what*?"

"He's dead."

Jess felt as though someone had punched her in the gut. "Rattlesnake?"

"I don't know. I found him out b-by the garage. I didn't see any marks on him, b-but with his thick fur, that would b-be easy to miss."

"We have to take him to the vet."

"Jess, he's really and truly gone."

"You think I don't know that?" she snapped. "I want to get him an autopsy."

"I think the vet would call it a necropsy."

"Whatever. We need it."

Kevin thought for a moment. "You know, those are pretty expensive."

She hesitated, thinking about the dire financial straits they were in. "I know, but this is important."

"Of course it is, b-but . . . well, you know our financial situation b-better than anyone."

She looked at him with moist eyes. "You're right," she said softly, "but I need this. Please."

He swallowed hard. "Okay. Let's do it."

* * *

Dave and Kevin sat next to Jess on the front bench seat of the pickup, with Wallaby in the back. Every time they hit a bump in the road, her eyes would flick to the rearview mirror, where she could see the stiff body of her beloved dog, random tufts of fur blowing in the wind. The lump in her throat increased in size until it felt like it might choke her. Not a word was spoken all the way to the Center Point Veterinary Clinic.

It took the vet nearly an hour before she came out to give them the news.

"He ingested a good quantity of bromethalin," she said, "which is a common ingredient in rat poison."

Dave shook his head. "We've always been careful when baitin' our traps."

The veterinarian nodded. "I understand, but the Australian shepherd is one of the smartest breeds out there. It's amazin' what they're able to learn on their own, though they're not the only dogs that figure out how to get into baited traps." She smiled ruefully. "We have cremation facilities on site. I'm sorry for your loss. People refer to our companion animals as pets, but they're much more than that."

Jess headed for the door. "If you guys are okay to settle up, I'm gonna wait in the truck."

"How much do we owe you?" Dave asked.

"Let me do up the invoice." She walked around the counter to her computer station, where she began punching in numbers. "At least he had a good last supper."

"What do you mean?" Kevin asked.

She smiled. "Not everyone gets a steak dinner for their last meal."

Dave glanced at Kevin, then bolted for the exit. "*Jess!*" he called from the door.

She walked in with red eyes and wet streaks down her cheeks.

"Let me guess," said the vet. "You didn't feed him any steak, did you?"

"Oh my God," Jess said.

"No," Kevin replied. "He's b-been a vegetarian since he was a puppy. Except for the occasional critter he'd catch."

The vet frowned and pushed her desk phone toward them. "Y'all need to call the sheriff."

CHAPTER FORTY-FOUR

Wears Valley, Tennessee
October 1965

Paul Stevens sat in his recliner reading the paper, his sister Marty's cat purring loudly on his lap. It had been a good day, mainly because Sheriff Keene was off attending a missing persons task force in Gatlinburg led by the Tennessee Bureau of Investigation.

"Your sweetheart called two more times this afternoon," Marty said, walking out of the kitchen.

His first thought went to Anna Mae before realizing his sister was talking about Peggy June. Of course. "Uh-huh," responded Stevens.

She waved a cooking spoon at him. "Is the phone at the station broken?"

"No, but we have an agreement that she doesn't call me there." He glanced at his sister. "I wouldn't want to get fired."

"Sheriff Keene wouldn't fire you if you spray-painted his patrol car pink. He knows what a good deputy you are."

Stevens turned a page. "Don't be too sure about that, Marty. He often reminds me how expendable I am."

"Of course he does, but only 'cause he's a frustrated and grumpy old bachelor. He's not stupid, though, and knows he needs you. Are you breakin' things off with Peggy June?"

He lowered his paper. "Whatever gave you that idea?"

"What gave me that idea is that I'm now tellin' you for the second day in a row she's been callin' you, and I don't see you jumpin' up to call her back."

Deputy Stevens felt a pang of guilt. Marty was right. He was neglecting his fiancée. Even though he and Anna Mae had only made love once, they'd had a few intimate lunches. He was always glad to see her when she'd stop by the station for a quick chat or to drop off some sweet tea, which she'd only do when Sheriff Keene wasn't in.

"I'll call her. I just—"

"If you're gonna break things off with her, then do it now. You know what Goethe said."

"Remind me."

"That action has magic, grace, and power in it."

"I'm actin'." He held up the newspaper and grinned. "I'm readin' the paper. Tryin' to, at least. And it's good to know your fancy college education hasn't completely gone to waste."

"Joke all you want, but we both know you're just puttin' off the inevitable."

"I'm—"

"Just call her."

"I will." He'd do it tomorrow. Why spoil a perfect day?

Anna Mae had stopped by the office at lunchtime with her picnic basket, and they'd enjoyed their meal there. It felt good to be around her.

The doorbell rang, and Stevens was surprised to see his fiancée standing on the front porch.

"Peggy June, what—"

"Did you not get my messages?" she asked bitterly, her eyes moist and red.

"I did, but I was just . . ." He opened the door wider. "Come on in and tell me what's wrong."

She sniffed and shook her head. "This won't take long. I just need to say . . ." Fresh tears welled in her eyes, and she gave him a sad smile.

Stevens felt terrible. He should have returned her calls. That was no way to treat anyone, especially his fiancée. "Peggy June," he said softly, "please come inside and sit down." Marty was right. He had to end this. It probably wasn't a good time, but there never would be a good time. Anna Mae was his future, and Peggy June wouldn't take that well no matter when he told her.

She shook her head again. "No. I just need to tell you . . ."

He waited for her to continue. When she didn't speak, he stepped out on the porch and moved to hug her, but she held up a hand to stop him.

Chin quivering, she closed her eyes. "I'm pregnant."

* * *

After a long, sleepless night, Stevens sat at his desk thinking about his next move. What he wanted and what he knew he should do were two different things. Keene was away until mid-afternoon, so the timing was right. He sighed and dialed Anna Mae's number.

She answered on the second ring and sounded happy that he'd called.

"Wonderin' if I could see you this mornin', Anna Mae."

"Of course. I was plannin' to bring lunch by." She paused. "Or you could come by here and make sure my house is safe. Papa's on a long-distance run to El Paso, and Mama is at work, so we'd have the place to ourselves." She giggled. "Not that we need the whole house."

"Um . . . I have to be on duty here at the station, and lunch isn't a good idea 'cause Sheriff Keene might get back early."

"So, what would you like me to do, Mr. Deputy? Ask, and ye shall receive."

She wasn't making it easy for him to say what had to be said. "Do you think you could just come on down here?"

"What's wrong?" she asked, finally picking up on his tone.

"Nothin's wrong," he lied. "I just need to talk to you."

"We're talkin' now, ain't we?"

"We need to talk in person."

She paused. "Oh. You mean *that* kind of talk."

"Anna Mae, I think it'd be best if—"

"Wait," she said with a quaver in her voice. "Don't you think we should give this a chance? Give *us* a chance?"

Stevens rubbed his forehead. Anna Mae would find out about Peggy June's pregnancy soon enough, as would everyone else in town, but he wasn't ready to tell her. One thing at a time. "Please, can you just come down here? This is important."

"I'll bet it is," she said and hung up on him.

* * *

On the walk to town, Anna Mae asked herself why she was doing his bidding. After all, it was pretty clear from the phone conversation he was fixing to end it with her before they'd really even started. How had she not seen that coming?

Stevens stood when she came in. "Good mornin', Anna Mae."

"Is it?"

He looked miserable, though he'd seemed so happy to be with her the day before.

"I don't know the best way to say this . . ."

"But you don't want to see me anymore."

"It's not that. I still want to be friends, but—"

"You want to be *friends*?" Something between a laugh and a sob escaped her throat. "I can tell you right now that ain't gonna happen."

"It's just that I'm engaged to Peggy June and—"

"You also slept with her, didn't you?"

His silence answered her question.

Of course. How could she have been so stupid? "When?"

"Before . . . us."

"And since? I mean, it's ultimately none of my bidness, and you don't have to tell me."

He looked away. "No, not since. It's just that . . ."

"It's just that you slept with two different girls but only made a promise to one." She blinked back tears. "Did I get that right?"

He nodded glumly.

She turned to leave, paused with her hand on the doorknob, and briefly considered telling him she was pregnant. But what would be the point? Even if he chose her out of a sense of duty or obligation, did she really want to share a life with a man who'd rather be with someone else? After a few tense moments, she left without another word.

The walk home seemed to take forever, and she was grateful that no one drove past to see her cry. The first thing she did when she arrived was to go through her mother's writing desk and take out a pen and a piece of fancy stationery with a wavy pink line around the edge. She sat down to write a quick note and didn't care that her tears dripped on the paper.

She folded it in half, set it on the kitchen table, then went to her room to get the bus coupon and pack her things.

* * *

It took Anna Mae more than half an hour to walk to the bus station, her small suitcase heavy by the time she arrived. The sign in the ticket window said it opened at 6:45, still several hours away. She could've called first, but what difference would that have made?

She sat on a hard wooden bench with the names and initials of professed loves carved into it and frowned at the messages, wondering if Troy still loved Jodie. Or did that change once he got what he wanted? She acutely felt the stress and emotional turmoil of the day. Her eyelids heavy, she curled up on the bench and fell asleep, only to abruptly wake from a terrifying dream.

In the dim light of the dream, the sight of a man walking through the woods with a young girl filled her with dread.

It was just after six by the station clock. She could call the sheriff's office from the phone booth. But what would she say? That she dreamt she saw someone walking through the woods with a teenage girl? She wouldn't even be able to tell them when, where, or who—only that the dream scared her.

If Deputy Stevens answered, he might even think she was doing it to get back at him. No, she had nothing useful to tell them. Besides, Wears Valley would soon be in her past.

The ticket window finally opened at 6:50, and Anna Mae handed the agent her coupon. "One way to Kerrville, Texas, please. What time does the bus leave?"

He opened his timetable and sighed dramatically, as though Anna Mae should have already known that. "Bus leaves at nine p.m. and arrives in Kerrville at six-thirty in the mornin.'"

"Well, that's good," she said. "I thought it would take longer than that."

The ticket agent looked over the top of his glasses at her. "Honey, that's six-thirty in the mornin', day after tomorrow. There are a lot of stops, and you'll have to change buses twice."

"Oh."

"That'll be two dollars and eighty-three cents."

Anna Mae's mouth fell open. "I thought this coupon would cover the trip."

"It did at the time it was bought, miss," the clerk said, "but it was purchased when prices were lower. That's inflation for ya. You're only payin' the difference."

"I don't have that much on me," she said, determined not to cry.

"Sorry, nothin' I can do about that. Is there someone you can call?"

"No, the only person I could call is in Texas, and—" She froze as the realization hit that her parents must have read her note already. Her father would be madder than a cat in a sack and probably out looking for her. She shivered at the thought of what he'd do if he found her.

"May I have that back, please?" she asked, reaching for the coupon.

She set her suitcase down next to the station's pay phone, placed a quick call to directory information, then dropped in a dime and dialed the number.

CHAPTER FORTY-FIVE

J ess lay in bed staring at the ceiling, feeling the previous day's loss of Wallaby with the help of some Napa Valley Merlot. Her grief had become like a living thing, its cold hands squeezing her throat so hard she could barely breathe. The latest news from the bank was also bad. They told her additional loans of any kind were out of the question and said that the foreclosure process was already irrevocably in motion. Everything they had worked so hard for over the years was going down the toilet. She spilled wine on her pillow more than once, but it didn't matter. Nothing mattered anymore.

The deputy who showed up the day before at the veterinary clinic had asked if they suspected anyone. Jess opened her mouth to speak, but Dave silenced her with a quick gesture. "We can't imagine who could've done somethin' like this," he said, keeping a warning gaze fixed on Jess. He shook his head slightly to make sure she got the message.

Of course she got the message. But why not tell the deputy Earl Kidwell had threatened their dog and was probably still upset about her fat white chauvinistic ass comment. Earl and his son were the only ones with possible motives—and the means. As ranchers who probably had fourteen freezers full of steak, that's what they had most likely given Wallaby. Nothing else made sense.

Dark thoughts swirled through her mind as she started on her second bottle of wine. By nightfall, she was well and truly drunk, browsing aimlessly on YouTube.

After watching "Funniest Fails of the Year," she searched "World's Smartest Dogs" until she saw an Australian shepherd that looked way too much like Wallaby, balancing a dog biscuit on its nose. That one brought tears to her eyes. She searched "Jess Atwood paintball," and found a video clip where she dispatched four opponents in the Blitz Paintball Arena within about fifteen seconds. A wicked idea came to her the second time through the clip.

She checked the hallway first. Kevin was in his room with the door closed, most likely playing on his Xbox, while Dave watched *Game of Thrones* down in the family room. The TV's sound was loud enough to cover any noise she might make. That was good because she stumbled halfway to the landing while tiptoeing down the stairs.

After leaving through the back door, she gathered her paintball equipment from the shed behind the house and lugged it to the pickup.

Ignoring the voice in her head telling her to give it up and go back to her room, she chose the glow-in-the-dark fluorescent pink pellets—her signature color. Getting the hopper on her high-performance Tippmann gun filled up took multiple tries. Damn thing wouldn't hold still, and she was getting more pellets on the driveway than in the gun. Choking back grief over the loss of her beloved dog, she finally finished loading and climbed into the pickup truck, setting the paintball gun on her lap. She waited another couple of minutes, thinking about her plan.

Normally, she wouldn't consider driving while under the influence, and the memory of her mother dying at the hands of a drunk driver gave her pause. But they were out in the middle of nowhere, the roads were virtually empty, and she wasn't going far. Besides, at that moment she just didn't care about anything. She was going to do this for Wallaby. Starting the truck, she threw it into drive and pulled onto the road, clipping their mailbox on the way out.

She drove slowly, pointed the barrel out the open window toward the

Kidwells' house, and held the trigger down, watching the colorful pellets arc through the air. At first, they fell short. She aimed higher and watched as the stream of paint-filled balls intersected with the house, some hitting the siding, some splattering against the windows, and several exploding on the roof with satisfying little pops. Mission accomplished, she floored it to Logan's Bend, where she pulled off the road and backed in behind trees and bushes until she was out of sight.

She shut down the engine, turned off her headlights, and heard the distant roar of Travis's GTO.

She hopped out of her truck and stumbled through the underbrush, approaching the road just as a pair of headlights turned out of the Kidwells' driveway and headed in her direction. She ducked behind the bushes and watched the rapidly approaching car.

He had to be doing well over a hundred miles per hour and didn't seem to be slowing for the curve. What if he went off the road, right into her? She bolted back toward the truck but hadn't taken more than three strides before she tripped and fell face-first, scraping her elbow and getting a mouthful of dirt. She was still picking herself up and spitting out soil when he thundered past.

Travis pulled a U-turn fifty yards beyond the bend. Jess ran the rest of the way back to her truck and squatted down beside it. She heard the sound of his car heading back in her direction and wondered if he'd already seen her.

The fear of getting caught weighed heavily on her mind. How embarrassing would that be? Slowed to walking speed, the GTO came closer but eventually passed by. Once out of the bend, Travis floored it and headed back toward home.

Jess tried to ignore the sinking feeling in her stomach. The Kidwells deserved it . . . or did they? What if someone else had poisoned Wallaby? As much as she hated Earl Kidwell, in hindsight, she questioned whether he'd be the kind of person who'd kill someone's dog, despite his threats.

She climbed back into her truck and turned on the radio to pass the time. After a few seconds, "Let It Be" started playing.

"Really?" she asked the radio. "Is that the song I get?" She slapped the steering wheel. "'Cause I didn't exactly let it be, did I?"

She opened her door and vomited outside the truck.

* * *

A half-hour later, Jess pulled up to her house and spent a minute listening to the clicking of the engine cooling before going inside.

Dave was waiting for her in the living room. "Travis came lookin' for you."

"What did he want?"

"Well, let's see. After handing me some pink paintball pellets he found on our driveway, he demanded to know where you were and why you'd paintballed their house." He raised an eyebrow at her. "He seemed upset, though I can't imagine why."

"What'd you tell him?"

"I told him I didn't know where you were."

She nodded. "That's what he needed to hear."

"You know, Jess, I've been sober for two hundred and thirty-two days."

"Well, congratulations." She glanced at her watch. "I'm goin' to bed now, and—"

"Don't bother tryin' to pretend, okay?"

"Huh?" She looked at him with what she hoped was a steady gaze.

"Not only do I know you've been drinkin'—"

"Is that a skill you picked up at your AA meetin's?"

Dave closed his eyes before answering. "No. That's a skill I picked up from bein' a drunk."

"Well, you *are* the expert. If the lecture's over, I'm goin' to bed."

"I'm sorry about Wallaby."

"Yeah, me too."

"But I reckon you may have jumped to conclusions about the Kidwells. Again."

Jess didn't respond, afraid that he was right.

"I know there were a few years when I wasn't always there for you and Kevin," he said.

"Really? I never noticed."

"You have every right to be mad about that."

"Ya think?"

"I do. And I will apologize until you don't want to hear it anymore. But I'm here for you now."

"Better late than never, right? If that's all . . ."

"That's not all," insisted Dave. "I'll not have you drivin' drunk."

"Oh? And how many times have you driven back from Clancy's three sheets to the wind?"

"Far too many. But you of all people should know about the potential consequences."

"Gee, Dave, thank you so much for dredgin' up that painful memory."

"It's a painful memory for all of us, and I'm done with tryin' not to feel it."

"Well, good for you. Fortunately, I'm fine, and I certainly don't need anyone tellin' me what to feel."

"Are you really fine?"

She rolled her eyes. "Dave, I—"

"No, hear me out, Jess. Paintballin' the Kidwells' house may have seemed like a great thing to do while under the influence of alcohol and anger, but it was plumb ugly. You need to think things out before you act."

"Think out what? We're done. When I was at the bank earlier, they told me the foreclosure process had already started." She stared at the ceiling. "I don't know if gettin' another loan would be a solution anyway. We're already chokin' on the payments we have."

"But we're still here, aren't we?"

"Yes, but—"

"But nothin'," Dave said. "It ain't over 'til it's over."

"Well, it *is* over. Today was the last straw."

"I understand what you're feelin' right now, but it's not like you to quit."

She started up the stairs. "You know what they say," she said, doing her best to keep her voice as steady as possible. "There's a first time for everythin'."

CHAPTER FORTY-SIX

Wears Valley, Tennessee
October 1965

Anna Mae breathed a sigh of relief when the Studebaker with faded green paint pulled into the bus station parking lot. Pastor Blaine greeted her warmly, then drove her to his house, thankfully without asking her a single question.

He showed her where she'd be staying. "This was Rebecca's room before she went off to college. Make yourself right at home."

"Thank you kindly. I don't plan on botherin' you for long."

He waved off her comment. "No bother at all. I get kinda lonesome these days. Jocelyn's been gone nearly ten years, and Rebecca was the only family I had left. I mean, she's still family, of course, but now that she's married and livin' up in Connecticut, I see little of her."

"That must be hard for you."

He smiled ruefully. "Some days it is. But at least I've got the congregation. Y'all are family to me." He cleared his throat. "Even though I haven't seen you in church for ages."

"I'm most grateful you consider us family."

"Of course. If there's somethin' I can do for you, just let me know. I've got some errands to run in the mornin', so if you need me to pick up anythin' for you, I'd be happy to."

"I don't suppose you're goin' anywhere near Main and Beauregard?" Anna Mae had decided to let Deputy Stevens know about her vision in person so he'd know what to be on the watch for. She'd also decided to tell him about her pregnancy and let him make a fully informed decision about who he would spend the rest of his life with.

"Oh sure, that'd be easy," Pastor Blaine said, "but the community center is closed for repairs right now."

"I didn't know that, but I need to visit the sheriff's office."

"Is everythin' all right?"

She felt her cheeks warming. "Of course. It's just that I helped them out some time back and thought I'd check in."

"Okay then. I'll be goin' in around ten o'clock if that works for you."

"That'd be fine, thank you."

"Don't forget to congratulate Deputy Stevens while you're there."

"Whatever for?"

He smiled. "Haven't you heard? For tyin' the knot next Sunday with Peggy June. About time, too. They've been engaged forever." He frowned at Anna Mae. "Honey, are you okay? You look pale."

"I'm okay," she fibbed. "I just need to lie down for a bit."

"That's fine," he said, speaking slowly. "Like I said, make yourself right at home."

* * *

The next morning, Anna Mae closed her eyes and tried to think of why she shouldn't call. In hindsight, her plan to go to the sheriff's office in person was silly, as was her hanging onto the irrational hope that Deputy Stevens might change his mind.

But things had become clearer, thanks to the vision returning of the man and girl. This time she saw them walking toward the barn she'd seen deep in the woods long before. The familiar sense of order was back with a feeling of great urgency. She had to pick up the phone and make the call.

The problem was that she didn't want to. What happened in Wears Valley was no longer her business, and she was going to catch the nine p.m.

Greyhound bus later that day. Pastor Blaine had been kind enough to give her the five dollars she requested without asking why. It would be enough to cover the ticket and get her some food on the long bus ride. That was all well and good.

The vision, however, wouldn't leave her alone. The pastor had made her a sumptuous breakfast, but she felt no hunger: only a hard knot in her stomach. What she'd foreseen kept replaying itself in her mind. It wasn't like her to not follow a vision and keep things in order.

Why hadn't she seen that Deputy Stevens and Peggy June were getting married so soon after Anna Mae had slept with him? She may have been wrong to lure him to her house and seduce him, but he could have refused her, knowing he was getting married within a few weeks. He wasn't much better than Andy, after all. Never had she felt so betrayed, not only by Stevens but by the visions themselves. How could she trust them anymore when they were so often wrong?

The world wouldn't end if she didn't pick up the phone.

Yet this vision disturbed her more than any she'd ever had. She couldn't see the face of the man in it, but he had a dark energy. The girl with him had an innocent glow but was in grave danger.

There was no way she *couldn't* call. Stevens answered the phone and sounded surprised to hear from her. Anna Mae felt the emotion in his voice. It seemed something was there, but obviously not enough to choose her over Peggy June.

She tersely explained what she'd foreseen about the girl in danger.

"Tell me where. I'll check it out immediately."

"I need to go with you, Deputy Stevens, and we have to hurry before it's too late." The thought that she might be putting their unborn baby in danger crossed her mind, but everything would be fine as long as things stayed in order. She knew it beyond a shadow of a doubt.

"Well . . ."

"Please."

"All right. Where are you?"

"Pastor Blaine's house."

"Be waitin' out front in ten minutes. And Anna Mae . . ."

"Yes?"

"You better not be leadin' me on a wild goose chase."

"I'm not. Cross my heart."

CHAPTER FORTY-SEVEN

Twenty days after the foreclosure notice arrived, Jess found Elena in the storage shed taking inventory of the non-GMO seed stock. "You know the farm is up for auction in a week, Elena."

"That's what I hear," she said without looking up from her work.

Jess handed her an envelope, which she folded in half and shoved into her back pocket.

"Aren't you gonna open it?"

"No, I trust you," she said, picking up a jar. "Somebody put these Italian kale seeds in the wrong place."

"Besides your regular check, there's pay for your built-up vacation time and all the days you never took off. We covered you through the end of the month, plus your extra days, and added eight weeks of severance. It's all there in the envelope."

"That's very generous, thanks."

"It's just a small token of how we feel about you." Jess sighed. "I guess I'll see you around."

Elena just nodded and kept sorting seeds.

"You know, we're good."

"I know."

"I mean, you don't have to work anymore."

All she got from Elena was another nod. She'd never been a woman of many words.

Jess walked back to the house, reflecting on how her life had been centered on their farm since she was five. As difficult as those twenty-five years had been at times, she found it hard to imagine living without the Heart of Texas farm. They were all starting over, but who could say what that meant? Dave had begun playing guitar again and was doing a few gigs here and there—while staying sober.

Kevin sat at the kitchen table watching a YouTube video on his iPad.

"Whatcha up to?" Jess asked.

"I'm learnin' how to design video games."

"Is that right? No farmin' for you today, huh?"

"No farmin' for anybody, really." He raised his eyebrows. "How does that sayin' go? Somethin' about when you get to the last page, you need to close the b-book?"

"Well, I never thought we'd come to that last page. I always thought instead of closin' the book, we'd just find a new chapter."

He gave her a weak smile. "Don't b-be gettin' deep on me, Jess. I might not be able to handle the shock."

"Right. Well, I'm gonna go take a nap, 'cause I can for a change."

But when she lay on her bed, her mind spun, thinking about the farm and how much work, focus, and energy they had invested in it over the years. Lately, though, it felt like trying to bail out a sinking ship.

"Sometimes your best may not be enough," Kat used to say, "but at least it's your best." Jess could give herself that much.

* * *

Outside Polk's Hardware, Jess stared absently at the big roll of bubble wrap she'd just tossed into the back of the pickup. The only thing left was to head home and pack.

She thought about where she could go for at least the tenth time that week. Austin and San Antonio had potential, but they weren't Center Point, and they weren't home. Jess didn't see how they could ever be.

Her heart fluttered when she noticed the late model SUV in their driveway. Agent Mallory was back! Then she noticed the Tennessee plates.

Walking in with the bubble wrap under her arm, she found Dave and Kevin sitting in the living room talking to an elderly white-haired man who looked vaguely familiar. The conversation abruptly halted, and the stranger rose to his feet, looking at her intently.

"Oh my God," he said.

"And a good day to you, too." She cocked her head to one side, trying to place him. "Have we met?"

The stranger shook his head. "I don't reckon so."

Dave nodded toward the older gentleman. "Jess, this is Paul Stevens, who knew Granny Mae back in Tennessee."

That caught her by surprise. "Really?"

Stevens stepped forward, extending his hand. "I must say, you remind me of your grandma."

Jess frowned and shook his hand. "Not that I'd know, 'cause we've never seen a single picture of her."

"Your resemblance to her is truly remarkable, especially your eyes."

"But . . . she was white."

He nodded slowly. "She was, but I see a lot of her in you." He scratched his head and sat back down. "I don't know of an easy way to tell y'all this, but . . ." He looked uncertainly from one Atwood to the next and took a deep breath. "Well . . ." he glanced around again at the expectant faces hanging on his every word. "I reckon I'm your grandpa."

Jess's mouth fell open. "You couldn't be!"

"Oh, I am. Katherine was my daughter."

"Then how come you weren't here long ago?" Jess asked. "Maybe you would've been around when we were growin' up. Or maybe at least you would've sent a card or somethin' once in a while for Christmas or on our birthdays."

"Come on now, Jess, you're bein' right hard on the man," Dave said.

"Right hard on him? This man who had nothin' to do with Mama's life or ours comes in here claimin' to be our grandpa, and you say I'm bein' hard on him?"

"That's exactly what I'm sayin'. Give him a chance to speak, will you? And show some respect for your elders."

Jess glared at Stevens, then her mouth fell open as she realized why he seemed so familiar. He looked like a much older, male version of her mother.

Stevens stood. "I reckoned this would probably be a shock for y'all." He handed Jess a diary with a locking cover, then retrieved a key from his pocket and gave that to her as well. "This diary belonged to Anna . . . your Granny Mae. She left it to me in her will, and—"

"Granny Mae left a will?"

"She did, in the hands of an attorney by the name of Pete Carson, here in Kerr County."

"We've worked with his son, Victor," Jess said.

Stevens nodded. "He was the one who contacted me. Anyway, there was no money or real property in the will, only instructions for Katherine's custody and well-bein' along with the transference of that diary."

"Why'd you take so long to say anythin'?" Jess asked.

Stevens hesitated, staring at the floor. "We lost my wife Peggy June about a month ago, and I only got the diary in my hands this past week. Anna Mae stated in the will that she wanted me to have it after Peggy June had passed away. There are only six entries, but they say a lot. I never knew your mama existed or where Anna Mae had gone until I read it. There's also a letter in there that she wrote to your great-uncle Rudy and his wife, Molly." He smiled sadly. "Your Granny Mae was an extraordinary person."

Jess stared at the words written one above the other down the front of the diary:

This
Too
Shall
Pass

Stevens pulled a folded piece of paper out of his front pocket and handed it to Kevin. "Here's my address, phone number, and email. If y'all want to call or email me, please feel free. And I'd love for you to visit any old time."

Dave stepped forward to shake Stevens' hand. "We appreciate you comin' all this way, Mr. Stevens. Can we offer you some supper?"

"Please, call me Paul. Thank you kindly, but I reckon this might not be the best time. Better to let things soak in, if you know what I mean. Besides, I need to head back to Wears Valley. I got a daughter to comfort and grandkids to be with." He noticed Jess's startled look and smiled. "Yeah, I got me three other grandkids, and each of them is special." He nodded to Jess and Kevin. "As I'm sure you both are. You've got an aunt by the name of Ellie Mae, who is the same age your mama would be . . ." His face clouded for a moment before he forced a smile and continued, ". . . and she'd love to meet you. I think you'd like her—she's quite a character."

"Ellie Mae's name sounds a lot like Anna Mae's," observed Jess.

"That it does." He glanced around the room. "Love your house," he said, smoothly changing the subject. "Might be the only one like it in all of Texas."

Dave smiled. "Yeah, Uncle Rudy built it like an old Tennessee farmhouse, and I reckon it was his only connection to where he was born and raised. He probably also did it to impress his sister."

"I wouldn't doubt that one bit. I barely knew Rudy Cole directly but know enough to believe he was always lookin' for ways to make other folks happy." He frowned. "I was sorry to hear he died so young. Folks back in Wears Valley say it had somethin' to do with him bein' poisoned by some of that Agent Orange stuff in Vietnam. I don't know if that's true, but either way, it's a tragedy, 'cause I tell ya, the world needs people like Rudy Cole to live long lives."

"Never met the man personally, but based on everythin' I heard from Kat, I'd have to agree with you," Dave said.

Jess cleared her throat. "I heard the Agent Orange story too, but Kat said he died of a broken heart three months after losin' Molly to cancer."

Stevens smiled sadly. "I believe that. Losin' the one you love can be . . . hard."

He glanced at his watch. "I'd best be goin'. I aim to hit Dallas before nightfall and drive the rest of the way home tomorrow." He nodded. "Good meetin' y'all. You got my contact information," he nodded at Kevin, "and I hope you'll use it."

CHAPTER FORTY-EIGHT

Wears Valley, Tennessee
October 1965

The silence in the patrol car felt thick as water. When Stevens asked how she was doing, Anna Mae replied that she was fine. Conversation over.

They parked where she showed him, and as they climbed out of the car, Stevens pointed at her shoes. "You leavin' them on?"

Surprised, Anna Mae hesitated. Deputy Stevens understood her better than anyone else, maybe even more than Rudy. Such a shame he'd chosen Peggy June. Without a word, she slipped off her shoes and socks and tossed them in the back of the car. The cool soil gave her a thrill, followed by an intense feeling of urgency. She started walking with only a quick backward glance at Stevens, who followed closely.

It took an hour of awkward silence to hike to the barn.

As they approached, she heard voices inside. One look at Stevens and she could see that he did, too. His lips pressed tightly together, he drew his revolver, motioning for Anna Mae to stay put. He approached the closed door and banged on it with the butt of his pistol. "*Sheriff's department! Come out with your hands up!*" He stepped to the side and waited, his gun ready.

A few seconds later, the heavy, weathered door slid open. A teenage girl came out with her hands in the air, eyes opened wide. Stevens nodded toward Anna Mae. "You go over and wait with her, honey. And you can put your hands down." Still off to the side, he banged on the wall next to the door. "You in there: *Get out here now!*"

A tall, clean-cut man with a goatee and a baseball cap came out smirking.

It took Stevens a second to recognize him without his Beatle haircut. "*You!*"

Phil Daley smiled. "We meet again, Deputy. How's the bottom rung over at your little hole-in-the-wall sheriff station?"

Anna Mae shook her head in disbelief. Daley was the man with the dark energy from her vision. Of course.

Stevens kept his gun trained on his adversary. "You are filth, Daley." He pointed at his chin. "Got a new act goin', do ya?"

"Aw, is that any way to greet an old friend?" He nodded toward Anna Mae. "How nice, you brought one of your girlfriends," he said, eyeing her up and down. "I declare, this one's pretty as a peach. Even though she seems hell-bent on runnin' me over every time we meet. Ain't you gonna properly introduce us?"

Stevens clenched his jaw and waved his gun toward the inside of the barn. "Is that your bag?"

"Sure is."

"Get it, and let's go. Just don't try anythin'." He turned his head slightly toward Anna Mae, keeping his eyes and gun fixed on Daley. "Will you two be okay? We won't be a minute."

"We'll be fine," Anna Mae said as Stevens followed Daley inside.

The girl was visibly shaking and had started to cry.

"Everythin's okay now," Anna Mae said to her. "Deputy Stevens is about to take that man into custody. Did he do anythin' to you?"

"Well," she said between sobs, "he told me to take my clothes off or he'd hurt me in ways I couldn't even imagine, but then the deputy banged on the door."

Anna Mae awkwardly patted the girl's shoulder. "There, there. Everythin' is gonna be fine." She was trying to think of something more comforting to say when the girl suddenly gave her a tight hug. Anna Mae went stiff and almost pulled away. Instead, she rested her arms gently on the girl's back and breathed deeply. She could do this. "What's your name, honey?"

"Susan," she said, letting go. "My friends call me Susie T since my last name's Twiller."

"Well, Susie T, that man in there is goin' to jail. Deputy Stevens is arrestin' him right now." She shot a worried glance toward the barn, where she could hear muffled voices. "Probably handcuffin' him this very moment."

Susie T also glanced at the barn. "Can we go? I need to call my mama."

"Of course. Soon as Deputy Stevens finishes arrestin' him, we're gonna—"

"*Drop the knife!*" Stevens' shout echoed inside the barn. "*NOW!*"

They heard a muffled reply.

"*Stop, or I'll shoot!*" the deputy yelled. Half a second later, a gunshot exploded in the barn, making both girls jump. Anna Mae ran inside to see Daley lying on his back, clasping his bleeding chest and soundlessly moving his mouth as if trying to say something.

Stevens holstered his gun and shook his head. "He shouldn't have rushed me with that knife."

Her eyes immediately went to the man's empty hands.

"He dropped it when I shot him," he said, as though reading her thoughts. "Wait outside, Anna Mae. You shouldn't be seein' this."

She nodded but kept staring.

"Anna Mae, did you not hear me?"

Finally, she turned away and joined Susie T outside.

* * *

Later that day, Sheriff Keene had a few questions for Anna Mae, including how to reach her. She truthfully told him she was staying with Pastor Blaine but left out the part that she'd be on the bus out of Wears Valley that evening and no one in all of Tennessee would know where she was going.

CHAPTER FORTY-NINE

"I told you my plan would work," Johnny boasted to his brother.

Carl felt a headache coming on. "Seriously? We've got less than $30,000 on hand. The property will go for many times that at auction. So, no, that plan isn't working."

"That's not my fault. I told you I'd get the organic fruitcakes to leave, and it's happening."

Carl looked at his brother incredulously. All that mattered to Johnny was being right. "They're leaving because they can't make the payments."

"And they can't make their payments because they can't sell the mushrooms. That was exactly what I'd planned, and it worked like a charm, capeesh?"

"Except now we don't have the cash to follow through."

"Only because Jorge told us we had to wait. "

"Without the money we need, we're not—"

Johnny slapped his hand on the table. "*Dammit*, Carl, do you hear yourself? I'm sick and tired of your negativity. I told you I'd take care of this. We just need to ask Jorge for an advance."

"But he always pays us in cash and gold. Do you think he'd just send it to our bank account by PayPal? Or maybe Venmo? No, we'd have to go down there to get it, which is impossible because he told us to wait. You know as well as I do that there are always consequences when someone doesn't do what he says. Besides, there's no way in hell he'll give us an advance. He only pays on delivery."

Johnny shook his head in disgust. "You are so negative."

"I'm so realistic."

"No, here's realistic: We've got almost two weeks before the auction. We can do this. We *have* to do this. It's our big opportunity."

"You think you can come up with $400,000 in cash in the next thirteen days?"

"I do! That's why I'm the visionary here. There are so many possibilities. Maybe Jorge will change his mind and let us deliver the girls." He shrugged. "Or maybe the farm will go for way less than $400,000."

"It might go for less, but not $30,000. Or, more specifically, $28,762, which is what we have on hand. And have you ever seen Jorge change his mind? Yet we've seen what he does to people who irritate him. Do you want to be one of those people?"

Johnny glared at his brother. "There you go, acting the part of an old lady again."

"And there you go, acting the part of an asshole again. When you come up with a plan that might have a possible chance of success, let me know. I'll be down on the dock, trying to forget this stupid conversation," he said over his shoulder before slamming the back door behind him.

* * *

The morning the farm was to be auctioned off on the courthouse steps, Jess sat at the kitchen table, staring out at land that wouldn't be theirs for long.

Part of her felt relief. No more stressing over mortgage payments or worrying about the business's success. She'd miss the planting, the harvests, the unpredictable weather—and the multitude of other challenges. Even being at war with all the pests had given her something to focus on.

Kevin asked if she wanted to go to the courthouse and watch the auction.

"What for? I don't need the pain of that. You goin'?"

"Naw, I don't need that pain either. Besides, I got too much to do. Aren't we supposed to b-be out of here in five days?"

"Unless a miracle happens."

* * *

That afternoon, Jess stared at her phone for a minute before making the call.

"Paul Stevens here."

"Hi, um . . ."

"Is this Jess?"

"It is."

"I'm happy you called."

She drew a deep breath. "I want to say how sorry I am for bein' so rude when you came out here."

"Don't worry about it. I can't even imagine what a shock it must've been for you."

"True, but that's no excuse for how I acted . . . and for what I said."

"Apology accepted." After a brief pause, he asked her what she thought of her Granny Mae's diary.

"Honestly . . . it made me cry. I didn't know her father was so abusive. I can see why she wanted to cut all connection with Wears Valley and everyone in it. And you, well, you're a different story. I reckon she was very much in love with you, but out of respect for your marriage, she ended all contact and didn't tell you about my mama."

"Yeah, that's what I think, too. I'm sad I never got to meet Katherine, but at least I understand the reasonin' behind it. Your Granny Mae was such a beautiful soul. I can't tell you how much I've missed her all these years." He was quiet for a few seconds. "Arrangin' for the diary to go to me after Peggy June passed on . . . that was so like her. Everythin' she did had to be in the correct order. One thing followed another, and that was just how it had to be."

Jess sighed. "To see what she went through, well . . . it was good to read her entries, but kind of difficult, too, hearin' about her doubtin' the visions and all."

"Have you also had visions?"

"Oh yeah. Big time. And so did Kat—I mean my mama."

"I'm certainly fine if you call her Kat. I like that name. I also like cats, so that's even better."

"You're funny. I don't know, it just felt so . . . familiar to read about Granny Mae strugglin' with her second sight and how it'd get her into trouble."

"So you're also a troublemaker?"

"More than you can believe. Not that I try to be, but let's just say I've had more than my share of conversations with law enforcement." She cleared her throat. "By the way, you didn't tell us you're a deputy sheriff."

"Was," he corrected. "Got elected sheriff back in '75. But I'm long since retired, now goin' on fourteen years."

"If I'd known that, maybe I'd have been even ruder."

"Somehow, I doubt it," he said with a laugh, "but yeah, let's just say I met Anna Mae by the grace of the sheriff's department."

"So I gathered from the diary. I'll tell you one thing, though. Unlike Granny Mae, I'm not romantically involved with any law enforcement personnel with whom I've had the great pleasure to meet."

He chuckled. "Good to know. So, what else is goin' on?"

"Well, our farm is bein' auctioned off at the courthouse today."

"Sorry to hear that."

"I don't really mind the idea of startin' over. You know what's funny, though?"

"What's that?"

"There've been times when I've thought about gettin' out of Center Point and away from this farm, but now that the door has opened itself wide, I'm not exactly itchin' to do anythin' else. I'm not gonna stay around here without the farm, but it gave me purpose."

"Of course it did, though I'm sure you'll find a whole new purpose."

"I hope so."

"I'm sure of it."

A comfortable silence grew between them.

"Speakin' of purpose, I love that Dave has picked up his guitar again," Jess finally said.

"I reckon we all need somethin' important to focus on."

"I agree. And without somethin' good to focus on, we might just focus on somethin' . . . else. I know his drinkin' was his way of grievin' the loss of Kat, but he got into such a downward spiral that he was eventually grievin' his own life. He's been stone-cold sober for almost a year now, though, and I can talk to him again like a real person."

"That must feel good, but I can't imagine how tough it must've been for y'all to lose your mama."

"It was, unbelievably so. It's still tough not havin' her around. She's been gone more than ten years now, but every once in a great while, I'll make a mental note to talk to her about somethin' before I remember I can't." She paused. "Can I ask you a question?"

"Of course. Anythin' at all."

"This is probably a dumb rumor, but do you know if Granny Mae ever killed anyone?"

"Not to my knowledge, but her father—your great-grandpa, Jefferson Cole . . ."

"What?"

"Well, back in '78, he nearly beat a man to death with a tire iron."

"Seriously?"

"Yep. And he did it in broad daylight where a half-dozen witnesses saw him. It took three men to pull him off. The fellow he attacked had been a dentist out of Pigeon Forge and spent a month in the hospital afterward. The attack essentially ruined his nerves and his business. Your great-grandpa accused him of havin' an affair with his wife Lucinda, who'd worked for that dentist nearly twenty years."

"Unbelievable."

"You're tellin' me. It was the most sensational case to come along around here since . . . a congressman's son was shot back in sixty-five. Your great-grandpa caught pneumonia and died a half-dozen years after the attack while servin' an eight-year sentence in Brushy Mountain State Penitentiary for aggravated assault."

"My goodness."

"I wasn't surprised when I heard he'd attacked someone so violently 'cause he'd been known to fly off the handle."

"Would you say he wasn't right in the head?"

"For sure. You've read the diary, so you get an idea. On the other hand, Anna Mae was the sweetest person you could ever meet."

"I believe it."

"I can tell you one thing, though."

"What's that?"

"If killin' someone had been within what she considered the proper order of things, I reckon she wouldn't have hesitated."

Jess suddenly got a funny feeling. "Is that, um . . ."

"That is somethin' I can relate to, yes."

CHAPTER FIFTY

Wears Valley, Tennessee
October 1965

Anna Mae sat next to an empty seat most of the way to Memphis, where she changed to a bus that would take her to Dallas. It was a later one than the bus she was supposed to take. The bus she'd been on had stopped at every little town between Gatlinburg and Nashville. It had also broken down outside Knoxville, where they had to wait for a mechanic to get them going again.

She'd called Rudy collect from the bus station in Wears Valley, letting him know when her bus would arrive in Kerrville. Now she was way behind schedule, however, and didn't know if she'd make her next connection. Filled with anxiety, she considered returning home and imagined what it would be like walking back into her parents' house. Papa's belt would be in his hand and ready before she even set her suitcase down.

Then there was the humiliation with Deputy Stevens. She didn't know if she could bear seeing his face again. He'd made himself clear enough, and there was no way she would degrade herself by begging him to want her. Besides, he'd be married by the time she got back.

As they entered Dallas after dark, the size of the city amazed Anna Mae. She'd thought Memphis was huge when they'd passed through it the day before, but Dallas looked even bigger, with its towering buildings and heavy traffic still going strong after eight p.m. She wondered if they would pass the Texas Book

281

Depository where Lee Harvey Oswald had shot and killed President Kennedy. Perhaps someone would make an announcement as they drove by.

But no announcements were made until they arrived at the Dallas Greyhound terminal. As the bus hissed to a stop, Anna Mae hurriedly gathered her belongings and asked the driver where to find the Kerrville bus. He leaned over and pointed down the long row of vehicles. "It's usually in bay twenty-three or twenty-four, right down that way. You'll see. It'll say Kerrville on the front." He glanced at his watch. "You better hurry, though. I believe that leaves soon, and the next one won't be off 'til this time tomorrow."

She waited impatiently for him to offload the luggage, and as soon as she saw her suitcase, she grabbed it and ran, finding her bus with only minutes to spare. The Dallas-to-Kerrville leg was much like part of her trip from Wears Valley to Memphis, but with even more stops. At least they didn't break down.

Anna Mae couldn't remember when she'd last felt so exhausted—and so desperate for a shower—yet a sense of hope grew in her with every passing mile. She was beginning a new life with her beloved brother and his wife, Molly. Baby Katherine would make her appearance in another eight months or so, and she'd be a welcome addition to Anna Mae's world. The pain of the past was behind her. One of her favorite quotes was from Will Rogers about not letting yesterday take up too much of today. Now she had the perfect chance to practice that.

As they came into the outskirts of Kerrville, the rising sun dramatically illuminated a pair of massive silos painted with enormous red-and-white checkered patterns. Those must be the silos Rudy told her about that had inspired him to look for purpose in his life. She remembered how Pastor Blaine used to end his sermons by encouraging everyone to choose inspiration and hope over despair and discouragement. Before, they had just been words to her, but traveling through the Texas countryside lit by the soft orange glow of the early morning sun, she decided she could also choose inspiration and hope, just as Rudy had.

She saw the Greyhound Bus Terminal sign up the block when they turned onto Main Street. For the hundredth time since she'd left Wears Valley, her mind flew over all the reasons her trip had been foolish. Then she spotted Rudy on the sidewalk, frowning and watching the bus coming toward him.

His face lit up when he saw her, and he trotted alongside as they pulled into the brightly lit garage. Every negative thought Anna Mae had experienced on the trip, every doubt, and every question she had about whether she was doing the right thing evaporated as she watched her brother. Her tears started before she left her seat and only increased when she ran into Rudy's arms. She hugged him for a long minute before he whispered, "Careful of that right side, honey."

She let go and wiped her eyes. "I'm sorry. I'm just so glad to see you."

"The feelin's mutual, but I'm a bit bruised from where I slipped on the tractor step the other day."

"I'm sorry, I didn't know."

"Oh, miss?"

Anna Mae turned around and saw the driver holding up her purse.

"My God, I'm such a birdbrain."

She ran back and gratefully took it from the driver, who winked and said, "Welcome home, honey."

She almost corrected him but said nothing because he was right. She was indeed home.

* * *

Deputy Stevens sat at his desk, staring at the wall. He'd often heard that you can't know what it's like to kill someone until you do it. Apparently, that was true even for squashing a lowlife maggot like Phil Daley. The Tennessee Bureau of Investigation had impounded Daley's pickup truck and found a hidden latch that could allow the passenger door to open from the outside only. Stevens wished he'd taken decisive action against Daley sooner.

To make matters worse, he couldn't get Anna Mae off his mind, agonizing over whether he'd made the best decision. His mind told him he'd made the only reasonable choice, but his heart told him something else. He needed to snap out of it because he and Peggy June were going to have a baby and a life together. The sooner he forgot about Anna Mae, the better. Some things, however, were easier said than done.

His sister had noticed him acting strangely and admonished him again for not ending the engagement. She obviously hadn't heard Peggy June announce she was pregnant, but that was one thing she'd find out in due course. She didn't know they were getting married that weekend, either. He knew he had to tell her but was not looking forward to that conversation.

The phone made him jump. After the second ring, Sheriff Keene gave him a dirty look. "Do I look like a switchboard operator, Stevens?"

He reached for the phone, shaking the cobwebs out of his head. "Wears Valley Sheriff's Department, Deputy Stevens here."

It was Jefferson Cole reporting his daughter missing. Stevens' heart beat so hard he wondered if Keene could hear it.

"How long has she been missin', Mr. Cole?" he asked, hoping the other man wouldn't pick up on the emotion in his voice.

"Monday mornin' was when we saw her last. This is an urgent situation, and you need to start the search now."

"You can come in and fill out a report if you like, though if I'm not mistaken, your daughter is over the age of eighteen, and we can't organize a search unless we have cause to believe there was—"

"You got a missin' girl who's not right in the head, and you talk to me about 'cause to believe?' What if she's in the trunk of someone's car right now? Would that give you cause to believe, Mr. Deputy Sheriff?"

"Please simmer down, sir."

"My mentally retarded daughter goes missin', and you want me to simmer down?"

"I've met your daughter, Mr. Cole, and I wouldn't say she's retarded. In fact—"

"You think you know her better than her own pa? For God's sake, I've lived with the girl her whole life."

Stevens rolled his eyes. "Okay then, any sign of foul play?"

"Finally, the master detective comes up with a genuine question. Of course there was foul play. Have I been speakin' to a deaf man this whole time? She even left a note."

"Did she say she was threatened, kidnapped, or otherwise in danger?"

"Not exactly."

"Then what—"

"She says things in the note she'd never say to her mama or me."

"Can you read it to me, please?"

"You need to come out here and read it yourself. There's somethin' about it you have to see."

CHAPTER FIFTY-ONE

Center Point, Texas
Present Day

Jess let her phone ring a few times before answering so she wouldn't appear too eager. "Agent Mallory, to what do I owe the pleasure?"

"Please, call me Ed."

"Whatever you say, Agent Ed."

That got a chuckle out of him. "Listen, I'm gonna be in your area in a few days, tryin' to figure out who was goin' to receive that call at the phone booth in Kerrville about the boy. We think they might be involved in multiple kidnappin's around the country. The FBI is also involved and coordinatin' with our division."

"I sure hope you catch them."

"You and me both. I'm sure you'd let me know if you had any other insights."

"Of course."

"Anyway . . . I was thinkin' maybe you and I could have a drink while I'm up there."

"Are you askin' me out, Agent Ed?"

"No, this would be strictly business, debriefin' all that's happened and discussin' future strategies."

He was definitely asking her out.

"You know, maybe some other time. You may not be aware, but we're goin' through foreclosure, and—"

"Sorry to hear that. I know how much that place means to you."

Jess sighed. It *did* mean a lot to her. "I was gonna say there's just too much to do around here to get packed up and closed down."

"All the more reason for a relaxin' drink with a friend."

"Thought you said it was gonna be strictly business?"

Mallory chuckled. "Well, maybe we can relax a bit, too."

It felt good to be wanted, and he was right. She needed to unwind a bit.

"I reckon you've at least earned a drink with me," she said.

"Let's hope so. I'm scheduled to be up there on Tuesday, but that might change. I'll call you the day before if that's okay."

"Of course."

"And Jess . . ."

"Yes?"

"You are amazin'."

CHAPTER FIFTY-TWO

Wears Valley, Tennessee, and Texas Hill Country
October 1965

Stevens took a deep breath and rang the doorbell. Seconds later, an angry Jefferson Cole yanked the door open.

"Took you long enough! Didja stop for coffee and donuts on the way?"

"Got here soon as I could," Stevens said to the man glaring at him through the screen door. "If you can show me—"

"Ain't you supposed to know what to look for?"

"Exactly, which is why I need you to show me that note. Let's start there."

"Why didn't ya say so?" Cole disappeared inside the house. "*You comin' in, or are you gonna stand out there like a lost doggy?*" he yelled after a few seconds.

Stevens took a deep breath and went inside. Cole thrust Anna Mae's note at him.

> *October 4, 1965*
>
> *Dear Mama and Papa,*
>
> *I'm starting a new life in a new place. Don't try to find me because I'd never come back even if you did.*
>
> *Thanks for all you've done and given me. Hopefully, I've contributed something to your lives as well.*
>
> *However, there comes a point when a person must decide when*

enough is enough. I've promised myself that I will not accept abuse
from anyone. Not anymore. Family or not.
Thank you for helping me learn that. I wish you both well.

Good luck to you, and God bless.
Anna Mae Cole

"You see there," said Cole, stabbing his finger at the note. "That was obviously written under pressure. Not once in her life has she been so disrespectful to Lucinda or me. We're her parents, for God's sake."

Stevens reread the note carefully before answering. "Mr. Cole, I don't see anythin' here that would prove she was bein' forced to write this."

"Are you dumber than dirt? Even an idiot could see she didn't write that on her own." He tapped the paper. "I ain't no detective, but those look like tear stains to me. This came right out of the blue, too—further evidence that she's been taken against her will. Ain't no chance she ran away. We need you to track her down and bring her back."

Stevens explained that he couldn't force Anna Mae to return since she was eighteen.

"You just don't get it, do you? A mentally incompetent girl has been taken advantage of. Do I have to talk to your boss to get somethin' done?"

Stevens struggled to remain calm. "Talk to whoever you want, Mr. Cole. I see no sign of anythin' other than her leavin' by her own free will, so I suggest you just let this go."

Cole scowled, his face turning red. "I suggest you just do your damn job."

"I am doin' my job."

"Doin' your job means findin' that ungrateful little bitch and bringin' her home. Do you think my Lucinda should do all Anna Mae's work?"

That revealed a lot. Stevens knew he was poking an angry dog with a stick when he said, "Maybe you could help your wife with some of that work."

Cole got right up in his face. "Do I look like a housewife to you? I'm a workin' man. I got major responsibilities with the railroad. Unlike some people 'round here, I do what I'm supposed to."

Stevens' hand automatically went to his holstered revolver. "I need you to take a big step back, Mr. Cole."

"Or what? You gonna shoot me, Deputy?" He practically spat the words out.

Stevens stared at him for a few moments, then turned to go. Some battles were not worth fighting.

"Didn't think so," taunted Cole.

"If you get any updates, let us know."

"Updates? What the fuck are you talkin' about? When are y'all startin' the search?"

"There won't be any search, Mr. Cole. As I told you before—"

"You ain't told me shit."

Stevens walked out, but Cole's profanities followed him to his patrol car. He started the engine and glanced back to see Cole still going strong, his face bright red. Anna Mae had done the right thing by removing herself from a bad situation. On his way back to the sheriff's office, he tried to convince himself it had all worked out for the best.

* * *

Anna Mae couldn't take her eyes off her brother as he carried her suitcase out to the street where he'd parked his '54 Chevy pickup. He opened the passenger door and offered a hand to help her up. "Hope you don't mind the truck," he said. "It was all we could afford."

"Are you kiddin'?" She slid her hand across the dash. "I love it. It's so . . ." She smiled at her brother. "It's so *you*, Rudy Cole."

He winked at her, closed the door, and walked around to the driver's side. "Ready to go see your new home?"

"You betcha."

"We're about fifteen minutes away," he said, backing out onto Main Street. "I think you'll like it there."

"I'm sure I will."

It didn't take them long to get out of town, and they soon passed by the same huge silos with the red-and-white patterns she'd seen from the bus. "Are those the silos you told me about?" she asked.

"Yep. Rudy Cole's famous 'Silos with Purpose.' Molly and I laugh every time we pass by since we say they brought me to her."

"They're huge."

"Oh yeah. Just about everythin' here in Texas is big." They turned off at the next road they came to, following a sign that read sixty-five miles to San Antonio. He gestured at a farm they passed by. "Around here, people have to be practical. Mostly, they got lots of land, so their houses are flat and spread out. They call 'em ranch-style. Kinda plain, mostly. They love their big fancy gates, however."

Before long, they approached a curve in the road lined on both sides by tall trees. "This is Logan's Bend," Rudy explained, "named in honor of Patrick Logan, who died here a few years back due to a fatal combination of excessive speed and alcohol."

As they came out of the curve, he gestured to the left. "This is the start of the Kidwell Cattle Ranch. I reckon they got about two thousand acres—maybe more. It's the biggest piece of land around for miles. Kyle Kidwell's the one who sold us our property, and his son Earl is the wannabe cowboy I told you about way back when. Haven't seen him much since we hurt his feelings that time his hat blew off."

He waved his arm toward the river on the right-hand side. "That's the Guadalupe. Gives us water for crops, plus we got about two hundred feet of river frontage, which ain't bad at all." He pointed ahead and to the right. "You see them big trees yonder?"

"I do."

"Those are our pecans. We've got almost two acres of 'em, though peanuts are the crop keepin' us afloat."

They slowed as they approached a large grove of trees around a house. When they turned into the driveway, Anna Mae stared at the Tennessee plantation-style home nestled among the trees, with a balcony across the entire second floor.

"Well, what do you think?" Rudy asked.

"You didn't tell me it was so amazin'."

"We wanted you to see that for yourself. It's not all finished inside, but it's close enough for the three of us to make do." As they climbed out of the pickup, a petite, beautiful brunette walked out of the house. "This gorgeous woman and love of my life is Molly."

Anna Mae extended her hand, but Molly came in close and gave her a tight hug, catching her off guard. The bigger surprise was how wonderful it felt.

"We're so happy you're here, Anna Mae. Welcome to our little family."

"This is your home now," Rudy said, "and you can stay with us as long as you want." He nodded to his wife. "Ain't that right, honey?"

"Of course."

Anna Mae smiled hesitantly. "Well, there's somethin' you should know before you decide whether that's what you really want."

"And what would that be?" her brother asked.

"I'm pregnant."

He frowned and glanced at her belly. "You sure about that?"

Anna Mae closed her eyes and nodded. "I'm gonna have a beautiful little girl who'll do wonderful things in the world."

Molly walked over and hugged her again. "Oh, Anna Mae, y'all are both welcome here."

Rudy looked thoughtful. "Is the daddy anyone we know?"

"It's not Andy if that's what you're wonderin'. The daddy and I won't be havin' any contact, and if it's okay with you, I'd rather not say who. He'd want to help if he knew, but . . . it's a long story."

"Okay." Rudy smiled and shook his head. "You might be a bit annoyin' sometimes, but you're part of this family," he nodded at her belly, "and so is your baby."

"I already know what I'm gonna call her."

Molly gently placed her hand on Anna Mae's arm. "Wouldn't you rather wait to tell us when you're sure it's a girl?"

"I'm already sure, and her name will be Katherine, with a 'K.'"

Rudy hugged her. "Katherine it is, like our sister," he said with a slight quaver in his voice. "But Anna Mae, there's one condition I must make."

"What's that?"

"I don't want to hear any more talk about you dyin'."

"But I've had—"

"You've told me many times about your visions. But death isn't a good preoccupation for you. Do you know exactly how you're gonna die?"

"Well, no, but that's 'cause—"

"I know. We've already had this discussion. But those visions make no sense when you compare one to another. Point is, you don't know how or when you're gonna die. Is that true or not?"

"That's true, I guess."

"It certainly is true, which makes you just like everybody else. None of us know how or when we're gonna go, do we?"

"No, but I've had—"

"Anna Mae, now hush. I can't tell you what to think, but I insist you don't talk about your death while you're here. I'm makin' it a condition for you stayin' with us. You good with that, honey?"

Anna Mae hesitated, then nodded. "I'm good with that."

As Rudy opened his mouth to respond, she continued, "Even if you are bein' a bossy big brother."

He grinned. "Sorry, sweetie, it's my birthright."

CHAPTER FIFTY-THREE

Center Point, Texas
Present Day

Jess rested her elbows on the balcony railing and sighed. The battle to save their farm and business was over, and they'd lost. Foreclosure was no longer something to fear. Now it would be an embarrassing and painful part of their past.

On the bright side, she'd had some good dates with Ed Mallory. She wasn't head over heels in love but felt great being around him, and it was a welcome diversion from the rest of her life.

The sound of a vehicle racing up Johnny's driveway startled her. Through the trees, she glimpsed something big and white, moving fast. She ran inside the house to the back window of Kevin's room and waited a few seconds until she saw a white Mercedes van speeding along the driveway. It stopped for the gate, then drove out of sight behind trees that used to be theirs.

That must have been where the van disappeared to all those months ago and would explain why she had the vision in the first place. She had to find and warn the man with the blue-and-white bandana, even if he was one of their rude neighbors.

She called Mallory's number as she walked outside but only got his outgoing recording. She pictured him rolling his eyes as she left a message, hoping her voice didn't betray the emotion she felt. At least she'd done what he asked and kept him in the loop.

She hopped in the pickup, drove to the end of the driveway, and stopped. Drumming her fingers on the steering wheel, she knew she had to act but dreaded seeing Johnny. Yet the vision of the shooting had come to her for a reason. At least three people would still be alive if she'd done the right thing all those years ago. She tried Mallory again but hung up when his recording started. She contemplated calling the sheriff's office, but that would be silly. All she could give them to go on was a violent, unconfirmed vision from months ago and a Mercedes van she'd once chased down the road—if it even *was* the same one. They'd think she was crazy for sure.

She took her foot off the brake and rolled the truck forward. At the last second, instead of turning into Johnny's drive, she crossed the road to the Kidwells' property. As much as she hated asking Travis for help, it would be better than facing Johnny alone. Hopefully, Earl wouldn't be home.

The third time Jess knocked on the Kidwells' massive door, she heard a faint, "Come on in."

She stepped inside. "Travis?"

"In here."

"Where's 'here?'"

"Just follow the sound of my voice, Sherlock."

She found him in the kitchen, newspapers spread out on the table, cleaning the biggest pistol she'd ever seen. He had a couple of aerosol cans and a small wire brush in front of him, with a roll of paper towels off to the side.

"How'd you know it was me?" she asked.

He held up his phone and grinned. There was a clear view of the front porch on his screen. "It's this thing called technology. You should try it sometime."

"Hilarious." She pointed at the gun. "That thing is huge."

"Oh yeah. It's a Colt Anaconda .44 Magnum with an eight-inch barrel," he said proudly. "Not somethin' you'd want to get shot with."

"I'll try to remember that."

"What brings you over here, Miss Atwood?"

"Well," she said, sitting across from him, her eyes still on the gun, "I'm pretty sure that white van I told you about has somethin' to do with those people who bought the pecan grove from us."

"You must be referrin' to those prime two acres of riverfront that you should have sold to *us*."

"As we've said before, we didn't know y'all wanted it." She paused. "And we were a little desperate."

"Apparently so." He spun the revolver's cylinder and aimed the gun toward the window. "This is now officially clean."

"Hallelujah. Now seriously, Travis, I'm concerned." She paused. "And . . . I was wonderin' if you'd go over there with me."

"I feel ya, Jess. I'd be deeply concerned if one of my neighbors was drivin' a white van all over the countryside. That would worry me to no end."

"You are simply impossible. I come here askin' for help, and all you have for me is sarcasm."

"Seriously? No apologies for me havin' to pressure-wash fluorescent-pink paintball splotches off our house?" He raised his eyebrows. "By the way, Earl says we need to bill you five hundred dollars for that."

"Five hundred dollars?"

"Yep. You're lucky we didn't complain to the sheriff. It took a long time to wash off your handiwork."

"You're such a big baby."

"You're such a slow learner." He waved toward the front door. "I'll see you around unless I don't."

She hesitated. "Look, I really am sorry about paintballin' y'all. I was havin' a terrible day and was kinda wasted."

"Maybe I'll eventually consider forgivin' you."

She shuddered as a wave of dread swept over her. "We need to get over there now."

"What's the hurry?"

"Somethin' terrible is about to happen to the driver of that van."

"Come on now, Jess. What business is that of yours?"

"I don't know, but I believe some poor man is about to get shot."

"And you're sure this is the same man you saw before?"

"I didn't exactly see him this time."

"You didn't even see him?"

"No." Jess felt her cheeks flush. "But I saw the van, and I've got a strong feelin' about it. When I passed him a few months back, I thought he might have driven onto your property, but he must have turned into Johnny's." She tapped the table for emphasis. "Which is why I was hopin' you'd go over there with me. Somethin' isn't right."

"Grow up, Jess. We live in a world where *most* things don't seem right if you look at them in a certain way."

"What's that supposed to mean?"

"It means if you try hard enough and use your imagination, you can find what you're lookin' for in almost anythin'. Even in some wacky dream."

She pushed her chair back and stood. "Wacky dream, huh? I should've known how much help you were gonna be. I'm gonna go warn him myself."

"You're gonna go warn who?" Earl asked, walking into the kitchen.

"The driver—"

"Just hold your horses," he interrupted. "Didn't you throw my fat white chauvinistic ass out of your house a while back? Right after you accused us of arson and right before you shot up our house with your little pink paintballs? And here you are, like Jezebel herself, standin' in my kitchen talkin' to my boy when he's got work to do?" He shook his head. "Some folks got all the nerve."

"Look, Mr. Kidwell, sir—"

"Oh, so now I'm 'sir,' am I?" He squinted at her. "Young lady, I don't rightly know what kinda game you're playin', but I want none of it." He pointed toward the door. "I'll thank you kindly to leave now."

Travis raised an eyebrow at her but said nothing.

"Fine," she said and stomped out, slamming the heavy front door behind her.

CHAPTER FIFTY-FOUR

Wears Valley, Tennessee
October 1965

The week after he shot and killed Phil Daley was a nightmare for Paul Stevens. He expected questions and possibly an investigation but was surprised when he wound up on administrative leave and couldn't even drive his patrol car. While he was sure he'd done the right thing, Special Agent Davis from the Tennessee Bureau of Investigation had his doubts. Davis interviewed Susie T and wanted to speak to Anna Mae, but she'd disappeared without a trace, which he found suspicious. Neither her parents nor Pastor Blaine had any idea where she was.

If Daley hadn't been the son of a congressman, Stevens was sure the TBI wouldn't have been involved.

The event had garnered national headlines. A news anchor from WKYU television in Knoxville kept trying to weasel his way into the sheriff's office, camera crew and all, but Keene chased them away each time. The segment they eventually aired showed the announcer outside, saying the sheriff and deputy both declined to comment. He said it with his eyebrows raised, and his tone of voice declared Stevens guilty. The headline of the *Maryville Gazette* read: "Congressman's Son Gunned Down by Deputy." The article hinted that Daley had been unarmed, even though a pocket knife with his fingerprints on it was found near the body. The *Sevierville Herald's* headline was "Police

Shooting Under TBI Investigation." The *New York Times* called it "A Tragedy in Tennessee." Sheriff Keene told Stevens not to worry, that they were just trying to sell newspapers.

Special Agent Davis repeatedly mentioned the TBI's most significant concern: Deputy Stevens had known the perpetrator and testified against him in an abduction case in which Daley had been acquitted. Stevens openly told people at the time that he thought the acquittal was a poor decision.

It was humiliating to have Keene drive him to work, where Davis questioned him extensively for the second day in a row. The tedious and unproductive ordeal stretched well into the evening.

The last thing Davis said as he left was an ominous, "We'll be in touch."

Stevens almost told him to give Congressman Daley his regards but was smart enough to hold his tongue.

"Suppose you'd like a ride home?" asked Keene.

Stevens nodded and stood, saying nothing.

They drove through the gathering twilight in silence. Finally, Keene said he couldn't believe Daley had been so stupid. "To attack a deputy holdin' a thirty-eight special on him when he's armed with nothin' more than a pocketknife don't make no sense."

"I know," said Stevens. "Some people just do the dumbest things." He shifted in his seat and looked out the window. "But what he was doin' . . . that was pretty dumb, too."

"Well, some things are beyond dumb. Some things you just gotta call evil." He glanced over at Stevens. "You know the funny thing?"

"What's that, Sheriff?"

"Daley had the same kinda knife I used to have."

Stevens looked straight ahead, his expression neutral. "You don't say."

"Barlow Huntsman, best pocketknife ever made." He glanced at his deputy again. "You have one of those too, don't you?"

"Yep. Got one around somewhere, I'm pretty sure."

They pulled up in front of Stevens' house.

"How's your sister?" Keene asked.

"She's okay, but reporters came knockin' on the door at least three or four times tryin' to get her to say somethin' they can use to make a mountain out of a molehill. It's all a bit too much for her."

"I'll bet. How's your nephew?"

"Niece. She's still goin' through her terrible twos even though she's almost three and a half, but otherwise, she's fine. Asks a lot of questions, but you know, kids do that."

"Of course they do."

Stevens got out and started to close the door. Keene leaned across the front seat toward him. "Deputy Stevens."

"Yes, sir?"

"You know you did the right thing."

"Well, yes, sir. There aren't many options available when you're in close quarters and a man's comin' at you with a knife."

"Stevens."

"Sir?"

"You know what I'm talkin' about. Sometimes you just gotta put a sick dog down, regardless of its pedigree." The sheriff paused and raised his eyebrows. "I'm gonna stand by you on this, Deputy." The two men locked eyes for a long moment. Keene gave him a salute, which Stevens returned, then stood watching the sheriff drive off.

"What was that all about?" Marty called from the front door.

"Oh, just some follow-up from shootin' that kidnapper last week."

"Well, come on in, Paul. Supper's been ready more than an hour."

He turned and walked toward the house, keeping his eyes on the sheriff's disappearing taillights.

* * *

Later that week, Stevens again broached the subject of releasing Hobo Bill. Sheriff Keene poured himself a cup of coffee and gestured at his deputy's empty mug. He nodded, and as the sheriff started pouring, Stevens continued, "We both know he wouldn't hurt a fly. The pistol he supposedly had probably didn't even work."

"But it was still illegal for him to have it, especially on national parkland."

"I know, boss, but he's just tryin' to make his humble way through life." He sipped his coffee. "Besides, we didn't even see the pistol."

Keene gave him a severe look. "Why're you so interested in him?"

"I just want to see justice served. Look, we accuse the man of kidnappin' and murder. Then, even though we know he wasn't the one who did any of that, we still keep him locked up."

"Where he's probably been eatin' better than he has his whole life. Plus, it's the safest place he can be. Commissioner Baker wasn't kiddin' when he said he'd have his boys take care of things."

"That may be, but he needs to feel as free as you or I. Besides, now everyone knows it was Daley."

"Who put you up to this?"

"No one."

Sheriff Keene stared at him for a long moment, the corners of his mouth barely turning up. "Sure. Whatever you say." He scratched his head. "All right, I'll talk to the County prosecutor. But you're gonna owe me one."

CHAPTER FIFTY-FIVE

Jess parked at Johnny's closed gate. Travis had a point; this was none of her business. People died every day for reasons that didn't concern her. What was she thinking? Especially considering that Johnny had threatened her the last time she was on his property.

But her vision had connected her to a violent act seen through the eyes of a perpetrator. If another innocent person died because she didn't take action, she didn't know if she could bear that burden. She couldn't bring her mother or the young couple in the orange Camaro back to life, but she could do the right thing this time.

Jess climbed the gate, walked up to the house, and knocked.

Johnny opened the door. "What are *you* doing here?" he asked, glancing behind her, "and how the fuck did you get in?"

"I climbed your gate," she said, already regretting it. "I saw a van come through earlier that—"

"Who's there, Johnny?"

The man with the blue-and-white bandana from her vision walked up behind him.

Jess gasped. "You!" Both men seemed as surprised by her reaction as she was to see him.

Johnny opened the door wide. "Come on in and tell us what this is all about."

His sudden shift in mood alarmed her. This was a job for the sheriff's department. They might not listen to her, but she had to try.

She pointed her thumb behind her. "You know what? I'm just gonna go."

Quick as a snake, Johnny grabbed her arm, roughly pulled her inside, and slammed the door. "You're not going anywhere. Where do you know him from?"

"I was just lookin' for the driver of the white van that pulled in here," she said, struggling to keep her voice calm.

"So? Why is that an excuse for snooping around?"

"I wasn't snoopin'. I passed him on the road a few months back," she nodded at the man with the bandana. "I turned around and followed him 'cause he was in danger." If her vision played out, maybe Johnny was going to shoot him. She wished she'd thought of that before knocking on the door. She had to get out of there and find help. "I saw him again today and needed to warn him."

"You needed to *warn* him? Are you fucking crazy? You pass people all the time and don't turn around and follow them." His eyes narrowed. "You're lying to us. Why would you think he was in danger?"

"'Cause he was drivin' way too fast." With her mind paralyzed by fear, it was the best she could come up with.

"So, now you think you're a traffic cop? You're even worse than I thought."

A loud knock startled them all.

"Carl, keep her out of the way," hissed Johnny.

His brother pulled Jess aside and whispered in her ear, "Say one word and I'll cut you." He slid his hand over her mouth, and she felt the sharp point of a knife under her chin.

"The hell do *you* want?" Johnny asked when he opened the door.

"I'm lookin' for Jess, the woman who lives on the front property."

She shook her head free. "I'm here, Travis—*ow*!" she cried out as Carl poked her with the knife.

"Hey, Jess, we have to get to that meetin' with Earl."

"Why don't you come in so we can talk?" Johnny offered.

"Oh, thanks, but we have to get goin'. My pa is expectin' us."

"I insist," he said, drawing a compact automatic pistol from the back of his waistband. "Why don't you come in and join the party?"

Carl made sure Jess felt the knife point again. The pain of it rippled through her. She could already feel blood dripping down the front of her shirt from the first wound. "You just stay right where you are," he said.

Johnny waved his gun at Travis. "Inside, *now*."

"Okay, relax." He raised his hands in surrender. "I don't want any trouble. We just need to get to our meetin' and—"

"*Shut up!*" Johnny snarled. "Keep talking, and the only meeting you go to will be with God. Get your ass inside, *now*."

From that moment, things happened almost faster than Jess could track. Travis walked in the open door as Carl pushed Jess out from behind it. Travis glanced at her and gave the door a mule kick, smashing it into Carl an instant before punching Johnny in the throat, who dropped his pistol and gasped for air. Travis grabbed Jess's hand and pulled her out through the doorway before she could fully register what had happened.

"*Run!*" yelled Travis.

She started running toward the road, but Travis headed toward the river. "*No, this way*," he hollered. "*There's more cover*."

He'd almost reached the trees, Jess a good twenty feet behind him, when Johnny stumbled out of the doorway and aimed his gun at her. Travis picked up a rock and hurled it at him. "*Keep goin'!*" he screamed as Johnny ducked the rock and fired back at Travis. It missed and splintered a small tree to his right.

Unfortunately, the trees weren't dense enough to give them much cover. "*Zigzag!*" yelled Travis. "We'll jump in the river and stay underwater as long as possible."

"What if—" began Jess, before the next shot spun Travis around and landed him on his back with a loud groan.

"*Travis!*" she cried.

She started toward him as another bullet hit the tree next to her.

"Don't stop," he sputtered, blood moistening his lips.

If not for all the adrenaline in her body, Jess surely would have fainted. She ran to the right, toward a large garage-like building.

Another shot rang out, the bullet so close she could hear it whiz past. She made a sharp zag left, then dove right, taking cover behind the building.

CHAPTER FIFTY-SIX

Dear Diary,

Last night, I dreamt I slept for weeks and couldn't wake up. It was scary, and I don't see the order in it.

As Rudy said, some of my visions don't make sense when comparing one against another. Yet they can be so real they save someone's life. I love that we rescued Susie T from Daley and that Deputy Stevens protected us by shooting that sick man.

Ralph Waldo Emerson said we have to overcome a daily fear to learn life's lessons. I'd feel good if I could conquer one every month. Will I ever overcome my fear of not seeing the order of things? It's less scary than it used to be, but without order in my life, sometimes I feel like a cow on ice.

Speaking of cows, now that I'm nearly nine months in, I'm looking very cow-like. Rudy calls me Watermelon Girl because he says I look like I swallowed one whole. I'm ready for this to be over so I can hold my baby.

Rudy and Molly took me to a doctor who checked me out from A to Z. Baby Katherine seems perfectly healthy. Strong little heartbeat, the doc said. Probably a boy. Ha! What does he know? He didn't say that she's also got a strong little soul, and she's going to shine her light into the world. That's not something you can measure with a stethoscope.

We're only twelve minutes from the hospital, which I reckon is good. Rudy and Molly learned first aid, CPR, and other valuable skills from the Red Cross. Rudy doesn't want me talking about how I'm going to die, but he also takes what I told him seriously enough to make his own preparations, just in case.

I'm also taking things seriously, so I saw Mr. Pete Carson and got my legal paperwork done.

I feel more connected to this little baby inside me than I've ever felt to anyone. Not even Rudy or Deputy Stevens.

Molly and Rudy are so kind to me, yet there are days when I miss my deputy. Most days, actually. But he married the woman of his choice, and it sure as hell wasn't me.

Besides, I have love here, and he's got love there. Some folks would say what I've got with Rudy, Molly, and Baby Katherine is a different kind of love, but love is love. It's all perfect when you think about it the right way. If I keep telling myself that, I may eventually believe it.

Rudy built me a little dock on the river where I can sit, dangle my feet in the water, and read to my baby, who hears everything I say. Today it was The Cat in the Hat, by Dr. Seuss. Every time I stopped reading, Katherine would give me a little kick, which was pretty funny. I wonder if she'll be bossy?

Every time I go down to the dock, Rudy tells me to watch out for alligators, but I don't reckon they're anything to worry about. That's just him being a protective big brother.

Molly says I should take it easy and rest. I told her I've been resting up my entire life for this. Serving the people I love fulfills me. I cook, clean, do laundry, fix clothes when they need it, and help in the fields whenever I can. Rudy also tells me to ease up, but what he doesn't get is that this IS my ease.

Some days I feel bad for Deputy Stevens, but if he knew he had a daughter here, I don't think he'd be able to stay away, which might destroy his marriage. I deceived him by putting those pinholes in that condom so it would break and by having my agenda in the first place, not telling him I wanted his baby. It seemed perfectly in order at the time and might just be the last piece of order left in my life.

Right now, I have no idea what the future holds and reckon I'm happier NOT knowing for a change.

* * *

"*Anna Mae,*" Rudy called out from the kitchen, "*do you have a minute?*"

She hurried in, concerned by his tone of voice. "What's wrong?"

His eyes flicked to a face-down envelope on the table. "There's a letter for you from Mama."

"*No!* How'd she find me? If she knows I'm here, then Papa must too."

"Don't worry. She has no idea where you are. Pastor Blaine put her letter inside one he sent to me, sayin' that she'd come to him beggin' to know where you were. He didn't tell her anythin', which suits me perfectly fine."

Anna Mae remained silent for almost a full minute. "Would you mind readin' it to me?" she finally asked.

"You sure?"

She nodded, and he tore open the envelope.

"*Dear Anna Mae,*" he read aloud, "*I understand why you'd be mad at your father. He was way too strict with you. We often argued about that, but you know how stubborn he is. I don't know if this letter will reach you, but I pray that it does, so that you will know how sorry I am for your troubles while you were under our roof. We both know how difficult living with your pa is, though it was probably worse for you than for me. If this reaches you, and you decide to give him another chance, I'll make him promise to never lay another hand on you. I already told him if that happens even one more time, he'd never see you or me again. We miss you, Anna Mae, both of us.*

"If you can find the kindness in your heart to forgive him and return home, I promise we'll greet you with open arms, and everythin' will be different." Rudy cleared his throat. *"If you need money to get home, just let me know. Life has not been the same since you left. I've never been much good at sayin' how I feel, but losin' both of my daughters would be just too much to bear. Your sister Katherine is long gone, but if there is at least a chance to get you back, it gives me a reason to keep on breathin'. Please come home so our family can be whole again. Your lovin' mama, Lucinda Cole."*

Rudy placed the letter on the table and crossed his arms, smiling sadly at his sister. "I'm here for you, no matter what you decide."

"I know."

"So, what are you gonna do?"

"Don't know yet. I've never heard Mama talk like that before," Anna Mae shook her head, "and she doesn't know she's gonna be a grandma."

"No, she doesn't." He sighed. "This is your decision and no one else's. You know you're more than welcome to stay with us as long as you wish."

She looked up at him, her eyes moist. "Thanks, I get that." She wasn't about to tell him she wouldn't be staying long.

CHAPTER FIFTY-SEVEN

Center Point, Texas
Present Day

Jess took cover behind the garage and thought about making a run for it. She might have a chance if she kept the building between her and Johnny. Hopefully, someone had heard the shots and called the police. She wished the message she'd left for Mallory had been more urgent, or even better, that she hadn't left her phone in the truck.

She ran with every bit of energy she could muster but wasn't even halfway to the river when another shot rang out. She changed direction and bolted toward a large shed.

A door with a panic bar facing out was on the far side of the building. Briefly wondering why anyone would install the bar on the outside, she pushed it, and the heavy metal door opened smoothly.

A skylight with a thick wire mesh lit the interior, revealing a set of stairs leading underground to a dimly lit passageway. A flicker of hope sparked within her. Maybe it led to a secret escape route. She tried to lock the door behind her, but it only had a pull handle and an electronic keypad. She wedged a fire extinguisher in place to hold the door closed and ran down the stairs into a long hallway with several doors she could barely see in the dim light.

Jess tried every door, each one secured by an electronic lock, but none of them opened. She paused, thinking she'd heard someone call out. Was Johnny upstairs at the door? Would the fire extinguisher keep him out?

The door at the end of the passage opened into the dimly lit room from the vision she'd described to Mallory. The surprise of it nearly took her breath away. Several free-standing closets stood around the room, but she saw no exit other than the way she'd just come in. She felt panicked by the semidarkness and wished her night vision was better.

She heard a dull clang as the fire extinguisher she'd wedged against the door upstairs fell over. Short on options, she opened one of the closets and hid inside. Less than a half-minute later, Johnny yanked open the closet door, pointing his gun at her and grinning like the Cheshire Cat. "You love to play games, don't you?"

"Please don't kill me," she said. "I promise I won't say anythin' to anyone."

"Do I look that stupid? We'd be crazy to let you go. Get your butt out here, and I'll give you some good news."

Trembling, she stepped out. "I can't wait."

Johnny laughed. "I love the fire in you. It's *so* sexy." He shook the gun at her. "The good news is that I'm not going to kill you." He smiled at the surprised look on her face. "Yeah, baby, this is your lucky day! You get to join our little family, but only until a high bidder decides he wants some of that brown sugar in his bed." He smirked and waved his gun. "Then we say goodbye. I think you'll go for a good price. Let me show you to your room, and we can get better acquainted later." He looked her up and down. "Maybe I'll come sample the merchandise."

Jess's revulsion almost outweighed her fear. Everything she'd heard about modern-day slavery and human trafficking ran through her mind. Years ago, she'd seen the movie *Room*, inspired by a true story about a woman kidnapped and held captive in a basement. She was raped and bore a child to her captor. Jess shivered involuntarily. That could be her fate—or something worse. "Please let me go."

Johnny grinned. "You're even sexier when you play the submissive role. You'll be popular with the boys."

Jess felt like she was about to throw up, and her eyes filled with tears. "I beg you, please—"

"Drop the gun and turn around, hands in the air."

Earl Kidwell stood in the doorway wielding the huge Colt revolver she'd seen on his kitchen table ten minutes earlier.

Johnny began raising his hands, then in one fluid motion, he ducked and shot twice at Earl, who cried out and fell to the floor.

As he crumpled, he fired his big gun with a deafening boom and blinding flash. Unfortunately, it missed Johnny, who just laughed. "Nice try, Tex."

It horrified Jess to see Earl sprawled on his back, the big useless pistol still in his hand, now splashed with blood that looked almost black in the dim light. Johnny walked over to him, keeping his gun trained on Jess. He swung his leg back to kick the revolver out of Earl's hand just as the big man swung the barrel up and squeezed the trigger again. This time he didn't miss, and Johnny collapsed with a surprised yelp.

Jess ran to Earl and checked for a pulse. Nothing. Through the acrid smell and haze of spent gunpowder, with a dull ringing in her ears, she picked up Earl's bloody gun and started for the door just as Carl appeared. He looked dazed, a lump the size of a plum on the right side of his forehead from where Travis had kicked the door into him. He pulled out a mother-of-pearl butterfly knife in a smoothly executed left-handed move and waved it at her. Jess gasped, recognizing it from the Dallas kidnapping vision she'd had months before. Chilled with the realization that she faced an experienced killer, she pointed Earl's gun at him. "Don't move," she said, trying to sound as confident as possible.

He laughed, the sound of it far away and tinny. "You're not going to shoot me. I'm getting out of here now, and we're both going to live long and happy lives, far away from each other." He glanced at his brother's body and swallowed hard. "Just put that down," he said, walking toward her, his knife held high, "and I promise not to hurt you." He was only five feet away when she pulled the trigger, producing nothing more than a loud click.

He flinched, then grinned. "Bad choice, bitch." He nodded at Earl's bloody pistol in her shaking hand. "Looks like your friend didn't take the time to fully load up. I'd call that a fatal mistake." He moved his knife in a small circle. "Now it's my turn."

Jess felt nauseous with fear and humiliation. In desperation, she tried the trigger again. Click. And again. Another loud click. *What had Earl been thinking, bringing a partially loaded gun?*

Carl lunged at her. She reflexively dropped to the floor, just as she'd done hundreds of times in the paintball arena, aiming the gun upwards. Her head hit the floor hard as she pulled the trigger again—more by reflex than anything else. Jess was unprepared for the slippery gun's explosive kick, knocking it out of her hand.

I've lost, she thought, before seeing the look of surprise on Carl's face as he stumbled back and fell to the floor, butterfly knife still in hand, a rapidly expanding dark circle in the center of his bandana.

She scrambled to her feet and stared at Carl, his bandana drenched with blood, then at Earl, who'd just sacrificed his life for her.

She felt as though the world was moving in slow motion as she ran down the hallway and up the stairs, ears ringing, her feet pounding but virtually soundless to her. She had to get to Travis.

Thankfully, the door had closed on the fire extinguisher, keeping it from latching shut. She opened it, hearing far-away sirens, which she quickly realized were close by, thanks to all the flashing red and blue lights. But she wasn't immediately concerned with her temporary hearing loss. Running toward where Travis had fallen, she heard someone yell "*Stop!*" as though from a great distance. She knelt beside him moments before a Department of Public Safety trooper arrived, shouting for immediate medical support into his shoulder mic.

Jess placed two fingers on Travis's neck, just below his jaw. His shallow breathing matched his weak pulse. Blood flooded the ground beside him, and a small stream of red trickled from the corner of his mouth.

The DPS trooper gently pushed her aside as a couple of EMTs ran up. They loaded Travis onto a gurney and rolled him to the nearest ambulance. She shuddered at how still and gray he looked.

"Is he gonna make it?" she asked. If anyone heard the question, they didn't answer. She tried to climb in behind him, but the paramedic attending him told her they needed all available space. She watched in a daze as they closed the two rear doors and drove away with lights on, siren off.

Police and FBI agents were all over the property, exactly as her vision had shown her months earlier. A muffled thumping cut through the ringing in her ears, and she looked up to see a helicopter hovering overhead. Mallory must have gotten her message. Or maybe Earl had called 911 on his way over to save them. Or both. She just hoped it wasn't all in vain as far as Travis was concerned.

CHAPTER FIFTY-EIGHT

Anna Mae stared out the kitchen window at the swirling yellow-and-brown storm cloud, brightly colored by the setting sun. "*Rudy, can you come in here, please?*"

"What is it?" He took one look out the window and gasped. "Oh boy. *Molly, come quick.*"

Anna Mae placed a protective hand on her swollen belly, over the baby who was due any day. "Is that what I think it is?"

"That's a twister for sure," said Rudy. They watched it grow larger by the second. "Looks like it's goin' to the west of us, but you never know; those things can change direction in a heartbeat. Let's hunker down in the cellar, just in case. In ten minutes, this'll all be over."

Molly pulled back the throw rug in the hallway and helped her husband open the hatch.

Rudy nodded to his wife. "Why don't you go down first so you can turn on the light and help Anna Mae? I'll go last and secure the hatch."

Molly had just started descending the stairs when they heard the haunting moan of the wind.

"Has this happened to y'all before?" Anna Mae asked, her heart pounding.

Rudy motioned for her to follow his wife down into the cellar. "Oh yeah," he said calmly. "This is very Texas for you."

Anna Mae couldn't help noticing some unsteadiness in his voice, however. She was only halfway down the steps when he started in after her, pulling the hatch closed as soon as he was clear. The moaning of the wind and the house creaking under stress increased rapidly in volume.

"Let's sit over there." Rudy motioned to some sacks of unshelled peanuts against the far wall. The noise from above grew louder. They sat on the sacks and held hands, Rudy in the middle, his sister and wife on either side. He turned to Anna Mae. "You all right?"

"I will be soon as this house stops moanin' and groanin'. And you know what they say."

"What's that?"

Anna Mae stroked her belly with a shaking hand. "A wise man once told me that no matter the situation, it too shall pass."

"Ah yes, but it took a wiser woman to listen and take that to heart." The solitary light bulb blinked out as he finished the sentence.

Anna Mae drew a sharp breath. "What happened?"

"Don't worry," Molly said, "this is normal when twisters come through. It might take 'em a bit to get the power back on, but they always fix it."

"I should've grabbed the flashlight from the kitchen," Rudy said.

It sounded to Anna Mae as though a freight train was passing overhead, right through the house. "You really go through this all the time?"

"I wouldn't say all the time," he said, "but we caught sight of one a few months back."

"Has it ever come this close?"

"No," Rudy said, "but don't worry, we're safe down here."

"Are we?"

"Absolutely. This is the best place on the property we could—" A resounding crash from above made them all jump.

"What was that?" Molly asked.

"Don't rightly know," Rudy said. "Soon as things settle down, I'll find out.

The main thing is that we're safe and together."

Anna Mae stared upward through the darkness, wishing the ordeal to be over. "Rudy," she said, "I've decided about goin' home to Wears Valley."

"We don't have to talk about that now, sis."

"I *want* to talk about it now. Not that I think anythin' is gonna happen to us down here, but . . . I'm not goin' home, 'cause I'm already home, more than I ever was back in Tennessee."

"We're glad you feel that way," Molly said.

Anna Mae took a deep breath. "I might feel different if Mama took some responsibility for the way things were, but she's just blamin' it all on Papa."

Rudy squeezed her hand. "I wasn't gonna say anythin' about that."

"Maybe she really would leave him if he whipped me again . . . but there are things almost as bad as bein' whipped. I can't help but wonder if she isn't missin' havin' a free live-in cook and maid."

"Honestly," said Rudy, "that thought also crossed my mind."

After a tense wait, the roaring leveled down somewhat, then drifted off more quickly than it had started. Within seconds, the sound of the wind had died to almost nothing.

"Twisters have been known to come around in a full circle," Rudy said. "We need to hold tight and make sure it's all clear."

They waited another few minutes but heard nothing.

"I'm gonna go up and look around," Rudy said. "You two wait here."

Once he made it up the ladder and got the hatch open, Anna Mae listened to his footsteps fade away as he went to check things out. He returned a minute later, shining a flashlight down into the cellar. "The coast is clear. Come on up."

"What was that crash?" asked Molly as Rudy helped Anna Mae up. Once his sister was safely up in the hallway, he reached down to offer his wife a hand.

"You know that hickory tree with the dead limb I said I was gonna cut down in case it fell on the house one day?"

"Of course I do."

"Well, that old limb finally decided to break loose."

"Oh no. Where'd it hit?"

"Smack dab in the middle of the balcony. Smashed right through the railin', and it's puttin' a lot of weight on the balcony floor." He gave his wife a wry smile. "I know what I'm gonna be doin' tomorrow," he said, not knowing how much his life was about to change.

Chapter Fifty-Nine

Jess sprinted toward her truck but only got twenty feet before a determined-looking female paramedic grabbed her arm as she tried to run past. "Whoa there, not so fast. Let's check you out."

Jess tried to pull free. "I have to get to the hospital right away."

"That's not a problem. We have an ambulance right here," the paramedic said in a soothing voice. "I'm Angie, and I'm here to ensure you're okay. What's your name, hon?"

"It's . . . it's Jess. But listen, I really need to go."

Angie opened her field case. "You're bleeding under your chin," she said, quickly taping a gauze pad in place.

"*Jess.*" Kevin ran up, his eyes wide, staring at the blood on her shirt. "What happened? Are you all right?"

"More or less." She shook her head, blinking back tears. "I need to get to the hospital and see Travis. They shot him, and he looks terrible. They, um . . . they got Earl."

"What?"

For a few seconds, Jess couldn't speak. "Earl and Travis saved my life," she said with a lump in her throat. "But they've both been shot. Earl is gone, and Travis . . . "

Angie strapped a blood pressure device to Jess's arm and shushed her. "No talking for a minute, honey. We need an accurate reading." As the machine did its work, she checked Jess's eyes with her flashlight. "One of your eyes is dilating a lot more than the other. You have a concussion." The monitor beeped twice, and the paramedic glanced at the reading. "A hundred and sixty-two over ninety-five. Your blood pressure is way too high."

A DPS trooper jogged up and started firing questions at Jess.

Angie turned to him. "She can't talk now, but you can ride in the ambulance with her." She glanced at her watch. "But she probably won't be fully coherent for at least an hour. She has a concussion and is in significant shock. Plus, I'm about to give her a little something to ease the pain, reduce her stress, and bring that blood pressure down."

"I'm fine," Jess pleaded. "Truly, I am."

Dave ran up, nearly out of breath. "Jess, are you okay?"

"More or less, but . . . they shot Travis. I don't know if he's gonna make it."

Angie gently touched the swelling at the back of Jess's head. "You've got a nasty bump back there."

"That's probably from when I dropped to the floor to get my shot."

"Your shot?" asked the trooper.

"That would explain the concussion," said Angie.

Jess looked from the trooper to the paramedic. "If it's all right with you two, I really need to go."

The trooper opened his mouth to object, but Angie spoke first. "No problem. You get an express ride to the hospital." She pulled a small hypodermic syringe out of her bag. "Here's a little somethin' to calm you down."

"I don't need to calm down. I just need to go. I can drive myself, thank you very much."

Angie shook her head. "Sorry, honey, but you're not fit to drive. You barely even knew your own name two minutes ago. Not only are you in shock with at the very least a moderate concussion, your heart rate and blood pressure are way too high." She held up the syringe. "This is a fentanyl cocktail. You can refuse to take it, but for your own wellbeing, I highly recommend it. Either way, we're putting you in an ambulance and taking you to the hospital. Trust me; it's the fastest way you're getting there." She smiled. "And don't worry, your boyfriend is receiving the best care possible," she said, wiping an area on Jess's arm with an alcohol swab.

"He's not her b-boyfriend," Kevin said as Jess frowned.

Angie swiftly administered the injection, then gave the spot another wipe.

"Hey, I thought you said I could refuse?" Jess rubbed her arm where she'd just received the shot.

"I did, but you didn't, so you got it." She winked at Jess and waved to a couple of nearby EMTs who rushed over with a gurney. "You're about to feel much better and more relaxed." She patted the gurney. "Can you lie down on this for me, please?"

"I don't need that. Really I don't."

"Just let them help you, Jess," Kevin said.

Angie smiled. "Trust me, honey, with what I just gave you, you're gonna be glad you have something to lie down on." She nodded to the EMTs. "Get her up there, guys." They guided Jess onto the gurney and started strapping her down. "Do either of you want to ride with her?" Angie asked Kevin and Dave.

"I will," they said in unison.

The paramedic watched the EMTs finish strapping her to the gurney, then turned to Dave. "Are you her daddy?"

"I am."

If that surprised Angie, she didn't show it. "You're going with us then." She nodded to Kevin. "You good to drive yourself?"

"Sure."

"That's my bro," giggled Jess as they wheeled her up to the back of the ambulance.

Angie chuckled. "That concoction I gave her makes people a little happy. It's got some heavy-duty anxiety modifiers in it."

"Can she take it in a daily tablet form?" Kevin asked facetiously.

"I heard that," Jess said as they lifted her in.

CHAPTER SIXTY

Center Point, Texas
June 1966

Rudy spoke with Molly and Anna Mae over breakfast about what they needed to do to clean up after the tornado. The top priority was to move the massive limb off the balcony—where it rested precariously—before it could cause additional damage. He gave his sister a kind smile. "Why don't you just take it easy today, Anna Mae?"

"I'm happy to help. I know there's a lot to do."

"There is, but much of it's heavier stuff, and there'll be broken glass and other hazards."

Anna Mae set her spoon down. "You know, I feel so cared for by both of you, but really, I'm fine. Plus, I like the idea of fresh air and exercise. It'll be good for me and good for the baby." She winked at Rudy. "Don't you worry. I'll be fine."

* * *

The property was a mess, littered with branches, leaves, random trash, scraps of sheet metal, and pieces of fertilizer bags. Rudy put his hands on his hips and shook his head. It would take days to clean up and repair things. Thirty feet from the house, he turned and looked up at the balcony, damaged by the huge hickory limb. Considering how close the tornado had come, they'd been fortunate.

He was fortunate on many fronts, he thought, watching Anna Mae pick up debris. "You know you don't have to do that," he said.

She just smiled and kept right on working.

"You sure that's good for the baby?"

"Yep."

He shook his head. Once Anna Mae made up her mind about something, there was no changing it.

* * *

Rudy cursed as he tried to start the chainsaw. After yanking the pull cord until his arm was sore, the saw finally coughed twice before sputtering to life in a cloud of pungent blue-and-white smoke.

Cutting and removing the tree limb wasn't as easy as he'd imagined. Around ten inches in diameter, it kept binding against the saw, repeatedly stalling it.

Down below, Molly used the tractor to pull on the limb with a rope to release a bit of pressure, but it wasn't helping much. Some things functioned better in theory than in practice. Rudy found that to make progress, he had to work the chainsaw one-handed and push on the limb with his other hand as the tractor pulled on the rope. His one-handed trick wouldn't win any safety awards, but it worked.

Several things happened nearly at once. The rope creaked loudly before suddenly snapping with a loud crack. A branch hit him in the head as the limb took another part of the balcony railing to the ground. The chainsaw bucked up, and the bar with the sharpened moving chain gouged his shoulder.

He screamed and dropped the saw, blood spurting from his wound. Through blinding pain, he remembered his Red Cross training and immediately lay on his back, trying to stanch the flow of blood with his opposite hand.

Anna Mae rushed out the door and onto the balcony within seconds. "*Rudy!*" she yelled, running to him.

He squinted up at her. "I'm gonna need some help here."

She stepped over him to the edge of the balcony. "*Molly!*" she called out. "Rudy's hurt. We need to call—" She slipped on the expanding pool of blood and grabbed a damaged section of railing that pulled loose in her grasp.

Just out of reach, Rudy watched helplessly as his pregnant sister went over the edge of the balcony with a surprised yelp, still gripping the piece of railing. He got to his feet despite the searing pain and went down to help.

"Oh my God, look at you," cried Molly as he stumbled out the front door. "Sit here with Anna Mae while I call for help."

She guided him to a sitting position next to his sister. Every little movement brought fresh waves of pain, but he almost didn't notice.

"How is she?" he asked as Molly dashed for the front door.

She glanced over her shoulder. "Not good, I'm afraid."

Anna Mae was breathing but unconscious. Unable to take his hand off his wound, Rudy could do nothing for her. Even if he could use both hands, he wouldn't know how to make things right.

After what seemed an eternity, Molly came running out with towels and ice. "Lie down, hon. We've got to get you taken care of."

"Forget about me. Help Anna Mae."

"You lie down, mister. There's nothin' we're gonna be able to do for her until the ambulance arrives. The operator said they'd be here in less than eight minutes. By the looks of your clothes, you've lost way too much blood and—"

"*Help me!*" Anna Mae cried out, grasping her belly with both hands.

CHAPTER SIXTY-ONE

The doctor attending Jess insisted she stay in the hospital overnight so they could keep tabs on her concussion. He didn't think her condition was critical but wanted to keep her under observation in case of internal swelling or hemorrhaging. She'd needed six stitches under her chin, but that was over and done with.

Her head felt like she'd been kicked by a horse, which didn't make it easy to answer all the questions from the DPS trooper. Finally, he thanked her and left, allowing Dave, Kevin, and Elena to come in.

She smiled at their business manager. "You missed all the excitement this afternoon, girlfriend."

"So I heard. Why does all the fun stuff happen whenever I try to take a day off?"

Jess's smile faded, and she asked about Travis.

Kevin shook his head. "They're not tellin' us anythin' since we're not family." He cleared his throat. "Speakin' of which, Agent Mallory is waitin' outside. He said he didn't want to overwhelm you with too many people at once."

"That was nice of him." Jess closed her eyes. "This is unreal."

"I know," Dave said. "I can't believe what those lowlifes were doin' right under our noses."

"Were they really takin' kidnapped girls and women over the border?"

"That's what the sheriff told us. They'd kidnap young women, then take 'em to their underground holdin' cells—on what used to be our property. When they got five or six victims, they'd put 'em in their van and sneak 'em into Mexico."

"Where they'd get sold to the highest bidder," Elena added.

Jess frowned. "That's disgustin'."

"It is," said Dave, "and I'd bet you a hundred dollars they're the ones who poisoned Wallaby and set our mushroom buildin' on fire."

She wished her head would stop pounding so she could think straight. "Why kill an innocent dog? And burnin' down our mushroom operation makes no sense at all."

"We don't know, but they might have been tryin' to run us off so they'd have more privacy. Maybe they thought we'd sell the rest of the property to 'em if they put us out of business. But you put an end to their plans—whatever they were. There were already five girls and women in those underground holdin' cells."

"No way!"

Dave reached out and gently squeezed her hand. "Yeah, three minors and two adults. They'd been missin' from all over the country for months." He gave her a faint smile. "How does it feel to be a hero, Jess?"

Not this again. "I'm not a hero. I just—"

"That's what all the heroes say," Kevin interrupted. "'I was just doin' my duty,' or 'I only did what anyone else would've done under similar circumstances.' It makes you seem like even *more* of a hero 'cause you're so humble."

"Kevin, can you please lean a little closer so I can get a good punch in?"

"Fat chance."

"I was gonna say that I was just tryin' to make things right." She closed her eyes again for a few seconds. "It feels as though I did."

Everyone in the room agreed.

She frowned. "But I wasn't the only one. If the Kidwells hadn't done the right thing, I don't even want to think about where I'd be." She paused. "I wish

I could take back every mean thing I ever said about Earl."

Dave shook his head. "We've all said and done things we regret, honey. It's more important to remember when you've chosen to do the right thing. Accordin' to Reuters, the FBI thinks Johnny and his brother were involved in at least a dozen unsolved kidnappin's around the country. Hopefully, they can figure out where the previous girls had been taken and get 'em back to freedom." He paused. "You know, your pictures were all over the news today."

"You're jokin'?"

"It's true," Kevin said. "Y'all put Center Point on the map." He smiled ruefully. "You and b-both Kidwells. I think the Associated Press headline was 'Ranchers Foil Kidnappers.' They're makin' Earl out as a hero who sacrificed his life for others. Personally, I thought they should've given you more credit."

"It's fine, Kevin. What the Kidwells did was truly heroic."

"B-but you're *our* hero, Jess." One side of his mouth turned up. "For real."

"Well, I deeply appreciate the kind words and support. From all y'all." She took a deep breath. "But right now, I just need to get some shut-eye."

They wished her well. No sooner had they left when Agent Mallory knocked on the door frame. "Is this a good time?"

It wasn't a good time. "I'm not in a very presentable state, I'm afraid."

Missing the hint, he walked in and sat in a chair beside her bed. "You are absolutely presentable, Jessica Atwood. I would've been here sooner, but I was in Dallas when I got your message. The FBI had a team in Kerrville, so I called them and the DPS. Guess they all got there pretty fast."

"Not fast enough for Earl, unfortunately."

"That's too bad. How's his son doing?"

Jess gently shook her head and winced when it throbbed painfully. "They're not tellin' us anythin' 'cause we're not family, but from what I saw at the scene, he's not doin' well."

"Sorry to hear that."

"Me too." She gave him a weak smile. "Thanks for soundin' the alarm and gettin' the cavalry out there."

"Of course."

"Well, I appreciate you stoppin' by, Agent Ed, but I've got the worst headache you can imagine, and I'm just about all talked out."

"I understand. If I promise not to talk, are you okay if I stay here with you?"

"Thanks, but I'll be fine. The doctors and nurses are keepin' a close eye on me." She nodded at the saline drip connected to her arm. "And they're not takin' any chances."

Mallory looked uncertain. "If you're sure . . ."

"I'm sure. I'd love to get a ride back tomorrow, though. They plan to release me around noon."

"Of course."

He stood and glanced at the door, then back at her. "Reckon I'll be goin'."

"Ed. I appreciate you bein' here." She raised a hand toward him.

He gently took it in both of his. "I appreciate you, Jess."

She smiled as best she could. "See ya tomorrow."

He looked as though he was about to say something, then, letting her hand slide out of his, he nodded and walked out. Jess wasn't sure, but he seemed to be on the verge of tearing up. She felt many conflicting emotions. Anger at the kidnappers, gratitude for Ed Mallory, grief for Earl Kidwell, concern for Travis, sadness for the kidnapped girls, relief for the ones who'd been rescued, deep affection for her family, and profound thankfulness for being alive. All competed for center stage in her heart—but only one compelled her to act.

Minutes after Mallory left, she reached over, peeled the tape off her IV needle, and pulled it out, instantly regretting it. It hurt more than she'd expected, and saline fluid streamed out of the needle, puddling on the floor.

She made a mental note to deal with the mess later and swung her feet over the side of the bed. Head pounding and sore all over, she tied the strings on her hospital gown and put on slippers the nurse had left for her. Jess peeked out into the hallway, saw no one, and quickly headed for the elevator. Once inside, she pushed the button labeled "ICU 3rd Floor."

Intensive care reception was directly in front of her when the elevator doors opened. The male charge nurse behind the desk frowned slightly and looked at Jess over the top of his reading glasses. "May I help you?"

"I'd like to see Travis Kidwell, please."

"Are you family?"

"Not exactly."

"Sorry, but we can't let you see him."

"Well," she lied, "we're in a relationship. And I'm the only family he's got left."

The ICU nurse eyed Jess skeptically. "You coulda started with that."

"No one really knows. We've kinda been keepin' it a secret."

"I see," he said, drawing out the words. He removed a folder from his file drawer and opened it. "First of all, nobody but doctors, nurses, and other intensive care personnel are seeing him for the time being. That's gonna be true at least until the day after tomorrow at the earliest."

"Is it that serious?"

"'Fraid so. The bullet missed his heart by only half an inch and punctured his right lung before hittin' the back of his sternum. That put fragments of bone and lead in multiple places, creating significant secondary damage." The nurse flipped another page. "He's lost a lot of blood and has had two transfusions so far." He glanced at Jess and pointed to a nearby chair. "You look pale. Sit."

"I'm fine. I just—"

The nurse stood and emphatically pointed at the chair again. "Sit now, then we'll talk," he commanded.

Jess complied as he came around the reception desk.

"Lean forward and rest your head between your knees," he said, then raised an eyebrow. "Are you supposed to be walking around in your condition?"

"Probably not." She leaned forward, the stitches under her chin throbbing painfully. "But we went through this together, and I have to find out if he's gonna be okay." She remembered she had a story to maintain and slowly sat back upright. "'Cause I really care. I . . . I love him."

"You know, I hear interesting stories from all kinds of folks. For me, reading people isn't just a hobby. Sometimes it can mean the difference between life and death. What's funny is when I hear someone tell the truth when they think they're lying." He smiled and walked back behind the reception desk.

"Can you tell me the rest?" she asked.

"You sure you want to hear more?"

"Please."

He looked at her thoughtfully and chewed his lower lip. "In the seven and a half hours since they brought him in, he's gone into cardiac arrest twice. We might have lost him if a nurse hadn't been standing by with the defibrillator. The second time, it took four tries before his heart started again. Dr. Mason is the cardiologist on his case, and right now, she's only giving him a one-in-three chance of survival. They're doing everything they can, but . . ." He sighed and gave her a gentle smile. "Sometimes, that's just not enough." He closed the folder. "I wish I had better news, but you should prepare yourself for the worst. This may not end well."

* * *

A call from a number Jess didn't recognize came the day after she got home from the hospital.

"Hello?"

"Jessica Atwood?"

She hated sales calls. "Who wants to know?"

"My name is Leon Houk. How are you today?"

"If you must know, I'm pissed 'cause my name is on the national do-not-call list, yet here you are callin' me anyway."

"I'm with the United States Paintball Association."

"Say what?"

"We read about your adventure with those kidnappers on the internet. The article also mentioned that you're a paintball enthusiast. I did a little research and found out you not only teach paintball; you're an outstanding competitor."

"Well, that may be a bit of an exaggeration."

"I don't think so. I spoke to Brad Rose at Blitz Paintball in Kerrville, and he said you're the best paintballer who's ever walked through his doors."

"I reckon he was just bein' kind."

"I think he was just being honest. How come you've never competed at the national level?"

"'Cause I'm a farmer and can't just take off whenever I want. Besides, those things take a lot of money with travel and all."

"That's why you get a sponsorship. You think Tippmann Paintball Guns wouldn't jump at the chance to have their name on the vest of a national champion?"

"Of course they would, but—how do you know I shoot a Tippmann?"

"I didn't, but they sell to more pros than all the other brands put together, so it was an easy guess. I'm sure they'd be delighted to know that you shoot one of their guns."

"First off, I've never won a championship, and second, I'm no pro."

"But you could be. What's the highest level of competition you've been in?"

"Only the local tournaments at Blitz, though I once entered a regional match in San Antonio. That was fun."

"Let me guess, you got first place, right?"

"Well, the competition wasn't very stiff."

Leon chuckled. "Compared to you, I'm sure it wasn't."

"I don't know about that, but our farm is gonna be closin' down soon, so I'll have time to compete in more tournaments."

"Which fits perfectly into why I'm calling you. We're looking for a top-notch instructor who can train national-level competitors."

"Thanks for askin', but I've only trained some local guys—and the occasional girl."

"Brad Rose says whoever took your class became a far better competitor. He said your class has a weeks-long waiting list."

"That's 'cause I'm the only one givin' classes there."

"Listen, Jess, I appreciate your humility, but here's our offer: You'll get A-level trainer status with unlimited practice time on our thirteen-acre tactical field. We want you to go national and would love to be one of your sponsors. You know, business is more about publicity and marketing than anything else. You're already known as the woman who used her paintball skills to take out a pair of dangerous kidnappers."

"I only took out one of 'em."

Leon laughed. "That still makes you pretty badass. You're someone a competitor on their way up would love to train with."

"Well . . ."

"Here's the best part. As you may know, we're based in Virginia, just outside Richmond. We'd pay all of your relocation expenses and can offer you a starting salary of $63,000, full medical and dental, and three weeks of paid vacation per year."

"Really?"

"Really. But that's not all. You get a hundred-dollar bonus for every one of your trainees who wins bronze in any national competition. Silver means a $200 bonus, and each gold nets you $500."

"Wow."

"And that doesn't even include what you'd make with sponsorships—from us and others. We're talking at least another $20,000 per year once you win some high-profile tournaments. Paintball is a rapidly growing sport, and the US Paintball Association wants you to help us look good." He paused. "So, what do you think?"

"I'm flattered you think I'm that good."

"Is that a yes then?"

"That's a strong maybe. I need time to think about it and talk to my family."

"I understand, but we need an answer from you within a week, so we know if we have to look elsewhere."

"I'll get back to you before then," she said, but couldn't help thinking it all sounded too good to be true.

CHAPTER SIXTY-TWO

Rudy had experienced excruciating pain when the chainsaw hit him, but it was nothing compared to what he felt over the possibility of losing Anna Mae. His carelessness ultimately caused the fall she'd warned him about because he hadn't taken her visions seriously. Things happened more or less the way she predicted, but he hadn't believed any of it until it was too late. The guilt from that weighed him down like cement shoes.

He hoped with all his heart that she was wrong about the dying part. Her coma had just entered its fifth week, and the doctors were annoyingly vague about her chances of survival.

Rudy sat on the living room couch with his right arm in a sling and a bulky bandage on his shoulder. He stared at his wife and baby niece, feeling things more deeply than he had his entire life—more than when he saw fellow soldiers die in Vietnam and more than when he saw his father slapping his mother or whipping four-year-old Anna Mae when she spilled a glass of milk on the kitchen table.

Visiting his sister in the hospital became a daily ritual. Their young peanut crop suffered from neglect, but that made little difference to Rudy. Anna Mae was all he could think about, and the fear of her not surviving consumed him every moment of every day. Besides, working the farm one-handed didn't allow him to do much. The doctors said he'd most likely recover the full use of his arm, but not for at least a few months. The painkillers they gave him did nothing to soothe his emotional distress. His eyes filled with tears as he looked at Baby Katherine. Such a beautiful little girl. If only Anna Mae could have held her before falling into the coma. The ambulance attendant who'd delivered her on the way to the hospital said Anna Mae had taken one look at her baby girl, smiled, and then lost consciousness.

Rudy had been right there next to her, but they said he'd passed out as they put him in the ambulance, so he missed the moment. He hoped Anna Mae had sensed he was there and that his presence made a difference. The love he felt for his sister nearly took his breath away.

He felt his wife's anxiety as well. Just a couple of months before, Anna Mae had comforted Molly when the doctor told her she'd be unable to have children. She thanked him that night for bringing his sister into their lives. And now they had a baby to take care of—to help Anna Mae take care of, he fervently hoped.

The doorbell's ring startled him. He rose from his chair too quickly and groaned at the flash of pain in his shoulder.

The well-dressed man on the porch with a briefcase in his hand looked grim. "Mr. Rudolf Cole?"

"That's me. What can I do for you?"

"I'm here on behalf of your sister, Anna Mae Cole."

"Say what?"

"I've been her attorney of record for the past seven months and have business on her behalf."

Rudy wondered if he'd heard the man correctly. "Her attorney?"

"That's right. The name's Pete Carson, out of Kerrville, listed with the State Bar of Texas and duly licensed to practice law here. I have the last will and testament, custody documents, and other miscellaneous wishes of Miss Anna Mae Cole to be executed in the case of her demise or unconsciousness for a month or more. May I come in?"

Rudy opened the door wider and stood aside. "By all means," he said, shaking his head in disbelief. He motioned toward the living room couch. "Please have a seat."

Molly nodded nervously to him and gave her husband a puzzled look.

"This is Mr. Carson, an attorney Anna Mae hired," Rudy explained.

Carson gave her a thin smile. "I'm sorry for the difficulty of the situation, ma'am. Anna Mae made plans in case she was in a coma or killed."

"I had no idea."

"She said something about not wanting to talk to either of you about it," Carson said, "but she had visions of being in a coma and dying, which, as you know, has come to pass. The coma part, that is," he added quickly, setting down his briefcase. He pulled out a set of papers and handed them to Rudy. "First, these are your custody documents, legally notarized by Anna Mae, referencing any children of hers in the event of her death or incapacitation." He nodded toward Katherine. "Though I believe this is the only child she had in mind."

"Hang on a minute," said Rudy. "We saw her today, and she . . . she's fine. We're not gonna talk about her like she's already gone."

Carson nodded sympathetically. "Of course not. Her complete recovery is what we all hope for." He cleared his throat. "But her will states that if she's comatose for a month or more, then I am to carry this out, and I'm legally and ethically bound to do so." He reached into the briefcase again and pulled out another document. "She states here that if she's unresponsive for forty-five consecutive days, then her request is to have all life-support removed . . . which would include the respirator she's currently on."

"But she'd die," Molly said.

Carson nodded slowly. "She figured that after forty-five days, she doubted she would ever really come back. Plus, she didn't want to be a burden on you both."

"A burden?" exclaimed Rudy. "No way could she ever be a burden on us."

"I tried to tell her you'd probably feel that way, but she was adamant."

Rudy couldn't believe his ears. "But that's only . . ." He did a quick mental calculation. "That's only a week and a half away." He looked at Molly, whose face registered the same shock he felt. "You can't make us do that."

"Technically, it's only a request. It's ultimately up to you, but it's what Anna Mae wants. I have a letter she wrote, addressed to both of you. May I read it aloud?"

They each nodded, too shocked to speak.

> *"Dearest Molly and Rudy,*
>
> *Never in my life have I wanted so badly to be wrong about something. I respected your wish, Rudy, and haven't talked about my death. I've also had dreams of being in a coma and decided not to bring that up, either. I don't know whether any of my visions will come true, but as you can see, I've made plans in case any or all of them come to pass.*
>
> *Perhaps one day in my old age, when I'm playing with my grandchildren, I'll remember this letter I gave to Mr. Pete Carson to hold back in 1966. I'll laugh and call Katherine to let her in on the joke.*
>
> *If one of my visions was accurate, you might be reading this after I've passed on or become a vegetable. Please forgive my forty-five-day request. My wish is that you kindly honor it.*
>
> *People say that it's all over when we die, or we get a new life, or our soul goes to be with God. Honestly, I can't say for sure what happens or where we go, but I don't believe we ever simply end. We just continue on in a different form, maybe in a different life, maybe in heaven.*
>
> *I know without a doubt how deeply I love you, my dear brother. You were always there for me. You made the difference for me between what could've been a miserable life and one worth living. You showed me what unconditional love is, and thanks to you, I'm closer to that than I would have ever been without your help.*
>
> *Molly, Rudy was not exaggerating when he told me he fell in love with the most wonderful woman in the world. Thank you so much for taking me in, caring for me, and treating me as family.*

Hopefully, you have both accepted Baby Katherine as your own. At least, that is my prayer. She could not have two more excellent, compassionate, loving individuals as her guardians and parents.

You'll eventually find this out anyway, but you should know that she will also see things before they happen. She'll have doubts about it and will need you both to believe unconditionally in her and her gift. She appeared to me in a dream back in Tennessee before I got pregnant with her, saying I see like you, so I know she'll foresee future events. She'll be a happy baby who will grow into a loving, caring adult. I know she'll have your support, which will make all the difference in her life.

I assume Mr. Carson has already given you the legal custody papers, and I have another request. My closet has an old shoe box with a locked diary in it. The key should be in the drawer of the nightstand next to my bed. Please give both to Mr. Carson. I've instructed him to send them to Katherine's father after a certain someone in his life passes on, whenever that may be. I believe it'll be quite some time in the future.

Please maintain our agreement to not have any contact with anyone in Wears Valley about me or Baby Katherine, even after I'm gone, and forgive me for not sharing the name of Katherine's father with you. I will only say that he's a good man, very much like you, Rudy. Also, like you, he's someone I love and respect. Although he doesn't even know Katherine exists, he will when Mr. Carson gives him my diary.

I wish you and Molly the most incredible lives imaginable. I wish you as much love as your hearts can hold, then double and triple that. I'm deeply blessed that you are my family.

You know how much I love you. Please don't think my death would ever change that. My eternal love to you both and to Baby Katherine.

Anna Mae Cole

P.S. Please put this letter in the diary to go with Mr. Carson. I want Katherine's father to read it one day."

Rudy wiped a tear from his cheek. "She's gonna be here to raise her daughter, Mr. Carson. I know it."

Carson smiled, but it seemed forced. "That would certainly be the best possible outcome." He cleared his throat. "Well then, if you agree to Anna Mae's request, I'll take the diary, letter, and key into safekeeping and be on my way."

Rudy stood. "I'll be right back." He nodded to Molly, whose eyes glistened. By the time he returned, even Carson seemed to be misting up.

As he handed over the diary, Rudy felt the irony of the words written down the front:

This
Too
Shall
Pass

CHAPTER SIXTY-THREE

Center Point, Texas
Present Day

Jess was surprised when she heard the good news about Travis. After he spent two weeks in intensive care and another ten days in a regular hospital bed, the doctors predicted a complete recovery.

The same week he was released, he stopped by one morning for the third time in two days. Jess had long since given up pretending to be annoyed when she saw him, especially since their relationship was clearly in the friend zone. Not that it had been romantic before—at least not recently—but now that she was dating someone else, her relationship with Travis was more straightforward. That took some pressure off, and Jess enjoyed their friendship. The last time he was over, she was surprised to hear he'd been meditating daily. She'd never known him to have much of a spiritual side.

Things were going well with Ed Mallory. A couple of weeks before, he'd taken her back to his hotel room, and though she politely turned down his wine, she graciously accepted the rest of what he had to offer. It had been too long since she'd slept with anyone, and it was good to be back in the saddle.

Jess felt she had the best of both worlds: a potential boyfriend on the one hand and a newfound guy friend on the other. While Agent Mallory was charming, clever, and romantic, Travis was true to his boots, as he would say himself in his down-home country-boy manner. Several times when she was out with Ed, she wondered what Travis was doing at that moment.

They'd argued about him a couple of weeks earlier. All she'd done was to bring up something funny Travis had said, and Ed mentioned that she talked about him more than was usual for friends. She tried to explain that the amount she spoke of him was perfectly normal. Mallory didn't accept that and became upset when Jess accused him of being jealous. The date ended on a sour note.

Travis had generously paid the Atwoods well over market value for their old thirty-horsepower John Deere tractor, which they all appreciated. Now he surprised her by saying he was taking his ranch in a new direction.

"How's that?" she asked.

"I've been lookin' into regenerative farmin'. The Central Texas Cattle Show is happenin' in San Antonio next month, and I'm puttin' my livestock up for auction."

"All of 'em?"

"Yep. Not that I have that many. Earl already thinned the herd last fall."

"If you want to practice regenerative farmin', you need to keep those animals on the land."

"Really?"

She cocked her head to the side and smiled. "Thought you said you studied it."

"I said I was lookin' into it."

"You gotta do more than that if you want to make a difference, cowboy."

"Look, I didn't come over here to argue with you. Thought you might be happy to know I was tryin' somethin' different, especially since it's right up your alley."

"Sorry, I just get excited about this stuff. So, congratulations."

"Thanks." He looked uncertain, as though he had more to say.

"Travis Kidwell, what did you *really* come over here for?"

"Well . . . I've been thinkin' about what it'd take to make sustainable organic farmin' a profitable business."

"I can tell you right now it would never make as much as your cattle ranch."

"I don't know about that. I researched it, and there are some very profitable organic farms. I read about this farmer up in Wisconsin. Everyone told him the only way to succeed up there is dairy farmin', but he set his mind on makin' his organic cranberry farm succeed. Last year, as one of the largest organic cranberry suppliers in the US, he made over a half-million dollars in profit. It took him more than ten years of hard, focused work with many setbacks to get there, but he did what many folks swore he couldn't. Inc. magazine even interviewed him after he made their top-5000 list of the fastest-growin' small businesses in the United States. You know what he told them when they asked how he did it?"

"No, but I'm just about dyin' of suspense."

Travis shook his head and grinned. "He said he ran his business as a spiritual practice and saw everythin' that happened—the good, the bad, and even the ugly—as part of that practice. He also vowed that he'd learn somethin' from everyone he interacted with, be they friend or foe. That made all the difference in his life and business. Readin' that, I asked myself why couldn't I run *my* business as a spiritual practice?"

It took Jess a few seconds to realize her mouth was open. "I swear, Travis Kidwell, you never cease to amaze me. I wish you well with that." She glanced at her watch. "I need to get goin' here, but I reckon I owe you a debt of gratitude."

He started to protest, but Jess held up her hand. "We both know I wouldn't be standin' here if you hadn't cared enough to come across the highway after me that day."

Travis scratched his chin. "I was just doin' the right thing."

"That's my line," she said with a laugh. "Don't we make the perfect little soap opera? I can see it now. Netflix starts a new miniseries called *As the World Turns in Center Point, Texas.* Yee-haw."

They both laughed, then she excused herself, saying she had to get her things packed and out of there before the new owners came in with the sheriff to carry her out kicking and screaming.

"I don't think that will be necessary, Miss Atwood."

"No, for sure it is. The notice from the courthouse says we have to vacate before noon tomorrow."

"I heard the new owner wants you to stay on."

"That isn't gonna happen. I don't need anyone rubbin' my face in our failure."

"You didn't fail. You just found a way that didn't work. Besides, ownership is overrated. We don't carry our titles or deeds with us when we die." He raised an eyebrow. "Or our GTOs."

She smiled at the thought. "Be that as it may, I'd be happy to help someone get their business goin' under different circumstances, but I'm done here."

"I think the new owner wants you to run it as your own business and profit share with him."

"And just how would you know that, Mr. Kidwell?"

"'Cause that new owner is me."

"You're jokin'."

"Not at all. Got a heck of a deal on it, too."

"Wait a second, didn't . . ." She called out to the other room, "Kevin, who did you say bought our property at the auction?"

"The Guadalupe Land B-Bank, or somethin' like that."

"The Guadalupe Land Trust, to be precise," Travis said. "One of three trusts Earl set up years ago. I've been an officer and signer on them since they started."

"Unbelievable."

"Believe it." He laughed. "Anyway, the invitation is for you to stay here and run your farm any way you please, and I would just take a cut of the profits. Or . . . I have a bigger invitation."

Jess sat on the couch, afraid she might faint. "And what might that be?"

"For you to help me create one of the most successful organic farms in the United States. I'm good with the business side of things, but I'll need a lot of help with ladybugs and such."

"Talk about a babe in the woods." She paused. "I don't know. I need some time to think about it."

"And ask your boyfriend," he said with a wink.

"That wasn't what I meant, and he's not my boyfriend. Not really. We're just datin'. Or were. I haven't heard from him for some time."

"I see," he said, drawing the word out, trying not to smile. "Take all the time you need. I've considered this for weeks, and as of this mornin', I'm fully decided. I'm happy to keep your guys employed, though I reckon Kevin might want to be movin' on."

"You got that right, b-buddy," he said from the other room.

"Just so you know," Travis said to Jess, "I'm not lookin' for a committee to help me make business decisions."

"Didn't think you would be."

"I'm offerin' you a full partnership in a new enterprise we're gonna create together. We'd share decisions equally. Whatever we make out of this will be fifty-percent yours. All the property will be under my name, but with your share of profits, you can buy into that whenever you want."

"That's a noble offer, Travis."

"I'm hearing a 'but' in there somewhere."

"The day after I got out of the hospital, I got a call from the USPA."

"The what?"

"The US Paintball Association, offering me a job trainin' national-level competitors. It's the kind of thing I've hankered for since I was in my teens."

"I know how much you love paintball." He shrugged. "But I'd love to be in partnership with you . . . " He turned bright red. "In business, of course."

"Of course."

"You'd have to be one hundred percent into it. I'm confident we could turn it into somethin' that will do a lot of good for a lot of people and would make us decent money. But obviously, you'd have to want it just as much as I do. If you decide to accept my offer, I'd need an absolute commitment from you. Do some serious thinkin', talk to whoever you trust, and see what they say. But let me know soon, so I can begin makin' plans." He started to leave, then snapped his fingers when he was halfway to the door. "Oh, and that two-acre parcel by the river you sold to those evil people?"

"Yeah?"

"It went on the County's seized assets auction three weeks ago, though not many folks seemed to notice. The GLT noticed, however, and snapped it up."

"GLT?" Jess asked.

"The Guadalupe Land Trust."

"You mean . . ."

"Yep. You can go down there with your favorite book and soak your feet off that little ol' dock whenever you fancy. And it looks like we got us a lot of extra storage space all of a sudden. That is, if your answer is yes." He examined his fingernails for a few seconds. "To be completely transparent, buyin' up your two pieces of property put me well into the red, so I'm under some financial stress right now. It'd be a bit of an uphill climb for a while, but I was thinkin' the house the kidnappers built would make a great little Airbnb. It even has a fireplace and will help our short-term cash flow."

"Travis . . . why are you doin' this?"

He paused with his hand on the doorknob. "I think a better question would be, 'Why not?'" His expression hard to read, he touched his hat and walked out the door.

* * *

Jess glanced at Mallory's number on her phone and waited a couple of seconds before answering. They hadn't spoken for a while, and his responses to her texts had seemed distant and somewhat cool. "Agent Ed, to what do I owe the pleasure?"

"I apologize for takin' so long to call, but . . . things have been busy."

"No doubt."

"I wanted you to be one of the first to know I've been promoted to captain, mostly 'cause of you and your visions."

"Thanks, but I just did what was right."

"You went far above and beyond just what was right, which brings me to the other reason I'm callin' you."

"Uh-oh."

"Don't worry, this is somethin' good. With the help of Interpol, the FBI, and the Mexican authorities, we've tracked down ten of the thirteen missin' girls so far. Would've been eighteen if you hadn't interfered with their dirty little operation." He paused. "Remember that girl with the white-blonde hair you told us about?"

"Ashley. Of course."

"She was one of the five bein' held there on the property where you had your little shootout. I was present in East Dallas when she was reunited with her family, and I have to say it was the most emotional event I've experienced in my life. Everybody was cryin'."

"You mean everybody except you," she teased.

"I mean everybody. Thanks to you."

"Well, it wasn't just me."

"Maybe not, but it was *mostly* you."

"I was just tryin' to—"

"Jess. Take it in. You did great."

"Okay, if you say so."

"I do. And Jess . . ."

"Yeah?"

"You really are amazin'."

She tried to let that sink in, but something about it felt hollow. "Thanks, but what are you not tellin' me?"

"What makes you think I'm not tellin' you somethin'?"

"There *is* somethin', isn't there?"

"Well . . ."

"Here we go."

He sighed. "My ex-wife has been in touch with me."

"I thought she wasn't speakin' to you?"

"She wasn't, but now . . . now she wants to talk about reconciliation."

"That's a pretty big shift from not talkin'."

"I know. She says our son keeps askin' about me."

"Your *what*?"

"Our—"

"How is it you never told me you had a son?"

"I was waitin' for the right moment. I swear I was gonna tell you."

"Sure you were. How old is he?"

"Six."

"I can't believe I'm only hearin' this now! How old was he when you divorced?" There was a few seconds of silence. "Agent Mallory, how old was he?"

"Technically, we're not exactly divorced."

"Not *exactly* divorced?"

"We've been separated for nearly a year, which is practically the same thing."

"Please tell me you're jokin'."

"Jess, it's not as bad as it sounds."

"I gotta go."

"If you just give me a chance to explain—"

"You've already had *many* chances to explain. Sounds like now you've got some important business to take care of that has nothin' whatsoever to do with me." She ended the call without waiting for a response.

CHAPTER SIXTY-FOUR

Center Point, Texas
July 1966

Neither Rudy nor Molly mentioned it when the coma entered its seventh week, but they were both aware of the slim number of days Anna Mae had left before they would unplug her respirator. The doctors told them the longer a coma continued, the less likelihood there would be of a complete recovery. When he wasn't at the hospital, Rudy constantly worried about his sister. They had visited her that morning, and she looked slightly paler, her breathing shallower than they'd remembered from the day before. The nurse on duty told them her CCM showed her heartbeat as irregular and appeared to be weakening.

"Her what?"

"Her CCM. It means continuous cardiac monitoring. We only just got the equipment a few months ago. It tracks a patient's heart activity and alerts us if anything goes wrong. We only use it when a situation is serious or critical." She shook her head. "I hate to be the one to tell you this, but she may not bounce back."

"Really?"

"I'm afraid so. We've seen no eye movement under her lids for a few days now."

"We're not givin' up," Rudy said.

"Of course not," she replied in a practiced, reassuring voice. "We all hope for the best."

* * *

They'd only been home from the hospital a few hours when the phone rang. The nurse on the other end asked them to come back in immediately. Rudy's heart sank. It was the call he'd been fearing for weeks. He asked her to tell him more, but she said she was just passing on the message from the head nurse, who was currently in with Anna Mae.

The trip to the hospital was tense and quiet, except for Baby Katherine, who seemed to enjoy the ride immensely. She cooed and made baby chuckles all the way there.

As they entered the intensive care ward, the head nurse smiled warmly at Molly and Rudy.

"Thank you for coming down so quickly. I don't want to give you false hopes, but Anna Mae has been stirring."

Relief washed over Rudy. "Can we see her?" he asked.

"Of course. She may even sense that you're in the room." The nurse smiled at Katherine. "And you brought her baby. That's wonderful."

She led them into Anna Mae's room, where a doctor was checking her vitals. He looked up and frowned. "What are they doing here?" he snapped at the nurse.

"I called them since the patient was—"

"This is important work, in case you haven't noticed." He nodded toward the door. "And visiting hours are long over."

Molly turned to go, but Rudy spoke up. "If it's all the same to you, sir, we'd love to be near my sister for at least a few minutes. I promise we won't get in the way."

"I'm afraid that's out of the question. We have visitor policies for a reason." He raised his eyebrows at the nurse. "Please show our guests out and give them a copy of our visitation schedule. You might want to take one for yourself while you're at it."

Once they were walking down the hall, Molly glanced back over her shoulder. "That doc was pretty rude, wasn't he?"

"He sure was. But did you see Anna Mae? She looked different, like she was dreamin' about somethin'. I think I saw her face twitch."

"I didn't notice," Molly said. "I was payin' attention to Katherine, afraid that nasty doctor was gonna make her cry."

"She sure picks up on things, doesn't she?" He smiled at his niece and pressed the elevator button.

Molly gave Baby Katherine a little bounce, and she giggled in response. "She sure does."

The elevator doors opened, and Molly stepped in with the baby. Rudy glanced up the hall and saw a nurse running into Anna Mae's room. He stared as another nurse ran in right before the doctor hurried out, yelling something at the remaining nurse at the station. The elevator doors started closing, but he stuck his hand in to stop them. "Molly, somethin's going on with Anna Mae."

She stepped back out of the elevator. "Should we go see?"

"Wild horses or rude doctors couldn't stop us." He put a gentle hand on her arm. "Come on."

No one challenged them when they arrived at Anna Mae's room, where they stood at the door and watched. It was hard to tell what everyone was doing, but when Anna Mae's hand moved, Rudy's heart nearly skipped a beat. "Did you see that?" he asked Molly.

"I sure did. Oh Rudy, she's—"

Anna Mae turned her head toward them, her eyes blinking in the bright light. "My baby," she mouthed, managing a faint smile. She closed her eyes again as a steady, loud tone sounded in the room.

The doctor frantically motioned for someone to shut the door. The nurse who told them about the CCM earlier that day gently closed it without looking either of them in the eye.

CHAPTER SIXTY-FIVE

"I hereby call this meetin' to order," Travis said.

Jess rolled her eyes and rubbed her neck. "You wanna sit down? It gives me a crick havin' to turn around and look at you up there."

"I'm good, thanks, and way too lazy to take my boots off. You don't have to look at me. Just focus on the water. It might calm you down a bit."

"I don't need any calmin' down, Travis Kidwell. I swear, sometimes you exasperate me."

"Maybe we should've asked your big Texas Ranger to the meetin' so you'd be more at ease with him here to protect you."

"I don't need any protection, thank you very much, and besides, he's not *my* Texas Ranger. We're ancient history."

"I'm terribly sorry to hear that."

"You are not one bit sorry, Mr. Kidwell."

"Guilty as charged, Your Honor."

"Right. So, are we gonna get somethin' done today? Maybe meetin' here on the dock wasn't the smartest move in the world."

"I was gettin' down to business, and *you're* the one who got us off track." He paused. "Besides, what better place to have a board meetin' than on a dock made of boards?"

"You're hopeless."

"I know, but there isn't much we can do about that, is there? Shall we go

355

over the minutes from our last meetin'?"

"What minutes? You're the CEO, and I'm president of our little LLC. You're management, and I'm the pretty face behind the brand."

"You're *so* much more than that. And don't be callin' our enterprise little. We're doin' big things in the world. At least we're goin' to."

"I've no doubt about that, but the real question is—oh my God!" Jess jumped up and was on her feet in less than a second. "Look at that!" She pointed to the middle of the river, grabbed Travis's hand, and pushed back against him.

"What?" Travis chuckled. "Not just anyone would get so excited about a damn log. Jess Atwood, you are one special woman."

Jess pointed again, shaking with excitement. "Since when do logs have eyes?"

"What in tarnation are you—holy cow, that's a *gator*."

"Great deduction, Sherlock."

They watched it lazily float past, and Travis let out a low whistle. "My entire life, I've never seen one of those in the Guadalupe. That's a big one, too. Must be at least four or five feet long. Didn't think they came this far up."

"Me neither."

It headed downriver until it looked like a floating stick in the distance. It was almost out of sight when Jess realized she was still pushing back against Travis, still holding his hand.

Jess momentarily tensed as he put his other arm around her.

"So . . ." he started.

"Hmm." She felt secure in his arms. "So?"

"I've got a little surprise for you."

She turned to face him. So that was why he wanted to meet on the dock. What better place for a first kiss? "What's that?" she asked in her most sensual voice, her eyes half-closed.

"Follow me," he enthusiastically said as he turned and walked briskly to his pickup truck. He held the passenger door open and laughed. "You just gonna stand there frownin' at me, or you want to find out what the surprise is? Grab your boots, and let's go."

They drove across the highway and parked near one of his garages. He pulled a remote opener off the truck's visor and jumped out, motioning for her to follow.

"What's all the fuss about?" she asked as they stood in front of his pickup.

Travis pointed the garage door opener at her. "You're about to find out if you can practice a bit of patience."

"I've got more patience in my big toe than you've got in your entire being."

"Sure you do, but let's not fight in front of the kids."

"What on earth are you goin' on about?"

The sound of the garage door opening caught her attention. When it was only eight inches up, a tiny puppy came running out, making excited little yips. "What the hell?" she exclaimed with a giggle, watching the puppy enthusiastically wag its stubby tail, running on short little legs toward her. "Is that a dog or a guinea pig with oversized ears? He's so cute."

"She," corrected Travis. He gestured at the dog as it arrived at Jess's feet. "Meet Peanut, the eight-week-old corgi with too much attitude for her own good."

Jess bent down to pet the excited little dog, but Peanut circled Jess twice without slowing down before running to Travis. He picked her up and scratched behind her ears. "Want to hold her?"

"Are you kiddin' me?" She held out her arms. "She is so unbelievably precious."

Peanut started squirming almost as soon as Jess had her.

"Just so you know, she gets restless right quick," Travis said.

Jess laughed and set her back down. The puppy immediately started running circles around her again. "She's just a little bundle of energy, isn't she? And she does look like an animated peanut."

"She sure does." He paused. "Her name is a nod to your great-uncle Rudy's peanut operation, long before it became the soon-to-be world-famous Heart of Texas Farm."

"Aw. That's sweet." She smiled at him. "But I'm surprised you didn't get a proper cattle dog since you're keepin' some livestock on the land."

"You mean a cattle dog like Wallaby?"

She closed her eyes for a moment. "Yeah, like Wallaby. Accordin' to Earl, he was a natural at herdin' cattle, especially when he wasn't supposed to."

"True, but the thing about corgis a lot of folks don't know is that they're also cattle dogs."

"You're kiddin."

"I'm not. They nip at the bigger animals' heels and are low enough to the ground and fast enough to avoid any kicks coming their way."

She bent down again to pet the tiny puppy, who this time rolled onto her back, making Jess giggle. "Will you look at that?" She shook her head and rubbed the little dog's belly. "She's perfect for you."

"I don't think so."

"Why in the world not?"

"'Cause she's your dog."

"Oh, I couldn't—"

"I'll keep Peanut if you don't want her. I just thought she'd make a wonderful partnership gift."

Jess looked at the energetic puppy—again circling her legs, making the occasional excited yip—and her eyes welled with tears. She opened her mouth to say something clever, but words wouldn't come. She put her arms around her new business partner and gave him a very unbusinesslike kiss.

CHAPTER SIXTY-SIX

Center Point, Texas
September 1979
(Eleven years before Jess is born)

Katherine let the screen door slam behind her, dropped her books in the hall, and stomped up the stairs.

"How was school, Kat?" Molly asked, walking out of the office where she'd been working on the farm's accounts.

"Awful," she mumbled as she reached the top of the stairs and turned down the hall toward her room.

Molly shook her head. It had been Kat's first day at school in almost two weeks. It was bound to be difficult, considering what she'd been through. The coma itself had lasted five days, and there were times when they thought they might lose her. The doctors said she'd had an acute allergic reaction to the rattlesnake bite and recommended another week of rest after she got home.

Molly sat back at her desk. The stressful ordeal reminded her of thirteen years earlier when they lost Anna Mae after she'd been in a coma for nearly two months. Thankfully, Kat had completely recovered, which was a blessing for them all.

Other things had also been going well. Profits were up, thanks to the ever-increasing consumer demand for peanut butter. Best Foods alone had bought fourteen tons of peanuts from them in 1975, all destined for Skippy Peanut Butter. The next few years had been even better, and they'd harvested an average of twenty-three tons annually. They'd been able to afford a used thirty-horsepower John Deere tractor that spring to replace their old International Harvester Farmall. In 1970, she'd tried to talk Rudy into a more diversified set of crops, but he insisted the demand for peanuts would keep going up.

She sighed and reopened their book of accounts. He'd definitely been right. Just like he'd been right when he kept telling her Kat would make it. Despite all his confident talk, however, Molly suspected her husband had been more worried than he let on.

But their niece was alive and healthy, which was all that mattered. Kat might not love middle school, but that wasn't unusual. Molly absently tapped her pencil on the ledger. She'd always dreamt that she and Rudy would have children of their own, but in a greater sense, Kat *was* their own.

* * *

Rudy sat bolt upright and wondered what had woken him. He'd been dreaming about Kat and her close call earlier that month. She'd morphed into Anna Mae in his dream and didn't survive. The actual situation had been way too close for comfort. Few people died from rattlesnake bites, but according to the doctors, Kat had been in grave danger because of her allergic reaction, and Rudy was afraid they'd lose her. He felt a tsunami of relief when he found out she'd be okay.

According to one nurse, the day before she'd come out of the coma, their niece had said strange things in her sleep about guns and girls. Rudy and Molly felt guilty that they hadn't been in the room when that happened, but as the nurse pointed out, their presence wouldn't have made a lick of difference. She explained that comas occurred in various ways, and people often had nightmares as they came out of them. It was a powerful sign that Kat's brain activity was returning to normal. The nurse had smiled and told them not to worry.

"*Watch out!*" Kat yelled from her room.

Rudy's feet hit the floor, and he ran to the hallway.

"Everythin' all right?" Molly asked sleepily.

"*Kat's havin' a nightmare,*" he called over his shoulder, hurrying down the hall. He ran into her room, and from the pale moonlight streaming through the window, he saw his niece flopping around on the bed like a fish out of water, saying words that made no sense.

Molly arrived moments later. "Oh, my. Do you think this is another reaction to the snakebite?" she asked.

"Not sure. Do you think we should wake her?"

"It might be better to call her doctor first."

Rudy frowned. "Maybe, though it looks like she's startin' to calm down."

"Jess, be careful," Kat said. "So much danger."

Rudy looked at his wife. "Who's Jess?"

"No idea. I wonder if that's a kid in her class?" She stared at Kat and chewed her lower lip. "And why would she be in danger?"

"You got me."

Molly pursed her lips. "You don't suppose she's having some kind of . . . vision?"

"Could be. Anna Mae said in the letter she wrote us all those years ago that her daughter would see the future."

They watched their niece settle down, her movements becoming less intense, her breathing gradually returning to normal. She sighed in her sleep, rolled over, and murmured something they couldn't make out. Within a minute, she had a peaceful look on her face.

"What do we do now?" Molly asked.

Rudy shook his head, still watching Kat. "It might be a good idea to mention somethin' to the school—or maybe even the sheriff—in case there *is* a Jess in danger."

"They'll think we've only got one oar in the water."

"Possibly, but we have to say somethin'."

Molly sighed. "You think she'll have more episodes like this?"

He tugged on his earlobe. "Don't know, but I reckon we'll find out."

～

THANK YOU

Thanks for taking the time to read this book. That means a lot to me.

I'd appreciate it if you left a review on Amazon so others can know what you thought of *The Reluctant Visionary*. Reviews and word of mouth are the best ways people can find out about this book. If you liked it, others will too.

This is my second novel. My debut novel, *Different,* won twelve literary awards, and I am already enjoying the process of writing a third novel. Your review will encourage me.

With gratitude,
Datta Groover
Loveland, Colorado
February 16th, 2023

Stay tuned by liking my author page on Facebook:
Facebook.com/DattaGrooverAuthor

You can also connect with me at: *DattaGroover.com*

ACKNOWLEDGMENTS

My profound thanks to everyone who supported me in writing this book.

The Awakened School® Team—I couldn't have done this without you. Your encouragement and emotional and practical support have been invaluable to me.

Thanks to my editors: John Paine, Karen Collyer, and Joshua Essoe.

Thanks to my book creation support team: my proofreaders, beta readers, cover designer Patrick Knowles, and interior designer Mark Thomas.

Thanks to all my friends, supporters, and others who believed in me: you know who you are and made more difference to me than you could possibly know.

Thanks to my family: The Kennedys, Groovers, Freemans—and extensions thereof. You all helped make me who I am.

Thanks to my dear sons: your belief and trust in me was at times all that kept me going through life.

Thanks to my mentors: George Horan, Gary Ferguson, Furman Riley, Jayananda, and Swami Prabhupada.

Thanks to the extended family of courageous souls I've had the honor of working with, in the roles of clients and/or friends.

Most importantly, I want to thank my wife, who has given me more support and encouragement than could ever be measured. Rachael Jayne Groover, you are my best friend, the love of my life, visionary business partner, Australian Language Consultant, and travel buddy on the road through life—all rolled into one.

ABOUT THE AUTHOR

Datta Groover is the founder of The Inspired Writer® training. He has been honored to train and coach many writers and founded Deep Pacific Press to help other authors achieve their writing dreams and goals. He has personally received fourteen literary awards as of this writing. Two of those awards were for this book.

He loves dance, photography, hiking, exploring, meditation, and playing music—all of which energizes his writing.

Datta firmly believes that any one thing we do is always influenced by every other thing we do and by the people we hang out with. "Therefore," he says, "we should pick our activities and associations carefully."

When they're not on the road, the Groovers live in the hills outside Loveland, Colorado, with their corgi Maya and rottweiler Sophie, surrounded by lots of wild critters and vast natural beauty.

Like Datta's Author page on Facebook: *Facebook.com/DattaGrooverAuthor*

Connect with Datta: *DattaGroover.com*

Writing Resources

The Inspired Writer®
This writing retreat and support program has a focused, intentional purpose:
To receive the book your soul wants to write—in days instead of years.

Our powerful writing process will guide you to connect to an unlimited divine source of information so the stories and topics of your book come through clearly.

First-time authors are often inclined to take too much time on their first draft and get caught up in never-ending questioning about whether their book is any good. Sadly, they frequently never finish this significant first step.

We're going to make the process of writing and revising your book fun and magical.

To learn more about The Inspired Writer, visit: **TheAwakenedSchool.com**

Deep Pacific Press - Published Author Program
This program will show you how to complete a book manuscript known as a "page-turner," be it a memoir, how-to non-fiction, or fiction. We'll show you how to take your message to new heights, using moving stories and powerful descriptions that put the reader directly in the scene. Learn how to use realistic dialogue that flows and a climax that will make people want to share your book with others as soon as they are done reading it.

We'll use our design and marketing experience and skills to work with professionals who will create a kick-ass cover, a beautiful layout design, and high-quality printing, creating a book that you—and others—will love.

To learn more about the Published Author Program, visit:
DeepPacificPress.com